# THE BONE Parade

ALSO BY MARK NYKANEN:

*Hush*

# THE BONE Parade

## Mark Nykanen

HYPERION NEW YORK

*To my mother, Veronica Coyne Nykanen,*
*who told us many dark and funny stories*

# THE
# BONE
## Parade

Ba-WAAAAH-WAAH-WAH. *The trumpets were huge, impossibly long, and their sound carried down the mountains and across the valley and shook my belly till it felt as hollow as the thin air itself.*

Ba-WAAAAH-WAAH-WAH. *The trumpets rose over Bhaktapur, Katmandu's sooty sister city. I heard their squall as I walked to the rear of the foundry, passing the crude furnace and a plume of blackened brick where the flames had once licked their shadows.*

*My guide led me down a corridor with a ceiling so low that I had to duck. His skin was as dark and shiny as a hard brown nut, and his nails looked to be claws, grown to grotesque lengths, curling back on themselves as the nails of the dead are said to grow in the secrecy of the grave. He was a Hindu in a country to which Tibetans had fled, bringing their lighter skin and godless God. A Hindu who worshipped all manner of beings.*

*Our way was lit by a single bulb, as unadorned as the sun, and as hard on the eyes. The corridor's mud walls appeared as stark and brittle as all the other elements in this difficult land.*

*I heard a scratching sound and watched where I stepped. Then*

*my guide spoke his ragged English, "No ladies. No ladies,"
though none accompanied us. I had come to Nepal alone, trekking
first in the mountains with their strange monasteries, chants, and
songs, and now in the final days of my trip I had found my way to
this foundry.*

*"No ladies," he repeated, and now he sniggered, and I sensed
the insincerity at once, laughter freighted with another meaning
entirely; in this case its dark opposite, for he led me from the tight
corridor into a cavernous room filled with the undraped female
form, shelves shiny with these polished bronze figures perched in a
vast variety of positions. It was a bold, blazing array. And then on
the wall directly to my left, rising several feet above my head, I
saw bronze women that looked as ravenous as the hungry hea-
thens in a medieval mosaic, predators eying not the meat but the
soul, their feet splayed, their sex brazenly pried open.*

*Bizarre? Yes, absolutely so, but appealing. I could not deny
this, not even then, not even when I knew that denial was most important, and that to turn away was critical. But I could not pull
back because I saw that the bronzes looked as real as life itself,
and that even to glance at them was to understand the terrible turbulence that lies beneath the sleeping skin.*

*If one of them had moved, had taken a step to embrace me, I
would have been no more surprised than a cat when the shadows
in the corner come to life and scurry toward a crumb. That was
how I felt standing there, no more significant than a bit of flour
and fat, salt and sugar: the crumb awaiting discovery.*

*I was like the man who sees an unsettling sex act for the first
time, who witnesses its rude depredations in a dive in Bangkok, or
in a window along one of Amsterdam's narrow, infamous streets.
Or who happens across a whole new world on the Internet, a
strange, shifting carnal alliance that changes him in an instant,
that forces him to fix on the act he has just seen for the first time,
and who finds—deliriously, dangerously—that he must have it
again and again and again. I had discovered the new fire that*

*burns up all the others, that leaves nothing but ashes in its wake.*

*This was the knowledge that had lain in wait through all the years. It had sought me out with a suddenness that was shocking, that forced me to say with a breath I could hardly bear, "I was this, but now I am that." This was the knowledge that had proved most disturbing of all because it gave the lie to all that I had been, to all that I thought I was. I saw in that searing moment that kindness and decency and even the barest sense of propriety can slip away in a blink and leave us not as we would choose, but as we have been chosen.*

# CHAPTER

# 1

I WALK MY NEWEST BEST friend along the northern edge of the subdivision, pause while she pees, and brush past the tall trees that crowd both sides of a wildly overgrown dirt road. It might have been formed by the cement and lumber trucks that hauled their loads up here more than forty years ago. I'm guessing the age of these homes, but I've gotten quite good at this, and base my estimates on the size of the trees and shrubs, and the style of construction. This is pure sixties ranch. Some of them have add-ons, second floors and new facades, and an architectural flourish or two; but you can't really disguise them, and in my view they'd be far more appealing with the integrity of the original vision, however flawed. You certainly cannot hide the age; subdivisions, like people, show definite signs of decay. This one, however, is in its prime, old enough for each home to have had half a dozen or more owners. Lots of families. That's important to me.

The dirt road is about a quarter of a mile in length, a dumping ground for all the dogs around here. Just about every neighborhood has a poop alley. That's why I'd "adopted" her, to fit in as smoothly as one of these poplars or maples. If someone had seen me walking back here by myself, it would have been, Who's the guy hanging out in the woods? But with a dog I'm as natural as a breeze passing through.

She's a cutie, too, a Border collie. Black and gray and white, like the pups she left behind in the shelter. All of them had a date today with the needle. She's the kind of dog people melt over. Her life with me will be brief, no more than a few hours, and then I will release her from all future obligations. She should consider herself lucky, and if I were of the mind to bother with such banalities, that's precisely what I would call her.

We actually share similar physical characteristics—the gray hair and sharp features, middle age—as well as an outwardly friendly, even fawning manner; and as I walk toward the house I recall how often dogs and their owners really do resemble each other.

I watched them move in on Monday, and by this morning, garbage day, they already had their flattened cartons all stacked up for recycling. I admire their fastidiousness and resolve to get settled, appreciate far more than they can realize how a neatly arranged home suits my purposes far better than a haphazard arrangement of belongings, any one of which can be pried loose in violent protest. I imagine too, their art already building up neat rectangles of shadowed paint. Sometimes I respect their selections, but this is rare. There's no accounting for taste, and for the most part I don't see much of it, not in homes such as these, or on the walls of the wealthy either. It's usually crap. Will it match the couch, the carpet, Aunt Emma's crocheted cushions? These are the questions they ask, the criteria they use. It would be sad if it wasn't such a crime.

We come to a paved road where a metal post blocks cars from entering poop alley. I'm parked down the street, a van that rarely raises curiosity in a neighborhood like this. It's a windowless Ford Econoline, the kind florists and plumbers and carpet installers arrive in, though I once read that an FBI profiler called them the serial killer's preferred vehicle.

Just before we step on the pavement, she squats to relieve herself again. I appreciate her discretion, and feed her a biscuit to keep her interest keen.

The house I've been watching since Monday has two stories, two shades of gray, the darker on the ground floor. White trim throughout. A brick walkway cuts across a lawn as neat as a fairway. The green almost glimmers in the afternoon sun.

They've managed to hang curtains on the first floor, which I applaud—it's certainly to my advantage—though the day of the move I noticed that the interior stairway spilled right down to the front door. Bad Feng Shui, all that energy pouring out into the street. It bodes ill for anyone living there. I doubt they know this, but they will, and shortly too.

"They" are the Vandersons. Four of them: a husband; wife; teenage daughter no more than fourteen with skin so perfect you'd want to touch it, stroke it, never let it go; and a son, perhaps nine or ten, who looked annoying even from a distance, preadolescent testosterone all balled up and ready to binge. No dog. That's very important. *Their* dogs get in the way; even the small ones can set off an alarm. Cats, on the other hand, can be amusing in their treachery. After I've finished with a family, I've had them rub up against my leg as if to say, Thanks, Buster, I never really liked them all that much anyway. But even the cats cannot remain unclaimed, not if they're part of the household, although I have delighted in dispatching a family's canary or parakeet to their eager jaws. I'm not above satisfying the long frustrated desires of felines, and I've learned a thing or two by watching them hunt and eat these birds. Parakeets, for instance, fight the hardest, and canaries sometimes die of fright. After they've been cornered, or swatted to the floor, I've seen them stare into a cat's mouth and literally drop dead.

People are pretty much the same, they have all different levels of fear, but the wonder of it is that the families I meet usually share a common degree of kindness, and I've never failed to make them feel it when it counts the most for me. I'm guessing the Vandersons won't be any different; they appear as normal as fence posts.

They moved here from Pennsylvania. Harrisburg, to be precise. Public records are extraordinarily revealing. I always use them. I simply don't want a family that's moved from one side of town to the other, or from two streets over. Better they've made the big move, far from those who know them or might miss them in an hour, an evening, or on the day that follows. Give me a day and I'm gone for good. And so are they. Never . . . to . . . return.

I feed her a final biscuit, a blessing of sorts to her good-natured self. She wolfs it down and wags her tail. If she misses her pups, it's news to me. Together we stroll up the front steps. "Easy now," I tell her, and ring the bell. I listen carefully to make sure it works. It's not a good idea to stand around any longer than you have to. You never know who's watching. This one chimes melodically.

The door swings open. It's the boy. He promptly scrunches up his skinny face and stares at me before gazing at the dog. She wags her tail and tries to lure his interest—she's doing her job admirably—but the kid doesn't take the bait.

"What do *you* want?" he says as if he's known me long enough to loathe me.

"I wonder," I say as I lean my head in the door just enough to glance around, "is your mom or dad home?"

"Mom," he bleats. "Mom!"

He turns as a bustle from the kitchen grows louder. She's even kinder looking than I thought from a distance. But her voice— "Yes . . . can I help you?"—is so hesitant, so . . . suspicious.

Usually they're trusting, what with all the new neighbors stopping by, greeting them, welcoming them. What is this? An unfriendly neighborhood? Hasn't anyone come by with a bottle of wine, or a tray of cookies? I've waited a few days for all of that to pass. By now I should be nothing more than a new face. And then I remember: they're from Back East.

I introduce myself as Harry Butler. Harry is such an unassuming name, untainted by association. Tell them Ted, and they might think Bundy; John, and they might think Gacy. But Harry? If they're young, they think of Potter; and if they're older, Truman. That's if they think of anyone at all.

"I'm so sorry to bother you, but I used to live here when I was a child, and I wondered—I know this is unusual—but I wondered if I could just come in and have a quick look around and see my old room. I've just come from my mother's funeral, I've got her things out there," and here I offer a feint to the van, "and before leaving town I wondered if I could see my old house. It's been a long time since I've seen it, and I have so many great memories of the place."

This is always a key point in the transaction: by implication, I praise their taste, and show that we share a fondness for the house. That's what it's all about at this stage, finding common ground. Keeping the moment gentle.

She is ever so attractive, in a dress of all things. You don't realize how few women wear dresses at home anymore until you start doing this. I wonder if they're Mormons, if I've come upon a coven of them. Now that would be sweet payback for all those freshly scrubbed missionaries with their neat haircuts and name tags who have violated my privacy over the years. It's the dress that has me thinking. I know she hasn't spent the day at work, I've been watching. It's nothing extravagant, mind you, but the kind of frock—forgive me, but it's true—that old June Cleaver would have worn.

I am wildly stimulated. I don't know if it's her, the dress, her pantyhose, or bald anticipation, but I have to choke down the desire to keep talking, to fill the silence with words. That would be a terrible mistake. It would make me seem much too eager, like a salesman, which of course I am: I'm selling myself and the whole notion of a lost childhood in these halls.

Some women have an especially sharp sense of survival, and have sent me on my way, and I know that if she says, No, I don't think so, I'll have to thank her for her time, turn around, and leave. I can't force the issue, and I remind myself of this as her eyes cloud and her lips clamp tightly together. But before she can speak, I am saved by her husband. I see this the moment he ambles up, all geniality and king of the castle, a big jolly looking fellow who welcomes me and says he's always wanted to go back to his own childhood home. Come in, come in, come in.

He gives me his meaty hand and leads me with practiced ease over the threshold. I hear the delicious click of the door closing. They're finished.

It's not difficult to subdue a family. You focus on the children, and let the worst fears of the parents keep their own panicky impulses in line. I have that Jolly Roger of a dad bind his son and daughter with duct tape, insisting that he do a fair job of it, or I'll do it myself.

He does do a good job, particularly with the girl, and I detect more than a little veiled hostility in the way he wraps the tape around her mouth. He does it so tightly that I can't help but wonder if she's been mouthing off of late.

When he works on his wife, her dress gets bunched up around her thighs, and I can see the panty in the pantyhose. It lures my interest, but not for long. I can ill afford a lapse, and I never suffer one. Never.

Then it's time for Jolly Roger himself to place his hands behind his back. I have the handcuffs out. I need only one pair, and I save them for this critical moment because once he cuffs himself, I can go to work on him, and then on to the other three as well; he has merely bound and gagged them, and so much more remains to be done.

"No way," he says with a sneer. "You're not putting those things on me."

This is what I've been dreading, pigheaded resistance. It's not unusual with big men, who despite all evidence to the contrary sometimes believe they're mightier than a bullet. I'm sure he sees himself as a hero. I think he's a creep. He binds his family, but not himself? What's with that?

"You don't have a choice," I say as if to a three-year-old. "Not if you want to leave here alive." And there is truth to that statement. I point the gun at his head. It's an impressive weapon, and his wife, voice muffled, starts making *oompf-oompf* sounds and shaking her head frantically. I can tell that she's run into his stubbornness before, and has no more patience for it than I. Her son takes her cue and follows suit. There's a veritable chorus of *oompf-oompfs*. The daughter looks on hollow-eyed.

"The vote's going against you," I say with a smile.

Then I cock the hammer and thrust the barrel right into his face where he can see the muzzle and smell its blue steel breath.

"Your cooperation, or . . ." I shrug, and the barrel moves an inch or two, grazing his nose as I intended it to, though truly I am reluctant to use it.

"What do you want?" he demands. It's not the first time I've heard this question of late. She asked me too, in a way that indicated she'd give me *whatever* I wanted. I laughed at her. I'll kill him.

He's still staring at the gun when I hand him the cuffs. I direct his hands behind his back, and he snaps them on, shaking his head.

"Hold still," I tell him.

"What for?"

I slap the tape on his mouth. There, there's his answer.

The dog sniffs his wife, then snorts grotesquely up her legs. The beast has a most appalling interest in her crotch, and June is squirming in real fright, as if she considers this part of the plan, that I would countenance bestiality.

I watch, and while I appreciate the added glimpses, I pull the dog off her and dispatch the creature with a bullet to the brain. This stills her eager snout, and their protests as well.

It's growing dark as I back the van into the garage. I save June for last. When I begin to unbutton the back of her dress, she stars *oompf-oompfing* again. An hour ago she was willing to bargain with her body; now she's acting like it's the sacred trust. But just at the point when I'm really losing patience, she relents, resigned to her presumed fate. Perhaps she thinks I'll spend myself on her, and spare the children.

Her arms slip out of the sleeves, and I raise it up over her head. This way I can take my time looking. Control top? Unquestionably, though you wouldn't think she'd need it. L'eggs? Or No Nonsense? No Nonsense, I'm all but certain of it. And industrial gauge underpants with a bra that has all the appeal of day-old bread.

Her knees fall open, but no more than a foot because she's still bound at the ankles, and will remain so because I have no interest that has not already been sated. I fold the dress and put it aside, lug her to the van and promise slow death to both of their children if any of them decide to start banging on the walls.

I spend the next forty-five minutes cleaning up the dog's blood, her carcass, which I toss in the back with them, and scraps of tape. Then I vacuum over and over, and wipe down surfaces till neither fiber nor fingerprint can survive my diligence. I remove the vacuum bag and toss it into the back of the van as well. I put a new one in. They have vanished *without a trace.* I can see the headlines already. They're as predictable as murder.

We have a long drive ahead, and I can hardly take a room for the night, so I pull into a McDonald's drive-through and order three large coffees. It's horrible stuff, but with a family of four trussed and bundled in the back, I'm hardly going to troll through this miserable town for a Starbucks.

They don't shift an inch as I pull up and pay, and minutes later we join all the other headlights on the interstate. Fifty miles away,

I pull into a rest area where I dispose of the vacuum bag and paper towels. It's still too risky to dump the dog, so her ever stiffening, ever ripening corpse will have to accompany us even farther. All of them are lying back there in the dark. None of them move. They don't dare.

# CHAPTER

## 2

LAUREN REED STEPPED OFF THE bus and caught the walk sign as it started flashing red. She hurried across the four lanes of traffic, casting a wary eye at the impatient, early morning drivers lined up to her right. One of them gunned his engine. Idiot.

Bandering Hall towered above her, six stories of gray concrete, slab upon slab of faceless floors and tall windows, ugly and urban in the mode of most modern architecture.

Her coat felt too heavy, too warm, and she decided that she'd have to retire it for the season. Spring, fickle as it was in the Pacific Northwest, had finally settled in. She'd already moved her morning run from the indoor oval at the Y to the streets and parks of Portland.

Today was critique day. As she eyed the foundry's exhaust fans protruding from the second floor of Bandering, she calculated that she could devote eight minutes to each student's sculpture. That's all she could spare, and that was figuring on no more than ten minutes for start time. Of course, some of them would wish for even less once the discussion of their work turned taut, but others would feel cheated by such miserly attention to what they considered their masterpiece.

Running late was not an option because the faculty meeting started at noon, and the chair wouldn't brook tardiness. Those who tarried faced truly unpleasant committee assignments every fall.

She passed the elevator as its doors clunked open, and climbed the stairs to her third floor office, feeling the effects of her daily run. Routines, she'd found, were vital when you weren't living at home, although where home was precisely had become a question with no easy answer. Portland, where she taught and rented a room in a fine old Victorian that had once been a B&B? Or Pasadena, where she kept her studio? And where Chad lived, she reminded herself, pleased to realize that his star was finally fading and that he wasn't foremost on her mind anymore. He'd been her boyfriend for seven years. Seven *years*, and when she'd said to him at Christmas, "Look, I love you dearly but I really want to get married and maybe even have a family," he'd bolted. Not physically. Emotionally. Backed out faster than a bank robber with a bag full of money.

Her studio was still in his house, but she'd found a small apartment nearby, all of which made the abode question so nettlesome: the room in Portland, or the one in Pasadena?

She unlocked her office and unloaded her shoulder bag before hurrying down to the student union in the basement of the adjoining administration building. She bought a tall cup of hot water for the chai tea that she stored next to her iMac, which had been sleeping all weekend.

As she sat at her desk, she jarred the computer screen to life. She glanced over to see her schedule neatly beaming back at her. Oh-no, she'd spaced on the writer who was coming to interview her in what? Eight minutes. That number had begun to haunt her. He'd said he was researching a book about contemporary sculpture, though she could not understand why: who would buy it? But she was flattered to have been called, hardly ranking herself among the foremost practitioners of her art. Hardly willing, in fact, to call herself an artist at all, preferring "sculptor," and believing that if she ever did really, *really* good work, then she could call herself an artist. But she hadn't, not yet, and her last show had been a disappointment to her, if not to the critics. She felt she'd been repeating herself, and for the first time a feeling of stagnancy had overcome her when she worked, a miasma as real as the smog that often enveloped her studio down in California.

She wondered briefly what the writer would look like, imagining an owlish man, a Mr. Peeps type, or a geeky twenty-something working wholly on spec on his first book, which would turn out to be his first big professional rejection a year or two hence.

What she most assuredly did not expect in the Ry Chambers who had spoken to her on the phone was a guy about six foot four with dark hair, thick as shearling, and a wedge-shaped torso sprouting from tan cargo pants that hung loosely around his hips because he had no belly to speak of.

His age? Thirty-five? Forty? Not any older. Not likely. No way, she told herself: no crow's-feet.

She was standing, shaking his hand, looking into his eyes, looking away, then with a most unpleasant jolt remembering that along with the appointment, she'd overlooked something even more vital on an urban campus:

"The parking pass! I'm so sorry. I completely forgot—"

"Don't worry." He shook off her concern as he unfolded his narrow reporter's notebook. "I found a space on the street. Just a few minutes from here," he added, as if she needed additional consoling.

She did. She *never* forgot details like this. Except she had, and all she could utter was "Good-good. It won't happen again. I promise. I don't know how I did that . . ." She was starting to babble, could feel the nervous urge to blather, and forced herself to shut up, but then she popped off again, like a champagne cork that refuses to seal, that yields to all the fizzy pressure rising from below. "Do you want some coffee? Tea? I could get some. It's right down—"

"No," he interrupted her again. "I had a cup on my way here. I'm fine, really. Thanks."

She felt her brow tense, and forced it to relax. *What are you doing?* Then she caught herself scratching her arm, another nervous habit.

"You're writing a book? About sculpture?"

He talked readily about the project, his publisher's willingness to risk a modest advance on a field so fallow of interest that the most well-known art critic of our time, the author Robert Hughes, who also labored for *Time* and public broadcasting, had barely bothered with it in his groundbreaking book about modernism, *The Shock of the New.* Ry Chambers mentioned the names of three other sculptors he'd already interviewed, all men, she noted to herself, and brought the conversation around to her: when had she started, and what was the nature of her early work? Before she realized it, she'd talked right up to the start of class, an entire hour, and felt acutely self-conscious for having monopolized the time. Had she asked him even a single question about himself? She didn't think so, and when she told him the experience had left her feeling "bloated with self-indulgence," he laughed, closed his notebook and said, "Good, that's the way it's supposed to be. I'm interviewing you. I want you to talk about yourself."

"You're not going to make me look like a fool, are you?"

He smiled again. "I'd say that would be an impossible challenge."

The computer screen chose that moment to jump alive with a rattle she'd never noticed before, and as her schedule began, once again, to beam, she assumed she must have bumped the keyboard, not considering in those first few innocent moments that it was the building itself that had moved, was moving. Shaking violently. He sprang to his feet at the very moment she did, and they leaped to the open doorway. The walls shook so furiously they blurred. Then she spotted gray dust raining down in the hall, and heard a vicious rumble as the concrete ceiling cracked open. The seam raced toward them, widening in sudden shifts from an inch, to two, three.

"Stop-stop-stop," she implored, but her voice could not be heard above the terrifying rumble.

From the ceiling in the hall her eyes fell to the floor of her office where the wheels of her chair jumped angrily, like drops of water on a hot greasy grill. The heavily laden bookshelves raged with a frenzy she felt in her own body. Two thick volumes spilled out and landed on their spines, then jittered insanely on the floor.

The quake ended seconds later, and she found that their hands now rested on each other. She noticed—she could not help herself, she was a sculptor attuned to touch—that his arms were firm, the muscles in relief as he steadied her, and she steadied him, and they both, perhaps, unsteadied each other.

Together they rushed downstairs to the street where scores of students had gathered. She'd walked up this sidewalk little more than an hour ago. The sun had been shining, the traffic thick, her thoughts anxious with the minutia of minutes. Now she felt lucky to be alive, uncrushed, if not unfazed.

A general giddiness filled the air as everyone tried at once to share stories of other quakes. Everyone but him. His reserve, even here, surprised her. Pleased her in a way that she recognized quickly: It seemed that every man she'd met in the past twenty years, except Chad *most of the time,* hadn't been satisfied until he'd let her explore the deepest recesses of his soul. Solipsism masquerading as sensitivity.

"They've started looting," a student joked. "We better get back in there and get our stuff." Most of them laughed, but not so hard that they didn't start filing through the doors immediately.

. . .

Forty-five minutes later Lauren's floor was cleared for occupancy. Five yellow plastic sawhorses had been placed in a pentagon under the crack in the hallway ceiling, though she wondered how they had determined that this area alone could possibly, just maybe, collapse. Wasn't there likely to be unseen collateral damage? Hadn't the quake sent shivers of destruction elsewhere? Wasn't that the nature of chaos theory, after all? What were all those butterflies in China doing at this very moment anyway?

She'd spent most of the down time trying to find out what had happened. The quake had been every bit as powerful as it had felt, registering a six point eight. It had killed a man in Seattle, and injured dozens of people in both cities. There had also been tens of millions of dollars in damage.

Now she made a grand attempt to put aside her worries, and called the chair's office. The faculty meeting had been postponed till one. At least she'd regained her eight minutes per student, assuming that they could stay an hour later, which might be assuming too much: most of them worked, or had children, or both, and schedules as tight as seamen's knots. It was a commuter campus, so she'd have to find out who *had* to leave at noon and work around them.

The first three pieces surprised her. Skillful, inspired, "eye candy," as Kerry, tall and henna-haired with a perfect dimple in the middle of her chin, called the soapstone statues they'd just viewed.

Lauren had quibbled with the installation that Kerry had chosen for her own sculpture, the first one they'd critiqued, a vaguely feminine, anthropomorphic figure reclining as a woman might, buttocks back on her heels, head forward to the floor. But the human form was an illusion, for Kerry's creation had no arms or legs, or any other discernibly human features, and that's what made the piece so effective: it evoked, it did not spell out, and Lauren saw that no one would "get" the work in an instant. They would have to linger, walk away perhaps, and return. They would have to give it thought because the form was girded in mystery. Remarkable for an undergrad, but not for Kerry, whose work had been among the best student sculpture that Lauren had ever seen.

But Kerry's mistake was to place it on a pedestal, and Lauren had her move it down to the floor. She accomplished this with the aid of an apparently gay, neurasthenic young man, who appeared incapable of lifting his own arms, much less half of this substantial work. But he did, with surprising ease. And once the figure lay before them it possessed, paradoxically enough, much more power.

They now came upon a piece that exemplified what Lauren found most uncomfortable in so much student art: banality. One of her better students, no less, had wrapped purple fleece around three oddly shaped, chicken wire forms. Protruding from each were shards of clear broken glass. It looked like that children's critter, Barney, had gone on a binge and landed on a case of broken gin bottles.

She saw Ry looking at it earnestly, too earnestly, as if he might betray his real feelings if he suffered even a momentary lapse of attention. Not so for Kerry and a couple of other students who kept shooting glances at him, evidently—and justly—finding him both more attractive and interesting than the work before them.

"It's very bizarre," said Lauren, finally unable to spare her student's feelings. But the girl was not offended or startled by her frankness, she was gratified.

"Thanks. It's about people. The way they get their defenses up." The girl swept her long curly hair over her shoulder.

"Why did you choose purple?" asked Kerry, who had survived her own eight minutes of critique with little but praise, and now had a pass to open up. Not that she necessarily would, but she was an exceptionally bright girl with a sharp tongue.

"Purple?" The artist retrieved a strand of curls and wrapped her finger around it, then gazed at her work as if pondering her color choice for the first time. Lauren hoped the girl had an answer to this, the most basic of all questions. She was rooting for the young woman's grade, even as the girl brushed her hair aside and shrugged. Feeling defeated herself, Lauren offered that purple was the color of the gods.

"I was thinking of children, especially when I made that one," the young woman said, as if she hadn't heard Lauren at all.

The artist was pointing to the smallest of the three shapes, a shriveled, pathetic offspring, presumably of the purple parents, who appeared much larger and clearly capable of slicing and dicing their wee one to bits.

They moved on, a tour that included a painfully obvious performance piece by an anorexic girl in black nylons, garter belt, and satin half slip, who'd had herself bound unpersuasively with rope and tied with no more ardor to a bathroom stall, beside which lay a whip and highly specific instructions on how to flog her, along with pedantic passages extolling the virtues of outré sex play. It made the Barney piece, as Lauren now thought of it, look like a Brancusi.

Thankfully, they finished on two high notes. The first was a duct tape shell of a female body with a puffy white lining. The artist had created the piece by having herself completely sealed in the silvery tape while sitting on a simple wooden chair. A poster sized photograph documenting the original, mummified state hung eerily on the wall behind the sculpture. When she looked from one to the other, Lauren saw how the artist had torn herself out of the mold, leaving behind a particularly convincing chrysalis.

The final piece pleased Lauren even more. At first glance, Melanie was the most normal-looking student in the class. Her girlish, frail frame generally skipped or flounced around in the loose fitting cords and tired pink sweaters that she favored. She looked altogether ingenuous in her pigtails and beaded bracelets until the warm weather stripped her down to a halter and revealed her childlike back, which was nearly blanketed with tattoos.

Lauren saw that Melanie's piece worked in much the same manner, by revealing meaning in layers. She had formed three bras and a single thong from grapefruit and orange skins. The rinds had dried and shrunk, leaving undergarments that would fit only a very young girl. Chillingly, she'd constructed the thong out of the skin of a blood orange, then installed each of the "garments" on elegant white hangers, as their satin and silk counterparts were often displayed in high-end boutiques. Lauren loved the piece, the installation and the imagination that had given rise to both. Whimsical at first sight, but horrifying as the hints of brutal eroticism and the oversexualization of children began to reveal themselves.

Ry walked with Lauren back to her office to get his denim jacket, which he'd left draped over a chair. They talked easily about the quake as they stepped around the yellow sawhorses. She unlocked the door, passing the threshold where they'd watched and felt the building shake.

"There it is," he said needlessly as he reached for the jacket. She detected the slightest unease in him for the first time.

"So, next Wednesday at eight then? Does that work for you?" he asked.

"Yes, I'll be here. And I promise to take care of the parking pass. I'll walk it out personally."

He thanked her for her time, and as he slipped his jacket on, she stole a glimpse of his torso, and imagined him as a nude model on a stool, a pleasant if entirely brief reverie because Kerry burst in holding up a letter.

"I got it! I got it."

"What did you get?" Lauren tried to remember what Kerry had been angling for with such keen enthusiasm.

"The internship with Stassler."

"That's great. Congratulations. When do you start?"

"Next month."

"Stassler?" Ry said. "You're going to intern with Ashley Stassler?"

Kerry turned her attention to him and nodded. Lauren noted the light in the girl's eyes, as she had earlier. Kerry was flashing interest, smiles, and way too much sexiness for a woman her age.

"Yup. *The* Ashley Stassler."

"That's interesting because I'm scheduled to interview him at the end of May at his home. We're talking about the place just outside Moab, right?"

"Yup!" Kerry snapped the letter in the air, and her smile widened to include all of her face. Lauren considered it enlivened as much, perhaps, by the prospect of interning with a renowned sculptor out in the Utah desert as by Ry's imminent association with both.

"Say," Kerry said, appraising Ry openly, "anybody ever tell you that you look like that journalist guy Sebastian . . . I can't remember his last name but he wrote *The Perfect Storm*."

"Yup," he parodied her gently, "I've heard that a few times."

Kerry's eyebrows rose and fell while her gaze remained steady, and Lauren wondered if another reason men found young women so attractive was their utter lack of subtlety. It was as if the fertility festival taking place in their bodies could beat only the loudest possible drums.

Kerry finally turned to Lauren. "I'll be gone for two months. Thanks so much for the letter."

Ah, the letter of recommendation, Lauren remembered.

"You're welcome."

"This is *so* incredible! Totally, totally awesome."

It is indeed, Lauren thought as Kerry ran down the hall, and Ry Chambers ducked out. An internship with one of the premier sculptors of our time, though his work no longer appealed to her. Far too representational. Families—children, mothers, fathers, pets even—cast in varying degrees of strictly enforced terror, bronze figures bearing "the ever present latency of unendurable pain," as a noted critic had written about Stassler's huge show last winter at the Guggenheim.

But the weakest aspect of Ashley Stassler's work, as far as Lauren was concerned, were the faces. They were clichés. Every eye appeared too stark, every brow too furrowed, every cheek and chin too rigid. The mouths were even worse. Even the lips of the children appeared uniformly contorted, twisted, never quite sealed. It was as if he'd taken the undeniable agony of the bodies, each of them unique in the bald expression of the most abject suffering, and mated it to a stereotypical portrait of facial pain.

But what she saw as a weakness was considered a great strength by the most influential art critics. Only last year, in a review of the Guggenheim show, the editor of Europe's most highly regarded arts journal had written about Stassler's "metaphorical use of the mouth, as if bound by the brutal constraints of convention, rendered silent by the screams that no one can hear."

Lauren had squirmed when she'd read the review, squirmed because she herself had praised Stassler, though less eloquently, when she'd written that the mouths of his subjects "called out with words to a world that could never be known." But that had been more than twenty years ago, back when she'd been an undergrad overwhelmed by much of the art she saw, and not surprisingly enamored of Stassler's work, which had been placed on loan to her college. Enamored, too, of bronze, the immortality it promised. She'd sent him a copy of her review. He'd never replied.

# CHAPTER

3

THEY'RE TOO TIRED FOR TERROR anymore. I can see it in their faces. They're not only tired, they're cranky, thirsty, and hungry. I've seen it before. I'll have to give them food and shelter and clean clothing before they'll focus on anything outside of their selfish little selves. I'm going to have to nurse them back to terror.

Not a peep out of them. Going on twelve hours in the van, and they might as well be as dead as the dog. Ol' Missy was pretty rank by the time I gave her the boot. Opened the doors and five pairs of eyes stared back at me. Did any of them blink? I don't think so. Certainly not that sweet little hound. Starting to get pretty stiff too. I stood her on her hind legs and kind of shook her paw to wave good-bye. That's when the girl laughed. I wasn't sure at first because of the duct tape over her mouth, but her mother gave her one of those *Don't you dare* looks, and that's when I knew. She laughed again when I made the dog dance on her mother's legs, dragged those claws right across her pantyhose.

I'd better open the curtain I've got drawn across the cargo area, let some air in back there. It's starting to get a little warm. I need to water them. I saw a billboard for a Safeway a few miles back. That would be perfect. Pull in, duck back there, and give them all a drink. And get ready for the complaints: *I have to pee. I'm hungry. What do you want?* (more often, *What the fuck do you want?*). *Where are we going?* So first I'll tell them that if anyone says a word, one word, then it's no water for any of them. Nothing.

There's the Safeway. It comes up faster than I realize, and I wonder if I'm starting to nod off. I find a space not too close and not too far from the nearest cars, and lean back, letting my eyes look over everything from left to right. No patrol cars, none of those wide-bodied barges favored by detectives in these parts. Nothing but the early morning bagel crowd of overweight Mormons.

I eat two more of the chocolate-covered espresso beans that have kept me going most of the night. I'm close to finishing the entire bag. Chocolate and caffeine, and water. I really do need to pee, but I can't leave them, so I take the pee bottle back there with me.

Now this is a form of torture, making them watch me when their own bladders are ready to burst. It's been twelve hours or more since any of them have had a chance to go, and I wonder who will break first. I've had others pee in their pants. June looks away, so does that Jolly Roger hubby of hers and their son, but daughter dearest stares right at me, at *it*. She's a bold one, isn't she? Doesn't look worried. Not like her mom when I was taking off her dress.

Oh no, I smell it before I see it, and when I switch on the dome light I see that Sonny-boy has messed himself. His sister is having none of it. She sounds like she's swearing at him behind the tape. It must be so because June is back to shooting her dark looks. Roger just looks sick. He's probably feeling very guilty, dragging me in the house like that. And now look at them, after just half a day with me! Tied up, hungry, thirsty, messing their pants. And you thought Harrisburg was bad, didn't you, Jolly Roger?

"All right, listen up." This gets their attention. I haven't spoken to them since we got started. "It's time for some water. Who wants to get a drink first?"

I knew it. Daughter dearest lifts her head and moves her legs, and when I look at her I think she might not be as young as I thought. She could be sixteen. Seventeen? Possibly.

Everyone nods when I tell them what the deal is. Everyone except Sonny-boy, who seems too ashamed to open his wet eyes.

I peel the tape off his sister's mouth, and notice her lips, fluted, like a champagne glass, and full. I help her sit up, feel the ridge line of her back. Then I run my hand up her spine, feeling every little bone, and her skin—it's so firm—and her neck, narrow and smooth. I keep my hand there as she drinks, and feel the liquid rushing down her throat.

"Not too much," I say softly. "You're going to have to hold it."

"Like *him*." She whispers a disgust so pure that I can only crouch there and admire her. But that's all I do because she's violated the agreement.

"If you say another word, they'll get nothing."

"Really?" She brightens. "And what happens if I scream? Will you kill them?"

I clamp my hand over her mouth, though my body shakes with laughter. And she knows it, I can see it in her eyes. And then—I don't believe it—she slips her tongue against my fingers. What a wench. What a dirty, filthy wench. I love her.

June is having an altogether different reaction to our tête-à-tête. She's trying to kick, yes *kick* her daughter, and I'm beginning to sense some serious family issues here.

"Stop that," I snap at her mother. "Get a hold of yourself."

"*Oompf-oompf.*"

"Oh, *oompf-oompf*, yourself." Even her pantyhose is starting to lose its appeal.

She'll be the first to go, I can see that already. You make sacrifices for your art. Sure, everybody does, but June Cleaver here has been on my nerves since that Sarah Bernhardt routine over her dress. A real drama queen. You get all types in this line of work, let me tell you.

I tape up her daughter, and move over to Sonny-boy. He doesn't respond to my warnings, so I turn to that Jolly Roger of a dad of his and patiently explain the deal once more.

He might be listening, I can't be sure. He looks exhausted, eyes heavy and hooded, like all his piss and vinegar have drained away; but there's no telling with some men, especially the big ones who try to make themselves look even bigger by doing something stupid.

"She," I point to the girl, "got away with it because she's cute, but you're old and ugly, Roger—" he looks confused when he hears his assigned name— "so don't go getting any ideas."

He nods as if to say, "Sure-sure, gimme a drink," and downs a full quart before I cut him off.

June's turned away from me, on her side, no doubt pouting over her plight, so I snap her bra, pull it all the way back like it's a slingshot, and let her rip. I haven't done this since high school, and it feels great, and brings her right around. But the *oompf-oompfing* has a snarling sound to it now, so I simply announce, "You lose," as I trickle water over her head and cap the bottle.

Now she starts kicking, it's a tantrum, and this forces my hand. I pull out my knife, a switchblade I bought in Sonora, Mexico, five years ago, a real beauty of a blade with turquoise inlay in the handle and gold bands on the top and bottom, and a stainless steel edge so sharp that all I have to do is nick Sonny-boy's cheek and a red blossom blooms. I pick him because I'm beginning to suspect that if I nicked his sister, Mom would never stop kicking. One of those tit for tat, mother-daughter things.

Sonny-boy's scratch is nothing, but it's enough to shut up June.

I wipe the blade off on her hip, on the panty part of the pantyhose, but feel none of the thrill that first captured my attention. It's extraordinary the way intimacy can breed animus.

When I look at the girl again she nods, and if I were to guess—and let's face it, that's precisely what I'm doing at this point—I would have to say that what I've just done meets with her complete approval. But what's really odd, what's never happened before, is that she has met with mine.

Four more hours to go. The nicest part of the trip, through the high desert of southeastern Utah. Rolling hills of red rock, beautiful mountains, open country. But it cooks around here in the summer, and even now the temperature is getting up there. I realize I'd better turn on the a/c and crack the curtain a little wider or they'll roast back there.

I keep thinking of the daughter. She looks absolutely delicious, completely ripe. When I touched her skin, I wanted to touch more of it. I wanted to run my hand over every firm inch of her. She's at that age when her skin is stretched to its maximum, when it couldn't be any firmer, when you really could bounce a dime off her belly. I had all I could do not to reach around and feel her breasts. She has such nice ones, high and proud. Of course she's underage, and *I wouldn't want to break any laws, now would I?*

What kind of childhood could produce so much hate: If I scream, will you kill them? I think she was serious. I don't think she'd mind at all if I offed them right now. They seemed so normal. That's why I went after them. The only thing missing was Lassie, and I have a Lassie or two lying around somewhere. Plus the bone parade, so they can spend their time thinking about what could happen, how they could end up. Time to think means time for the terror to sink in. I want them secreting adrenaline into every cell, until they're flush with it, like cattle moving down the slaughterhouse ramp, bellowing hopelessly as an endless rush of chemicals comes crashing through their brains.

Maybe she was molested when she was little. Nowadays, you

can't help thinking it, it's the first thing that comes to mind. I really despise child molesters. To prey on children like that is a disgrace. That can really twist a kid into an emotional pretzel. They should all be shot.

But it could be that she's just a bad seed. I'm sure that's what they'd say about me. I had a perfect childhood. No one buggered me. I think I was spanked all of two times. Mom stayed home. Dad worked. And I got to play all the time.

All in all, I turned out fine. The only fetish I have—if you could even call it that—is this pantyhose thing. I'm not the only one. Search under "naughty pantyhose" on the web, and dozens of sites show up. You think I'm kidding? You want up-skirt shots of big-breasted Asians in pantyhose? No problema, as they say down south, way down south. British schoolgirls in knee socks and sheer pantyhose? Ditto. These pantyhose freaks even have their own lobbying group. They want to make Hollywood filmmakers show pantyhose in sex scenes, instead of nylons and garters, which are so ridiculous anyway. On Valentine's Day maybe half the women in a restaurant have them on, but the rest of the year it's pure pantyhose, and thank God for it.

I've tried them myself—there are even sites for that, men in pantyhose, usually men with giant erections—but the thrill was fleeting. By the time I'd worn out half a dozen pairs, I didn't really have any interest in wearing them anymore. I guess it was cross-dressing, but there's nothing unusual in that. Every Halloween party I've ever been to half the guys are in drag. Are half the women in drag? No. They're goblins and fairies and witches. But the guys? They're secretaries and tarts and sweethearts in miniskirts, pushup bras, and pumps.

So I'm hardly tweaked, not by contemporary standards. I'm a lot of things, but I'm not tweaked. It's not as if I get off on these abductions. I do them because I have to. It's work. I'm certainly not getting any erections out of it. I'm not like those freaks who climax when they kill. The only thing I'll admit to is ambition, but that's it. I take pleasure in the fame. And why shouldn't I? I deserve it. Every bit of it. The work I do is unique, first-rate, and unforgettable. I take the human mind and bend it and bend it and bend it, and right at the moment it breaks, I capture the entire length of the naked body as it tenses and shudders. That's what I saw in Nepal, the terrible turbulence that lies beneath the sleeping skin. I wondered then how he'd achieved it. I wonder still. I know how I do it.

But you build terror, just like you build anything worth having. It takes time. Lots and lots of time. It's like I have to sweeten them up, the way you sweeten a pear by putting it in a paper bag. Day by day the pear softens, the juices rise, until finally it's ready to burst. Then again, she could be gaming me. Trying to play me for the fool. God knows, others have tried, but never so early in the game. They did it after they saw the compound, and the cage.

Then, in a week or two they'd tried to seduce me, with their husbands right there! They took me for a fool. But she was willing right from the get-go. She seemed thrilled by it. Maybe life with Mom and Dad and Sonny-boy is so boring that even this is better.

I feel a sudden rush of sympathy for her, and tell myself to watch it.

It feels like I've been driving forever, but at last I turn off the highway and head down the dirt road. All I see in the side-view mirrors is the funnel of dust we leave behind. On a day like this—no wind, no humidity—it can hang there for an hour, slowly drifting back to earth. Every time I pass a mountain biker on one of these roads I feel sorry for them, sucking up all that dusty air. But if I could I'd send them all back to wherever they came from. I moved here for the isolation, and now suddenly we're the mountain biking capital of the world. About a million of them pour in here every year to ride the trails on the slick rock, and some of them get off course and end up out this way. I've been tempted to immortalize one or two, but never have. Every step has to be planned. I just smile, tell them they're lost, and how to get back. And then I watch them carefully to make sure they go on their way.

I stop at the cattle guard and open the gate, pull through, and lock it back up. It used to be a working ranch until I bought it. I had no use for the land, just the privacy it gave me. The biggest selling point was the single feature I couldn't see, that no one sees—the cellar. These Mormons love their cellars. They fill them up with enough food to keep themselves stuffed for a year or two. It's part of their religion. So they have cellars, but I'd never seen one like this. The first time I walked in, I was astounded by the size.

They'd built it right below the barn, which was huge with half a dozen horse stalls on either side, and a tall ceiling with a two-thousand-square-foot guest quarters above that. Post and beam. Beautiful. I use it for my home. But the cellar, for my taste, was glorious.

The entrance is completely hidden. It's in the last stall on the left. Rake out the hay, and there's a heavy oak door set flush with the floor. It has a recessed, hand carved O-ring that blends right in. I didn't even notice the door until they pointed it out to me. Turn the O-ring and the door opens to a steep set of stairs that descends fifteen feet to the floor below. The cellar is the full size of the barn. Very raw in appearance, with unfinished cinder block walls. There's a composting toilet on the far end, the "kitty box," and cold water pipes running out of the ceiling nearby.

When I viewed it for the first time, it was stacked with all these survivalist foods: hundred-pound sacks of rice, oats, flour, huge boxes of dried fruits, dehydrated milk, beef jerky, plus cases of tortilla chips, pretzels, Twinkies, Sno Balls, you name it. Cookies, instant cakes. Those Mormons were a bunch of couch potatoes waiting for the apocalypse.

It looks much different down there now.

. . .

I drive right into the barn, close the double door, and lock up. And then I listen. I listen very closely. I've never found anyone here, but this would be the worst possible time for an oversight.

It feels odd to me. I realize that it's probably nothing, just the effects of a sixteen-hour drive, but I inspect each stall. They're all empty. Except for the hay, they're as shiny clean as the Mormons left them more than fifteen years ago.

Still uneasy, I walk upstairs to the guest house. It's as quiet as a cathedral in here. I look up at the timbers crisscrossing high above me, but see nothing but a single silky strand fallen from an unseen spiderweb. It's snagged on a beam and catches the silvery light.

A long kitchen bar extends along my right as I enter, with the living area to my left. When I looked at the guest quarters for the first time they had their Christmas tree over here, a giant, the largest I'd ever seen inside a home. It must have taken days to decorate.

I walk past the furniture and enter the hallway, darting into my bedroom on impulse. But there's no one there. There's no one anywhere in the guest house, and feeling reassured I go back downstairs and open the back of the van.

Phew, it smells. I cut the ankle bindings on each of them and let them lean against the closest horse stall. I don't know if any of them have slept, but the girl's eyes now look puffy and red, like she's been crying. Not so saucy anymore, is she?

I unlock the O-ring and twist it. The door rises easily. Lots of gears. I march them down like prisoners. June looks ridiculous in her pantyhose, and the boy affects a bowlegged gait, which I assume is the result of his mess. Which reminds me to tell them about the kitty box.

As they enter the cellar, I watch their eyes closely. I want to see their reaction. This is important to me.

They all startle. All of them, as a group, rear back to the wall when they see what the cellar holds, and I can hardly suppress a laugh.

"Move on. Keep going."

This is the richest moment of all because they're seeing the bone parade for the first time. Their eyes fall on the remains of the desperate and the dead, the smashed and the scattered, all the pathetic people who finally gave up on hope and good fortune, survival or escape. The skeletons stand before them, draped in the clothing they once wore. I'm not a sculptor for nothing; I've used my blowtorch to weld the figures into positions familiar to anyone who's seen my art, though not once in all the times I've done this has anyone ever made that connection. Sculpture is so far below the radar screen for most Americans that it doesn't even raise a blip. If they don't care about me, why should I care about them?

But they do care about their fate, and they know death when it stares back at them. That's what the dearly departed do, they stare from their empty eye sockets at every newcomer; and from the darkness of those orbital holes they speak too, of the future, the not too distant future when the newcomers will join them, and the bone parade will grow even longer.

"You should feel honored," I tell them. "Not everyone gets to see this side of my work."

They look confused, this is denial at work, and I herd them along. I don't want open rebellion. I've got my gun, but I'd rather not use it. And now, yes I can see, they're looking at the cage. This is truly a magnificent structure. It rises to the ceiling and stands as wide as the cellar itself. I also welded this together. It's sculpture in its own right, made from found art. Mostly metal, steel from old car parts and wrecked trucks, chrome and copper from plumbing supplies, rebar, even old sewing machines and drill presses. If your only point of reference is popular culture, think *Waterworld*, or better yet think of any of those cheesy futuristic epics set in dark subterranean worlds where hopeless prisoners stare out from behind thick bars.

I've also woven in the sun-bleached skulls of cattle (think Georgia O'Keefe now), along with the bones of dogs, cats, and animals more feral than these. Their prison's a tomb built from the rusting remnants of our culture. And it is strong. They can climb on it—and most of them are all over it at one point or another looking for a way out—but all they do is cut themselves on the bones and old car bumpers.

There is no way out—no climbing, no tunneling, no picking the locks—but only Jolly Roger seems to sense this. He has not followed his family into the cage. He stands at the entrance surveying everything before him. I have to prod his awareness with my gun before he joins his brood. I close the door, an irregular series of open spaces and harshly welded joints, all metal, all tested.

I throw the lock, and tell Roger to come over.

"Turn around." He does this without protest. Perhaps he trusts me not to hurt him, not right now. Perhaps he no longer cares.

I have him press himself up against an opening so I can unlock the handcuffs. Most of them immediately rip the tape from their mouths, so impatient are they with the urge to scream. But he stands unmoving, a big man who's fading faster than cheap denim.

June hurries over and pushes him aside, then turns around so I can cut the duct tape from her hands. As soon as she's free, she tears the tape off her mouth and tries to shout, but can't. Her throat is so dry she hacks, and when she finally forms words she sounds like Linda Blair in *The Exorcist*, every syllable torn and frayed, ripped from a parched throat.

"What is this? What do you want with us?" Her eyes race to the creatures we have passed, and she gasps, "Who are they?" But she knows who they are. She knows.

I signal her daughter to come over, and as she approaches, June smacks her face, and gasps,

"You horrible . . . girl. Laughing at your brother, playing along with him."

June's eyes flash at me, and I see fury in them, and hear it in her crusty voice when she turns back to her daughter.

"Don't you *dare* start playing your games."

The woman shakes as she tries to restrain herself from taking another swing. Seeing this stirs Roger to life, and he takes his wife's arm, grunting—the tape is still on his mouth—as he leads her away. I can see it's going to get testy down here.

I free the girl's hands, and she turns to me as she peels the last of the tape from her mouth. "See what I have to put up with?"

Then she walks over to the kitty box, pulls down her pants and underpants, and without ever turning away pees long and hard. It's as if she's replaying what I did in the van. She never takes her eyes off me, not even when Jolly Roger finally pulls the tape off his mouth and starts shouting "Cover up!" June joins in. So does Sonny-boy.

None of this fazes the daughter, who calmly stands, her pubis brazenly naked, and slowly pulls her underpants up. Her lazy movements seem designed to incense her parents further, and they succeed splendidly with her mother, who leads the "Cover up!" chorus to a shrieking finale.

I'm on the verge of cuffing June for the girl's protection when she collapses at her husband's feet and pounds the floor weakly. Once, twice, and then she is spent.

# CHAPTER
# 4

LAUREN HEARD HIS FOOTSTEPS, AND realized that she could now actually recognize the sound of Ry Chambers walking down the hall. This was getting to be a regular Wednesday morning routine. Eight o'clock sharp, he strolls into her office and starts asking questions. By eight-oh-five she's immersed in memory or theory or art, and quoting the likes of Kandinsky and Heidegger (last week it was *Building, Dwelling, Thinking*), offering the edifice of her thought to him, opening up as earnestly as she'd ever opened up to anyone, including all the students she'd ever taught. She loved it! She'd been seduced by the experience. Being interviewed was great. He was paying her more attention than she'd ever known. Three weeks now, going on four. Seduction, that's exactly what it was. And never having been interviewed in depth, she had no idea if her reaction was simply to the attention, or more troubling, to the man who provided it. She suspected the latter. Why else would she have dressed like this: heels, inch and a half (nothing outlandish, but enough to lift her all the way to five-three), when she could have worn her Birkenstocks. Isn't that what half the city wore? And a black skirt with silver piping that ran up the middle from the hem almost to the waist, falling short by a few critical, suggestive inches. Then there was the black sweater, which didn't quite cover both black bra straps at the same time, leaving one or the other to sport coquettishly with the world. With him. To be frank.

Plus the makeup, the red lipstick so striking against her pale skin and blond hair, nicely cut just yesterday at a pricey salon she'd read about in the paper.

*Seduction.* Except she was doing all the talking. Talking herself into it. Into what? More than a book, it seemed. All he'd done was look into her eyes and ask short questions, and off she'd roar. Short questions produced long answers. She'd discovered the guiding principle known to all good interviewers: the length of the answer is inversely related to the length of the question.

The more she talked to him, the more she told him about herself, and the more she told him about herself, the more she brought him into her world, her family, her history. Her father's get-rich-quick schemes. How he'd started raising exotic birds in their backyard in Connecticut. Beautiful birds with the most amazing plumage. How she'd taught a macaw to perch on her shoulder. But this was New England, and guess what? Every one of those birds froze to death the first winter. What was he thinking!

The bankruptcy too. She'd told Ry all about her father ordering them downstairs for a family meeting. "And bring your piggy banks," he'd said. "That's when I knew we were in trouble," she joked, and Ry laughed hard, a good honest laugh. Nothing quiet about it. She had too. All over again. As she had when she told him about her father's hypochondria, the way he'd lie on a couch and tell his kids that "this could be it. You'd better be kind to your old dad. I might not be here much longer." And her mother saying, "Oh, Jay-sus, Martin, you've got a common cough." Him, lying there, shaking his head, murmuring, "You don't know that, Lillian."

She recalled uncomfortably that a novelist had once said that writers were constantly betraying the people closest to them. She felt distractingly close to Ry now. Was he going to betray her too? Take all those words and make her a fool? Her father had made fools of them, left them, all of them, for another woman. Then returned at five A.M. a week later to say it was the biggest mistake of his life, that what they all needed was a good vacation. A good vacation? They barely had the money to pay the rent. What did he have in mind? The Riviera? Provence? After he'd left them, she'd cried herself to sleep every night, cried till her insides ached, so she was glad he was back, but even then part of her was thinking, It's five o'clock in the morning! Couldn't you have done this at any other time?

Three days later he was gone again. And this time he didn't come back.

She'd told Ry things she'd never told anyone else, not Chad, not Gene, not any of her boyfriends, lovers. Not even her therapist. Opening up her mouth, herself, opening up at every opportunity, so naturally she listened when he'd looked in her milky blue eyes and said that no one would ever care about what she had to say as much as he did.

The arrogance! To state that so baldly. But the truth of it landed right in her gut, because no one else had ever listened as closely as he did; and if no one ever had, why at age thirty-nine should she expect that anyone ever would?

Ironically, for all of her preoccupation with him, he startled her when he finally did walk in. Jumping like that had always made her feel fragile, like a canary, which had been one of her nicknames in high school, a biographical detail she had not divulged.

Lauren led Ry to the foundry ten minutes before the pour was scheduled. They could feel the heat from the furnace as soon as they stepped in the room, and she questioned her sanity for dressing like this. She noticed his water bottle, and asked him to put it on a shelf by the door.

"People get nervous about water in here. If any of it gets splashed on the crucible or mold, they can explode. They get that hot."

"Consider it done."

When he came back, she handed him a fireproof coat and a hard hat with a Plexiglas face shield.

"This is really going to make it hard to take notes," he said.

"So will a hole in your head. That stuff," she nodded at the glowing crucible of bronze, "is twenty-one-hundred degrees, and if a drop of it splatters and lands on your head, it'll burn right through your skull and kill you."

"Say no more, I already have enough holes in my head."

He slipped them on, and they walked to the periphery of the pour.

She'd spent her first two years as a teacher at a private school in Texas. Ross Perot's grandson had been among her students, and the Secret Service among the onlookers. It was the '92 presidential race, which she'd been aware of only distantly. She'd spent so much time casting bronze with those kids that she'd learned to regulate the air and gas in the foundry furnace by the degree of vibration it triggered in her diaphragm. When she'd told Ry about this, he'd asked about a temperature gauge—didn't the furnace have one? She'd said they were never as accurate as the vibrations. Then she'd looked up, as if she'd snapped out of a trance, and said, "Oh my, that's so ooey-dooey."

"Ooey-dooey? Is that some kind of technical term?"

He'd been smiling, but still she'd blushed, felt the blood rush right into her face. "So New Age."

Two students held either end of a six-foot steel rod with a cradle in the middle that held the crucible. She explained to Ry that the young man who had his back to them was the pourer, and the person who held the other end was called the shank. Despite the face shield, Ry took notes.

It took muscle to do the job, she pointed out to him, but it wasn't nearly as macho an ordeal as most of the men who worked in foundries would have you believe. Though the psychological tension, she allowed, could be intense.

"Why's that?" he said.

"You're pouring everyone's work, not just your own. A lot of students, and even some artists for that matter, work directly in wax. You blow the pour, that's it, all their work goes down the drain."

"Have you ever done that?"

"No, but I've seen it happen."

"Do you miss . . . bronze?" He held up his reporter's notebook, as if holding a bar of it.

She'd told him about the bronze phase of her career, but not how she felt about the material itself.

"Yes and no. There's something very primal about bronze. It's so ritualistic. You're taking something hard—metal—and you're making a liquid out of it, and then suddenly it gets hard all over again in a whole new form. And all of that is wrapped up in this weird sense of permanence. Even bad sculpture can appear impressive in bronze. You see it all the time. It's mediocre art, but it looks meaningful because it looks immortal. Look—here they go."

The shank and the pourer lifted the steel bar with the steaming crucible, and stepped toward the molds clustered on a dirt floor inside the pouring area. The bronze blazed, and even with all of her experience, it was difficult for Lauren to remain unimpressed. So much was at stake: so much work and so much inspiration. All art was a gamble, a casino with its own roulette wheels and baccarat tables and rolling dice and deadeye dealers. You staked a good part of your shaky financial status on a piece that had taken perhaps months to finish, handed it over to a gallery owner who would take fifty percent of the sales price, and bet on the buying whim of the public; but all of that was loose change compared to turning your sculpture over to others to cast. Here was a liquid that could betray you in a second, yet so cunning in its artfulness that it could fill the farthest reaches of a mold and lend itself to the most exquisite shapes—curves and angles and contours that would outlast life itself.

Already great puffs of invisible scent rose from the mold, the slightly sweet odor of the metal as it began to harden and give new form to the world. Thousands of hours at stake. She could see the pressure in the bent back of the pourer, the way he remained so tightly in control, and in the intensity of the shank's eyes as he looked out from behind the face shield. But wait, that's Kerry, Lauren said to herself as she glanced again at the shank. The girl must have finally come up for foundry duty; students had to wait months for a chance to work in here. Kerry was staring at the pourer, following his every cue, letting him lead, a richly choreographed pas de deux with a blazing sun between them, holding them firmly in its orbit.

They finished filling the first mold, took two short rehearsed steps to the right, centered the crucible, and the pourer started to turn it on its side. But then he hesitated.

"No-no. Don't!" Lauren whispered, painfully aware that she could do little more than plead as a splatter of bronze fell to the top of the mold, flattened, and instantly began to harden.

From where she stood, she couldn't see if the chute had been splashed, inadvertently sealed, destroying all the efforts that had gone into creating this piece of sculpture.

Kerry's head rose. Lauren could see the tension in the girl's eyes. It wasn't her fault, but it was her first pour, and Lauren considered it entirely likely that she would blame herself.

"You're fine, girl. You're fine." Lauren again found herself whispering from behind her face shield, overheard by no one.

The pourer took a small step, repositioned the crucible, and this time poured cleanly into the mold, which accepted the bronze.

Lauren took a welcome breath of the foundry's warm air as drops of perspiration ran down her sides. She'd always perspired heavily for a woman. Why-oh-why had she worn these clothes?

She hung her helmet on one of the hooks by the door, and shed the heavy coat. Her fingers rose to her brow, then ran through her hair, harvesting perspiration from both. Her wan complexion had turned as red as a stoplight.

Ry's skin certainly looked moist. Beads of sweat had formed above his upper lip, and she had to resist the urge to dab them away with her finger.

When they stepped into the hall, the normally tepid air felt cool.

"So what did you think of your first pour?"

"Except for feeling like I was in a sauna," he wiped his face with the crook of his elbow, "I thought it was really impressive." He drew deeply on his water bottle.

"Did you notice the little mistake that almost turned it into a disaster?" she said as they headed up the stairs to the third floor.

"Is that what it was? I wasn't sure. I noticed the guy facing us staring at the guy who was doing the pouring."

"That was Kerry. It wasn't her mistake."

"Kerry? Really? I couldn't tell."

"It's pretty hard with everyone in face shields and coats."

They stepped around the sawhorses that still formed a pentagon outside her office.

"Are they ever going to fix that thing?" He looked at the crack, which had been crudely patched with cement.

"I have no idea. They never tell us anything." She unlocked the door. "They did seal it."

He looked back at the barrier. "They obviously don't trust their own work."

"By the way," she walked over to her desk, "I found this on the net. I thought you might want to take a look at it."

She handed him a copy of an article called "The Triangle of Life."

"It turns out that we did everything wrong when the quake hit. You're not supposed to stand in doorways. The fatality rate for people who do that is extremely high."

"No kidding? I'd always heard doorways were the safest places in an earthquake."

"Me too, but now they're saying that you're much better off finding the nearest solid object and standing by it, or curling up next to one if you have to. Then when the ceiling and walls fall in you have this triangle," she demonstrated with her hands, "between a file cabinet or a desk, let's say, and the chunk of ceiling that's leaning against it."

He looked at the article she'd copied, then her. "So it's really true: you *do* learn something new every day, if you're not careful."

He was smiling as he tried to hand it back.

"No, go ahead and keep it. I made that for you."

"Thanks. Look, you've been so generous with your time, how about if I take you to lunch. Or dinner?"

The way he'd said "Or dinner?" made her realize that they'd reached a crossroads: Lunch was safe. Dinner was sex. The distinction felt as real as the crack in the ceiling.

"I can't go to lunch, not today. I'm supposed to meet with one of my students. But dinner . . . dinner would be nice. Tonight?" She thought that's probably what he meant; he had to drive all the way in from the coast.

"That would be great. Seven sound good?"

She nodded, part regret, part pure anticipation. A jumpy feeling in her stomach.

"Where shall I pick you up?"

She gave him her address, and they shook hands as they had each time he'd left. She wondered how they'd say good night. The student she had to meet with was Kerry. She hadn't wanted to know if the prospect of the girl's presence would spark Ry's interest, make him linger; and she definitely didn't want to put up with Kerry's flirting again.

Kerry arrived a few minutes late, as was her habit. Lauren could not get accustomed to this any more than she could get used to seeing her students piercing their bodies with rings and bars and studs. Kerry, she'd been pleased to see, had confined her self-mutilation to her belly button, nose, and the obligatory half dozen holes that ran along the outer fold of each of her ears.

Lauren had noticed that the most oft punctured students, the ones who looked aggressively unattractive, like furious warriors from a sci-fi flick, inevitably turned out to be the sweetest kids. She had come to believe that excessive body piercing was a means of warding off sexual interest, perhaps the predictably sad response to a culture that had sexualized them from childhood, through ads, music, and movies, and sometimes, most grimly, through touch.

Kerry wrapped her long legs around the base of the chair, and rocked forward. "Guess what?"

"What?"

"Stassler says I can stay in a room in his house. He says he has a guest house above a barn that he stays in, so I can have the big house to myself. He says he's so far out in the country that getting in every day would be a drag."

"That's accommodating of him."

"I'm bringing my bike anyway."

"How far is his place from town?"

"From Moab, it's about twelve miles."

"That's a long way to ride."

"Not really. I've been racing mountain bikes every summer since I was sixteen. I can do twenty, twenty-five miles like it's nothing."

Kerry was feisty, and Lauren could see why she'd be so appealing to men. There was sexiness in that sort of zip. Looking at her features in isolation, you wouldn't consider her a beauty, but put it all together—the dimple in her chin, her henna hair cut in a strange V on her forehead, those bright brown eyes and straight nose, and truly perfect lips—and you beheld an extremely attractive combination.

"It's the mountain biking capital of the world," Kerry said. "I've always wanted to go there."

"I hope that didn't influence your—"

"No way! Come on, there's plenty of good riding around here. I want to work with Stassler," she said with conviction. "His vision is so, I don't know, dark, but real."

Yes, thought Lauren, dark, but real. As an undergrad she'd also been impressed with all that dark but real, Sturm und Drang crap; but she'd outgrown it, and thought most other artists did too. Only a few insisted on wallowing in it, mostly the ones unlucky enough to have found early success, and who then sentenced themselves to the prison of popular expectations where they repeated themselves ad nauseam. She thought of the painter who had his first big commercial success more than two decades ago with highly stylized hearts. He was still painting them. He lacked either imagination or courage. She asked herself which one applied to Ashley Stassler. But it wasn't her job to criticize him. Better to let Kerry reach her own conclusions in her own time. As she herself had. When Lauren had set up the internship program, her goal was to put budding sculptors together with the men and women they admired. Stassler had surprised her by his willingness to cooperate. For that she was grateful, even if she now thought of him as more artisan than artist, good with technique, but absent of any original vision. But hers was a minority view, and unlikely to prevail.

"Okay, let's review your goals for the next two months." It was important for a student to keep her own objectives in mind, lest she become an errand runner for an artist. Part of the compact required the sculptor to help the student with her own work.

Kerry opened her portfolio, spilling out copies of the material she'd sent Stassler, including black-and-white photographs of the pieces she planned to cast under his supervision. Her drawings also fell out, along with her curriculum vitae, and a color photo that showed her kneeling by the piece she'd exhibited on critique day. But there was nothing vaguely anthropomorphic about Kerry in this picture: she was wearing a short skirt and a snug halter. Lauren had to repress a groan; her stomach felt as if it had sunk to her knees.

"You sent this to him? All of it?" Her hand moved over the material, including the sassy picture of Kerry herself.

"Yup," Kerry said. "I wanted him to see everything," she added with no self-consciousness whatsoever.

Lauren felt badly for her. Kerry's photograph would have been bait for a lot of men. Perhaps this was especially true for a man who lived in the desert by himself. Maybe Kerry had intended this, but Lauren didn't think so. The girl could be flirty, no question about it. But sexually scheming? No, Lauren didn't think so. More than anything, Kerry was obsessed with sculpture.

The work she planned to cast was impressive. So were her drawings. If he helped her in the foundry, then he would be giving her a great gift. They could not reasonably ask for more from a sculptor of his stature. Except, of course, for him to keep his hands off her.

Lauren planned to dress down for dinner. She had no idea where Ry planned to take her, and didn't want to appear overly . . . Overly what, she demanded of herself. Overly . . . eager? Overly . . . interested? Overly . . . sexed?

When was the last time I felt like this? She held a red sweater up to her chest and looked in the vanity mirror, which nestled in the corner of the tiny room and revealed the double bed and comforter in the background. She began to hum "Norwegian Wood," the words flitting across memory, teasing her with certain sweet possibilities,

*She asked me to stay and told me to sit anywhere, so I looked around and I noticed there wasn't a chair.*

The sweater had a fetching split up the back that stopped an inch or two above the waist, and flared away on both sides. Oh hell, she tossed the sweater aside and slipped on a white blouse.

No, absolutely not. You look like a schoolmarm. I *am* a schoolmarm. Kind of.

Off with the blouse, on with the sweater. And a calf length gray skirt that buttoned down the front. The last time she'd worn it had been to an opening with Chad in December, the night before she'd told him that she wanted marriage, maybe a family too. She'd unbuttoned it to just above the knee. For all the good it had done. She moved to button it up, but then didn't.

Now she applied more of the red lipstick she favored, touched up her mascara, and froze when she considered cologne.

Do it, she ordered herself.

Over dinner at one of Portland's better seafood restaurants, she finally got him to open up. It had taken almost a month. He surprised her by saying he was the second of four children, all raised by their mother; his father had fled when he was four.

"The four of you, by herself?"

"She's an amazing woman. Very smart."

"Did she work? I mean, outside the home?"

"You bet. She had to. She had a masters in counseling. She was a therapist. My sisters and I used to tell everyone that she treated severely emotionally disturbed people, and then she went to work."

Lauren laughed. Ry smiled, clearly pleased that an old family joke had succeeded once again.

"I'll bet you were pretty healthy kids."

"We were. We are. I missed having a father around, but she never missed a ball game, or a school play, or anything that was important to us."

"Plays?" She had designed and built sets in college. "Did you act, or work behind the scenes?"

"I did some acting."

"Did you pursue it at all?"

"Only in the broadest sense: I was an anchorman."

"TV news? Really?"

"Don't look so shocked."

"You seem . . ."

"What?"

"Too . . ."

"Too?"

"Too smart."

Now he laughed. "We're not all dummies. I did it in Minneapolis, and then I worked in Miami for almost ten years."

"Why did you leave?"

"In a word, I got sick of it." He squeezed lemon on his grouper. "I just couldn't do the work anymore, and when I told them, they said, 'Don't worry, come in when you want. As long as you're here to do the news at six and eleven.' But that was ridiculous. The vibes in the newsroom were ugly. Everyone else was working these long hours, and I was coming in at five-thirty, just in time for makeup. It wasn't comfortable, and I'd been doing it forever. I'd made plenty of money, so I decided to get out and try something different."

"A book about sculpture?" Her incredulity sounded a raw note.

"Everybody has a story, and some people have great ones. You just have to listen. And besides, I have a feeling about this one."

"A feeling? What are you doing now, warming up for the Psychic Friends Network?"

He laughed again. She liked the way his merriment turned his face from handsome to mischievous.

"That sounds like something my mother would have said."

"Your mother?" Lauren asked.

"It's a compliment. Trust me."

This was the moment. Walking to the door. Saying good night. It felt awkward in high school. It felt awkward in college. And it still felt awkward at thirty-nine.

They stepped up on the porch, and the light over the doorway suddenly appeared too bright. She heard that Beatles song again, and wondered if she did invite him in, where *would* he sit? There seemed no halfway ground, standing here or sitting on the bed, and then he gestured at an old church pew in the shadows at the far end of the porch.

Once they'd settled, she asked about his interview with Stassler. He wouldn't be leaving for two weeks, but she'd set aside studio time for herself down in Pasadena, and might not see him again until after he got back from Moab.

"How long do you think it'll take?" She hoped not more than a week or two.

"It's more a question of how much time he'll give me. I'm a glutton for time, in case you hadn't noticed."

"I haven't minded at all. I've enjoyed it."

He sat closer, and leaned his body toward her. She felt a pulse of delicious anxiety. Scared in a good way.

Their knees were touching. She wasn't clear on the precise moment when this had come to pass, only that she welcomed the contact. She looked down and saw that her skirt had fallen open, past the button that she'd decided to leave undone. The knee that was touching his, along with a few inches of thigh, appeared brazenly on view. When she resisted her reflexive urge to cover up, she experienced a deeper, even more delicious pulse.

His hand rose to her chin, and she let him guide her lips to his. She felt so young and nervous and giddy, and surprised that a kiss could still excite her so, make her mouth moist with longing; but it also made her feel more than a little naughty, for she was kissing and touching a man other than Chad for the first time in seven years.

# CHAPTER

## 5

*FAMILY PLANNING.* THAT'S THE TITLE I used for my first piece, and then later I decided that the whole series ought to go under the same name. *Family Planning #2, #3*, and so on through *Family Planning #8*.

Jolly Roger, June Cleaver, Sonny-boy, and Diamond Girl will be *#9*. I have yet to configure them. Usually a family's pecking order is pretty predictable, but this crew has confounded all my expectations. First of all, Diamond Girl—her name came to me as naturally as daybreak: she's hard and beautiful and seems capable of cutting anything—runs the show, whether her parents accept this or not. They key off her moods, as I suspect they have for years. Even June reacts to Diamond Girl more than she *acts* on her own behalf.

Early on I exacerbated this dynamic by announcing that Diamond Girl was the decision maker, their master. That if they wanted anything, they had to go through her.

They all wanted something. June, for instance, spent the first two weeks demanding, and finally begging for clothes. Her pantyhose had more runs than the American Kennel Club, and her underpants had become embarrassingly discolored, so I told her, "You'd better ask Diamond Girl. See what she says."

"Diamond Girl?" She looked around clearly perplexed—Who else could it have been?—before staring at her daughter. "Ask *her?*"

June's hand rose to her mouth like an Indian about to make a war cry in one of those old John Wayne movies. But she appeared too stunned to attack. I think she'd been struck dumb by the news that the natural order of things wasn't the natural order after all, though I was only making official what had long been their practice. Any fool could have seen that.

Her eyes changed color. I'm not kidding. They darkened from brown to black, and widened to the size of soup spoons. She reached for the cage to support herself, and gripped the skull of a cat. Her pinkie actually curled into the creature's empty eye socket, a violation of the dead that she never appeared to notice.

"What's going on?" she said to her daughter. "Why are you doing this to us? You think he's going to be nice to you if you're like this?" And then suddenly she stopped talking, and her features flattened, as if she'd been splashed with a cup of cold water. A word sputtered on her lips, which I couldn't hear. It might have been "Wait." Her eyes overflowed, and her cheeks and brow clenched into hard furrows. More than anything, they made me think of a freshly plowed field. The harvest came soon enough.

"I get it," she said in a choked voice. "I do. You planned this whole thing, didn't you? The two of you."

As she spoke, she let go of the cat skull and edged closer to her daughter. Roger, roused from his lethargy, intercepted her.

"No, she didn't. She wouldn't do that. You're upset. Calm down."

But Diamond Girl smiled and never denied the role her mother had assigned her.

Some people are born to the manor.

■   ■   ■

A day later, after June had wept for hours and implored her daughter to talk to her, Diamond Girl announced, without ever looking at her, that she would be "permitted" (yes, she chose that very word, the precisely correct word under the circumstances) to wear a thong, but no bra, and absolutely no top.

Now why she would have assumed that I had a thong lying around, I don't know, but the fact is that I had two of them, a satiny purple, and one with a floral pink and white design.

June went off like nitro. I'd been expecting this. All those tears, all that pleading and paranoia and motherly resentment, that's a volatile mix.

She shot to her feet and ran over to Diamond Girl, kicking and screaming at her. Diamond Girl balled herself up and waited for Jolly Roger to perform his paternal duty, which he did, but not without injury to himself, so far gone was June by this point. The blow that drew blood was the one she landed on his nose, and that brought Roger back to life for the first time since he'd entered the cage. He pushed her away and threatened to kick the shit out of her if she didn't quit. Truly, this family is evil.

I couldn't resist inflaming them further. Right then I walked back upstairs to the guest quarters, grabbed the thongs, and returned posthaste to the cellar.

"Diamond Girl has spoken. Which will it be?" I held them up, each thong no bigger than the palm of my hand. June stared at them. "They stretch to fit," I assured her. She turned away before I could demonstrate.

Roger said, "Gimme the pink one. How about both? Something she could change into?"

I shook my head no, and tossed him the floral print. June did not change right then, but the next time I looked in she'd put on the thong.

"Your bra?" I held out my hand in expectation. She knew the deal, but shook her head.

"Then Sonny-boy doesn't get to eat."

The bra came off. The maternal instinct is so strong. Sometimes. She glared at Diamond Girl, who crossed her arms, mimicking her mother, whose attempt to maintain even a small degree of modesty was doomed.

For most of the month, food has been an issue for them; indeed, a divisive one, though that wasn't my intent. Jolly Roger and June are hungry almost all of the time because I'm trying to reduce their body fat to single digits. This may not be possible for June, because women cling to fat like sap to a tree. It's evolutionary, I'm sure. But I'll get her down to about twelve, thirteen percent, and given her overall tone, she'll look great. Roger, even as he loses weight, doesn't look good at all. It's his lack of tone. He has the body of a man who has eaten too many quickie airport meals—too much fat and too much sodium—and hasn't had nearly enough exercise. It's not that he's fat. It's that despite his size, he's beginning to look feeble. And now that I've seen him naked, it's hard to imagine that June ever got excited at the prospect of having sex with him. She may be off her rocker, but she's got a nice body and a kind face that completely belies the fury that comes out on an almost daily basis now. It's reached the point where I expect her to scowl and screech whenever I address her.

"You're looking good, June," I say as I come down the cellar steps. She turns away, hiding her breasts but exposing her butt. The truth is there aren't many moms in their late thirties who can wear a thong, but telling her this does not improve her mood. She swears at me, having given up all pretense of civility.

"Look, I try to flatter you and all you can do is snarl. That's it, no petit fours for you today. I'm giving yours to Diamond Girl."

June stops, just freezes in her footsteps. I can almost read her mind. *Petit fours. You mean those luscious little chocolate and cream cakes that come in apricot and cherry and raspberry and mocha?* Yes, *those* petit fours, June.

I wasn't planning on giving them to her anyway. Petit fours, to someone who needs to lose body fat? That's like giving Jack Daniel's to someone who's trying to dry out. No, this is a special treat for Diamond Girl and Sonny-boy, neither of whom needs to lose weight. In fact, I'm more concerned with keeping them just the way they are, which is damn near perfect.

"You do that," June spits without looking back at me. "You just *do* that."

"And prayer service will be held at five today."

"What?" Now she whips around, her face as wrinkled as a rag. Even Jolly Roger looks up when he hears this announcement.

"Isn't that what you said, Diamond Girl?"

"Yeah," she snorts. "Prayers at five. Bring your Bibles and get ready to thump."

This kid is great. She's quick, and she plays right along. I'm going to miss her.

June, realizing she's been had, swears again, which causes the greatly aggrieved Sonny-boy to burst into tears and complain,

"You never used to say those bad words, Mommy."

June shakes her head, which makes her breasts jiggle in a most appealing manner, and walks over to her son. He throws his arms around her, pressing his face into her naked belly. She hugs him and whispers, "I'm sorry."

It's a touching moment, if you're touched by such things.

This parceling of food has created a great deal of tension. It's clear to me now that Jolly Roger and June resent the wholesome meals I prepare for Sonny-boy and Diamond Girl, and if past experience tells me anything, I'll soon see the total breakdown of the family. June, I'll bet, will attack Diamond Girl to get her food. Roger won't intervene; he'll be too busy trying to wrestle an extra portion away from his son. You think the family that suffers together stays together?

I had this happen with *Family Planning #5*, a fivesome from Kentucky. I am *never* trolling in that state again. It got so bad I had to set up a temporary shelter for the children. If I hadn't, they might not have survived for the sculpture.

The parents' problems were greatly aggravated by the most extraordinary nicotine addiction I've ever seen. After a day without tobacco they were screaming and shouting over the pettiest differences, and by the second day they were openly beating each other sans any excuse at all.

I had to cast them sooner than I wanted to, and #5 is the weakest piece in the entire series. Even the critics agree. If they'd only known what I had to go through, they might have been a good deal more forgiving in their reviews.

Slimming down my subjects is such a hassle that I wouldn't even bother except that the gaunt, hungry look increases the appearance of terror. Muscles stand out more, so do veins, and in those final seconds of resistance, at the very moment when they have a vision of their death, there's a definition to their bodies that wasn't there before.

But this takes more than diet and supplements. More than anything, it takes the planned introduction of terror. This is how you really stiffen them up over time, make them jumpy and nervous and wary so that their reflexes are in overdrive, their glands alive with adrenaline.

I roll the television and VCR up to the cage. The screen is large. I have speakers, big ones hanging on the walls facing them.

"Show time," I announce.

Diamond Girl wanders up and glances at the screen. "What's it going to be?" she says with more good nature than even I deserve. "*Henry, Portrait of a Serial Killer*, or were you thinking of something a little less obvious, like *Texas Chainsaw Massacre*."

"Don't incite him," Roger says sotto voce, but I hear him.

"What?" Diamond Girl snaps at her father, "you think if we're good he'll give us *Nick in the Afternoon*?"

"How about some Julie Andrews," I say.

"Shut up!" June screams, and I'm forced to order them all to cease and desist.

"Now, I can't make you watch, but if I were you I would. I'd watch very carefully. What you're about to see is your future, if you don't cooperate with me, if you don't follow *all* my instructions. And who knows?" I add blithely, "Maybe by watching you'll figure out how to get out of here. Maybe I've *missed* something."

"Yeah, and maybe she's Anne Bancroft in *The Miracle Worker*," Diamond Girl shakes her head at her mother, "but I don't *think* so!"

She's a pistol, and apparently a bit of a film buff to boot. Well, let's see how she likes this one. Let's see how they all like this one.

I dim the lights and turn on the tape, and as promised up pops Julie Andrews singing in *The Sound of Music*.

But then there's a rough cut, if you'll excuse the pun, and they're no longer hearing the marvelous voice of Ms. Andrews but the screams, and they are chilling, of a young girl. *Family Planning #8*'s, as a matter of fact. Just a little younger than Diamond Girl. She's strapped to a table, and she's staring to the side. She pulls at the leather restraints, and each effort produces a show of muscle that I suspect only I am appreciating, though Sonny-boy's eyes are wide open. Perhaps he's never seen a naked girl, aside from his cellmates. I presume their bared flesh holds little interest for him, though there's no telling with this family.

The camera looks down on her. The lighting is harsh (I'm no cinematographer), but the focus is good. And now the camera starts to tilt in the direction the girl is looking. Slowly, we begin to see that she's watching another TV where the writhing figure of a woman lies on a stainless steel table beneath a cover of what appears to be green clay. It is, in fact, alginate, the gummy material dentists use to take an impression of teeth. The woman is choking to death; her ghastly green body has become one long spasm. Her grunts are extremely disturbing.

"There's more to come," I say with impressive eeriness. At least I think so, but Diamond Girl doesn't miss a beat:

"Oooo," she coos, "real spooky, dude. Can I go first," she adds in a bored voice. "So I can get the fuck out of here."

But she's the only one talking. June, for once, is speechless. Jolly Roger stares at me, and Sonny-boy has lost all fascination with frontal nudity, and is crying again.

"That was her mom, right? The one that was choking."

"That's very observant of you, Diamond Girl."

I can hear the wariness in my voice. She's done this to me, made *me* wary. I don't like that, not one bit, but I'm intrigued.

"So I'll get to see something like that too?" She smiles at her mother, who isn't looking; she's leaning against the cage with her head down.

"Maybe I'll make you go first, and let her watch," I say.

"No," she says, cocky as a one-eyed whore in the land of the blind (to give a new twist to an old line), "you're not going to do that. You're going to kill her first, then my dad, then my brother, and then you're going to kill me."

She's right, but how does she know? I actually want to ask, but I'm not going to concede her anything. Then, as it turns out, I don't have to because she says, "I know because that's how I'd do it."

I observe them for hours on a monitor in my bedroom. I have three cameras, two set into the walls and one in the ceiling right above them. I'm certain they haven't noticed. There's not that much to see; a camera's eye is quite small, and the walls and ceiling are unfinished, rough in appearance.

But I see a great deal. June has just finished playing another in an interminable round of tic-tac-toe with Sonny-boy. This one went on for more than two hours of drawing Xs and Os in the dirt, then smoothing them over with her palms, playing without talking. They've been doing this for weeks.

Jolly Roger sits leaning against the wall most of the time, and when he does move he grips his lower back, like he's got a disc out. He hasn't complained, hasn't said much of anything in days.

Diamond Girl watches her family as intensely as I do. When Jolly Roger tried to talk to her yesterday, she told him to "back off."

I've caught her staring at the walls and ceiling too, as if she suspects that I'm watching; and after what she said about the order of death, I can't help but wonder if she's looking for the camera because she knows that she'd be watching too.

I've also become convinced that she's trying to seduce me. I know that statement would probably raise a Duh! from her, it's so obvious, what with her tongue on my hand in the van, and the way she went out of her way to expose herself in the kitty box when we first got down here. But even during the hours when I'm out of the cellar, I see the seduction in the way she moves. Sometimes she stretches, does a whole series of feline movements, and she's always, *always* positioned for optimum exposure, whether it's her ass rising up in the air when she's on all fours, or her breasts thrusting into profile when she's stretching her shoulders back.

After the first week, I became intrigued enough by her posturing to bring them all buckets of warm water, soap, and face cloths. Towels too. I set them within easy reach of the cage before retreating to my monitor up here in my bedroom.

First, June and Jolly Roger helped Sonny-boy clean himself up. Then they went to work on themselves, Jolly Roger in the bored, brusque motions of a man who's past caring about his own stink, and June with the furious scrubbing of a penitent, a woman who hates her body and all that it has brought her, who wants nothing more from a bath than to scourge her own skin.

Their daughter waited till they stepped aside, then shed her clothes and washed herself without the least hint of self-consciousness.

I've given them buckets and washcloths every few days since, just for the joy of watching Diamond Girl. I've just done it again, and once more make myself comfortable in front of my monitor.

Diamond Girl strips off her top and pants as she has in the past. All very businesslike. But now she's inching her panties down, as if the waistband were fraught with resistance, a motion that makes much of what is to come. It's a tease, and it's definitely different from what I've seen up till now. Maybe she really has figured out that I'm watching, and is taking full delight in my desire. I sit forward knowing I'd climb right inside that screen if I could.

When she does slide her panties past her pubis, she stops to scratch her dark patch idly, provocatively, her upper arms squeezing her breasts together with each movement, making them swell above her bra. I'm aroused by all of this, and filled with a heady sense of anticipation. I couldn't take my eyes off her if the barn were burning down.

She's still facing me when she bends over and slides her panties all the way off. Her hair falls forward, and for a moment she's the picture of modesty; but then she straightens up quickly, sending it flying up over her head and onto her back. She reaches between the cups and unhooks her bra. But again, she moves slowly, her fingers lingering over their promise.

I'm not the only one noticing. Jolly Roger shows a keen interest too, the slob, and June tells him to look away. He raises his hands in surrender, as if he's been caught, and as he turns around he forces Sonny-boy to do the same, on the theory, I suppose, that if he can't watch, then justice cries out for a similar sacrifice on the part of his son.

June hisses at her daughter, "What do you think you're doing?"

Diamond Girl ignores her, and with surprising grace reveals one breast and then the other.

June looks around, as if she suspects that Diamond Girl has an audience, then stares balefully at her. I'm staring too. It's as if I'm seeing her breasts for the first time. They are so abundantly the breasts of a young girl, so taut, so forcefully forward in their trajectory. They have not suffered from children or time or weight gain and loss, the seesawing vicissitudes of most female flesh. They are . . . perfect . . . and pale, a pristine white with tiny nipples and a tan line that plummets between them to form a nearly perfect V that's matched by the dark V down below, which lies in a field of white so alluring, so inviting, that I cannot look away. I find myself begging her, as I have each time she's bathed, to turn around so I can see her bottom, which I have until this moment only glimpsed. And now, just when she does precisely what I wish, her goddamn mother picks up a towel. I curse the woman, would strike her dead this instant if doing so would preserve the vision I treasure; but June holds it between her daughter and the male members of her family, which does nothing to sully my view.

I'm mesmerized by the pale panty outline on Diamond Girl's bottom. My breath is a veritable storm. She has satisfied my greatest desire so easily that it's as if she can clearly see what I'm doing to myself.

She walks to the wall of the cage, her mother holding the towel beside her, reaches to the last of the buckets, and proceeds to wash herself thoroughly and without haste, pausing—yes, I'm certain of it—*pausing* over her pubis. She is not businesslike today. She is bold. She is brazen. She knows what she's doing, she *knows*. She's infecting me with richer and richer fantasies, and I have to fight the urge to yank her out of there. Already I spend too much time thinking of her, watching her. Last night I even dreamed of her. She had a child she'd named Baby Peach in a stroller, and she pushed it up to me.

"Baby Peach," she whispered in my ear. Even in my sleep I felt her breath hot and moist.

Baby Peach? I thought but did not say.

"Yes, Baby Peach," she said as if she'd heard me anyway.

Now she turns her bottom to me again and reaches back, scrubs and scrubs and scrubs, bringing the cloth up along the length of her crack, wringing the dirty water out and washing herself again, leaving herself pink where she had been pale.

To dream of her? I have never dreamed of them. Never. My dreams have never been troubled by such trifles. Now I want to kneel behind her and cup those cheeks with my hands, feel their fond firmness, their waves of warmth as I spread them cleanly. I want my tongue to tempt the sweetest heat she has to offer, to remain encircled while I inhale her every scent.

She has driven me to this. She is to die, but of course she's right: she will be the last to go.

I turn from the screen as she bends over once more, fully displaying all that has inflamed me. I must clean up after myself, but even as I reach for the tissues I know that Diamond Girl's display has not truly satisfied me. My thoughts, which rarely disturb my calm, are roiling with possibilities, none of them kind, not even by the standards that I enforce.

# CHAPTER

## 6

NORTHERN LIGHT GATHERED AS GENTLY as a caftan around the empty vessel. Lauren stepped back, still studying the plaster finish, the wash of earthy pink and brown pigments. They were not unlike the hues outside her studio window, which faced the Angeles National Forest, an austere landscape hardly deserving of the name. She could see little more than a scattering of green out there, the desert bushes that managed to eke out enough moisture to survive, and on the hills beyond a risen trove of pines that bore only a bitter resemblance to their lofty cousins in the Northwest. The sun-baked trees appeared brittle, snappish in temperament, the stunted offspring of a sere land with strict demands.

She brushed her plastery hands against her jeans, took a deep breath, and turned away. The break between academic quarters was proving productive. She'd finished the last in the series with the funny French names. After this she had to move on. She wondered what the critics would say about this piece. She wished she didn't care, but she did. Most of them had been kind to her work, even if the labels they'd used to describe it had been confusing at times. *ArtWeek*, for example, had called her last show "postmod-

ern . . . minimalist . . . and feminist" all in a single sentence. Another critic had stroked her ego more directly by comparing her—
and this came as a shock—to Henry Moore, one of the past
century's most esteemed sculptors, saying her vessels "with their
primordial simplicity and rich interior existence echo the master's
own metaphors, even as they seek to invent a sensual language
more appropriate to these less laden times."

Whew! She'd had to take a breather after reading that review,
and remind herself that it could be artistic death to believe your
press notices. But *sensual language?* She had to admit she liked
that one.

She needed a run, but knew better than to go out there at this
hour. After ten A.M. the ozone count in the San Gabriel Valley
generally rose to unhealthy levels, but she could not bear to stay
inside a moment longer. Finishing a sculpture made her fidgety,
anxious, ready to roar. And the skies looked clear; she'd felt a
breeze earlier when she'd put seed out for the birds, so maybe
some of the smog had been swept away. Maybe she could even
avoid Chad, who had taken to coming home from work at odd
hours to check on her in the studio. She didn't need him to check
on her. Didn't *want* him to check on her, but that's what he did
every day, stopped by to see if she'd changed her mind, if she
wanted a rapprochement, which would mean nothing more than a
return to a physical relationship with no future.

Quickly, before he could show up, she pulled off her jeans,
pleased to see how loosely they were fitting; all those miles were
paying off. She slipped on running shorts, socks, shoes, and a
sports bra, filled her water bottle, and stuffed it into a waist harness. She grabbed her sun visor on the way out, and jogged down
the block to the entrance to the national forest.

The metal gate stood open, a space barely wide enough for the
mountain biker who nodded to her as he snaked through it.

She reached up and gripped the fence, weighting her back and shoulder muscles, feeling them loosen, draining the tension from the hours she'd spent working in the studio. She devoted a few more minutes to stretching her quads and hamstrings, then started down the crumbling asphalt road that led away from the gate. The canyon walls on her left rose higher as she descended, filling the ravines and dry streambeds with shadows, the only coolness these stretches of rock and sand and parched scrub would likely know until the monsoon season returned, though it hadn't done so for several years now.

The road turned to dirt before it crossed a concrete bridge that looked as old as the city itself, and she wondered as she listened to her footfalls how it had managed to survive all the earthquakes.

Now the dirt road, no wider than an automobile, curved right, and she began to run uphill. To her left the buff-colored walls grew taller, steeper, until she came to a washout where the road had been devoured by a mudslide several years ago. She picked her way over the rocky surface before stepping up her pace again on the smoother dirt.

Her breath quickened as the grade increased, and the sun came alive on her head and back. Three miles up, three miles down. Take about an hour. She was no speedster, knew she'd never win a race; but she'd been lucky enough to have been born with thin genes, and she wanted to stay trim. Despite her pretty blue eyes and the lovely softness of her face, she considered her legs and back and bottom to be her finest physical features. Plenty of men agreed, judging by all the nods and smiles and hellos she received from the runners and mountain bikers who overtook her on the trail.

Today she ran alone; she'd started too late for trail traffic. The mountain biker who'd squeezed through the gate had long ago disappeared.

In about twenty minutes she'd reach the national forest fire station, her customary turn around point. She planned to take in the station's broad view of the valley before starting back down.

Shadows blanketed her as she ran along a steep face, and the sudden rush of cool air reminded her that May still had its moments, even in southern California. The road switched back sharply under towering power lines, and as she came around a blind corner she almost ran right into a huge rottweiler.

The dog growled as she stumbled to the side, kicking up dust with her running shoes, never taking her eyes off the beast. Then she froze. She'd run into rattlesnakes, scuttled around them and kept on running, but the rottweiler filled her with fear. Where the hell was its owner? That's all she wanted to know.

She wished she could have shooed the dog away with the confidence of other runners who never seemed concerned about the hounds on the trail. But the rottweiler scared her witless. Muzzle like the mouth of a cannon. Probably just as dangerous. People were getting mauled to death by these things. She'd wait for the owner, they couldn't be too far off. They'd undoubtably wave, call the dog, and *maybe* apologize.

Even small dogs could give her a good fright. When she was five she'd been bitten by a cocker spaniel, of all things, a cute cuddly toy store sort of dog that had almost ripped out her left eye, which would have been a tragedy, given her life's trajectory. She'd taken six stitches right below the eyebrow, and if she looked closely she could still make out the narrow ridge of hard skin.

Now she faced a black-and-tan beast that weighed more than she did. At least the growling had stopped, but the dog was clearly in no rush to leave. Where *was* his owner?

Definitely a male, too; with his long balls hanging down he looked like the Bad Bad Leroy Brown of doggiedom.

Then she saw that he didn't have a collar. Not again. *Goddamn* them! She was furious enough to be profane. Another asshole had dropped off his dog in the national forest instead of taking him down to the shelter. She'd bet anything on it. They'd had problems with this in the neighborhood. Canines wandering out of the hills starving, thirsty, homeless, and hopeless. She'd called Animal Control a few times herself. Where were they now, when she really needed them?

He started licking the sweat streaming down her leg, and panting heavily. She backed away in disgust. He reminded her of certain other males she'd known, some even less appealing. Then it dawned on her that he might need water.

Oh crap, he was doing it again! His tongue felt *so* gross.

"No!" she shouted, surprising herself, surprised even more when he stopped licking her and stiffened.

Emboldened, she said, "Sit!" and lo and behold the beast sat.

For the first time in minutes, she caught her breath.

She pulled out her water bottle and took a quick drink. He cocked his head when he saw this, as supplicating a gesture as she had ever seen in an animal.

How the devil was she going to give him water? She looked around for a rock with a concave surface. Nothing, and the soil would soak it up in a second.

Would she piss him off royally if she squirted a stream in his face?

No way would she risk that. Then she thought about cupping her hand and filling it with water, shuddering over the prospect of that tongue again.

He continued to stare at her.

"Okay-okay." She squeezed the bottle, and her palm filled.

He dove right into her hand, a head as large as her own. His tongue felt like some huge slimy sea creature, and it never stopped squirming until she'd emptied the bottle.

He gazed at her and shook his dark stump of a tail. She looked around again. As far as she could see the trail was as empty as the sky above.

"Come on," she said, begrudging him her aborted run. "Let's go."

. . .

He was a perfect gentleman, settling on the patio outside her studio after inhaling a large stainless steel mixing bowl full of water, but turning his nose up at the organic Oatios she'd put out for him. Panting, panting, panting. She figured he was too hot to eat.

Huge. Absolutely huge, and she tried to calculate how much it would cost to feed him. That simply, he'd found a new master. The decision proved no more dramatic than her realization that she could surely afford to keep him, and that she didn't fear him. The practical considerations, such as Chad's reaction to having him here at the studio, and where the dog would stay during her extended trips to Portland, had not presented themselves yet.

"I'm taking a shower," she said to him firmly. "I'll be right back."

What are you worried about, she asked herself as she stepped inside. That he'll leave? Not likely. Leroy looked like the kind of guy who hung around for the duration. She'd known a few of his human counterparts. The last thing you needed to worry about was their leaving.

She closed the studio door, not about to trust him near the fragile vessels, and washed herself thoroughly, concentrating on the hand and leg that had been smothered by his tongue.

As she toweled off, she heard that growl again, but louder. It sounded like thunder, and someone—it must be Chad. Oh-no— was saying, "Easy boy. *Easy.*" But the growl was growing murderous. The beast, she now realized, hadn't really growled at her at all.

She raced out to the patio and found Chad, ashen-faced and frozen against the wall with Leroy's teeth fully bared, his muzzle wrinkled and fierce.

"Watch it, Lauren," Chad said shakily. "Don't come any closer."

"No!" she shouted loudly. Leroy glanced at her and stopped growling.

"Leroy, come here. Now!"

"Leroy?" Chad said.

The dog ambled over to her, Bad Bad Leroy Brown style, a gait that betrayed nothing but raw confidence.

"Sit," she commanded, starting to revel in her authority. The animal tucked his bottom between his hind legs.

"Good boy," she whispered. Leroy's stumpy tail swished back and forth like a metronome.

She looked over and noticed that one of Chad's body parts was also moving, though far less rhythmically: his cheek was twitching like the tail of a startled cat.

"I just found him," she protested.

"Your good buddy, *Leroy?* You just found him. Where? At some gang-bangers picnic?"

"Out there." She pointed to the forest. "He was all alone."

"I can't imagine why. He's such *good* company."

"He was nice to me."

"Well, that's all that counts."

"He was thirsty. He could've died out there."

"He could have killed you."

"No, you mean you were afraid he was going to kill *you*. He does fine with me. I like him. He's big, he's strong, he's handsome, and he's smart. And he listens to me." The perfect guy, she thought, but she restrained herself from adding this.

"Do you know that along with pit bulls, they're responsible for fifty percent of all the dog bites in the country each year?"

Chad was always doing that, coming up with some statistic to try to prove some point that she'd never agree with anyway.

"Does that include bites by police dogs?" That would surely up the ante.

"I don't know," Chad said honestly.

"Look, if he'd wanted to he could have had us both for lunch. He's nice."

"Nice!" Chad shouted. "He pinned me up against the god-damn wall," he said as he took two angry steps toward her.

Bad move. Leroy, who would forevermore be called "that shithead" by Chad, stood up and issued a growl so chilling that Lauren thought he was going to slaughter her ex-boyfriend on the spot.

"I think," she said in her most delicate voice, "that he doesn't like you shouting at me."

Though nervous herself, she reached down and petted Leroy's aircraft carrier head, and without realizing it reinforced his already strongly protective instincts. Chad swallowed with difficulty, and she noticed for the first time how unpleasant his Adam's apple appeared when it bobbed.

Leroy turned out to be a marvelous companion. He stuck by her side when she went for a run and didn't bother anyone, though his intimidating appearance kept most strangers at bay. Surprisingly, he was positively charming with the children they'd encountered at the apartment complex, suffering their awkward and sometimes heavy-handed pats with at worst indifference.

He just wasn't crazy about one particular big person, which made bringing him to the studio problematic. They'd tried having Chad feed him, but that didn't make a dent in the dog's deportment; Chad still caught a growl if he snapped at Lauren, which did have a salutary, if superficial, effect on his behavior. Chad's that is.

By the end of that first week, though, the tension in the house reached the point where it came as no surprise to Lauren when Chad said, "I don't want that shithead around here anymore." He said this with the unmistakable undercurrent of ownership, the unspoken *I own this place, and don't you forget it.*

"Oh Chad, sit down, you're making him nervous," she joked.

Once he might have laughed at that line. They might have laughed together, and their laughter would have been another sign of their love. When had they stopped laughing? Lauren wasn't sure, but she knew that Chad used to be a funny guy, and had laughed so easily at her antics that he made her feel funny too; but they hadn't shared those lighter moments in months, and the dry spell didn't appear to be ending anytime soon.

"I don't give a shit if I'm making him nervous," Chad said in a voice so mellifluous that unless you spoke human you'd never have known he was angry (in a single week, Leroy had trained him well). "He's big, he smells, and I don't want him hanging around."

"He does *not* smell." Lauren considered herself especially sensitive to odors, and Leroy most definitely did not have a bad one. "And besides, how would you know if he smells. You never get close to him."

"Is that a criticism? Is that a *criticism?*" Chad's voice rose, and Leroy growled as if bored—*not this again.* "You're kidding me, right? You're not actually suggesting that I should get close to that . . . that *thing.*"

"It's not about Leroy, is it?" She could as well have said, It's about *you,* Chad, just as it's always been about you: what you want, what you need, what you desire. But Chad flipped it around, as he always had.

"You got that right. It's not about the damn dog, it's about you! You've been incredibly distant for a long time now."

"Distant? What the hell did you expect? We broke up, remember? You didn't want to get married, remember?"

"That's all you wanted to do, *get married,*" he said in a snide voice. "We needed breathing room. We needed—"

"Breathing room! We had enough breathing room to launch the America's Cup. We had—"

"We needed to let our relationship grow."

"Grow!" She yanked on her hair so hard that she honestly feared she'd uprooted two thick fistfuls. "Did I really hear you say that we needed to let our relationship grow? It had *years* to grow. It grew so much it turned into a jungle, and then it started choking on itself."

"Yeah, and this is making me want to gag. I needed some breathing room and all you cared about was getting married."

"Fine. Breathe. Hyperventilate for all I care."

"That's not funny."

"Neither is the fact that I wanted to get married, and you treated it like the plague. I'm not going to apologize for that. I loved you."

"You *loved* me? What? You don't love me anymore?"

"I'm trying to get my life on track, okay? Maybe I should move my studio." What a headache, though.

"Maybe you should!"

Lauren drove Leroy back to her apartment, still fuming over Chad. What the devil did he expect? Sure there was a gulf between them, but did he think they were just going to go back to the same old same old? Still, she hadn't recognized how wide that gulf had grown until she'd met Ry, in the way an old sea captain might think about land only after passing an alluring isle.

Ry had been the one to back off that last night on the porch, saying that if she wasn't sure about inviting him in, then he should leave.

"You're right," she'd conceded. "I'm not sure at all. But I think you're wonderful."

He'd taken her hand, stood her up, and kissed her so passionately that she'd actually started to swoon. She could still remember the feel of his back as she clutched it greedily.

Then he'd left with a quick good-bye, and all they'd done since was exchange email: his follow-up questions, her answers; no reference by either one of them to their dinner, their date, much less their desire.

She'd also received an email from Kerry. The girl was on the road to Stassler's place in Moab. In no hurry, it seemed. She'd already spent a day mountain biking in the Columbia River Gorge, and planned to take another one to ride in Sun Valley.

Lauren didn't understand how anyone could feel such passion

for a sport, but she did understand the nature of passion itself, and had long pitied those who had never experienced its power. She had thought she'd known all about it, had experienced its many dimensions in her obsession with sculpture; but in the past few weeks she'd learned that passion exists well beyond the confines of a studio, and every time she saw an email from Ry Chambers the elevator dance in her belly reminded her of this all over again. She'd never felt this for Chad. She'd never felt this for any man. Even when Ry asked for a simple detail about a green patina that she'd used on a piece (as he had this morning), it thrilled her to read his words. The feelings she had for him rivaled even the passion she'd long felt for sculpture, which had also come alive in a single spark. On a spring afternoon her sophomore year in high school, her art teacher had given each of them a box of clay and said they were free to fashion anything they wanted.

She had worked a ball of it in her hands anxiously, unsure of the direction she should take, worried that she'd even find a direction. And then it had come to her, and in the hour that followed she'd roughed out the figure of her absent father, not as she'd known him, but as she had *felt* him, the inner life she'd endured thinking about him since his disappearance. The form had been abstract, and its abstraction had possessed a reality that only the emotions could ever know. Her teacher, who spent compliments with the mean, pinched face of a miser, had looked over her shoulder and spoken the one word that had changed her forever: "Excellent."

As a professor, she'd always strived to do the same for her students, to send them on to a larger life than the one they'd lived before meeting her. To let them feel the license of passion, the way it could unchain them from their more conservative impulses. Now Kerry was moving out from under her tutelage, taking her admiration elsewhere. In a way, it was like losing a lover, not the one you took in your arms but the one you took under your wing. And you had to withhold judgment. She could never say to Kerry that Ashley Stassler's work lacked vision, or integrity, that it was little more than the glitzy, fashionably macabre accumulation of appearances worshipped by a celebrity-conscious culture. Kerry would have to come to those conclusions on her own. Or not. Even thinking about Stassler's work in such critical terms made Lauren feel like an ingrate because he alone had agreed to work with an aspiring sculptor; none of her other students had secured an internship. Then again, to her knowledge none of the other young women had included a photograph of herself in a snug halter and short skirt.

Nevertheless, Stassler's willingness to take on an intern kindled Lauren's grudging—and wary—gratitude; he would be helping Kerry pursue her dreams. She'd send him a thank-you note tomorrow, wish him well, and remind him that in Kerry Waters she was entrusting him with her very best student.

# CHAPTER

## 7

JOLLY ROGER'S WEIGHT IS DOWN to the point where I think I can put him on a strength-building program without killing him. Until recently, he looked like he had a heart attack waiting in the wings, an understudy eager for the leading role in his life.

None of them know exactly what's in store, though the video of *Family #8* drilled real fear into at least three of them. But they've also gathered that they're on a health kick of some sort, what with all the supplements, lean protein, and low-fat foods. June even wondered aloud why I'd bother taking such good care of them if I had any "foul intentions." The camera mikes pick up their conversations, though there are few of them. For the most part, they're as sullen as oxen.

The free weights make a clanging sound when I pull them out from behind the bone parade, not pleasant to their ears, judging by the way June cringes, but like Mozart to mine. I like weights, the brutal struggle to lift them. I'm forty-eight years old, and I have a better body than most twenty-year-olds. Weights are the only reason for this. You can't do it any other way. You sure can't run your way to a beautiful body. Your typical marathon masochist looks as emaciated as a Nepalese beggar. Pumping iron gives you definition, but definitely does not make you look like the Incredible Hulk. That's a total misconception. To look like him you'd have to spend years eating your way through a mountain of food. That's not going to happen with the Vandersons; their calories are as carefully calibrated as the fuel for the space shuttle *Challenger*.

They'll hit every body part twice a week. It's what I do, and it's a very challenging regime. But if I didn't do it I'd end up looking like Roger. Dying like Roger.

I position the workout bench directly in front of the cage. I can raise or lower one end of it so I can hit different muscles, even different parts of the same muscle. That's what the uninitiated don't understand: you can't do one exercise for one muscle and get optimum development. Weights are your chisel. You hit a muscle from down below, the sides, and from the top. You chip away at it from every angle. After a few weeks of sweating, they'll see.

The aficionados of my art believe I sculpt my series out of clay, entire families rising into perverse perfection from the rich depths of my admittedly unusual imagination. It's what I've told them, and they, dutiful dolts that they are, believe me when I say that I make molds of the clay figures, and cast them in bronze. So simple. So false. So contemptibly common. I sculpt people alive.

Before I ever pour an ounce of bronze, I sculpt their living flesh. I forge it right down here, right before their very eyes. By the time I'm through, they have the best bodies of their lives. The Vandersons won't be any different. They'll have muscles where muscles are only a memory right now, if that. They'll have ridges and curves and sharply defined shapes, instead of all that loose flesh that hangs off them like moss (though to be fair, I'm thinking of Roger mostly). They might even become aroused by their partners again. I've seen that happen more than once. A few weeks into the regime I've seen husbands and wives start eying each other, then eying the children until they're asleep; and then

I've seen what they do with their new bodies, how they copulate in silence, running their greedy hands all over each other. I do them favors with this program, but they rarely recognize the benefits in the beginning. That's why acts of persuasion take precedence, though in the case of *Family Planning #5* nothing worked. They were so addicted to nicotine that the parents became irrational, and I had to speed up the schedule. I felt sorry for those poor kids, living with parents like that. Their folks wheezed like a couple of sour old cushions when I put them on the stationary bike, and even with the threat of death hanging over them like their favorite cloud of Marlboro smoke, they didn't make much effort with the weights. I cringe every time I think of *Family Planning #5*. They could have been a career breaker for me. Killing them was an act of mercy. For me *and* for them.

But Jolly Roger and June, Sonny-boy and Diamond Girl are going to work out. I mean that literally. Jolly Roger's back problem seems to have eased up. At least he's no longer gripping himself like he's got lumbago, and I'm dearly looking forward to watching Diamond Girl lie face down on the hamstring machine, hook the bar behind her ankles, and start curling those weights back. It's a movement that produces the most delightful effect. With every pump the buns rise hungrily, as if achy for relief, as if inviting the swiftest violation. On Diamond Girl, I expect this delectable sight will only be heightened by the cruel constancy of her firmly rounded cheeks.

They watch me with great interest. I understand why. It's boring down here. Weeks of tic-tac-toe with Sonny-boy would drive anyone to distraction. Yes, they do get to see ongoing episodes of *Family Planning #8*, but it's not precisely the distraction most of them would prefer. Only Diamond Girl continues to smart off, so much so that I'm beginning to think she could use some professional help. Why they didn't get her to a psychiatrist years ago is beyond me. Could any human being be that cold? That indifferent to her fate? It's got to be an act. She's got to be gaming me. I can't believe she's willing to die just to get away from her family. Although, who knows? Maybe if I'd spent fourteen or fifteen years—I still don't know exactly how old she is—with that clan, I'd be ready to die too.

I haul out the weight stand and take my time setting it up at the end of the bench. Then I go back for the barbells and dumbbells. I've cast them from bronze, the most handsome set I've ever seen. Diamond Girl stares.

"How old are you?" I finally ask.

"Eighteen," she says as June blurts out "thirteen," and Roger, the idiot, says, "sixteen." Roger is the only one telling the truth. June's trying to keep me away from her daughter by claiming she's little more than a child (admirable, given their obvious difficulties). Diamond Girl herself is trying to claim adulthood, and whatever prerogatives she presumes it holds in store. And Roger, good old guileless Roger, is hoping the truth is a talisman of some sort. I suspect that in the end, he will be most burdened by my duplicity. He will spend weeks forcing himself to get into shape, and will die feeling bitter and betrayed when he realizes that all his sweat and toil not only failed to buy his freedom, but assured the desirability of his death.

Sixteen, such a sweet age. I believe it was Bette Davis who said that the nicest thing about being eighteen were eighteen-year-old-boys. Much the same could be said for being forty-eight, and having Diamond Girl around.

The whole time they've been here I've had all of these barbells and dumbbells behind the bone parade. Now it's as if the Vandersons are suddenly finding out that they've been staring at a screen, and that when you roll it up you find the tools of the trade, the secret to all this success. It's called hard work.

That's my quarrel with the new generation of artists. They're not willing to really work, to commit themselves fully to their art. They have dalliances with their medium, but they never truly commit, which means they'll never be more than dilettantes. I give *everything* to my art. Everything. Always have. And so will the Vandersons. They'll work harder than they ever have before. They'll see the payoff, and if they're reasonable people, they'll be grateful. What do people have? Fifty, maybe a hundred years? Sculpture is for centuries, maybe forever. Look at Michelangelo's *David*. He'll be around long after we're all gone. He'll be around a thousand years from now, two thousand. And so will the Vandersons. They should thank *me*. When I think of the pleasure I'll have sculpting Diamond Girl, taking the impressions of her breasts and pudenda, her hard round bottom, I can't help thinking of Michelangelo chipping away at David's penis, fashioning his hard young ass, eventually unveiling in raw rock the physical expression of his own intense longing for adolescent boys. To say the master did his work lovingly is to understate the most obvious motivation of all: lust. That he did so much of his work for the Roman Catholic Church is the greatest irony of all.

It takes a full hour to set up all the equipment. I put on my fingerless leather gloves and tell them to watch carefully.

"Your lives depend on doing this right."

"He's fucking crazy," I hear June say under her breath. This from a woman I thought was June Cleaver, maybe even a Mormon. I let it pass. Who cares what *she* thinks. Crazy? Who's in a cage staring out at *me?* Who's been having more mood swings than the hunchback of Notre Dame? Who's been trying to scratch the eyeballs out of her daughter's head one minute, and playing tic-tac-toe with her son the next? If anyone needs to take her meds around here, it's you, Juney.

"I'm starting you off with the stationary bike. Easy at first. I don't want to see any heroes out here. You'll come out one at a time, and you won't even *think* about trying any funny business." I pull out my gun and wave it in the air. I feel like a Wild West cowboy on his bronc. "You hear me?"

They actually all mumble something. I think it's "yes."

I set the resistance on low and begin to pedal. "I want you warming up slowly." I can see it now, Ashley Stassler, Personal Trainer. I suppose if this sculpture thing goes south, I could always do it for a living. I have had some amazing results with some really out-of-shape people. Unfortunately, they don't let you hold a gun to the head of the folks who join health clubs. Too bad, really, because the threat of murder is a marvelous motivator.

"You see, my legs are not pumping away like mad. I'm going nice and smooth."

I don't want Roger and June to pull any muscles or injure themselves. That would set everything back. I'm not so concerned about Sonny-boy and Diamond Girl. I'll work them enough to bring out some muscle, but it's very hard to do much with a young boy's body. He's so lean to begin with, and his sister is as close to perfection as I'm likely to get. It's Roger and June who need the work.

"I'm perspiring. See?" I point to my brow and climb off the bike. "Now I'm ready to lift weights, but even now I'm going to start off slow."

I slip light weights onto the barbell, and crank the upper part of the bench until it rises to a thirty-five-degree angle. I begin to pump out incline presses, fifteen of them.

Now it's time to strip off my warm-up jacket. Underneath, I have a body builder's shirt on: sleeveless, with extra narrow shoulder straps, and cut low on the sides to expose much of the back and chest, and all of the shoulders. They'll learn the names of these muscles—pecs, lats, deltoids, traps—as we go on. Right now, I don't expect the Vandersons even know they exist.

It takes me about fifteen minutes to complete all three sets of incline presses. I point out how critical it is to rest for a couple of minutes between each set. I'm knocking down eight to twelve repetitions every time. That's lifting to failure, which means until I can barely push the bar back on to the rack. Then it's on to more lifts, again with three sets apiece.

I'm dripping wet by the time I'm through.

"You see how hard I've worked?"

Jolly Roger looks worried. You can almost see the cartoon bubble above his head: you expect *me* to do *that?*

"You're going to work even harder. You know why?"

They stare at me blankly, then Diamond Girl pops up, "Why's that, Arnold?" in a bad German accent.

I assume she means Schwarzenegger. I'd lie if I didn't say I'm flattered, though I have none of his bulk, don't want it either. I have lean hard muscles, and every one of them "pops" when it's worked. I also have veins that look like they're going to rip right through my skin.

"The answer, Diamond Girl, is that you're going to work out like this because your life depends on it."

I'm almost sure she's going to make another crack, she has that smile on her face again. I race to anticipate her words, humoring myself again, this time with the thought that perhaps she'll suggest I make an exercise infomercial. I even toy with titles: *Finding Your Perfect Body: Health or Homicide with Ashley Stassler.* Maybe something more to the point: *Get Lean or Die!* (though for accuracy's sake I suppose that should be *Get Lean and Die!*). But instead she reaches up, clasping her hands together high above her head, stretching as she shifts her hips from side to side, and says, "Cool. When do we start?"

*We* don't start. June starts. At gunpoint I back them all up against the kitty box. I bring her out and lock the cage.

"Put these on."

I toss her generic gray sweats, and she throws them on over her pink thong. She even looks grateful. She shouldn't be. I want her warm. I don't want her throwing a muscle.

"Now get on there and pedal."

"Yeah, pedal for your life, *Mother!*"

Diamond Girl doesn't exactly constitute a cheer section. But June does pedal hard. Too hard too fast, and I have to slow her down. She's a classic overachiever, I can see that already. She'll be buff in no time at all.

After she breaks a sweat, I tell her to get off the bike and take off her top. She's beyond protesting. I point to the bench. When she lies back her breasts flatten like a couple of eggs sunny side up.

She's weak. She doesn't look weak, but she is. She can barely bench press the lightest weight four times. She's straining, not faking at all.

"Try these," I snap.

I hand her two five-pound dumbbells and stand over her, guiding the weights straight up from her sides. She completes nine repetitions. That's acceptable.

By the time her chest workout is done, she glistens with sweat. When she was lifting I saw some definition in her triceps, anterior delts, and pecs. She should have started pumping iron years ago. She'd be totally buff by now. I hand her the sweatshirt, and she says thanks. It's the first civil word she's had for me.

Roger—no surprise here—is another story. He's trying, but he's not much stronger than his wife, and lacks her determination. I have to point the gun right into his face to remind him that I'm not kidding. Then I do get some honest effort, but I can see it will take lots and lots of work with Jolly Roger. I'd hoped to pull this off within a couple of weeks of that intern getting here. I could use her help with the molds, but at this rate it'll be iffy. I'm not above carving the extra pounds off him with a scalpel. Fat cuts away as easily as confetti; but it's messy, and often exhausts their terror before I can get a proper impression. Still, it *is* an option, and if he doesn't come around quickly, I'll point this out to him. I could, I suppose, always get started by casting June and the kids; but then Roger would realize that having muscles equals murder, an equation that would unquestionably prompt reluctance with the workout routine. That's why it's essential to bring them all along at roughly the same rate. Believe me, I've learned.

. . .

Sonny-boy is so scared I can't get him out of the cage. His knuckles are white from gripping June's leg, and he's crying. This kid's a real weeper. For several seconds I think his mother will smack him loose in disgust. She's come close before, but she suffers his death grip with saintly reserve, and I decide I can't accomplish a thing by shooting him. It would be hell on their morale, and this is team building time. I give him a pass. As long as he stays the same, he'll be fine. I thought the exercise would do him some good, but if he wants to whine and cry, he can do it on his own time. Attitude is everything, buddy boy, but I can see you haven't learned that yet.

Besides, I'm itching to put Diamond Girl through her paces. She springs out of the cage, throws on her sweats, and jumps right on the stationary bike. She makes a show of nestling her butt down on the racer seat until even I have to admit that it's a rather unseemly display, considering the crowd. But on the other hand I find her cheekiness appealing. Where did she learn to behave like this? I'm certain it's not from her mother. Much as June irritates me, she's not sleazy. More like a cheerleader grown bitter, who's learned that life, no matter how much you smile and stick out your chest, just won't let you score a whole bunch of points. The young man she married so many years ago has turned out to be a lazy slug, a provider of marginal means and little more, and her daughter is someone she probably hasn't understood since birth. Out of the womb and out of your life has been the arc of Diamond Girl's development. A fool could have seen it from the get-go, though perhaps not a mother with sweet plans for her baby girl, birthday parties and frilly dresses, team cheers, and maybe even a homecoming crown. Certainly not this sluttish mix of Gidget and gangsta rap groupie.

"I'm sweating like a pig. Can I take this off?"

Diamond Girl startles me from my thoughts.

"Sure," I say without considering her request. Just that quickly she whips off her sweat top *and* her T-shirt, so now she's wearing only that bra that fastens in front.

Her whole chest moves as she pedals. Not like June whose breasts jiggle. Diamond Girl's aren't loose enough to jiggle. Everything is too firm, everything moves together.

She must see me staring.

"This too?"

And just that quickly she unfastens the front and drops her bra to the side.

"Put it back on," Jolly Roger growls.

"Why, Daddy?" she says, mock innocent. "You like them. You've been staring at them every chance you get since I was twelve."

June shoots her killer look at Roger, who's shaking his head. She mutters, "You're disgusting," and turns away from him and Diamond Girl.

Daughter dearest takes her hands off the bar and sits up straight, still pedaling hard, making a real show of herself. I am not unaffected. I dreamed of her again last night. No Baby Peaches this time, nothing so elliptical. I saw her hanging by her legs from a jungle gym, with a short pleated skirt having fallen down over her face. I was staring at her white underpants. She didn't move to cover up, and I spied a curly black hair poking out from the elastic band, and the shape of her vulva, even the slight crease in the middle.

She runs her hand over her chest. "I'm hot now. Can I get off?"

I nod. I'm as hard as the bones in this basement. So hard it must be apparent. It is. She's looking right at it. She pulls off her sweatpants and panties, and bends over the bench where the barbell rests on the weight stand.

"Don't!" cries June, with none of the harshness I've heard before. She's pleading.

But Diamond Girl is having none of it. She's settling her knees into the earth, legs apart, looking back over her shoulder. I'm facing those buns that have tantalized me for weeks now.

I approach her quickly. This is no time for thought, no time for careful consideration.

"I want you on your back."

She lies on the bench, opening her legs and smiling in what I judge to be itchy anticipation.

When I lean over her, she's forced to take it in both hands.

For a moment I think she may spit at me, but then she lowers the barbell and pushes it back up.

"I want fifteen reps."

"Fuck you," she whispers.

Art is everything.

# CHAPTER
## 8

LAUREN'S ARM FELT AS IF it had been yanked out of her shoulder socket. Bad Bad Leroy Brown had wrenched it during his early morning encounter with a female golden retriever in the Angeles National Forest. Granted, the animal was in heat and its harebrained owner had no business whatsoever walking it in public. Granted, a Doberman with a particularly satanic leer had already attempted the coupling that Leroy so zealously sought to complete. Granted, it's part of any creature's nature to want to reproduce. But Lord, her arm hurt. She barely, *barely,* managed to pull him off that animal. Scary, too, what with all the growling and gnashing of teeth, and that was the retriever's owner!

She hung the leash on the door, and told Leroy to sit. As soon as he obeyed, his floppy gray scrotum with its two huge balls settled on the floor like an army blanket over a couple of rambunctious recruits.

"We're going to have to do something about you," she said as she scooped out four cups of kibble, which he devoured only after she stepped back and snapped, "Okay."

At least he had some manners, which was more than she could say for Ashley Stassler. What's with him anyway?

She flipped open her laptop on the tiny table in the tiny kitchen of her tiny apartment to check her email. She'd already had the department secretary rummage through her snail mail up in Portland, but there had been no word back from Stassler. She hadn't been badgering him, but she'd sent what? Three emails about Kerry's internship since he'd accepted her.

The first had been a standard thank you. The second had included the compact that she and Kerry had put together outlining the girl's goals for the two months she'd spend with him. And the third? Well, the third had been the one she'd sent two days ago. Lauren thought of it as her Mother Hen email, the one in which she'd tried to strike a familial and protective tone that she hoped he'd extend toward her finest student.

At the very least she'd expected a perfunctory reply. But . . . she clicked the email icon . . . nothing again today. No email at all, which in one sense and one sense only was good news because Chad, apparently, had given up his daily plea for a reconciliation.

Alas, no email also meant nothing from Ry, who was up at his home on the Oregon coast. Last night she'd emailed him a big "THANKS" for the bouquet of spring flowers he'd sent her, along with a note that said, "I miss you."

Never had those three words sounded so good, and she could think of only three others that would have sounded even better.

Their email had warmed up in recent days as Ry started revealing his feelings for her, but the zinnias, daffodils, and tulips had still come as a most pleasant surprise. The splashes of pink, yellow, and white commanded her gaze from an end table in the modest living room.

She'd called last night and left a message on his machine thanking him, but she really did want to hear his voice. Or see a note from him pop up on the screen. He would be in touch, of that she had no doubt. Ashley Stassler, in contrast, clearly considered himself above matters as mundane as acknowledging mail.

Still, she decided to knock out another note letting him know that Kerry should be arriving later today. She knew this because Kerry had turned out to be a marvelous correspondent, and had kept her apprised throughout her journey, including details of her quick side trips to ride her mountain bike, of which there had been three *after* Sun Valley.

Lauren had an article she wanted to send her about Stassler that had just appeared in the online magazine *Sculpture Review*. If all went according to plan, Kerry would receive it as soon as she logged on in Moab.

The hump in the highway rattled Kerry's teeth, and snapped her out of her mountain bike reverie. She braked sharply for the flagger and construction crew, offered her most winsome smile, a silently mouthed apology, and a wave. Then she sped off, taking the curves quickly in her old four-wheel-drive pickup, and imagining once more that she was on her bike in this gorgeous red rock country. What a totally awesome gig: Moab, mountain biking, and casting. Couldn't get any better.

The sign said fourteen miles to Moab. Already she'd seen a ton of billboards for motels and restaurants and river-rafting expeditions. Lots of white water around here, though she didn't expect she'd have much time for running rapids. Lots of rock climbing, too. Now *that* she might have to somehow slot into her schedule. She loved climbing, and had brought her shoes, harness, and chalk bag. Somehow she'd find the time. But the reason you're here, she reminded herself, is to get this whole casting thing down, totally dialed, and that's going to mean a lot of foundry time, studio time, time with Ashley Stassler! She could hardly believe it. He'd taken *her* on as an intern! Kerry Waters, third-year art student. A wannabe. But he must like her work. She'd sent him copies of her portfolio, and the papers she'd written about his series, *Family Planning*, the most amazing sculpture she'd ever seen. He could capture the human form as no one had since . . . since da Vinci. Since . . . Rodin. She had to find out how he did it. And then it hit her: just by working with him, she'd go down in art history.

Moab appeared first as a long line of motels and convenience stores. Kerry frowned. Not what she'd expected, not entirely anyway. An old mining town should look like an old mining town, not the heart of franchise America; but then with great relief she turned into Moab's downtown, a wide, tree-lined street with a pleasing hodgepodge of old and new, plate glass and white clapboard, red brick and green trim. She studied the storefronts searching for an espresso stand, and quickly spotted Screaming Beanies.

As she pulled over, she smiled at all the bikes parked on the sidewalk: mountain bikes, road bikes, touring bikes with fat panniers, racing bikes with spokeless rims, bulky bikes towing baby trailers, bikes with toddlers' seats. Yes! This was it. Bike heaven.

She rushed inside, eager for caffeine, figuring that if she wasted not a minute she could squeeze in a ride on the Slick Rock Trail, which she'd been reading about for years, and still get out to Stassler's by six.

Within five minutes, Kerry was back in her pickup and headed out of town with a double Americano and directions from the girl who'd served it.

She passed several groups of mountain bikers riding to the trailhead, and suddenly felt like too much of a tourist ferrying her bike on her truck. Never again, she vowed. If she hadn't been so pressed for time, she would have turned right back, saddled up, and joined the throng making the trip on pedal power alone.

Parking was tight—*lots* of tourists—but she wedged the narrow pickup between two mammoth SUVs from California.

She looked around. No one nearby. She unbuttoned her Levi's

and looked again. No one. Go for it! In the tight space between the two cars, she stripped off her jeans and panties and wrestled on her Lycra bike pants. Another quick look, and off came her cotton top and on with a garish bike shirt provided by her sponsor, a shop in Portland that gave her bike clothes, bike maintenance, and tires and tubes in exchange for her blood, sweat, tears, and torment.

Bike shoes next, then the hydration system, basically a body hugging backpack molded around a plastic pouch with a drinking tube she could flip in her mouth whenever she needed water.

Sunglasses and helmet. A new one. She'd taken a "header" a few weeks ago on Mt. Hood, and her old helmet had been the principal casualty. The Styrofoam shell had cracked open, but it had absorbed the impact and saved her skull. The shop had given her this one, and mounted the old brain bucket under a photograph of her atop the winners' stand at last year's Oregon Mountain Bike Championship. The new helmet looked as sleek as a Porsche. She wouldn't think of riding without one.

She reached up to the rack and unlocked her bike, holding it above her head as she maneuvered to the rear of the truck, careful not to scrape the forty-thousand-dollar Expedition crowding her from behind.

Bike gloves. Almost forgot them. She leaned her Cannondale against the rear bumper, hurried back to the cab, bent over the front seat, and grabbed them off the dash. Time to lock up. She slammed the door, turned around, and that's when she spotted the guy in the Expedition watching her through tinted windows, casually munching an energy bar. He gave her a thumbs-up, and she turned red, could feel her face burning as she realized that he must have seen her strip off her clothes and change. She hated tinted windows.

But he wasn't leering, and he didn't look sleazy, kind of cute actually, so after taking a deep breath she managed a nervous smile, and set off.

. . .

The ride was markedly different from the trails in Oregon. Up there you rode in trees almost all the time, lots of shade, except for the clear-cuts. But this was amazing. She could feel her skin come alive in the sun, like a duck finding flight after a winter in a marsh.

She sang to herself as she nimbly navigated up a twisting stretch of smooth rock, easily passing a group of guys, just smoking them, not even close to her lowest gear. Her legs were practically singing too. Endorphin high. She crested the rock and saw the sinuous line she'd have to take down the other side, so steep that if she didn't raise the left pedal to the twelve o'clock position, it would bump against the rock and buck her over to the right, and that would mean . . . the unthinkable. That's how steep it looked.

But her tires held the rock like they were made of Velcro, and she descended at an angle impossible on even the gummiest dirt. Fun riding, as long as you had the stomach to take the steeps in stride.

Kerry did. She had the *power*. She finished the ride in under two hours, nineteen miles of rock and sand and smooth, wicked descents.

As she pedaled back to her pickup, she drained the last drops out of her hydration system. She still felt about a quart low, so as soon as she opened the cab she pulled out a water bottle, downing about half of it before the murmur of a power window gave her a start. The guy in the Expedition.

"Good ride?" He looked like he was waking up. She wished he'd been asleep earlier.

"Yup, real good," she said, settling down. "You been out?"

"Did it twice today. I can hardly move."

He said his name was Jared. He sure was cute. Light hair, not blond or red, but kind of like the color of the rocks on the trail, and strong-looking shoulders. She dug that on guys, when the caps of their deltoids looked as hard and round as baseballs.

"You must be dyin' then," she said, checking him out some more, glad to have her sunglasses on, though not confident enough in the dark lenses to let her eyes wander too much. But the sculptor in her still wanted to soak up his musculature, the way his pecs formed nice clean inside edges before disappearing into his sleeveless shirt. Hard on top, hard down below. That's what she and her riot grrl buds always said. That and "A hard man is good to find." At least one of them would just *have* to say that, usually with more irony than intention as they whipped past some creep on a five-thousand-dollar ride. But this guy didn't look creepy, he looked cool.

"Yeah," he allowed, "I'm hurting, but hey, I'll be back out tomorrow." He paused to look her over; she could see *his* eyes. "You?"

"I don't think so," she said reluctantly. "Got to work."

"Yeah, you local?" He sat up straighter. "You work around here?"

"I'm just starting. With a sculptor. Ashley Stassler? Ever heard of him?" She hoped, really hoped that he had.

"Ashley Stassler?" he said slowly, as if the name might catch on some barb of memory.

He rubbed his chin, then shook his head. "Nah, I don't think so."

"He's like one of the top three or four sculptors in the world. I'm going to be working as his assistant for the next two months." She preferred "assistant" to intern.

"That sounds way cool."

"What about you? You live here?" She'd noticed the California plates when she'd pulled in, but maybe he'd moved.

His head shook again. "Vacation. Chilling for a week. I leave Sunday."

Two days from now. Already she was calculating whether she could spring loose long enough to spend some time with him.

"You want to go get a burrito? Have a beer?"

Now it was her turn to shake her head, say no. "Sorry. I've got to get out to the guy's place before it gets dark. He kind of lives out in the boonies."

"You got a way for me to call you?"

"Yup, that would be cool. I'll give you my cell number. Give me yours too."

He scrambled to find something to write on, and told her that he *would* call.

As she drove away she felt a familiar buzz, the post-ride endorphin high along with the kind of bubbly excitement that made her bike pants feel way too tight.

Stassler's directions sucked, and it took her an hour to find the cattle gate that he'd said was "right off the road." Right? Try *left* next time. And then maybe point out that it's another three miles!

She searched around the gate post before finding the key he said he'd stash away for her. The sun was all but gone, and she'd had to flick her headlights on about half an hour ago.

After pulling across the cattle guard, she locked back up. He'd been very specific about that. Ten minutes later she saw Stassler's compound, the barn with the guest house, and the old home that he said he didn't use. How could he not? It was beautiful, and huge, with an old fashioned veranda that stretched clear across the front and wrapped all the way around the side. Two stories. Real cedar board and batten. And the barn was almost as big, painted the palest yellow with white trim all the way up to the cutest cupola. The brick foundry, single story and the least impressive of the three buildings, sat back behind the barn.

No one greeted her. Thank God for that. Maybe she could slip inside and clean up before meeting him. She wished she'd found a place to shower and change before coming out here. She felt conspicuously grimy. Her arms were streaked with the sweat and dirt she'd picked up riding, and her hair was a mess. She worried that she smelled funky too.

She heard something, or someone, in the barn. The big double doors were open to the early evening air. She took a few steps toward the entrance as Stassler himself came striding out, still managing to startle her with his sudden appearance.

"Oh," she sputtered.

"You must be Kerry Waters," he snapped. "You'd *better* be Kerry Waters," he added so crisply that even if she hadn't been, she would have claimed the name.

"Yes-yes," she stammered, recovering awkwardly from her surprise.

"I'm Ashley *Stassler,*" he said, emphasizing his last name as if he had to, and stabbing his hand toward her. It took Kerry a moment to understand that he was extending it in greeting. She shook it, noticing the dry grip, the calluses, and knowing that her own hand probably felt just as abrasive.

He had a smile as sharp as a chisel, Kerry thought, or something a chisel might chip out of rock, a hard rock like granite, not sandstone or soapstone. Lean, too, and not much taller than she, which made him fall an inch or two short of six feet. Handsome, no denying it, his face familiar from the PBS documentary, and from all the photographs of him in the stories about the *Family Planning* series. She'd read them all, and had studied the photos: Stassler serious, Stassler laughing, Stassler straining to achieve perfection in his foundry. She figured she'd seen every variation of his face, but she'd never seen this, the canine curiosity of his eyes, the way they combed over her. Not like the boy in the Expedition. Way different. Like Stassler was taking stock of her, doing an inventory, studying her flesh, fingering her dimple with his gaze. She'd had a lot of men look her over, and had never liked it. She didn't like this either.

"I'll show you your room." He started walking toward the house, abruptly gesturing toward it with those rough hands. "It's all yours. For the next two months."

. . .

It was magnificent inside as well. Kerry had grown up on Portland's northeast side. A bungalow built in the twenties. Broken down, dry rotted, like a lot of other bungalows in the neighborhood. Gentrification hadn't come to her hood because it was a hood, and the dotcomers hadn't considered it tony enough, not with all the drive-bys and gangs and TV action news crews always looking for more of the gore.

She'd dated a couple of guys who came from money, seen their homes, their parents' homes, but nothing like Stassler's place. The foyer had a hammered copper ceiling, and maple wainscoting. The front hallway opened to an immense living room with thick carpets, stone hearth, and a beamed ceiling that rose at least twenty-five feet. It was a rugged, masculine manse with a dining area and a kitchen larger than the apartment she'd been renting near the university.

He'd taken the trouble to stock the refrigerator, one of those enormous stainless steel boxes that took up a wall. He also showed her the well-packed shelves of the pantry before leading her to the master bedroom near the rear of the house. Master bath, too, with a long bear-claw tub perched on black-and-white tile.

"This is really nice," Kerry said, trying not to sound impressed, like maybe she was used to all this, which only made her sound overwhelmed and underprivileged.

"It is, isn't it?" Stassler said. "Maybe I should live here, and give you the guest house."

"Sure. That would be—"

He waved her silent. "I'm kidding. I like living so close to my subjects. I can walk down . . . out to the foundry any time; it's only a few steps away. And this would be too much for me. I'm a simple guy."

She nodded, even though "simple guy" was the last thing Ashley Stassler would ever be. She sensed this after being in his presence for less than fifteen minutes.

They walked back to the front door. She couldn't imagine having a place like this and not using it, but the barn and guest quarters were closer to the foundry. She stared at the red brick building from the edge of the veranda. He followed her eyes.

"That's my favorite spot. It doesn't look like much, but that's where we do all the work."

"I can't wait."

"Tomorrow we'll start getting the molds ready for casting."

"We will," Kerry said excitedly. "A new part of the series?"

"No, I've got to repair one of the figures in #8. It got damaged during shipment. But eventually we'll do #9. It's interesting the way that one's turning out. Not quite what I'd had in mind when I started it."

She asked him what he meant.

"Only that I had envisioned a husband, wife, and two children, but there's only one child now."

"Couldn't you, y'know, go ahead and add the second kid?" Was she missing something?

He shook his head as if that would be the worst of violations. "No, you'll learn that you have to let the materials speak to you. As I got into the piece, I could only feel a boy and his parents. No girl."

"Right-right." She felt *so* stupid. Lauren had talked about this as well, letting the materials speak to you, the subjects too. No preconceived notions about how it *had* to turn out. That's how a true artist worked.

"But I do like #9. I feel like I'm getting to know the figures in the piece really well. I'm starting to see their bodies more clearly, the bones and muscles, the facial features. It takes time, but they're starting to emerge. Maybe in a couple of weeks they'll be ready for the molds."

"Can I see them?"

He shook his head without looking at her. "I can't do that. It destroys my focus if I let anyone see me creating them. It takes me a long time to make them come alive, and I can't risk any break in concentration."

Kerry nodded, then worried about her access to the foundry. "But how can I work in there," her eyes returned to the brick building, "if I can't see them."

"They're not in there. They're in my guest quarters." He pointed to the second story of the barn. "That's where I create them, and that's completely off-limits. Right?"

"Right," Kerry agreed immediately. "Don't worry, I can appreciate why you'd want to have some private space. I'll do whatever you need. I've been really looking forward to this. Thanks."

He left her then, and she got some eggs out of the refrigerator and scrambled them on the gas stove, the largest she'd ever seen in a private home, more like the range in the restaurant where she'd learned to smile for tips. She wolfed down dinner and executed a quick cleanup before heading directly to the master bath. The taps were sticky, and rusty water spilled out for almost two minutes before she put the plug in.

Even before it filled, she stretched out, letting herself luxuriate in the full length of the tub. Soon the water rose up over her entire body, and she grew groggy from the comforting blanket of warm water.

Half an hour later, she had to force herself to get out. Drying off seemed an ordeal, relieved only by the prospect of pouring herself into the four-poster bed.

She stared at the ceiling, remembering the night sky above a campsite she'd once made high in the Cascades. She'd lain on a soft pad of pine needles at ten thousand feet, and dreamed of Van Gogh's brilliant stars all night long. Now, with legs as heavy as steel wheels, she fell into a sleep so deep that her only dream was of darkness.

The next morning she woke to the creaking of a door. She bolted upright, her eyes scouring the unfamiliar surroundings, but nothing was moving in the room. The door to the hallway and the one to the bath were closed, as she had left them the night before.

A metallic clang prompted her to throw back the curtains

above the bed. Ashley Stassler was standing by the barn doors feeding a padlock through a hasp. With an angry expression, he slammed the U-shaped shackle shut with the heel of his hand. He looked around, his eyes alighting on the front of the house, though not with the imperious gaze she'd witnessed the night before. In its place she saw concern, and that made her wonder why he was locking up the barn. It had been open when she'd arrived last night. He'd been coming out of it when he said she'd *better* be Kerry Waters. She'd been planning to ask him if she could keep her bike in there. But his wary manner now made her uneasy, so when he turned toward her she instinctively dropped the curtain. She felt silly, certain she'd been seen. Oddly, she also felt warned.

She downed a quick breakfast, brushed her hair, and opted for a minimum of makeup: lip gloss, mascara. That's all, and only in deference to a new gig. She'd dispense with the minimum as soon as she could. She wondered how long they'd work today, and whether she should give that guy Jared a call, plan a ride for later. He said he was leaving on Sunday. That's tomorrow, she realized. What's the big deal? she asked herself. Another cute guy. Moab, she guessed, was full of them, like all the other sports towns she'd heard about. She'd read a story in one of the magazines—*Shape*? *Cosmo*? *Mademoiselle*?—about the best place to meet cool guys, and sports towns had been at the top of the list. So it's not like Jared was the only pair of buns on the block, but something about him turned her flywheel, made her feel "spinny."

As she stepped on to the veranda, Stassler shouted from the door of the foundry,

"Hey, sleepyhead, let's get started."

"I'm coming." She smiled and skipped down the stairs. The misgivings she'd felt when she first woke up burned away like a morning mist.

Stassler had already spread out several of the master molds for *Family Planning #8*, the repair work he'd told her about last night.

"Shit *does* happen," he grunted, and she laughed. The word sounded so strange coming from Ashley Stassler. In some ways he seemed prissy, incredibly fastidious. She wondered if he was gay. She certainly didn't sense any of the sexual vibe that most men give off. Of course, she was less than half his age. With the exception of some notable rock stars, that kind of age difference generally diminished her interest in a man, although she had found a couple of forty-year-olds appealing; but none she'd done more than kiss, and even then it had been out of curiosity rather than desire.

This morning, he explained, they'd prepare the master molds. That meant heating up wax and spreading a thin layer of it into each mold, then letting it cool.

"That's the only way I use wax," he said. "I sculpt with clay, and use the alginate to make an exact replica of the clay sculpture. The replica's what I use to make the mold. That way I don't have to take any chances with the sculpture itself. But the alginate," he looked right at her, "is the key. It's the only way to get a perfect impression." He glanced at a tub of alginate on a nearby bench. "It's what makes my work so special."

She'd heard about alginate, the green stuff dentists use to take an impression of your mouth. The gunk that always made you want to gag.

"What I like about alginate," he explained, "is that it captures *all* the details of a . . . my sculpture. When I'm finished, I want people to see the pores in the skin, the way a muscle or tendon rises. For that kind of work, there's nothing better."

Kerry loved this. This is what she'd dreamed it would be. Working by the master's side while he went on about materials, his technique, his art, his vision. But that's about all he said once they went to work. When she tried to prompt him with questions, he offered only the briefest replies.

After the first hour, the work became routine enough that her thoughts ambled along on their own, and they kept coming back to Jared, which annoyed her. Here she was with Ashley Stassler, and thinking about some other guy. Grow up, girl.

But at one o'clock, when he said they were through for the day, she burst out with a "Really?" appearing much more pleased than she would have wanted to let on.

"That's it. We're off tomorrow. I never work on Sunday. It's not a religious thing, it's just me."

She nodded.

"Go have some fun. I've got stuff to do."

"Do you want to see any of my work?" He hadn't asked about her plans, and she'd been nervous about bringing it up; but Lauren had insisted she establish right away that this was a two-way street: her labor, his expertise.

He waved her away, saying, "Not today," which would have made her feel like shit if her thoughts hadn't already run to Jared.

She called him as soon as she walked inside the house. He answered on the first ring, and they made plans for an easy ride, a getting to know you ride, as Kerry considered it.

It took them about an hour of moderate climbing before they'd pedaled all the way along the banks of Onion Creek to a vast plateau, the whole of a gigantic ranch that had apparently been there since territorial days. The sun had played coyly with them all afternoon, but now broke through a wide opening in the clouds. The light looked like a brilliant, fibrillating column extending from the land to the sky itself. Big boulders rose to their left, and they climbed them until they found one they could settle on.

Kerry stretched out, letting the sun bake her bare legs and the rocks warm her back and bottom.

Jared sat next to her unpacking a baguette. He broke off a piece and offered it to her, along with wedges of Gorgonzola cheese and apple.

"How gallant," she laughed.

"That's not all."

Out came a bottle of Pinot Grigio. "You're too much. You know that?" she told him.

He liked hearing her say this. She could tell by his smile.

They toasted the ride, and then he said, "To you, too," and they drank again.

The wine went straight to her head. She felt silly, giggly, and not at all like a riot grrl who could take control of any situation. She was still relaxing against the rock when he kissed her. She let him, and their mouths opened to each other as easily as the clouds to the sun.

She didn't do anything but kiss him back. No hands in his hair or wrapped around his hips. No extra encouragement. She was perfectly content to kiss up here on the rocks, to open her eyes and see the sun, and smell his warm body, moist from straining after her for most of the ride. She'd let him take the lead as they started out from the highway, and for the first fifteen minutes had been happy to check out the hardest buns she'd seen in a long time; but then the competitor in her had come to life, the riot grrl who liked to lead, and who didn't mind if the right guy got an eyeful of her butt in tight bike pants as she rose up out of the saddle to send extra power to the pedals. She passed him, getting keyed up from all that keen attention. Keyed up even more now that she was in his arms, tasting his lips, his tongue, sensing his titillation, and sharing hers too.

But she wouldn't do *it*. In a weird way, the day was too perfect to screw up with sex. So when his hands fell to her pants, she clenched his fingers and said, "No, I don't want to." But she said it softly and she said it nicely, and he'd been trained well somewhere along the line because his hand rose back to her chest. She let him caress her for a few minutes more before he realized that, "No, I don't want to" wasn't going to turn into a boisterous roll on the boulders.

. . .

The ride back was a gentle downhill, which she was thankful for because after drinking the wine she'd discovered that her fine motor functions weren't feeling all that fine.

She had him drive her to the gate, where they'd met earlier, but no farther: she didn't think Stassler would appreciate any extra company. He helped her get her bike down off the rack, and promised to call her tomorrow.

"I thought you were leaving."

"I was, but now I'm not."

"Cool," she said with a big smile. "I'm glad to hear it."

*Yes!*

When she rolled back up to the house, Stassler was again exiting the barn.

"What do you have in there?" she said, out of breath but feeling as sprite as a wind-dancing dandelion.

"I'm trying to figure out what I can do with it."

"We can keep my bike in there," she joked.

He squeezed out a smile when she asked if she could look around. After a moment's hesitation, he said, "Sure, but there's not much to see."

At any other time she might have sensed his reluctance, asked herself what was the big deal; but she still felt those endorphins pogoing around her brain like it was their very own mosh pit.

The barn was almost sparkling clean. The only odd business, as far as she could see, was the straw on the floor of each stall. What was the point? Stassler clearly didn't keep horses. The barn didn't look or smell like a horse had been in it for a long time. But those big piles of straw did look inviting, and when she reached the last stall she flopped backward onto the golden mound, the picture of youthful exuberance.

Stassler froze, then reached to help her up, as if she'd tripped.

"Come on," he said. "Let's go."

Without waiting, he took her hand and pulled her up. They were out of the barn directly, as fast as if they were fleeing a fire.

She had the strangest feeling as she said good night and walked up the steps to the veranda. When she'd landed on the straw, it hadn't been as thick as she'd expected, and she'd kind of bonked her butt on the floor. But here's what was weird, it hadn't really felt like a floor. It had felt like . . . what? she asked herself.

The answer came a few moments later as she entered the house: it felt hollow, like when you bump against a door.

# CHAPTER
# 9

IT'S THREE IN THE MORNING, and the air is as chilly as an ice chip. You'd never know it was May. Not even a hint of desert heat at this hour. Even the sage is sleeping. I can barely smell it (not like at midday when the sun seems to suck the scent from the sap). No dust either. Everything's settled. Everyone's asleep. Everyone but me. I'm lucky in that I don't need much sleep. I can stand here and watch the way the darkness surges from the sky like the widest river in the universe, flooding the desert, the mountains, and every crevice and canyon, stripping them of their shadows and the simple condolences of light. But most of all, the darkness puts Kerry Waters to rest. Early to bed, early to rise. Such a wholesome girl. She sickens me. It's difficult for me now to believe that I ever harbored libidinal intentions toward her, even though she was brazen enough to send me a photo, along with a letter filled with the kind of adulation that usually signifies a willingness on the part of a young woman to give it her all, if I will just be kind enough (please!) to take her under my wing. Rock stars aren't the only ones who get groupies. It was reasonable of me to assume that Kerry Waters would do what so many other young women have done, and provide the stimulation that I otherwise pass up because of my cloistered lifestyle.

But then I had a bad feeling the minute I saw her. All that health and vigor, all that dirt and sweat from her bike ride. I suppose she thought she'd honor me with her body odor. She was as nervous as a child bride. "You must be Kerry Waters," I said, though I wanted to add in those first few odoriferous seconds that her patronym would have served her better had it been Soap, or Lather, because water alone could never rinse away such rankness.

Worse even in my estimation than the body odor was Kerry's ongoing good-girl enthusiasm. I could bear her earnestness as long as we worked in silence, and she didn't try to thrust her prosaic attempts at sculpture at me. As part of our compact, I have to look at them, offer some insights, cast a couple of these trifles; but as soon as she started with her wheedling I could feel my patience wither. In comparison to Diamond Girl, she's a chimp.

I walk into the barn, and take the stairs down to the cellar where my charges lie under Army surplus blankets.

"Wake-up time!" I shout, though they don't sleep deeply anymore. Correction, all but Jolly Roger sleep uneasily and can be disturbed with the slightest noise. When he curls up, he snores and snorts through one hour after another.

But none of them knows if it's day or night anymore, their circadian rhythms are all messed up. I wish I didn't have to roust them because rest is as important as exercise when I'm trying to get them buffed out, but this is simply the best time to avoid the curious eyes of Kerry Waters.

"It's show time!"

No more smart words from Diamond Girl. She's been smoldering since my rejection of her fanny thrusting overture. She stares at me, not sullen like her parents, but with contempt. I can feel it as clearly as I can smell the mold in the dirt down here. Her flirtations have taken flight, and now she's angry. I like her even better this way; truth be told, I find all the spite and resentment very seductive. If I stoke it carefully, it could explode in the most delightful fury. The fact that I still bother toying with her says a lot about her hold on me. She's the girl I could not stop thinking of in my high school calculus class, the one who wore short skirts and soft sweaters. She's the girl I bought an espresso from every day during my last year in college. She's every girl who ever pre-occupied me, all the Wendys of my life (for Wendy was the young woman with long blond hair I found every excuse imaginable to talk to during my year as a visiting artist in Madison, Wisconsin).

I'm about to add to the Vandersons' emotional imbalance by playing another episode of *Family Planning #8*, the one in which I take the final impression of their fifteen-year-old daughter. If anything can make Diamond Girl squirm, this is it.

Before I performed my legerdemain on *#8*'s dark-haired beauty, I'd given the girl a healthy injection of methamphetamine, the preferred drug of the working class, those poor plebes who must stay awake for two, three shifts at a time. I don't want any-one in my families passing out. Isn't that always the easy way? I despise fainting spells. It's such a weak response to terror, such an abject attempt to cheat the only emotion worth savoring. *There is no escape.* I tell the Vandersons this. I also tell them that the young girl they're about to see refused to work out, and what I did to her I'll do to each of them if they don't push themselves harder. After this, the weights will feel different in their hands. A little lighter, yet more real. A passport to that illusory land of safety, freedom.

I expect that even Diamond Girl will be affected. In a few sec-onds she'll see that *Family Planning #8*'s first born had a body not unlike her own. She'll be able to identify with her, and this, if noth-ing else, should greatly diminish Diamond Girl's own sense of im-mortality, or fashionable cynicism (whichever it happens to be).

Without another word I turn the tape on, and for once I see I'm right about Diamond Girl. She actually turns away when she sees what I've done to that young girl, and says absolutely nothing. And this is only the beginning of the show! There's so much more to come. I feel an elation unlike any I have known for weeks. Diamond Girl squirms! What is it that finally does it? What makes her tremble? It's the alginate. I have covered the front of *#8*'s entire body with it, and that includes the girl's face, her lips, and finally, with an oversized plug, her left nostril.

This leaves only the right one, the sole source of air. The girl's shuddering is visible right from the beginning (visible and outstanding!). She shudders from fear, from terror, but mostly from the lack of air. Try sucking in *all* your body's oxygen needs at a time of intense physical crisis through one nostril. Imagine yourself running up a steep mountain, and you have but one air hole. It *can* be done, but not with ease. And not for long. It's the fear of suffocation in a mind already twitching from a dose of speed, a mind hallucinating a rich grotesquery of meth monsters, that makes the impossible effort to breathe enough air as acutely painful as the amputation of a limb. Believe me, I know of what I speak.

I've used many methods over the years to generate fear. I've tried blunt force, sharp knives, and a variety of power tools. I've even pried loose more than a few teeth, and at one point had a whole array of dental tools at my disposal, including those delightful snaggle-shaped, needle-nosed scalers that the hygienist uses to scrape away tartar. But I've found that nothing, *nothing* works as well for obtaining truly sharp impressions than suffocation with alginate.

My theory about why it works so well? It's fairly simple. Trauma leaves a subject so singularly focused on a particular pain that the pervasiveness of terror can't be spread over the length and breadth of a body. But suffocation, so hypothetically pale in the spectrum of pain, produces a protracted struggle, and a remarkably revealing play of muscles as panic sets in and then *takes over*. With suffocation, true terror has the time to come to the fore, and come to the fore it does.

It's also an experience everyone knows. At one time or another we've all been underwater, unable to breathe, and fearful—if only for a moment or two—that we'd never take another breath. Some of us have known even more agonizing versions of this. But no matter the degree of experience, it's familiar to everyone, and therefore it has the most splendid effect on viewers like the Vandersons. It will impel them to the most vigorous participation in future workouts, at the same time bringing out the most remarkable definition in the body they are watching.

#8's face twists as she fights to breathe, and Diamond Girl and company can see the girl's hopeless battle for breath, the way she tugs viciously at the restraining straps, her quadriceps yanking for all their puny worth against the leather, and her hands, her fingers, trying just as desperately to claw at her face, to rip the alginate from her nose.

I'd gagged the girl's mouth with a hard black rubber ball that I'd purchased years ago from an S&M mail order outfit in Dubuque, Iowa. A wonderful device. It leaves the mouth incapable of breath, while the lips stay partially open, which gives them ample room for expression, for twisting and curling, those pathetic gestures of pain that everyone—not just young girls—exhibits at a time like that.

And all of this took place *before* I inserted the final plug of alginate into her right nostril. This was the moment I'd been waiting weeks for. You could say that that little green plug was my pièce de résistance. You could call it the most terrifying object in the world, and if *you* were *Family Planning #8*'s little girl, you most certainly would.

I brushed her nose with it, not rushing the insertion at all, giving rise only to the rich possibility that it, too, might soon find a home in her body, and with it would come the inescapable end of her meager supply of air. Each time it touched her, no matter how slightly, her body would heave as it sought to suck in all the air it could, an instinctive response to store as much as possible, as if that slim stream were acorns for the long winter ahead. So I brushed it over her nose several times, watching the girl's pelvis arch from all that effort. I tried offering the merest scent of it to see if it would work as well, and it did! Delightfully so. Just the slightest suggestion of sealing this final orifice sent her into shivers of distress, and I imagined—how could I not?—the tears leaking out from behind those sealed eyelids, and the monstrous energy of those limbs, of every cell in her entirely fibrous body writhing with the single need to escape. But she won't. No suspense there. Not for me. But for the Vandersons it's different. They can barely restrain themselves from pleading for her life, so real does that screen seem to them now.

We all hear the girl's guttural horror rising from behind the hard black ball that fills her mouth. Not the chorus of *oompf-oompfs* I heard in the van, but a sound infinitely deeper and more chilling, the sound of suffocation, that struggles for silence amid all this fear, because to grunt beneath that gummy layer of alginate is to use up tiny stores of air, and she must know this as a drowning man knows that panic burns up oxygen, but knowing something—and don't we all know this—is not the same as acting upon it. And who's to say what those meth monsters are doing to the fragile composite that now makes up *#8*'s mind, the demands these wildly imperious creatures make on a consciousness now soaked in the insanity of a premature death?

Again I pass the ball of alginate under *#8*'s nose, inciting an involuntary "No!" from June that makes me smile. And Jolly Roger, God bless his common touch, takes her in his arms and tries to comfort her. Him! Roger! Offering comfort. And she accepts it. That's how wounded June has become.

Sonny-boy whimpers, no longer the kid who threw open the door of his house and insulted me with his insolence on the day of their abduction. No, now he lies huddled at his parents' feet like a bear cub who wants nothing more than the hibernation it has never known.

Diamond Girl? Yes, Diamond Girl watches, and her facade of invulnerability vanishes. How do I know? I look for her hands. I always look for the hands because the hands give away far more than the face. And where are hers, you might ask. Where has she placed them? Why, under her sweet round bottom, an instinctive attempt to still them from flight, from the rising desire to grab her arms, her body, perhaps even grab her parents while pleading for the protection they can no longer provide. I also see her eyes squeeze shut. She shuts them as I make a third, and tellingly final tease with that plug of alginate.

I run its edge in a gentle, coaxing circle around that small opening. I coo at the girl, sing her a song of my own devising, though it owes to the inspiration of so many others. It goes to the tune of "Frère Jacques."

> *Shall I enter, shall I enter,*
> *I don't know. I don't know.*
> *If I go inside, if I go inside*
> *You will die, you will die.*
> *Ding, dong, ding.*
> *Ding, dong, ding.*

More guttural gasps from beneath that green layer, the spirited antiphony she offers. I lean over her, place my lips near her ears, and hum more of the same. Buying time. Buying more of her panic. Buying it by the bushelful!

Still, Diamond Girl's eyes don't open. Still, Jolly Roger plays paterfamilias. Still, June clings to him. Still, Sonny-boy weeps at his parents' feet. Still, the plug remains deliciously on the tips of my fingers. And still, yes, *still #8* suffers for air, suffers, too, from the monsters I have set loose in her brain, from the fierce imaginings of a madness that only the deepest fear of death can know. And all this time her muscles are pushing, pulling, straining so hard they're ready to snap. They are not dying. They are more alive than they've ever been. This is what I want! This is what I need. This is the goal of all my work, to sculpt terror in its most revealing moment.

Her pores tear open as sweat floods her skin and drenches the soft down of her arms, legs, and belly. She burns with the desire to live, but this is what will kill her, the ruthless greedy manner in which she sucks up those dribbles of air. Always wanting more, sucking on it so hard that her nostril collapses inward, squeezing off the little life it gave. Spasms run down the length of her body like sparks racing along an exposed wire. She is frying, her body, her brain, the lungs that will no longer let her live.

Suddenly, my timing turns out to be impeccable: Diamond Girl's eyes open. This is *too* perfect because I know what's going to happen in a second—two at most—and I know that Diamond Girl will see it too.

I jam the plug up #8's nose, forcing it in with the complete madness of that moment, feeling the moist interior of her nostril with my finger, the hollow enclave of her final hope. I pack it in so tightly that no exhalation will ever reject it, though that is the first thing they try—expelling the alginate with the little air they have. But her body steals even this hope, steals the very element that could free it. Yes, that's right, the muscles devour the oxygen, eating away at the only force that could expel the plug. So you see, I have not killed her. Her own body has killed her. In this absolute sense, she has killed herself. They are all suicides, this one no less than the others. I am but a witness to their crimes of weakness.

Violent convulsions follow, her body turns rigid, recoils, then goes rigid again. Not from lack of air, not in those first few seconds, but from the swift understanding that these will be her final moments of life. No reprieve. No gentle casting of tie-lines to the living. Just this suffocating, seizure-saturated withdrawal from life.

And then as her fright freezes every muscle, contorts her fine face to a mask of purely grotesque proportions, I peel away the alginate, peel it from her legs and belly and chest, from her neck and face too, until it lies in a long sheath, like a second skin. I leave in place only the hard black rubber ball in her mouth, and the two nose plugs, so she can die, as die she must, for her job is finally finished.

I have become a master of this. Two impressions for each of them—back and front. First, I have them lie facedown so I can do their back, for a reason that should be obvious: they are dead after I take the impression of the front of their bodies.

As for their faces, their real faces, not the ones I sculpt so carefully for public display, I have other plans. I take all the alginate impressions and make masks. I think of them as visual antidotes to the death mask where inevitably we see the eyes so respectfully shut, the features in such timid repose. My masks speak boldly of the body's greatest urgency, to live on, to survive, even as it knows both the dearness of time, and the nearness of eternity.

The masks are yet another gift I bequeath to the world. I've made dozens of them, and in my will I've directed that they be placed on display within thirty days of my death. I'm not the least bit concerned about loved ones identifying the faces of relatives who disappeared, for I will be gone, and so will any definitive explanation. Let them live with even more dreadful questions than the ones posed by the sudden absence of their dearly departed. It will be, to my way of thinking, my last hurrah.

"Pleasant dreams," I tell the Vandersons as I turn out the lights at quarter to four.

To my surprise, Diamond Girl calls out, "Pleasant dreams to you too, asshole!"

"That's right," mutters Jolly Roger.

I ignore him, but Diamond Girl? What fire! What spirit! It's that refusal to submit that I find most alluring. I've never run across it before. It's easy to imagine Diamond Girl becoming a national hero in another situation. Put her down in Paris, say, during the Occupation, and she would have been spitting in the eyes of those butchers.

No one is fearless, but she comes close, confirming my decision to save her, to keep her around for my amusement, though I worry that her defiance could become contagious. She's exactly the kind of rebel who could rally the troops. While it's highly unlikely that she could lead a successful rebellion down here, especially given her putative allies, it does give me pause. Already, Jolly Roger was joining her chorus. I wonder if I can get her out of the cage, but still keep her around. I'm not about to install her in the guest quarters, that's much too risky, so I don't have a lot of options. It's not like I'm running a hotel here. But I realize that even if I had a place to put her, the moment she disappeared from the cellar, June and Jolly Roger would assume that I'd killed her, and that would snap the only reed of hope I've given them: get in shape and survive.

Even now, even after seeing the delightful demise of *#8*, they think there's hope. They cling to my assurance that the girl died precisely because she didn't work out hard enough, and that so many of the others who came before them are still among the living. The bone parade, I point out parenthetically, has arisen from the more recalcitrant residents of the cage.

June believes me. I can see this in her ongoing effort to cooperate. A mother like her can make a man as weak as Jolly Roger believe anything, even in her love, which in my opinion has been a vapor trail for years. So no, I will not deprive them of hope, never that, not till the final moments, that last breath when their bodies will betray them as surely as *#8*'s did to her; but I do want to keep them on edge, uneasy, the cascade of adrenaline alive, coursing through their shaky systems. They'd all be candidates for posttraumatic stress disorder, if there were a "post" to look forward to.

Then in one of those inspirations that can make you realize how good life can be, it occurs to me that what I need to do is as simple as divide and conquer, a prescription for ruling as old as the poverty it so richly enforces.

It will entail making fine use of Diamond Girl's penchant for the bizarre, along with a gaudy display that I purchased from the same S&M folks who sold me the mouth plug. It's a chain and collar arrangement for a master and his dog. And we all know who likes to wag her tail, now don't we?

# CHAPTER
## 10

LAUREN AND BAD BAD LEROY Brown walked down Pasadena's Colorado Boulevard, past the Gap and Banana Republic and all the other franchises that had set up shop along the route made famous by the Rose Bowl Parade.

Even behind her tinted glasses, the sunlight made her squint, and she recognized that she'd become acclimated to the fuzzy edges and softer skies of the Pacific Northwest, a recognition that nudged her closer to making a permanent move north. Her relationship with Chad had ended, and her studio, while wonderful, couldn't compensate for his rude intrusions. He'd taken to coming home in the middle of the day to try to cajole her into the physical intimacy that had been missing from their relationship since New Year's Eve, when she'd broken her very first resolution by making love to a man with whom there was no future.

She'd remained steadfast ever since, and knew that if Chad whispered one more salacious suggestion in her ear she'd scream, or turn a chisel on him.

Her first priority was finding a new place in Portland. The dainty Victorian wanted no part of Leroy—she'd called, they'd been clear—and her room was hardly suitable for him anyway; he'd look like King Kong in a Tonka toy world.

Maybe she could find a decent place with a garage that could serve as—"Walrus! Hey man, how they hangin'?"

Lauren had no idea that this rowdy greeting was intended for Leroy until he started straining on his leash, dragging her toward a biker in black leather chaps. The man lifted his heavy frame off a Harley, and raised his hand in a high five. Leroy offered an anemic response by swiping the air a few inches above the sidewalk.

"Nah, you're forgettin' already, Walrus. We gotta whip your ass back into shape. Sit!"

Leroy sat and dutifully executed the paw to palm greeting.

"Son of a bitch! Where you been, boy?"

Without even looking at Lauren, the biker grabbed the dog by both sides of his big thick muzzle and shook his head with brute familiarity. Leroy shuddered with pleasure. Or something.

The biker yanked off the leash and collar, and tossed them at Lauren's feet.

"What do you think you're doing with my dog?" she said.

Again, without so much as a glance in her direction, the biker snorted and said, "Walrus is not your dog. He's mine. Went missing a while back when the old lady and me were going through a bad patch. But hey . . ." he looked up at Lauren for the first time, and she took in his beard, the mustache growing down into his mouth, the stringy vines of dark hair that he smacked away from his face, ". . . that's all over now. You hear what I'm saying."

It wasn't a question.

He kneeled in front of Leroy, and his meaty hands once more gripped the dog's muzzle, greatly abusing—from Lauren's point of view—his head, though Leroy hardly protested. As she witnessed this rough play, a sad sinking feeling spread through her body.

"What happened?" she managed.

"None of your goddamned business, what happened."

"No, it is my business. I've been taking care of Leroy."

"Leroy? What the fuck kind of name is that?" The biker shook his head. "But hey," he said again as he turned toward her, sending his vines of dark hair swinging over his shoulder, "you did okay taking care of him." He eyed the dog. "Still got his balls. Good thing you didn't go cutting them off. I wouldn't be liking that."

He stood to leave, his hand wrapped around the back of Leroy's neck.

"He would've died out there. Did you know that? He didn't have anything to drink. What did you do, drop him off in the middle of the night?"

She heard a small group gathering behind her, lured by her anger, his arrogance, the dog in dispute.

The biker wheeled around. "Don't be giving me any bullshit about Walrus. He's *my* goddamned dog. Now fuck off before you piss me off."

Leroy's response was *grrrrr*.

"Shut the fuck up, Walrus."

"He doesn't like it when people yell at me."

"What?" The biker thrust his face forward like a curious tomcat.

"I said he doesn't like it when people yell at me."

"Him?" He shook Leroy by the neck. "He's a pussycat." Then he looked back at her and shouted, putting on a show for the assembled, "He wouldn't give me any shit, not for you, not for anybody. He knows better."

But Leroy's growl grew louder, ungodly loud, and Lauren thought she'd never heard a sound quite so good. She fully expected that it would put an end to this repossession, if that's what it was. But the biker, arms like hams, dragged Leroy up by his front legs and shook him by the neck. The rottweiler bared his teeth. Lauren thought her dog was about to bite, but he didn't. Maybe the biker knew he wouldn't. Maybe that explained why he started clobbering Leroy with his fist.

"Asshole," a woman shouted.

Lauren leaped forward, tears in her eyes, and tried to pull

Leroy away. She was yelling, "Stop it! Stop it! Get your hands off him!" when the biker spun her around and shoved her back into the growing number of gawkers. Lauren tripped, cried out her dog's name, and he lunged for the biker's leg. Caught it too.

"You son of a bitch." The term was no longer an endearment. The biker looked at the slash in his chaps, and then at the animal growling ferociously, hair up along the length of his back.

Someone in the crowd—the same woman?—shouted, "Kick his ass, doggie!"

Lauren climbed to her feet and yelled Leroy's name, then "Come. Come!" fearful that he'd be quarantined—or worse—for biting. They were cracking down on dangerous dogs.

Leroy, as if begruding every bite now denied him, backed up slowly.

The biker, head shaking, hair vines jiggling, stared at the dog, then jammed a thick finger at the creature's new master.

"You just made the biggest mistake of your life, bitch. You don't go ripping off one of my dogs."

"Yeah, he really loves your ass." The same woman again, no doubt about it this time.

But the biker's eyes never strayed from Lauren. "Big fucking mistake."

He climbed on a bike with more chrome than a Detroit warehouse, kick started the engine with a massive black boot, and roared off.

Lauren's legs jellied as she watched him race down the boulevard. A hand rested on her back, which made her jump.

"I'm sorry. I didn't mean to scare you."

Lauren knew from the voice that it was same woman who'd been shouting. But she didn't look like a woman, she looked like a girl, mid-teens with nose and lip rings, black hair, pale skin. Surprisingly young for all the grit she'd shown. Lauren caught her breath.

"That's okay. I'm just a little shaky right now." She reached down and leashed Leroy.

"I wanted to see if you were okay."

"I think so."

"Does he know where you live? You think?"

Lauren shook her head. "I don't see how. Why, do you know him?"

"Not him, but I know the type, if you know what I mean."

Lauren found herself nodding, not that she'd ever known a biker, not this kind anyway.

"They'll hurt you," the girl said as she turned away. She wiped her eyes with the inside of her wrist.

"Are you okay?" Lauren said. Now it was she who rested a hand on the girl.

"I'm fine." Her eyes drifted back to Lauren. "Just don't let them catch you alone."

That's it, we're out of here. Lauren started packing the minute she walked in the door of her minuscule apartment. You need an omen? A sign? You just got a billboard.

After her clothes, she organized her portfolio. She'd have to return during the summer break to close down the studio, a far more complicated affair than moving her spare possessions. But as long as she kept paying the rent, she could probably keep it forever. Chad had started charging after she'd refused to have sex with him, which had put a price, and a revolting taint, on all the years they'd spent together. She had to pay him three hundred forty dollars a month for what was essentially a room (or, as she once calculated, she'd earned about forty-two dollars and fifty cents per sex act, figuring their average of eight per month. By the minute, she did much better. By the inch, she was a millionaire).

She rued having to toss the bouquet of flowers, but they'd wilted and looked too sad to save. She did pocket Ry's "I miss you" note, and reveled in the memory of last night's call when they'd exchanged stories of childhood, traded secrets of adolescence (in all its gangly awkwardness), and shared the intense intimacy of their first loves. She wished she could rendezvous with him in Moab, but told herself to quit pining after the impossible. This had been her break, and she regretted only that she hadn't been able to work on her sculpture *and* see him. That should certainly get easier with a move north.

Before unplugging her laptop, she checked her email to see if he'd written. She planned to be on the road all day with Leroy in her classic sky-blue '65 VW Bug. That's if she could somehow contrive to cram the beast into the back seat.

No email from Ry, but another message from Kerry. The girl reported that she and Stassler had continued the repairs on *Family Planning #8*, which had been more extensive than he'd first realized.

All of Kerry's emails had started to sound like a dry recitation of routine, which concerned Lauren. Yet it wasn't so much what Kerry said, but what she didn't say. The omissions—any sense of joy, wonder, or even much in the way of comment on her hero— might be telling.

Early the next morning Kerry stared at her computer screen, feeling her shoulders collapse to somewhere south of her hips. What was she supposed to say to Lauren? That the jerk hadn't even looked at her stuff? Hadn't even *peeked* at it? She'd been telling Lauren everything was going "just great," but everything wasn't going just great. Stassler was a real irritating asshole jerk. There had been lots of work, but not much talk. She'd tried, she'd really, really tried to get him to open up, but it was like talking to *Family Planning #8*, which she was still helping him fix. Did he thank her? Say anything? No! What the hell was she there for, if he wasn't willing to talk to her, help her learn about casting? But she knew the answer. She was there to be his foundry slave, because that's sure as hell what she had become:

"Here, hold this."

"Here, hand me the clamps."

"Here, take this, and this time squeeze it shut *carefully*." Like she was an idiot.

Here-here-here. She wouldn't have taken this shit from anyone, and she wasn't going to take it from him much longer. The emperor has no clothes, that's what she'd concluded. None. Zip. Butt naked.

She wrote Lauren a short reply. No hint of disappointment. She'd told everyone at school, Oh, I'm going to work with Ashley Stassler, and now she burned with embarrassment at the thought of going back there with her tail tucked between her legs. But staying here meant walking around on eggshells. The only time she felt comfortable was in the house with the door shut and the shades drawn. Not even on the veranda. Even out there she felt like he was watching her. It was creepy. The only really completely totally neat thing about this whole trip was Jared. And the mountain biking.

They'd go out almost every afternoon. He was a pretty strong rider, not as strong as she, but good. She thought it was cool when she learned that they'd both grown up on BMX bikes, doing front and rear wheelies, and tricks like hopping around on the rear tire. Both of them had even spent long afternoons in neighborhood parks jumping their bikes up onto picnic tables, and then back to the ground. She'd even learned to knock off a really gnarly spin by getting her bike up to a good speed and then pulling a rear wheelie that let her whirl all the way through a three-sixty. Kind of like a ballerina on a bike.

When she was a kid, she did that stuff for fun. She'd had no idea how much those skills would pay off once she'd started racing mountain bikes over boulders, stream beds, and up steeply sloping canyon walls that looked too crazy to even crawl.

She'd also learned about Jared. Definitely from money. Lots of it. He'd grown up in a place called Palos Verde in L.A. She'd emailed Lauren, casually asking about it, never mentioning a guy, and Lauren had said Palos Verde had some of the most expensive real estate in southern California. Which was about what Kerry had figured all along: Jared had that Expedition, two-hundred-dollar sunglasses, and never sweated the small stuff. The rich kids she'd met were relaxed, never worried about things that drove her crazy, like how she'd pay the rent, or next year's tuition. But most rich guys were assholes too, used to having everything they wanted, and kind of assuming that everything included you as soon as they met you. But Jared was different. Plus his ego could take the fact that she really could outride him. Better tricks, stronger legs.

They'd gotten close, but she still wasn't sleeping with him. The feeling she'd had that first afternoon when the whole experience was too good to screw up with sex had evolved into something a *little* bit different. It now felt so good that she wanted sex to come at the perfect time, not just because she was feeling itchy, or worse, because he "had to have it." How many times had she heard that line? Guys who made their sex drive sound like pure viper venom, and she was the only antitoxin.

She and Jared had played around, enough to know that she loved the feel of his body, his scent, the taste of his skin, his sweat even, but not enough to know much more.

Thank God for Jared, though, because the other man in her life was El Creepo. She shook her head and wondered where the hell Stassler was anyway. It was already seven-thirty, and usually they'd be working in the foundry by now.

Screw it. She threw open the front door and walked directly past his Jeep to the guest quarters. Time to take the initiative. She'd tried the nice little intern routine, and he'd treated her like a dishrag. Maybe she'd get some respect if she was more like her real self, a riot grrl on a mission.

She knocked. No answer.

That's weird. She looked at his Jeep again. Definitely there. She knocked harder, and still no answer. She wondered if he was all right. She'd heard of guys his age suddenly dying of a heart attack, or something like that. She checked the handle.

The door opened to stairs that led her up to the guest quarters. She spoke his name softly, using it to try to ease her way into the one place he'd told her not to go.

Nothing. But he must be up and about; she could see his coffee mug and an empty bowl stacked neatly in the sink.

She turned around, eyes filling with the beauty of the wood-beamed room. But where's the sculpture he said he was working on, *Family Planning #9?*

Down there? She glanced at the hallway that led away from the main room. She dared not go any farther. As long as he wasn't stretched out on the floor, she thought she'd better get the hell out of there and never mention this morning's escapade.

She hurried down the steps, and was about to make her exit when she noticed a second door behind the one she'd left open. It looked like it went to the barn. She wasn't sure she'd actually go in there, but tested the handle anyway and peeked in. What she saw puzzled her. The horse stall where she'd flopped on to the straw had a wood floor. She could see this because all the straw had bunched up in the back of the stall. A wood floor? In a barn? She looked around. No wood on the floor anywhere else. Concrete. Strange, very very strange. And it had felt odd when she'd landed on it too. Hollow. Like a door.

Now she found herself creeping toward the stall, and that's when she spotted an O-ring. At first she simply touched it softly, silently. Then she lifted it up, feeling little resistance. As it rose, she understood that the straw had slid toward the rear of the stall when someone had opened the door. Stassler, right? Who else?

Lights were on down there. She thought she heard someone,

then she was sure she heard a moan. Oh God, he's in trouble! All of her ill feeling toward him vanished when she realized that he must have hurt himself.

She raced down the stairs calling his name. As she neared the bottom, her eyes took in the cellar, and she lost her breath so quickly it was as if all the air in her body had been sucked out by an approaching storm. A line of skeletons, posed just like his *Family Planning* series, stood before her, a long parade of bones garbed in pants and skirts, blouses and shirts, even eyeglasses and shoes, boots and belts. They stared at her, as if positioned to welcome the unwary.

A woman in a ghastly cage screamed at her to go, leave, now! Run! Get help! But in the confusion of the moment, Kerry stood at the bottom of the stairs glancing everywhere at once, at the skeletons and barbells and weight bench, and at the man, woman, and boy clinging desperately to the bars. She halted only at the sight of Stassler rising naked from behind a girl who was crouching on the dirt floor and chained at the neck to one of the support beams.

The woman in the cage gestured frantically and screamed again, "Run. Go. Get help! Please," as Stassler started sprinting toward Kerry.

She scaled the steps two, three at a time, his feet thundering right behind her. She stumbled as she climbed up into the barn, bolted right, saw the big doors, knew they'd be locked—they were always locked—and spun back toward the door through which she'd entered. As she ran past the stall, he was climbing out. He lunged for her feet, and almost grabbed an ankle. The touch of his fingers made her howl. Her heart surged so violently that it felt as if it would break apart the bones in her chest.

In seconds she made it through the doors and raced into the open area between the barn and the house. She ran toward her bike on the veranda, scaled the railing, and jumped on it. She pedaled madly for the stairs, determined to plunge right down them and straight into the desert—let him try to catch her out there—when she saw him running almost even with her down on the lawn, in a direct line to intercept her. She never descended, riding right past the stairs, and a second later, surely no more, again heard his footsteps pounding after her.

The railing on the far end of the veranda stood no more than thirty feet away. She raced toward it. He might have assumed that he had her trapped. Any reasonable person would have, but Kerry hung a wheelie and executed a jump that landed the rear tire on the edge of the wooden railing, pumped furiously on her pedals, and launched herself right into the air.

The ground lay a good six feet below her. She spotted her shadow streaking over the dry grass, and then tried to land on both wheels, crouching to absorb the impact; but her takeoff was unbalanced, and she suffered a vicious tumble that peeled the skin off her shoulder and elbow. She'd taken falls like this before, and though shaken from the impact, from Stassler, from all she had seen, she was back on her feet with surprising speed, grabbing her bike as she had in any number of races where she'd had to get started with other mountain bikers ripping past her like furious darts. But this time as she powered the pedal down with all the force she could muster, she found that the crash had knocked the chain off the front ring and jammed it between the crank and frame. It was frozen.

As soon as she grabbed the greasy chain to try to yank it free, Stassler slammed into her from behind, knocked the air right out of her, and ground her face into the earth. With her mouth mugged by dust and dirt, she couldn't even scream, though the pain demanded a swift response. Hers came in an uncharacteristic flood of tears.

He wrapped her in a choke hold and dragged her to her feet. He was naked, and she could feel his limp penis pressing into her bottom.

She thought she'd pass out from the struggle to breathe. Even so, she tried to fight him by grabbing at his testicles, but as soon as she did this he drove his bony knee up into her coccyx, stunning her.

"Stop, or I'll kill you."

He spoke with unnerving calm. She nodded as best she could. He gave her only enough slack for short breaths as he dragged her back to the barn and upstairs to the guest quarters.

"You wanted to see, right? Couldn't stay out, right?"

"I thought you were hurt," she gasped. "I was coming to help you."

"Your problem, Kerry, is you're not a very original thinker. The fact is, you're not smart enough to think. You're like all the rest of the world. You just drift from one stupid concern to another."

He pulled a pair of handcuffs out from a kitchen drawer and cuffed her wrists tightly behind her back. Then he reached back in the drawer for a two-foot length of copper wire.

When she started to plead for her freedom, he grabbed a fistful of her hair so tightly that she thought the roots would explode. He twisted her toward him and said,

"You got to be kidding. Let you go?" This made him smile. "I don't know what I'm going to do with you, but the one thing you can count on is that I'm not letting you go."

He snapped her head back and forth. The roots of her hair screamed and her eyes teared. Then he yanked her back down both flights of stairs to the cellar, forcing her past the girl chained to the beam. She was also naked, and still on her knees.

Kerry's vision was blurred, and she almost twisted an ankle when he shoved her to the floor. Stassler appeared above her as a dark, shadowy, indistinct figure. She couldn't make out what he was doing, but felt all too acutely the sharp point of his hip slamming into her shoulder, and a horrible stinging pain when he crushed her against the cage. She cried out, and tried to blink away the gathering tears, but seeing clearly wouldn't have helped: he was already bent over her back, threading the copper wire through the cuffs, binding her to the metal and bone prison. Then, just as the blurriness finally faded, he gripped her jaw and forced her to look up at him.

"Don't even think about trying to move. You hear me?"

Before she could make sense of his words, he pushed her head away and turned to the naked girl.

"All right now," he said cheerfully, "where were we?"

# CHAPTER
## 11

CONTROL. ALWAYS IN CONTROL. NONE of them answer me. But it's not as if after saying, "All right now, where were we?" that I really expect June to pipe up with, "Oh, you were having sex with my daughter. You know, the one over there in the dog collar and chain," although just once in my life I'd like my guests to show a little humor. Is that asking too much?

And to think the morning had started off so well. I had shaved and showered, breakfasted, and strolled down to the cellar with the "rugged but elegant" dog collar I'd bought from that S&M outfit in Iowa. Black, with steel studs on it. Really, those S&M freaks have no imagination when it comes to color. Their palette runs the spectrum from black to really black.

But they do sell a strong collar; one glance and you can tell it's for people who are really serious about their bondage games. You could restrain a mastiff with one of these, and the chain itself has outlandishly heavy links, sufficient to cause considerable damage if you weren't concerned with skin abrasions and broken bones. But I am, so I used the chain strictly to secure Diamond Girl, first to the collar, which has a delightful silver heart-shaped lock that snaps together along the vertical axis (a jagged affair no doubt meant to suggest that the heart had been broken but now, thanks to the benefits of bondage, is healed), and then to one of the cellar's structural beams.

Diamond Girl's smile didn't fade even after I'd ordered her down on all fours.

"You are a real son of a bitch," June snarled, which pleased me immensely. She'd been treating me like an ally, as if I had done *her* some great big favor by not having sex with her daughter during the time that I'd allotted strictly for working out. That's a thoroughly repulsive notion, bearing any kind of moral kinship with June *the* Cleaver, as I now think of her, so her opprobrium pleased me to no end. And to think I hadn't even really started yet. If it's true that you can tell a lot about a man by the enemies he makes, then it's even more important to watch who you end up with as friends.

"I beg of you, don't do it," Jolly Roger said with absolutely no conviction. He might as well have been reading from a teleprompter: "I . . . beg . . . of . . . you . . . blah, blah, blah." Have I ever met anyone so tiresome as these two?

Sonny-boy appeared as interested as ever in his big sister, especially as a certain sexual tension knotted the air, and threw a temper tantrum of a highly convincing nature when his mother snapped at him to "turn around."

The only one who seemed genuinely unflustered, other than me, of course, was Diamond Girl. She was down on all fours stretching her ass into the air like a cat rising from a warm cuddly nap.

Why was I doing this? I mean, besides the obvious pleasure? To anger them. To make them absolutely furious. To raise their rage to levels they haven't known since the day of their abduction. I've had to do this with every family to one degree or another. Raise the ante, their ire, and you build their fury, their hate because there's only one thing they get to do with it: work out even harder. *I'll show him!* It's almost hilarious to see how easy they are to manipulate, but you don't have to be a shrink to understand the response. The only power I've given them is the power to get stronger physically, which they equate, consciously or unconsciously, with the power to kill me. I do believe that some of the men have actually seen themselves as gladiators whose only hope is to grow so strong that they can bust out of their chains. And that is how I bet they see it too, *busting* out of their chains, like Russell Crowe, that pint-sized pudge boy who played the part in that awful movie everybody loved. You think they would have cast someone with at least a modicum of muscle tone.

I've done simply horrendous things to pets to get a family frothing. Nothing like messing with kitty to whip them into a frenzy. I can almost guarantee you that if I'd been about to sodomize a little pussycat of Jolly Roger's, he would have been a lot more worked up than that pathetic "I . . . beg . . . of . . . you . . ." business would suggest.

I've had them pump iron like monsters for days after one of my "incidents." As for Diamond Girl herself, I saw this as an opportunity to call her bluff, to see if all her fanny wagging would actually mean something.

As I settled behind her, she looked back and raised her eyebrows. She might as well have been asking me what I was waiting for. *Go for it, dude.*

I yanked her sweatpants down without any further warning, not a word to her or to the peanut gallery with their whimpering protests. I did it, I'll admit, with the urgency of a man who had been restraining himself for far too long.

Her panties were cockeyed from the force I'd used on her sweats, so before I cut them off I positioned them perfectly so that they were as symmetrical as a sweet summer peach.

I pulled out my switchblade, the one I used to prick Sonnyboy's cheek in the van, and the blade snapped open with a distinctly metallic click that proved impressive in the silence of those teeming seconds. Then I slid the blade under the right band of her bikini brief. I lifted it no more than an inch before the blade bit through the fabric and the elastic snapped apart with a most pleasing sound.

All of her right cheek and the top of her crack appeared naked before me. I saw that precious tan line, and the fabric gently rumpled against her skin. I leaned over and kissed her body's plushest flesh, avoiding the precariously balanced panty, as I felt no rush to disturb its delicately compromised position.

The silence in the seconds that followed was complete. I had, after all, a knife in my hand, and their daughter so fully at my mercy.

I sliced through the other side of the panty, and it fell as a place mat to the earthen floor.

At that point I stood, for I was still clothed, and folded the blade back into the casing with another definable click. I shed my shorts and T-shirt. My member was engorged, and I could see June stealing glances, her rabid eyes darting between it and Diamond Girl's lovely offering, as if she had defined the physics of space, and found her daughter wanting.

Then I heard her husband's boorish voice again,

"She's a virgin, you asshole."

Jolly Roger cracks me up. If there's an inappropriate comment, or time to say it, he homes right in. A virgin? He must have been hallucinating. The girl was no more a virgin than Madonna.

As it was, I restrained my humor and focused on the work at hand. I found Diamond Girl as silky as I'd imagined, and given the vividness of all my imaginings, she was living up to a great deal. And her enthusiasm was quite extraordinary. Her moans bordered on screams. That's when all hell broke loose.

I didn't even notice anything amiss until June started shouting, and when I did look up it was with the greatest reluctance, for my eyes had been feasting on the slope of Diamond Girl's lower back, the way all that lean, muscular tissue tapered into the firm cushions of her buttocks. Only moments before I had kissed her back, run my tongue up her spine, tracing the trail my hand had made when I first touched her in the van, when I gave her water and felt all those bony protrusions. I was still savoring the taste of her, the succulence of her taut youth, and experiencing her truly exquisite muscle control, the kind you generally don't find in women until they've learned their Kegels, when June started her inane, though helpful, screeching. At that particular moment, I had no more interest in a stupid blundering move by Kerry Waters than I would have had in partaking of a prayer service; but there she was, cow-eyed on the other side of the cellar performing her uncharitable act of coitus interruptus.

What actually infuriated me the most in those first few moments was the indignity of having to run off in the buff with my eager penis bobbing wildly and slapping my legs and belly like a punch-drunk boxer bouncing off the ropes.

Then I skinned my damn knee taking her down; but the biggest surprise came *after* I cuffed Her Rankness, tied her to the cage, and said, "All right now, where were we?" The answer that followed would have shocked most mortals. It even managed to surprise me. I looked down to see Diamond Girl kneeling like a dog begging for a bone, holding her hands up in front of her chest like paws . . . with my *knife* in her mouth. I'd run off without it. I'd left my shorts there too.

I took the moist knife from her, and rushed to search my pockets for the key to the cage and the one to her collar. Gone! But when I turned to her, she held them pursed between her lips.

She could have freed herself, she could have freed her family. It would have been a nightmare down here. But Diamond Girl didn't do any of those things. Instead, she betrayed her family, and her own possible survival.

From behind me I heard someone pounding the cage. It was Jolly Roger. At first he appeared speechless, suitably dumbstruck for words, and for once I thought I'd be spared his limited capacity for expression, but he finally found his voice and bellowed,

"You stupid fucking slut!"

"But Rog," I reminded him, all smiles, "you said she was a virgin. Remember? 'She's . . . a . . . virgin.'"

And I calmly turned back to the ministrations I'd been performing so well before I was so rudely interrupted.

Control. Always in control.

# CHAPTER

## 12

NUDE CLASS. LAUREN COULD FEEL extra energy in the air this morning, the added buzz that came when a lovely body would soon pose in the center of the studio.

All eleven of her students settled at their workstations. Only one remained empty, and when she saw it a feeling of dread swirled through her system. It would have been Kerry's, if she hadn't taken the internship. And if she hadn't taken the internship, Lauren reminded herself grimly, she wouldn't have turned up missing in Utah either. Stassler had reported her disappearance two days ago. Lauren had made frantic calls to the sheriff's office, Moab Search and Rescue, and to Ashley Stassler himself, though he hadn't bothered returning them. How could Kerry just disappear?

Lauren looked to her left and right, and realized that if the twelve tables around the posing platform were a clock, the empty workstation stood at midnight. Or noon? The question made her feel strange, superstitious in fact; but recognizing this did not settle the goose bumps that speckled her arms, or turn her thoughts away from the missing girl. Kerry had excelled with the human form, even when she chose not to replicate it exactly. She had the kind of control that let her allude to a muscle or tendon, or a feature on the face, and then transcend the literalness to find more in her medium than mere representation would allow. Lauren found it inconceivable that a girl with so much talent could simply be whisked off the planet, swept away like so much dust.

A piece of Styrofoam snapped loudly, like a branch over a knee, as Melanie, pigtails and pink sweater again today, wedged together chunks to bulk up the armature of her sculpture. Most of them had already roughed out the shape of the model's body with the Styro, two by fours, and empty water bottles, along with ample handfuls of dripping plaster. They would add more plaster this morning until they had enough mass to start cutting, chipping, and chiseling the legs and arms, head and torso, breasts and buttocks.

The model, Joy Anders, waited until the students started sorting out their supplies and tools before she took off her sweater, scarf, and kiwi-colored top. She wore no bra. No underpants either. She lay down on a white sheet, and adjusted an underlying layer of foam pads for comfort. Her skin was lightly tanned all over. Flawless.

"Here," Lauren said as she bent over her, "on your left side." Joy must have forgotten in the days that had passed since their last class. She was reliable, so she had a lot of work in the department. "That's it, with your calves and thighs at a right angle."

She gestured above Joy, but never touched her. The girl's legs came into position.

"Now, we want that little twist in your stomach again, with your shoulders back."

Joy moved as easily as a yogini, although the position wasn't that challenging: her upper body faced the ceiling at a slight angle to her hips, enough to emphasize the structure of her chest, ribs, and abdomen. Classic hourglass.

Most times Lauren hardly noticed the nakedness of a body in a studio. She'd spent hundreds of hours in nude classes, took them as a student, taught them as a professor, but Joy had the most amazing tattoos. An amber and aqua green fairy flared up from her sparse pubic hair to just above her belly button. The fairy was a generously winged creature, perhaps the most attractive tattoo Lauren had ever seen, which was saying a lot about very little because in her opinion tattoos were to art as bar bands were to music.

A more traditional black ink panther leapt from Joy's heel to her instep, while a dragonfly—again in amber but with a dark outline—hovered right over her upper spine.

But what lured Lauren's eyes was not flesh, however attractive, but the steel that pierced its most tender points. Joy had a one inch stud in each of her small, pink nipples. They looked terribly painful. And what would happen if she ever lactated?

Lauren asked Joy if she was comfortable, a question that felt freighted with extra meaning.

"I'm fine," she said.

Work had begun all around them, and plaster dust now hung in the air, swirling like brilliant white galaxies in the beams of light that broke through the blinds. Several students wore gauze masks to filter out the particulates. Sanding, scraping, and chiseling filled the air as well, along with the crinkling of big brown bags of plaster as students scooped out handfuls of the silty white powder and mixed it with water in plastic buckets.

Lauren eased by the empty workstation, and thought again of Kerry. Her fears about what could have happened to the girl had been shadowing her since she'd heard the dismal news. She had to force herself to move on.

A number of students heaped the damp plaster on their forms, but several of them had progressed to the point where they needed to use tools to start bringing out the shape of Joy's body.

Felicia wielded the chisel and mallet with the dainty reserve of a manicurist.

"You're too gentle," Lauren said. "Here, let me."

She took the chisel and gave Felicia's sculpture a good whack. A chunk of plaster came flying off.

"If you just chip at it at this stage, you'll never get it done. Work out the rough form, and then you can start taking out the smaller bits."

Felicia nodded, and when Lauren stepped back the girl applied marginally more force than she had before. Well, it was a start.

So far only Cornelia had captured the full roundness of Joy's hips and bottom. Cornelia had been a massage therapist for twenty years before returning to school, and her hands were intimately familiar with the shape of the body. Lauren felt this as much as saw it. When she touched Cornelia's sculpture, the heft of the human haunch filled her hand. Its warmth too, which always shocked the first year students who didn't know that plaster had the peculiar chemical property of heating up as it dried, becoming as warm to the touch as the human body itself.

Lauren checked the time, and ducked out of class to call Ry, who was supposed to arrive in Moab today. But when she got to her office, she found a message from Ashley Stassler. So he'd finally called back.

She dialed his number immediately, and got his answering machine again. The fourth time. As she began to leave yet another message, he picked up.

"This is Ashley Stassler."

"Hi, I'm Lauren Reed, Kerry's sculpture professor. Have you heard anything about her?"

"No, nothing I'm sorry to say. Not a thing. The sheriff's department hasn't found a trace of her or her bike."

"What do you mean, about her bike?"

"I thought you knew. She went out for a ride and never came back. They've had search parties out."

Of course she knew about the search parties, but a bike ride? "Where did she go riding?"

"We don't know. If we knew that, we'd be a whole lot further along," he said with a noticeable hint of impatience.

"Have you been out searching too?" She dearly hoped so. If for no other reason than to be able to tell her department chair that Ashley Stassler himself had been out looking for her.

"Me?"

"Yes, you."

"I'm *working*. I'm not running a search-and-rescue operation here. She went off for a ride and didn't come back. I called the sheriff. What else do you want me to do? They've been searching in helicopters, planes. Do you know my foundry is getting buzzed ten times a day since she took off, and every time they fly over the alginate shakes?"

"Sorry," she said with so little feeling that she surprised herself, but she was thinking mostly about the alginate. Figures that he'd use it. That green gummy stuff could capture the subtlest detail, which was undoubtedly important to a man concerned with the physical intimacies of terror.

"Yes, well so am I. This whole incident is highly regrettable, and a terrible interruption. I don't think I want to take part in your little program anymore."

"I don't think that's even an option, not after this."

"You're right about that. I don't mean to be rude, but I picked up because I heard it was you, and now I really must get back to work. Is there anything else?"

Despite his disclaimer, his rudeness surprised Lauren. Not that she'd expected a great deal of friendliness, not after everything she'd read about him, but maybe some commiseration, some heartfelt sense of remorse.

"No, nothing right now."

"Good day then." He hung up.

Lauren sat there staring at the phone until it started beeping.

She looked at the time and debated about calling Ry. Impulsively, she went ahead, but got only his message service.

By the end of class, only a few of her students had come close to approximating Joy's body in plaster. Most of them were frustrated—and humbled—by the difficulty of rendering the human form.

Joy came alive and slipped on her top, adjusting it carefully, so comfortable in her nakedness that she did not rush to pull on her pants.

Lauren walked her to the door and thanked her. Not every model was committed to a class to the degree that they'd show up consistently. And who could blame them if they didn't? Thirty dollars to remain absolutely still for three hours in an unnatural position with a single short break? A tough way to earn a buck.

After she left, Lauren wandered to the center of the room, surrounded by all the unfinished sculpture. Even the least of them had a rough form, and had gained size. Only the workstation that would have been Kerry's stood empty, stark in its solitude.

Midnight? Or noon?

Numerous online news stories repeated the little that was known about Kerry's disappearance. But Lauren did find an Associated Press account that included a quote from Stassler. His words almost made her physically sick. He said the girl had been unusually interested in abandoned mines. Lauren was sitting at her desk picturing Kerry lying broken and dazed, or dead in some dark mine shaft, when Ry returned her call.

"You don't sound well," he said.

"I'm not." She told him what she'd read.

"That would explain it," he said gravely. "There are abandoned mines all over here."

"What were they mining? Gold?" Those shafts could go on forever.

"Uranium."

"Uranium!"

"It's not as bad as it sounds. Falling into a uranium mine isn't going to be a whole lot more dangerous than falling into any other kind of mine."

Especially if you die in the process, but Lauren didn't say this. She heard Ry ask if Kerry had ever talked about old mines.

"No, but that's not saying she didn't have an interest. She had . . ." Lauren caught herself using the past tense, and winced. "She has an omnivore's interest in everything."

"She's big news here. Search and rescue's still on it, and there are posters of her everywhere."

She told him about her conversation with Stassler.

"I've heard he can be rude."

"Rude? Yes, that works," Lauren said. "So does insensitive, calloused. Let's see, what else? Can you imagine saying, 'I'm not running a search-and-rescue operation'? And then complaining about the search planes shaking your alginate? I wish he could have taken the call from her parents."

"You talked to them?"

"Yesterday afternoon. They're absolutely petrified. They're there too, in the Best Western."

"Then he probably has heard from them."

"When are you supposed to start interviewing him?"

"Tomorrow."

"You might want to call out there and see if he still wants to do it. He might not want to with all of this going on."

"There's no way I'm going to call him and give him a chance to back out. It's an old reporter's trick. You just show up as if nothing's wrong. It's a lot harder for them to turn you down that way."

"Ask about her, okay?"

"I will. It would seem strange if I didn't."

"This is just the thing to spice up your book."

"No, they'll find her, she'll be okay, and all of this will blow over."

Lauren didn't think anything was going to blow over, but it seemed heartless to admit this.

She imagined Ry in downtown Moab with the phone to his ear, imagining the town much more than she needed to imagine him, the kind face, square jaw, bright brown eyes, and all that hair that felt so good when she sank her hands into it.

"I'll be anxious to know if you get any kind of reading on him when her name comes up."

"Me too. I'll let . . . know . . . I . . ."

Ry was breaking up. She sat forward, and her foot nudged Bad Bad Leroy Brown, who'd been sleeping in her office all morning.

"I'm losing you. Ry? Ry? Ry?"

The line went dead.

Before she could help herself, Lauren was once again imagining Kerry in an abandoned mine. The possibility of such a fall made her squirm. It would be like falling into a dark crevasse, or a dizzying canyon. Like falling into hell. Lauren had always had a horrible fear of heights, and an even worse fear of falling into huge openings in the earth. She shook herself and stood.

"Come on, Leroy. Let's get lunch."

Leroy stood up and executed a perfect "downward dog": extended front paws, arched back, butt high.

"A yogi doggie." She smiled. It was the first time in two days.

They hadn't walked ten feet from her office when they ran into Dr. Aiken, the vinegary department chair. He grimaced at Leroy, but then ignored him; dogs were as common as calls to action on the campus bulletin boards.

"I *received*," he intoned in a lordly voice, "a visit this morning from President Nacin. She wants to know *why*," that regal tone again, "we didn't check out this situation a lot better before we let one of our students go *merrily,*" a sarcastic singsong, "on her way."

"I don't know what I was supposed to do. Let's be realistic here, the girl's an adult. She went off on an internship with a world-renowned sculptor. It's not as if we sent her off to the deepest darkest part of the Amazon without a guide."

"You might as well have," Aiken snapped.

Leroy growled.

Aiken stepped back.

"He doesn't like it when people raise their voices at me," Lauren explained.

"I didn't raise my voice."

"He thought you did. You want to discuss it with him?" Oh, the benefits of tenure.

Aiken ignored this, but spoke in a noticeably muffled tone when he said, "What do you know about Stassler anyway?"

"You mean besides being one of the foremost sculptors in the world? Besides having made the cover of *Time* in 1994? Besides having been the subject of an Emmy-winning PBS documentary? Not much. He was willing to take Kerry on as an intern after she wrote him."

"And *you* sent a letter of recommendation."

"She's one of my better students. One of the best I've ever had, so yes, I wrote—"

"One of the last you'll ever have." Aiken stood with lips so pinched they stuck out as far as his nose.

"What's *that* supposed to mean?"

"We don't *lose* our students around here."

*Grrrrr . . .*

"Get that dog off campus."

Lauren shook her head. "As long as the other *tenured* faculty can have their dogs, I'm keeping mine. And we didn't lose Kerry Waters 'around here.' She's lost somewhere in the desert of southeastern Utah."

Aiken stormed off. Leroy didn't give him so much as a glance, but Lauren watched his departing figure with a growing sense of regret. And what she saw after he turned the corner was her own reflection in a tall glass display case. She felt like she was looking into the academic version of an abandoned mine shaft. Sure, you can have tenure, but a vengeful department chair can turn your every day into torture.

# CHAPTER
## 13

DESPITE MY OUTWARD CONTROL, I am not without my concerns. They are deep, and they are obvious. They even have a name, though I am loathe to utter it. After I tossed that wretch into the cage with the Vandersons, I had to report her missing. But before doing this, I had to load her bike into my Jeep and dump it by the side of an old, deeply rutted two track way up in the mountains. Then I had to go back home and wait a suitable period of time before calling the sheriff's office.

Where the hell is she?

I rehearsed the disgust I really would have felt had she failed to show up the next morning to help me with my work, but even then I couldn't call the sheriff. Too soon. Wouldn't a reasonable man simply assume that she'd spent the night with her boyfriend, this Jared fellow she'd had the good sense not to bring around. That's what she told me, officer, that she and Jared were going for a ride. That she and Jared were going out to dinner. That she and Jared spent all their time together. A quick romance, very quick, as far as I could see.

And were they . . . intimate?

I don't know. She did confess that he was "pushy." Yes, I believe that's the word she used, but she liked riding with him, said he was very strong.

And when they tell me that they've found signs of a struggle near her bike, I'll shake my head in small wonder over the fabric I tore from the crotch of her bike pants and jammed around the chain. Then I'll look up and say,

Signs of a struggle? Well, officer, she would have given as good as she got. She was nobody's patsy, not my Kerry.

Yes, I rehearsed well for the procedural mind of the law, but I had not anticipated how quickly the sheriff and his chief detective would ask to look around.

"Yes, by all means," I told them. "Go anywhere you wish."

Neither had I envisioned how unsettling I would find the obligatory search of the compound. But had I said no, they would have been back with a search warrant and a set of suspicions as deep as the desert itself. They would have been scouring every inch of the foundry, the house, the barn, and the ranch, all seven hundred eighty acres. That would never do. But even so, I soon regretted my generous offer.

They poured through every door, the sheriff and chief detective, along with two toady deputies, minions. The chief detective wanted to know about a basement, so I led them without pause down the stairs from the kitchen in the main house, unable to recall what I had down there. Nothing, as it turned out; but those Mormons had left old building materials, a pile of tongue-and-groove boards, a couple of sacks of cement that had split open and spilled their gray innards, and a trowel.

The dirt floor apparently proved persuasive because after peering at it openly, and finding no disturbances in the surface, finding it, in fact, as compressed as concrete, they trudged back up the stairs. While I felt insulted that they would suspect me, even momentarily, of mimicking that crude painter of clowns, John Wayne Gacy, who turned his cellar into a cemetery, I also knew that it was wise for me to suffer my grievance in silence, if just this once.

They didn't even think to ask about a cellar in the barn. Who ever heard of such a thing? No one digs a cellar under a barn. They walked past the stalls, the sheriff asking if I ever boarded horses, a question I believed was more personal than professional—he probably has a nine-year-old daughter who just *loves* horses ("Can we get one, Daddy? Can we? *Please!*")—and then trudged once again heavily up the stairs to the guest quarters.

They looked through every room, opened closet doors and cabinets too. They found nothing. I made a point of chatting amiably as they moved along. I pointed out the storage room, which they might have missed, but that's all: I didn't want to appear overly helpful, overly anything.

I drove them out to the gate, and waved good-bye. I was open, aboveboard, honest. Well rehearsed.

Their search goes on. I know they're combing the desert. I told them about her interest in abandoned mines, told several reporters who called the same thing. Spread out enough hints and clues to keep even the dimmest bulb burning brightly. Now I feel comfortable returning to my nighttime excursions.

Kerry's arrival does have a single salutary effect: she has told the Vandersons that *their* disappearance is not a news story, that she hadn't heard anything about them, even though her hometown paper did report the story in the regional section of their Sunday paper. Not even the front page. Not that it would have mattered. I doubt Her Rankness would have noticed if it had been plastered across her forehead. Like most of her generation, she appears woefully uninformed, and I'm not at all sure that if pressed she could name the vice president.

But it's a wonderful service that she provides, this news to the

Vandersons that they are no news at all. I don't want them believing in miracles. I want them believing in muscles, and ultimately only in me. I say they live. I say they die. I am their one true God, their Jesus, and mahatma.

Other than her rapidly diminishing value as a bearer of bad news, Her Rankness would serve no purpose at all, except that she now appears to be striking up a relationship with Diamond Girl. For the first time, Diamond Girl is talking to someone in the cage. They whisper back and forth, like a couple of schoolgirls in the back of a classroom. It pains me that I cannot hear them. The camera mikes have no difficulty picking up the strident tones of June the Cleaver, the bellicosity of Jolly Roger, or the constant whining of their guttersnipe son, but whispers fall beyond their limited capacity.

Seeing Diamond Girl engaged with another young woman, even in such a subdued manner, has been fuel for my imaginings. I watch her on the monitor now. I watch her at every opportunity. She is as unlined as sand, the wind that rustles my tracheal calm. She utterly preoccupies me. My memory proves as insistent as a needle, always threading back to the mystery of her touch. I must hold her breasts again, rediscover their fleet buoyant weight and the radial heart of her bottom. But most of all, I want to feel her girlish pudenda nestle in the heated pocket of my palm.

I have not let her out of the cage since taking delight in her body, which I've thought about a great deal. I believe she climaxed at the same instant that I did; and despite her precociousness in the ways of the flesh generally, I don't think she could deceive me on something as vital as this. She is a hungry little cur, and her appetites are unusual only to the degree that she's willing to satisfy them at a staggering cost to herself and her family.

But I'm not so fool as to let her go, give her the run of the ranch, though I have imagined talking to her. I am intrigued by her treachery. It's difficult to find such purity of spirit in anyone anymore, but to find it in a girl so young, so delectable, constitutes nothing short of a treasure.

And besides, I have purchased an outfit that will suit her as well as it suits me. She shall wear it, along with the collar and chain; and she shall join me up here, the first of my guests to be welcomed to the guest quarters.

I wait until early evening. I want the light that dazzles the eyes, that softens the vision with dusk.

She looks up as they all do when I descend the stairs. They will work out in about six hours, all but Her Rankness; I won't waste precious workout time on her. For the first time, Diamond Girl will know when she settles on that stationary bike that it's the middle of the night, because in a few short minutes she will discover that it's early evening.

Her Rankness "demands" to know what I *"think"* I'm doing.

My head shakes. It's all the response she'll get. More than ever, I'm comfortable in the knowledge that I'm saving some poor slob a life of hell with this woman. To think of the accolades I would receive if the world only knew the service I provide, not only with Her Rankness, but with most of the subjects who end up here.

I wave them back as if I have the gun, though I don't and have always been extremely careful about bringing it down here. The gun is absolutely necessary for June or Jolly Roger's workouts, but less for Sonny-boy or Diamond Girl. The knife serves them well; they have both felt the blade, and the ease with which it cuts through a panty, or pricks the skin.

At this point all of them are sufficiently cowed as to require little coercion, and even Her Rankness joins the herd as it retreats numbly to the back of the cage. Only Diamond Girl remains by the door, assuming correctly that I've come for her. Indeed, I think she'd be disappointed if I hadn't.

She kneels once I have locked back up, and accepts the collar as easily as a cleric would accept his.

I lead her on the chain in the proper "heel" position, as I would a canine. We climb both sets of stairs to the guest quarters. Now I tell her to disrobe, and she complies with only a slightly amused expression.

Once naked, I hand her the box and tell her to open it. She does this with childish expectancy.

"Plaid?" she says when she sees the skirt. Then "pantyhose?" as an obvious question, which I don't deign to answer. She shuffles through the rest of it and says "Whatever" as joylessly as a wife whose birthday brings yet another gaily wrapped gift box with a pushup bra.

I'm tempted to warn her about her attitude, but my excitement is flowering, and as soon as she's dressed I hand her a page of written instructions.

Still holding her at chain's length, I watch her sit on the edge of the chair, as instructed, and cross her legs. The skirt, short by design, rises even higher until she's all legs and panties and hose.

Do I dare permit touching up here where windows could be broken, and doors could be opened? The question becomes moot. The dusky light itself begs a whole series of brazen revelations, and I am fighting far too hard to ever hold back. My hand retreats from my pocket, from the feel of the knife, from the bold grip of all that is hard. I never take my eyes from her. She watches me too, and washes away my last few grains of control as she moves down the list of instructions with the deliberateness that I demanded. To stand here and stare at her is to know without any uncertainty that she is every disturbance of every element that has ever passed through me. My urge to touch is no longer mere feeling, it is frenzy.

Afterward, she gathers up her hose and panties, skirt, blouse, and bra, and folds them up neatly, perceiving as she must that this is exactly what I expect. Then she sits at the kitchen bar, upon whose hard surface we finished, and drinks the water I have given her. She is naked, as am I. The collar and chain lie across the room, where they were flung in our fever. There are kitchen knives within reach. Her eyes, though, have not strayed from me. She has a look that pierces, and I realize that I've seen more warmth in the eyes of the dead.

For all the chill, I still find myself burning with the one question that has plagued me: When she had the knife, the keys, she didn't release herself, her parents, or Sonny-boy. Why not?

"Why not?" She mocks me when she repeats my question, and her head moves heavily from side to side, as if belabored by the obviousness of the answer. Still, I persist,

"Yes, why not? You could have."

"You might as well ask who I am, if you're going to ask that."

She is right, and I recognize this instantly, because only by knowing who she is can I possibly fathom the brutal beauty of her act.

"Okay," I say with a jauntiness that I do not actually feel. "Who are you?"

She taps her fingers on the bar, and I'm reminded of a prostitute I met several years ago in Harry's New York Bar in midtown Manhattan. She had the same bitter impatience when she realized that I wasn't going to be a paying customer, that my only desire was to talk, to probe, to furrow her brow with my questions.

But Diamond Girl's fingers stop their dancing quickly, and she is unflustered when she speaks,

"What you really want to know is, did my dad fuck me?"

She has brought me quickly to this question, directed us there as swiftly as a ship's captain navigates a dangerous but familiar crossing. It was the very first question I ever had of her, and the one to which I had planned to return. But the journey she made was much faster than the one I had in mind. My impulse was to thread my way slowly among the rocky shoals, but she's having none of it:

"That's it, isn't it? Something simple that explains everything you ever wanted to know about Diamond Girl. It's that her dad fucked her. See, there you have it—Diamond Girl, The Whole Story. Then it's on to the next one, since she's all figured out."

She flips her hair over her shoulder, "That's stupid."

She stuns me with her judgment, for its biting accuracy, and I'm left to watch her eyes, lest they lead her hands to a knife. But they don't stray, and remarkably I'm the one forced to look away. To admit painfully and without words that she is right: I do want the quick and easy answer. Now I know that she'll never give it. But I'm wrong again.

"Okay, my dad fucked me."

She lets the silence settle between us, and I feel a tinge of guilt for having taken her sexually after that lout downstairs has had his way with her. He *will* die slowly, even more slowly than the rest. So deep is my hatred of child molesters that I'm inspired to go to greater lengths than ever before to find an extraordinarily excruciating demise for Jolly Roger.

"Actually, he didn't. I fucked him."

I lean back. My surprise must be evident because she inches forward, as if to keep the distance between us stable. "The same as it was with you. He couldn't resist."

She chooses that moment to lift her feet up on to the stool so that when I look down I see her swollen sex staring back at me. It isn't until I begin to talk that I realize she's in the perfect position to kick me with both legs and send me flying. I grip the bar.

"But he's your father."

"Maybe," she snaps.

"Maybe?" Is she gaming me, even now?

"I came home from school early one day and found my mother doing the UPS guy. So who knows?"

I stare at Diamond Girl and wonder if this is true. She doesn't look at all like Jolly Roger, but who does?

She squeezes herself. "Now if I tell you I'm lying, would you believe me?"

"What?" I feel like an idiot, and none too patient with her game, if that's what it is.

"If I tell you I'm lying, would you believe me? Come on, think about it. Can you really see me fucking Jolly Roger?"

I smile at her use of his name.

"Yes," I tell her, "I can imagine it. What about your mother and the UPS guy?"

"What about my mother and Jolly Roger? Can you believe that too?"

"You're not as smart as you think, Diamond Girl."

"And you know what? Older men always say something like that just when they're starting to feel really stupid."

"So you think I'm stupid?"

"Do I think you *feel* stupid?" She looks up at the high ceiling after correcting my question. "Yes." Her eyes fall back to me. "But I don't think you are."

She's thrown me a bone. I know this, but still I am grateful. I *want* her approval. This is insane. I know this too, but consciousness does not equal cure. Consciousness equals only insight, and only sometimes, and insight itself can be madness. Whoever thought otherwise was kidding himself, Dr. Freud.

"What about school," I ask.

"What about it?"

"Do you like it?"

"What is this, a job interview?"

"If you like."

"Look, I'm fucking you because I want to. Okay?" She releases one of her legs slowly, drapes it over my knees. I stroke the inside of her thigh, and she adjusts to accommodate my apparent intentions. Then I quickly realize that they are not my intentions as much as they are her own because she takes my hand and draws it to her. She is moist, as moist as a warm sponge.

"School?" she muses. "I'm in accelerated classes. A college-bound girl," she says softly, but it's pure affectation. A deaf and blind man could tell. Even with my hand resting on her sex, the distance between us is that distinct. "Next year was going to be my senior year. I was planning to take a few hours at Washington State while I finished up. Nothing but four point O's. Does that surprise you?"

"Not at all. I would have been surprised if you weren't working up to your potential." I hate myself for saying this. I'm starting to sound like her father. Or *a* father (I distance myself immediately from Jolly Roger). I try to recover with some bromide about how it must be a good school, but she surprises me all over again.

"Yeah, you think so? Some of my friends carry guns to school every day. What does that tell you?"

"It tells me that your friends are thugs."

She laughs. It's the first time I've heard her do this, and I am shocked by the depth of her amusement. She laughs so hard her legs shift, and my hand falls away. The air feels cool on my wet fingers.

"You? You're calling *them* thugs?" This starts her up again. Her whole body shakes with laughter, and I find myself smiling awkwardly.

"No, I don't think so," she trills. "You see, there are some real creepy people out there. You have to protect yourself from them."

"From me?"

"Yeah, that's right, from you. But you know what?"

"What?" I look at her closely and spot a slinky disturbance in her eyes.

"You're not the only one."

When she says this it sounds so juvenile at first, a child's attempt at one upmanship, that it takes me a full moment more to understand that she has threatened me. Or more precisely, that I feel threatened. See, even here I can't be sure of who is the actor, and who is the play. But I will never let her know this. She can sense and suspect, but she is sixteen and doesn't really know anything for certain. She's good at this game, and it will keep her alive; but the time is coming when my breath will no longer seize at the sight of her, and the burden of her body will be lifted from me forever.

I tell her to fetch her collar and chain, and she climbs down off the stool and retrieves them as dutifully as a dog.

# CHAPTER
## 14

LAUREN *HAD* TO GET TO Moab. Her sense of urgency had only grown in the days since her chance encounter with the department chair. To hell with him. If he was determined to make her life miserable, let him find a teaching assistant to cover her classes. She needed to join the search, do whatever she could for Kerry. Unfortunately, getting out of town with Bad Bad Leroy Brown had become quite the task.

In the midst of keeping up with a crowded class schedule, following news reports about Kerry, and playing telephone tag with Ry, she'd gone ahead and had Leroy "fixed," though she doubted her dog viewed his loss so benignly. She'd planned on transporting him to the airport in her VW Bug for this morning's flight to Salt Lake City. True, she had considered boarding him, but had no idea how long she'd be gone, and little confidence that a minimum wage employee of a kennel would carefully administer his schedule of medication, particularly if her dog turned irritable (always a possibility, given the cause of his grief).

During a dry run late yesterday, she found that she could not cram his huge, convalescing body into the Bug, not even the front seat. It wasn't the most capacious of cars, and Leroy, God knows, wasn't the most nimble of dogs. After her lone attempt to load him, he staggered and collapsed under the influence of doggie downers. The only other obvious option—mass transit—would have demanded a white cane, dark glasses, and more gall than Lauren could ever muster, especially with a dog that looked no more alert than his favorite fire hydrant. Worse, none of the airport shuttles or Portland cab companies were willing to transport a rottweiler, a breed whose reputation really did precede it.

"Try Oregon Armored," cracked the dispatcher at Yellow Cab.

"But he's sedated," pleaded Lauren.

"Why's that?"

"He was neutered."

"So he's in a *really* good mood."

That clinched it. Early this morning, in a fit of frustration, she finally called Alamo, which didn't know any better when they leased her a white Chevy Impala, a full-sized barge for a dog that took to its broad back seat as naturally as a pasha takes to a pillow.

She pulled up to arrivals, hauled the huge dog carrier out of the trunk, and tried to rouse the drowsy Leroy.

"Come on, boy," she stroked his thick muzzle, "it's wake-up time."

Leroy lay as still as an artist's model.

Now she tapped his jaw with her hand, as you might gently slap a loved one's insentient face. Leroy moaned. The skycap who had just walked up reared back.

"He's harmless," Lauren said, not knowing exactly what Leroy was like in such an intoxicated state. Would his real self emerge? Would he be a barrel-chested, two-fisted bar brawler of a dog? Or might he be a sweetheart, happy to cuddle and riffle his rubbery flews with sighs of pure chemical contentment?

She'd heard that the best possible test of a man was to get him drunk. Then you'd see what he was like in his heart of hearts. Did he turn into a loudmouthed braggart ready to do battle with the world? There's your guy. Or did he slur sweet nothings in your ear as he rested his sloppily arranged body next to yours?

Leroy turned out to be neither. Leroy turned out to be comatose. This worried her. The vet said the pills would make him "woozy," and suggested giving him an extra one for the flight. This was not woozy, this was dead weight, one hundred twenty-five pounds worth.

She stood up and eyed the skycap. He looked capable.

"I do need your help."

"With that?" He pointed to the lump of black-and-tan fur.

"Yes, with the *dog*." A surge of impatience unsteadied her.

"This is gonna cost you."

She ground her teeth and did all she could to modulate her voice. "How much?"

Not that she had any choice. Although only a few feet separated the supine Leroy from the open door of the dog carrier, without some help the gap might as well be the Grand Canyon.

"We'll do it on a sliding scale," the skycap said. "Ten bucks if it's easy. A whole bunch more if he bites."

"He's not going to bite. He's drugged."

The skycap appraised the dog. "Gonna take both of us, one on the head and one on the butt."

"Fine. Which end do *you* want?"

"I don't want the head," he said quickly.

"Then I guess you get the butt end."

"Ain't it my life."

He climbed in from the driver's side and started pushing as Lauren pulled. Leroy moaned again, and this time one of his hind legs kicked out. The startled skycap scuttled back out the door.

Lauren asked him to come around the car. "I think we can do it from here now."

She was holding Leroy's head and shoulders; they felt like they weighed a lot more than the forty-pound bag of chow she'd bought him last week.

"Hey, Burt, get your sweet self over here," the skycap shouted.

Lauren saw a box-shaped man ambling over.

"What you got here, a dead one?" he said.

"We got what you might call one very passed-out puppy," said skycap number one.

"Then let's wake his sleepy self up," Burt said.

"*You* wake him up. Personally, I want him doing the Z's."

"Yeah, okay. What's his name?"

"Leroy," Lauren said.

"Leroy? I've known a few Leroys. Nasty boys. Hey, Leroy," Burt said to the dog, "you living up to your name? Having yourself a good time?"

"He's fixed," Lauren said, feeling more than a touch testy. "Look, are you going to help us?"

"Sure-sure," Burt said. "Here, give me his head. Take yourself a breather. Kenny, you can get his butt. You look like you could use some loving. Go on. We gonna do this on three."

On three they did do it, shoveled the sleeping one right into the carrier, which Kenny, skycap number one, snapped shut in a hurry before turning to Lauren.

"You got anything else?"

"Yeah," Burt laughed, "she's got herself an ocelot in the front seat."

"I just have a carry-on," Lauren said.

When she didn't reach for her wallet, Kenny's smile disappeared faster than free food in a Chinese restaurant.

"Oh, right," she said. "Hold on." She dug out a twenty. "Can you split this?"

"Can Siegfried and Roy make one of those big white pussycats go bye-bye?" said the latecomer Burt, filching it from her hand so fast that his buddy didn't stand a chance. But just as smoothly he peeled off a ten spot for him from a roll as big as Lauren's fist, and slapped the top of the carrier with his broad hand.

"See you, Leroy."


For Leroy, the flight to Salt Lake City proved restorative, although he still weaved a little as Lauren walked him out to the rental car.

She herded him into the backseat while a skycap loaded the carrier into the trunk.

Moab was about a five-hour drive, which meant a six o'clock arrival time. Perfect, because she had a dinner date with Ry.

She and Leroy left the city behind quickly, though its borders did appear to be expanding; everywhere she looked she spotted new subdivisions going up. They rose along the freeway like port towns along a river.

Leroy sat forward and placed both paws on the front seat.

"How are you, boy?"

She reached back and scratched his ear. He licked her hand, as he had her leg when they'd first met in the Angeles National Forest. It was an endearment that still made her squirm.

"Ready to do some searching?"

He yawned, and in the rearview mirror she saw his aptly named canines gleaming in the dark cavern of his mouth. What a mutt.


Finding a motel that would allow a dog turned out to be extremely trying. Perhaps it was *this* dog. One manager offered a "maybe," and another said, "It kind of depends"; but both had refused when they spotted Leroy looming over the front seat.

"But he's really very nice," she protested to the second one.

"Try the Green Glow Inn downtown," he snorted. "They'll take anything."

The Green Glow Inn looked like it had sprung up during the uranium fever that had swept through Moab in the fifties, and had fallen into disrepair ever since. The color of the neon sign that rose along the length of the second floor seemed like a reasonable enough facsimile of radium, but the lobby window had a five-foot crack that had been taped so long the glue had crystallized and the edges had curled up.

She found the lobby itself as beaten in appearance as the rug runner that led to the front desk. Behind it hunched a white-whiskered man with shrunken features and no discernible interest whatsoever in her presence, or in the business it could possibly represent. He was reading a hardcover book, and might just as well have hung a DO NOT DISTURB sign on his pointy beak of a nose.

"Hi," she said, trying to sound perky, but perky wasn't in her weary repertoire today.

After turning a page, he scowled and said, "What do you want?"

"A room?" she said hesitantly.

"Sign here." He thrust a yellowed form at her, along with a pencil that had been chewed down to a nub. Lovely.

"Do you take dogs?"

"Do I take dogs?" he repeated theatrically. "Does this look like a place that has any choice in the matter? What is it anyway?" He turned his rheumy eyes on her for the first time. "You look like the Pekingese type to me."

"Kind of."

"I thought so. Cash or charge?"

"Charge." She handed him her American Express.

"Don't take it. When you stay at the Green Glow Inn in Moab, Utah," he mimicked the old commercial, "you better have Visa, or you're outa luck, lady."

"I've got Visa."

"I've got a room for you and your pooch."

To his credit, he laughed when she walked in with Leroy. Then he said, "I like you, lady. I like your style. What's his name?"

"Leroy."

"He looks like a Leroy. I'm Al, by the way. Al Jenkins."

She waved as she started up the steps. They creaked like an iron wheel all the way to the second floor. No one ever ran out on a bill in this place, she thought.

The room appeared refreshingly clean and large. While it wasn't exactly Four Seasons plush, it did have a double bed and bath, which included, much to her delight, an extra long tub. The last time she'd checked into a hotel like this was in Flagstaff, Arizona, another old downtown building, where Zane Grey was reputed to have written one of his westerns during a three-week stay. She and Chad had proceeded to ring the springs on the old bed for a good half hour before heading out for the evening. When they'd stepped into the hall, they'd found three geezers perched on an ancient divan, a smiling smirking conspiracy. She'd turned every shade of red in the spectrum of embarrassment.

"Okay," she clapped her hands. Leroy looked up. "What do you say we take you for a walk, and then go get Ry?"

The huge hound wagged his stump.


Ry's digs were much more upscale than the Green Glow Inn. He was staying on the newly minted motel strip. HEATED POOL, CABLE, JACUZZI TUB, crowed the marquee.

She called him from the lobby phone. He appeared moments later bearing a smile, open arms, and a hug that turned into as much of a kiss as either one of them apparently wished to display in public.

They ended up at a Thai restaurant with outdoor seating, a blessing to Leroy who'd spent the day cramped in a dog carrier, or in the backseat of cars.

"He's a creep," Ry said when Lauren asked about Stassler.

"That doesn't surprise me."

"I should never have worried about him canceling. He wants the publicity as much as any politician I've ever met. And right from the start he had his own agenda, which included finding out if the book was going to be all about him, or if I was going to include 'lesser lights.' His words."

"You're right, he really is a creep."

"Then he wanted to know who these 'lesser lights' were, and when I told him he went off on how each of you," Ry smiled reassuringly at her, "didn't deserve my attention, or the 'benefits'—can you believe it?—of any association with him."

"Okay, cut to the chase. What did he say about me?"

Ry waved his hand as if the words of such a well-regarded sculptor were of little consequence.

"I want to know, Ry. Tell me."

"It hardly bears repeating, but if you really want to hear it he said that you've received a lot of attention because you're a woman in a man's field, and because you had challenged the 'hierarchal importance of bronze.'" Ry used his fingers to indicate the quotation marks.

"Which he would see as heresy."

"Yes, I think it's safe to say that that definitely offends him."

Ry reached across the table and took her hand. "Lauren, he's so obnoxious that I wouldn't even bother with him, but to do this book without including him would be like writing a survey of contemporary literature and ignoring someone like Norman Mailer just because you don't like his persona."

"Except Mailer is good. Mailer wrote *The Executioner's Song*—"

"And Stassler has done the *Family Planning* series. He's very good too."

Arguable, but Lauren was in no mood to press the point. Instead, she asked him what else Stassler had said.

"About you?"

"About me. And the others."

"He said you were a product of political correctness, and that as soon as it went out of fashion, your work would be forgotten."

"I never knew I was in fashion."

Ry laughed. "You should take it as a compliment. He got himself more worked up about you than the other three combined."

"But they're all men."

"True."

"Maybe it's not me at all. Maybe he hates women."

"He certainly doesn't have any of them out there. That's another thing about him, he's living in the middle of nowhere. He's got a big house, a big beautiful barn, and that foundry, and he's all by himself. Not even a dog, or a cat, not that I could see. Hundreds of acres, and no sign of any other living thing. If it seemed strange to me, I got to think it must have seemed really strange to Kerry."

"What did he say when you asked about her?"

"I didn't have to. He brought her up. And I'll tell you, he sounded really worried about her. He said he called the sheriff as soon as he realized she was missing."

"So you didn't pick up any strange vibes?"

"Sure, lots of them, but not about Kerry. He said the sheriff came right out, and he let them look wherever they wanted."

"How decent of him."

Ry shrugged. "He hates the publicity he's getting, reporters calling all hours of the day and night, and flying over his foundry. I think that's at least part of the reason he's going ahead with these interviews. The book's the kind of attention he wants. He said he really liked Kerry, by the way. He thought her work showed a lot of promise."

Lauren nodded, and only now noticed his hand on hers, so preoccupied had she been with the subject of Ashley Stassler. Ry's hand was soft, not at all like a sculptor's. She felt self-conscious about her calluses; more so when he peeled her rough fingers open and kissed her bumpy palm.

"I've missed you." His brown eyes held hers until she squeezed his hand and looked away, unbearably uncomfortable and not knowing why.

"You going back out there tomorrow?"

"No, not tomorrow. He said to come back on Thursday. I guess he's planning to put me to work."

"Did he say on what?"

"No, and I didn't ask."

"Better be careful," she turned to him, "those hands of yours might get a blister."

"A blister!" He held them up in mock horror. "Never. These are the hands of a reporter. Soft, like baby's butt," he said with a silly Russian accent.

"I've noticed," but she had to force the words as much as the smile that budded briefly on her face, and she realized that she was in no mood to flirt with the man she'd been longing to see for weeks. For this, and for so much more, she cursed Ashley Stassler in silence.

They drove into downtown Moab and parked, then strolled past several lampposts with Kerry's picture on them, as well as a dozen or so bicycles until they found an ice cream shop. It didn't take long; ice cream shops were as common in Utah as espresso stands were in Portland.

Lauren got a pistachio cone, Ry a mango frozen yogurt, and Leroy got to check out a standard poodle with a big red bow rising from a puff of white hair on the top of her bony head. Much to Lauren's shock, he promptly tried to hump her.

She pulled him off, but the poodle's owner wasn't mollified by Lauren's urgent apology. The woman acted as if her precious dog had been mugged in a park.

"He's fixed," Lauren said, lest the woman think anything truly untoward could have transpired.

But she was already hurrying Fifi away, although her dog, its red bow all cockeyed from Leroy's frisky overture, might have had other ideas (and perhaps a taste for rough trade) because she kept stopping to glance back at her roguish suitor.

"I thought deballing him would put a stop to that," Lauren appealed to Ry.

He cast a dubious eye on her hound. "I think we're talking habit here, probably reinforced by lots of positive feedback over the years. I'll bet he keeps trying to do that till the day he dies."

Leroy looked up with what Lauren could describe only as a leer, as if to confirm what his brother male had just said.

They lingered over shop windows as they walked back to Ry's Land Rover. Lauren had the feeling that they both found it uncomfortable to consider the question of whether they'd spend the night together, and right then she decided they would not begin their love life this evening. Something felt off. Maybe it was the phase of the moon. Maybe it was hearing about Ashley Stassler. More likely it was just a quirkiness on her part, but it didn't matter: she wanted them to start off in sync.

"Did you know that Kerry had a boyfriend?" Ry said as he started the Land Rover.

"No, I didn't. Here or in Portland?"

"Here. She met him the day she arrived. His name's Jared."

"Did Stassler tell you about him?"

Ry nodded as he pulled away from the curb.

"Where is he now?"

"I don't know, but Stassler said he told the sheriff about him. He figures they talked to him right away."

"Maybe we should too."

"That's a good idea."

But they didn't talk to each other again until they reached his motel, when the awkwardness Lauren had felt back in town became downright acute, rife with all the possibilities of what could go wrong, what had gone wrong with Chad and the others too. She said good night as soon as he pulled into the space next to her car.

"All right. Good night." He looked and sounded perplexed. She could hardly blame him. "Do I get a kiss?" he asked.

"Yes," she said. But this smile came with effort too, and he must have sensed it.

"Lauren, what's wrong? It's not that crap Stassler said, is it? You're a great artist."

"No, I don't think it's that, and I'm not a 'great' artist. I'm a sculptor of limited renown, and a pretty damn good teacher who's in Moab to try to find out what the hell happened to her best student. And I feel out of sorts and really, really wish I didn't."

He cracked open his door. "I guess I'll see you in the morning then?"

"That sounds good."

"Do you want to meet here, or at your hotel?"

"Why don't you come to the hotel, and then we can find a place to eat downtown."

He leaned across the seat and kissed her, and she remembered the soft invitation of his lips. Even on a trying night like this, they were as welcome as the smooth hands that settled on her face and cupped her cheeks with warmth.

Al Jenkins was at his perch behind the desk of the Green Glow Inn when she and Leroy returned. They'd made it to the stairs before he looked up from his book and asked where she'd gone to dinner.

"A Thai place," she said.

"Must be Manny's."

"Manny?"

"Manny Santiago's got the Thai Joint and the Burrito Barn. Most successful restaurateur in town. How was the grub?"

"Okay." She sounded tired. "I liked the spring rolls."

"You're being nice. Manny's food stinks, but no one comes to Moab for the fine cuisine. They come to bike, or go jeeping, but you don't look like the bike or Jeep type. What's your story anyway, if you don't mind me asking?"

"No, I don't mind. Did you hear about the girl who disappeared?"

"The one whose face is on those posters all over town?"

"Yes, Kerry Waters. She's a student of mine."

"So you're a teacher?"

"Actually, an associate professor."

"Let me tell you something." Al leaned his head over the desk as Lauren and Leroy walked back toward him. "You know all that stuff they're saying about her ending up in some abandoned mine by accident? That's what they're saying, right?"

"That's what I've heard."

Al shook his head. "I been in this town all my life, my daddy was a miner, and every time someone comes up missing they blame it on an abandoned mine, like there's a whole slew of them out there waiting to gobble up anybody stupid enough to step off a trail. They make it sound like those mines are nothing but big old vacuum cleaners sucking those folks right off the face of the earth."

Lauren studied him. Al Jenkins looked serious, and intelligent, a man who once could have commanded the attention of a room simply by walking in the door.

"What are you saying?" she said.

"What I'm saying is that they should be blaming the people that *pushed* them into the mine in the first place. A mine's dark, and a mine's deep. And it's filled with a lot of things you don't want to meet. You figure out who wants them in there, and you got yourself the killer."

He settled back on his stool.

A chill trailed Lauren all the way upstairs. She shivered as she climbed into bed. She pulled the spread up around her neck and tried to fall asleep, but she couldn't stop thinking about Al Jenkins' final words: ". . . and you got yourself the killer."

# CHAPTER
## 15

EVENTUALLY, JUNE WILL FIGHT, WILL blister her heart with her hatred of me, but for now she turns away and meekly puts her hands behind her back so I can reach through the bars of the cage with the cuffs. She even casts a kindly eye on Jolly Roger, and he, as addled as ever, waves to her. *Waves!* Doesn't rush to hug her, much less to try to hold her back from the horror. He waves as she steps to the door. And he must suspect, as June does, that this is their final parting. I took the impressions of their backs yesterday. They saw #8's young girl, so they know the possibilities. I wanted them to know. But perhaps they still fall prey to hope, or prayer. That's so sweet, sickeningly sweet, hilarious in a wretched sort of way when the sorriest among them start mumbling the most predictable of all prayers: *Our Father Who art in Heaven, hallowed be Thy name.* Blah, blah, blah, I whisper in their ear. Blah, blah, blah . . . Your God is not in heaven. Your God is me. *I'm* the one who decides if you live or die. You'll see. You'll see. So try praying to me, and forget your goddamned God. They do too, for the little it's worth. I like to leave them bereft of *all* hope, especially in a God so impotent that he can't even get it up to save them.

I have June walk ahead of me. She slouches, her shrill defiance is gone. She may believe she's resigned to her fate, whatever it is, but I know better. I know that none of them truly surrenders. I simply won't permit it. I need their most furious resistance, and one way or another, I always get it.

Their bodies have come around nicely, even Jolly Roger's. While he's hardly a candidate for the cover of a muscle magazine, he's as buff now as he'll ever be. It didn't take long to bring out their definition, not after weeks of rigid dieting melted away all that fat. It's easy to see a freshly pumped biceps without a pound of blubber in the way. But sculpting them with diet and weight lifting only roughed out their form. The real fine art begins now, when I take them out of the cage and strap them to the table. That's when I sculpt their minds, their deepest, most tender fears, the thoughts and images that leave them insane with the sharp edge of every passing second. I'm not overstating this in the least. Trust me, you'll see, for once they are on the table, there's no lollygagging. I always rise to the challenge of a new subject, and I find the prospect of doing so again tonight nothing short of intoxicating.

June's in her freshly laundered sweats. Freshly bathed too. I despise the smell of a sour body. I want only the scent of fear when I go to work on them for the last time. This morning June bathed, as did Jolly Roger, Sonny-boy, and Diamond Girl. Only Her Rankness refused, apparently determined to earn every stripe of her sobriquet. In time, peer pressure would force her to bathe, if she were to have both time and peers; but these are huge questions marks for Her Rankness, whose fate lies not so much in the balance, as in my mood of the moment. My interest in her whispered intimacies with Diamond Girl has faltered. I'd hoped, no, I had imagined much more from the two of them: young girls, caged together, barely clothed, would surely bow to the hormonal imperatives of prison. As it is, I'm left with an extra body lying around, and I'm still puzzling about what to do with her. Even if I could display her, an absurd and self-defeating notion because of her link to me, her form does not intrigue me enough to cast, and her skeleton would provide not even a grace note to the bone parade. In short, she does not inspire me to do anything with her at all. Let her languish until she turns as pale as an aphid. To be truthful, my only impulse is to ignore her. If I cared at all, I could compel her to do any number of things, including bathing, violating whatever sense of modesty and decorum she no doubt possesses in measures wholly out of proportion to her appeal. But that would be a misdirection, a terrible allocation of energy when I have so much to do, and so little time in which to do it. She can fester in her stink for all I care.

I see that June's eyes are wet. Her suspicions are turning to certainty as I order her to lie faceup on the table. Her family and Her Rankness line up at the cage to watch, though Sonny-boy is already turning away, beginning to bawl loudly. I'd give him a medal for this, so effective is he at reminding June of why she must offer me each wrist, each ankle, even as the alginate awaits her. Yesterday, as I worked the green gum into the rich valley of her fine buttocks, I told her that eunuchs make the best lovers. I repeat this now as I strap her down. Eunuchs make the best lovers, June. Just ask the Pope, or any sultan of the Turkish crown. Eunuchs (I use the word often for its frightful effect) have but one means of arousal, June, and they use it with a hunger known only to the most profoundly afflicted. They become *promiscuous,* June. Like the fingers of little girls free to explore for the very first time, eunuchs scamper among errant pleasures and renegade erections. And Sonny-boy has such a sweet fanny. I've seen it often, June, so lie still and don't fight me, not yet, or I will bring him here and make you watch. I will make you study the carefully applied tourniquet once known only to bishops and sovereigns and the boys to whom they devoted themselves so smugly. The knots and ties and twists of cord that saved lives and created such perfect, round-bottomed lovers. You see, June, your fears back at the house were not completely incorrect. You wanted to satisfy me in the hope that I would spare the children. And you hope this still, don't you? But you're about to see that I can't be sated by your body, only by your most indulgent death. Do you hear me, June? Your most *indulgent* death. You will be free to experience every sensation fully, richly, gloriously, and though your thanks will never come, your gratitude will be cast in bronze.

I bring out the dark rubber ball that protrudes from the middle of a thick black strap.

"Open your mouth."

She does this, but to protest, or to question me, bore me with "Why . . ." but I jam it in with a viciousness she hasn't seen, could never anticipate, and as she gags I crank the buckle as tight as a fat man who's trying to make his belly disappear. It will take her a minute or two to realize that the pain of the hard rubber ball is worse than the buckle digging into the back of her head. Until then, the ball and the buckle will feel like lovers trying desperately to copulate through her skull.

Alginate, dear June. It's your friend.

Now the fight begins. It's inevitable. No matter how self-sacrificing a mother, the body rebels, becomes the rage of slaves in open insurrection, slaves whose heads no longer bow in hope but rise in hate. I've seen this so often that it's as predictable as rain, as tears, as the rushing waters that carve the most beautiful canyons.

So revel in your revenge, June the Cleaver, take it all out on me. I want to see every inch of your body's rebellion. Die with hate curling your lips, broiling alive the cilia of your lungs.

I cut off her sweats. She has become marvelously lithe, always the overachiever, right June? She is appealing, and her legs are open, her sex available. I try to envision the cast. Do I want her vulva swollen, or in repose? This is also part of the sculpting, what I do with the sexual apparatus of the body. Some women had bodies that begged the violation I gave them, and have appeared ever since with the ruffles of flesh that define a well-satisfied woman in the momentary aftermath of intercourse, with whatever instrument I've chosen, producing "a singular sexual madness," according to the critic who liked this effect the most. Need I tell you he was a man? Who else could romanticize such derangement, though I hardly share the affliction, honoring as I do the separation of art from the artist. I am not that madness. I am but the medium of its expression, and this difference is not so slight as it might seem.

She must be shaved. This is a sudden inspiration. I can't answer the question of her vulva until I can see it clearly. I leave her strapped to the table while I steam towels and gather tools. These I do with some measure of practice, and return to my labors only to hear the baubles of conversation between June and her hubby. These cease with my appearance, and I will have to check the tape to see if they contain anything more than the most predictable pleas that punctuate certain lives at such moments.

The towels are hot, but not scalding, and after recoiling from the shock of their touch, June relaxes. I squeeze the nozzle, and take pleasure in the way the aquamarine gel transforms itself into a white foam as I rub it into her pubic hair. She squirms at my touch, and I smile because I know from past experience that if she's squirming now, her body will be screaming later. It's the very best prognosticator of pain, this aversion to all touch. It makes the greater violation as deep as the universe, and as horrifying to contemplate, the finite space of infinite pain.

Though I am sorely tempted to slip in a finger, two, maybe three, I force myself to abstain. If I choose to sculpt her as a sexual woman, then I will violate her with all the enthusiasm the act demands; but if I want her like this, with her outsides all but crawling into her insides to get away from me, then she must remain unmolested.

I use a straight-edge razor. I strop the blade against a leather strap, and find the whisking sounds so pleasing. Then I kneel between her legs and scrape away great tufts of black hair that swim in a sea of white cream. The purity of the colors, the arc of the spectrum here, is nothing less than bewitching. I'm extraordinarily careful not to cut her. I want to save myself from the odd nick that bleeds through the cream and black strands. While I'll admit that even the tiniest trickle possesses a lush insurgent beauty of its own, I prefer the stark clarity of black and white, and care not at all for the phony intrepidness of blood.

The razor reminds me again of how sculpting a body encompasses so much more than the feeble minds of my contemporaries could possibly contemplate. I have cut away a good deal of June over these final weeks of her life, and now I cut away the last vestiges of her womanhood. I see this most clearly as I dab away the last few flecks of cream with a towel. She looks like a girl again, a little girl, yet she is a woman, and the tension of this vision will arouse others, or disgust them, but it will *move* them all. I stare at her sex and consider again the violation, which feels to me as duty does to a soldier. What will generate the greatest edginess in the eyes of a patron: a girl's vagina on a woman's body that has been violated, and reveals all of its naked folds? Or a girl's vagina on a woman's body that has not been violated, but suggests through its unveiled appearance a virginal *vulnerability*, or is it a harlot's brazen *availability?* This, too, will plague patrons, the delectation of their own indecision, for it will speak to them of their own agonizing desires.

This dilemma is ennobling, because it is so completely uncoupled from any base considerations. They do not enter my calculations for even a moment. At last I decide that she will remain inviolate, that for most patrons the tension between appearance and possibility is so great that it will prove far more arresting than the fait accompli of intercourse. I bank, once again, on the power of the imagination's most sordid machinations.

My decision also conforms most closely to my initial sense of June, when she was simply June Cleaver, the might have been Mormon in the dress.

She has come so far for so much.

I spread alginate over her feet and calves, rubbing it in, making sure to create the overlap with the "skin" I peeled from her back yesterday. I smooth it over her thighs and into the creases that separate her bottom from her legs. When I press it against her bare vagina, she shudders. I do not kid myself, this is not from pleasure.

Half of her body is now a greenish gray.

I press it into her belly button and come to her breasts. The nipples look like they are trying to dive back into her bosoms. She is, I would guess, experiencing the antithesis of arousal. I've yet to meet a woman who enjoys this, but that's the point, to make them endure what they never thought they could endure; and then, just when they are fighting the hardest for breath, for a few more seconds of consciousness, to snap the illusion of life into pieces, the body as a vase that has fallen from an endless sky to a shattered earth, though at the time of its arrival I suspect that most of my subjects long more for death's final sedation than for the life they are leading.

The alginate covers her to the neck. I won't continue in such a linear fashion. That would be such a waste of anticipation. Instead, I encircle the instrument of breath until only it protrudes, making sure to smooth over the creases in the cheeks from the mouth-plug straps. I ignore the hair, it is not so interesting as most women think, not in their final repose. And then I dab alginate onto the bridge of the nose and down to the nostrils.

Already her breath has become ragged. The fear that grips her has extended its reach from her limbs to her lungs.

"Yes, June," I coo, "it's your turn now."

I am about to become truly cruel to her for the first time, but I must be blind to kindness if I am to achieve the sculpted effect of bottomless fear.

Into her right nostril I insert a plug of alginate so thick, so viciously viscous, that she suffers immediately; but not, as you might suspect from the halving of her breath, because this is not the cruelty of which I speak. This is:

"At least you can die a happy woman, June. You've lived a full life. No regrets, right? I want you to think about that now. You've achieved your dreams, haven't you? You've had a family, a *good* family, and a good husband in Jolly Roger. You've had everything a good American girl could possibly ask for: husband, home, happiness with children."

I've said all of this before to other women, but never has it proved so effective, never have I been such a provocateur. June twists her body, tensioning it like a screw boring into the hardest wood, a hickory or mahogany rail, contorts her face until I know that this will be a fine mask for my private collection, that it will capture not just horror but the grisly nightmare of becoming no more than you are for now and forever. But what bellows most loudly are the legs, the belly, the breasts and arms, the hands and fingers straining, scratching, thrashing as if each of them were an animal, a rodent left to claw its way out of a glass cage on the blood-raked backs of its brethren. This is delicious. She beats the table with her elbows, the back of her hands and wrist. Her head thumps dully, her heels too, a hopeless defeated dance of defiance. All this because the words I offer provide no comfort; they are incitement to the most agonizing realization: that her life as she lived it was the worst of all possible mistakes, and that now, in her final moments, she is forced to relive them with the full and terrifying recognition that she could have done so much better. Oh, how she knows this. I see it as clearly as she does. I have sculpted her body, and with my words I sculpt her mind, give form to all the misgivings, all the mistakes, all the madness she has known. I am but patina to her pain, the copper solution that turns her green with envy for the lowest of all life still crawling unfettered through the jungle slime. She really could have done better.

This is not illusion. Not for June the Cleaver. Though I have abominated her, loathed her to my core, she *could* have done better, much much better. She has the body, and enough of the cold calculator about her to have risen far beyond her humble rank.

What *does* she see as I slip the tiniest ball of alginate into her left nostril, blocking but a fraction of the passageway with a bitter intimation of the final closure?

Does her life pass her by already? Does she remember the doctor or midwife handing her baby girl to her? Does she remember Diamond Girl resting on her chest? And if she does, and I know she does because I am urging these memories on her with whispers, does she recoil from the bullet of bad memories that this little baby brought to her in all the years that followed? The girl who only days ago sacrificed her mother's life and her father's, and even her little brother's, to the icy game she's playing?

No, the memory of her baby girl cannot bring her peace, it can bring her only more agony, more remorse. I hear this in the greatly muffled *oompf-oompfs*, for she speaks the language of the dying as she struggles for a lasting breath.

Perhaps she remembers her wedding day, the flowers and the bridal train, the bridesmaids and the best man who looked at her with longing, and flattered her with the knowledge that she could have had so many, but she chose her one and only.

"Your one and only," I repeat with my laughter barely disguised because Jolly Roger poisons the whole conceit of a "one and only." He is as common as sand, as common as dust, and doesn't she know this better than anybody on the entire planet?

"You've got half of one nostril left, June. *Half*. Breathe too hard and you'll suck it all the way in, and then that's it."

But she's a smart one, she is. She draws in a long steady breath, quieting her arms and legs, and then exhales harshly, expelling the dull green ball from her left nostril as she would a blockage of phlegm. But the effort at controlling breath, parcelling it out so closely when it's in such short supply, costs her dearly, leaves her tortured for more air, trying to make up what she has missed. Her body thrashes about as she loses the last degree of control.

"Look at you," I say to her, but she doesn't hear, can't hear, not with the struggle to breathe growing feverishly frantic. She is a dull green creature from head to toe with nothing but one small dark hole connecting her to life, a single dot in the only universe she can call her own. Her entire existence reduced to this speck of emptiness that can be squeezed shut in an instant. But does she give up? No. She's an inspiration. She's managed to buy a few moments more. I admire her. I really do. Go, girl, go. But I have to confess that I'm laughing. I am laughing so hard that I can hardly catch *my* breath. I tell June to stop it. Stop it! You're killing me, June. You really are. And this makes me laugh even more. One tiny hole, and with that she engineers all she needs of hope.

"Breathe, June, breathe," I mock her, perhaps by bringing back the dull face of Jolly Roger by her bed, aping all the men he'd ever seen in movies who urged their wives to breathe during birth, as if this could lift them past the greatest pain they would ever know. Except it isn't the greatest pain they'll ever know, not for the women fortunate enough to have met me. For them the memory of childbirth becomes a holiday, a festive retreat. June, I'll bet, never thrashed like this, not even with Diamond Girl poking her bubble head out, tearing apart her body's tightest cords.

"Breathe, June, breathe," I repeat as I pass the alginate that will kill her over the tiny opening, a threat that can't last a second longer, for I have milked her death dearly and can't possibly squeeze out one more bead of anguish. She has entered the birthing room of her new life, the one she'll live forever in bronze. I jam a large plug of alginate into her left nostril, pack it in and smooth over the surface. I imagine her left in the darkening silence to remember Jolly Roger's words, *Breathe, June, breathe*, and the birth of Diamond Girl. Both tear at her now. Both rip open her lungs, her body, from the inside out, for the birth of death is mired in the worst understanding of life, and all who doubt this have only to wait for their own demise to learn that in the final moments they will not relive all the years that have passed, but all the regrets they have known. This is our one true horror, not that we die, but that we never really lived.

I peel the alginate from all but her nostrils as her struggle turns heroic. Yes, June, you are my hero, you and all the others. I will honor you well.

The green reflection of her body lies beside her now, and after a greatly weakened spasm she quiets. I picked the right moment, I can see this in the terror of the skin. Only now do I hear the screams that rise from the cage. They have been present through all of this, but dimly so. Such is the power of concentration. Such is the power of art. It is Jolly Roger, wailing on his knees. His fists have beaten two bowls into the earth, and his face is awash in tears. He surprises me, and I can see that my story of the eunuch might not be enough to quell such rage, even in a man, if a man he has become.

I lay June's second skin, the one cloaked in the greatness she could never have known in life, on a length of Plexiglas, and carry it out to the foundry as if on a giant serving platter.

The air is abundant with memory, for I've made this trip so many times, and each step has been graced with its own reward. I place June on a long table where she'll await her family, and my own labors later. Maybe I'll have Ry Chambers help me build the molds. I revel in the thought of him observing June and Jolly Roger and Sonny-boy in this state, a newsman who won't see the most amazing story in the whole of art history when it literally stares back at him.

Much as this tickles me, I know in my heart it's a disgrace, an utterly contemptible disgrace. There's no other word for it. I will never escape this judgment, no matter how hard I might try. I've waited years to have a book written about me, and what do I get for an author? Some ring ding of a TV reporter. But that's not the worst of it, the most *disgraceful* part of it. When he showed up, he told me with a smile (no less) that he's including four other sculptors. Lesser artists all. Am I supposed to be pleased? Am I supposed to feel *complimented?* That I have to share the first book of its type with a Lauren Reed? He's determined to mix the burnt wicks of four tiny candles with a klieg light. It's sickening, but I tried to appear flattered, showed him my work, my notebooks no less (the heart of my art), tried to show him without saying so directly that the work of the others—and that's all you can call it, *work*, because it's like pounding rocks to look at it—is tripe.

I feel fallen into some arid Oz to have to share a book with the likes of them. I hadn't even heard of Reed until Ring Ding came along. No, that's not true. I had *heard* of her. I'd seen her show at the Jenson in San Francisco several years ago, enough to recharge my arsenal of disgust for all this crap that passes for art. A whole century of it, starting with the modernists and their self-lauding abstractions, Mondrian lines (an inspiration to linoleum everywhere) and Kline's *gestures* (now there's meaning for you). Sculpture was far, far worse. Try Rauschenberg herding his pathetic goat through a tire (How very homoerotic, *Bobbie*). Or that impossible woman with her fur-covered coffee cup and saucer, much praised for its lesbian overtones. I wish I were exaggerating, creating hooey out of honor, but I'm not. These are but two examples of highly praised modern sculpture, and every first-year art student knows this is so.

June stares unblinkingly into the lone light that hangs above her. She is perfect now, the embodiment of all that should be held dear. Perhaps when Ring Ding sees these skins he'll understand why my greatness can never suffer so much as the shadow of these other so-called sculptors. My art and their work can't mix, any more than the day can embrace night, light its absence. Perhaps June and her family will provide the insight he so vitally needs, the one that will let him see what a waste it is to force me to share pages with a plasterer. That's what Lauren Reed is, a plasterer, and all the glowing reviews in the world won't change that at all. "Challenging the hierarchal importance of bronze." Another toady critic. When I read that I wanted to scream, "No, she's not, you idiot. She can't handle bronze so she's working with plaster." Making me share space with her is no less crude an insult than suggesting that the peasant who plastered the walls of Rodin's studio shared an artistic currency with the master himself.

I gave Ring Ding copies of several reviews that made the point for me, and because he worked in television and therefore probably has the attention span of a popeyed slug, I highlighted in yellow the statements that he should consider the most. I noted in as casual a manner as possible that a number of critics have "savaged" me for the "representative" nature of my art, as if portraying the world in its vicissitudes were not challenge enough for an artist. But the highlighted passages say it best, particularly the critic who wrote that my "gaunt, ghastly subjects are rife with metaphorical implications. Their hunger speaks of the wantonness of appetite even as it denies its reach, bestirring a recognition of the barren emptiness of so many lives, an inescapable truth writ powerful in the uncompromising art of the world's foremost genius of form." Thank you.

Top that, *Laurie*, with your plaster dust and negative space, your art that's all about "body," though no sane person could ever see a body in that morass of plaster. Better Rodin's peasant than the penury of *your* eye.

I turn from June, no longer daring to look, so distracted have I become by thoughts of these lesser lights. I recognize that I've grown too splenetic to work, yet I must return to the cellar. *Family Planning #9* is so close to completion. I want Jolly Roger's skin lying by his wife's side. Then Sonny-boy's. Then the bronzes will be born.

That will leave me with Her Rankness, whose fate could not interest me less, and Diamond Girl. I am still seized by the sight of her, and for this she should be grateful. The species endows most relationships with about three years of intense physical fascination, which is just long enough in most cultures for a man and a woman to meet, mate, and reproduce, to avail the curse of family. As for all the years that follow, that form nothing but harrowing footnotes to this initial passion, the species cares not a whit, for once the breeding is done, they might as well be dead. I could not possibly agree more.

# CHAPTER
## 16

THE REMAINS OF LAUREN'S OMELETTE looked passably obscene, and she turned from them as she would a leer or a curse. Old Al Jenkins was right about the Moab cuisine, but did "cuisine" have to include breakfast? Might it have the addled decency to apply only to those meals in the post meridiem? And couldn't Ry stop making so much sense? Lauren had been intent on driving directly to Stassler's to see where Kerry had been staying, tour the house the girl had described so vividly in her email, the barn and foundry too. Get some sense of the compound where she'd been seen last. And most important, talk to Stassler himself, get some sense of *him*. No matter how faithfully Ry reported his encounters, it could never substitute for her own need to see the sculptor, talk to him, eke out even the thinnest details about Kerry that might help them find her.

But Ry was proving persuasive. Since their first sip of coffee he'd been insisting that based on Stassler's brusqueness with her on the phone, and his well-deserved reputation for obnoxiousness, she'd probably get one chance with him, so why not gather as much information as possible first?

"Fine," she said, more shortly than she would have liked. "I see your point. I just thought if I went out there, I might find something out."

"But you might find out more if you wait."

"Patience," she said in an exaggerated drawl, "is a vastly over-rated virtue."

Ry laughed, but he also grabbed the check and rose, as if to forestall any further discussion.

Bad Bad Leroy Brown began to wave his stump as soon as they stepped outside. Lauren untied his leash from the parking meter, and had him hop into the back of Ry's Land Rover for the drive to the kennel.

Leroy had finished his meds, and it seemed safe to leave him in someone else's care for the day, especially at the Canine Castle. The "concierge," as the owner had referred to himself on the phone, had explained that they had three levels of "accommodations." Lauren had rolled her eyes when she'd heard this, but she was new to the world of pampered pets and had agreed to take the tour that he'd promised.

Yaps, barks, and howls greeted them even before the owner himself appeared in a crisp, new tuxedo T-shirt. He smiled, toothy as a horse, and hurried them past a basic chain-link run, barely noting that it was available for the "budget-minded." Then he flicked his wrist at a kennel with access to a heated outdoor concrete slab.

"It keeps them toasty," he said with the same horsy grin.

"It's hot," Lauren said. "Wouldn't they be happier on a block of ice?"

"At night," he snapped. "At night."

His pace slowed only for the top of the line, which featured a private suite with a bed and a doggie "bar" (liver snacks, chew toys, rawhide bones).

Lauren chose the chain-link run. The concierge shuddered.

*   *   *

They parked outside the county building a little after ten. The sun now burned right above them, and glinted painfully off the loops of concertina wire that crowned the second floor. Even in tinted glasses, Lauren had to shield her eyes as they approached the jail and sheriff's office.

"He's friendly enough," Ry said in a hushed voice as they started up the stone steps, "but the real reason he's talking is he's politically ambitious. He figures if it's a big book, he's big news. But he's not the type of guy you'd ever want to burn."

Ry opened the door, and Lauren escaped the glaring sunlight. The sheriff's office was on the ground floor at the end of a hallway filled with vending machines, a water fountain, and blond wood benches.

Sheriff Holbin welcomed them into his office and showed them to a pair of fat-backed chairs that faced his desk. Ry made the introductions, and the sheriff said he was pleased to meet Lauren. Perfunctory, but polite, and in the moments to follow she saw that he was also quick to the point.

"We got one of those good news bad news things come up early this morning," he told them in completely even tones. She watched his blue eyes take them in, and decided he was wary but willing to trust them. Handsome too, despite his big belly, lantern jaw, and prodigious nose, outsized features that would be natural targets for political cartoonists if he ever realized his ambitions.

"A couple of guys riding near King's Rock found her bike. They didn't know it was hers, but they saw some signs of a struggle, and had the almighty good sense to keep their hands off of it. They called us on a cell phone, and I sent my evidence guys up there pronto."

"When was this?" Ry asked.

"Early, about six."

"What kind of struggle?" said Lauren.

The sheriff pursed his thick lips and shook his head. "The kind you don't want to see when a young woman turns up missing. We found what appears to be the crotch," he said with evident distaste, "of her bike pants. It looks like it was ripped right out of them."

Lauren moaned.

"We're definitely considering this an abduction now."

"Any tire tracks? Any indication of who might have done it?" Any anything? she pleaded in silence.

"There's nothing but tire tracks out there. Bicycle tire tracks. SUV tire tracks. Jeep tire tracks. Tire tracks on top of tire tracks. My guys looked for a single clean track, but there was no way. And it's exposed up there too. Gets lots of wind. There's no telling if the tracks of the vehicle that took her are even up there anymore. That's if it *was* a vehicle."

He looked at Ry, then at her. She asked the obvious: "What else could it have been?"

"Could have been someone she was with. Another mountain biker could have dragged her off. That's why I've got the rest of my deputies scouring the whole area, fanning out in stages. You want to speed through town today, there'll be no one here to stop you, though I'd appreciate it if you'd take my point and stick to the limit."

Lauren sat there feeling sick, expecting the sheriff's phone to ring at any moment with the news that they'd found Kerry's body.

"Wait a second," she looked up. "If there's so much traffic around there, somebody must have seen something. Don't you think?"

"You'd like to think so," said the sheriff with a pronounced weariness, "but people don't notice much. They think they do, but they don't. We'll publicize this, just in case, but I'm not going to be holding my breath. You think an eyewitness is good? An eyewitness is a nightmare, if that's all you've got. Eyewitness has come to mean I-witless. Bad pun, but the sad truth."

"So what's the good news," Ry said. He'd been taking notes, and paused long enough only to look up.

"The good news is that she might still be alive. If she'd fallen into a mine shaft, the chances are she wouldn't be alive by now. Most times these creeps don't bother abducting them just to kill them right away."

"No, they do it so they can take their time," Lauren blurted.

"Sometimes," Sheriff Holbin allowed. "But sometimes it's the abduction itself that they're after. The thrill of it. An abduction, bad as it is, gives you hope."

"How much?" Lauren said.

The sheriff shrugged, then leaned forward as if to apologize for his body's sudden candor. "It's hard to say. It really is. Is she still in Moab? Is she even in Utah? Who knows? She could be anywhere by now. He says she's a strong girl," his eyes landed on Ry, "so did Stassler, so maybe she's going to be okay. That's what I told her parents this morning when I called them. If she was your daughter, you'd rather hear this than nothing at all. That's what I'm telling you too. Maybe she's alive."

Yes, and maybe the phone's going to ring any second now, thought Lauren.

"What about Jared Nielsen?" said Ry. "Have you talked to him about this?"

"I found out a little after six, and we had someone over there at seven. You bet. He knows he's not to leave town under any circumstances."

"What's to prevent him?" Ry continued.

The sheriff tilted his head and smiled. "Now Mr. Chambers, you say you've been a reporter for quite a few years, right?"

Ry nodded.

"Do you really think we'd put ourselves in the position of letting him climb into that two-ton SUV of his with the vanity plate EXTRMBK and take off?"

"So he's under surveillance?"

"So you could conclude." Holbin offered all this without rancor, and so it was received.

"How much of a suspect is he?" Lauren said.

The sheriff propped his hands on his belly. "I have an agreement with him," he glanced at Ry, "that because he's writing a book, and he's not some pain in the fanny reporter, I'll talk to him with the promise that none of this background stuff comes out until *after* the investigation is over, no matter how long that is. If it isn't over for ten years, then he doesn't use any of it for *ten* years. Do I have the same understanding with the girl's professor?"

He stared at her.

"Yes, you do." She felt as if she'd been sworn in.

"Okay, then. You bet he's a suspect. Number one on a very short list. That bike was found way the hell up there, a good four-thousand-foot-elevation gain. To ride that far you'd have to be in super shape. He's a strong rider. To rip her pants open like that, you probably have to be male. He's male. To get that close to her, you got to know her. He knows her. To commit that kind of violence, that *personal* kind of violence, ripping apart her bike pants, you got to be invested in her emotionally. He's invested in her emotionally. He said so himself. Said he was 'crazy' about her. We want to know how crazy."

"Who else is on that very short list? Stassler?" Lauren asked quickly.

The sheriff made a brief clicking sound with his tongue before he spoke.

"He's a strange one, but why would he do it? You got to look for motivation. That's why Jared Nielsen is getting such a hard stare. What's Stassler's motivation? None that I can see. Nothing like the things that have us looking at Nielsen. Stassler's associated with her, she was living in his compound. Okay, those are pretty strong links. And he was the one who reported her missing. It's not unusual for the perpetrator to make the initial call, although I got to tell you that in abductions that's kind of strange. But anyway, he did call. But then he never missed a beat when we told him we wanted to come out there right away, and he let us search his place. He didn't have to, but he did. So, to answer your question, Stassler is on that very short list, but I have to ask myself, what's in it for a world-famous sculptor to abduct some girl?"

"He's obsessed with pain," Lauren answered.

"Is he? Enough to snuff some young woman?"

Lauren recoiled at his words.

"I didn't mean to put it so coldly, but what I'm driving at is the absence of any motive on Stassler's part. In your basic financial-type crime, you follow the money. In a murder, abduction, you follow the motive. Who's got it? Who doesn't? With Stassler, we come up with goose eggs."

"Have you seen his sculpture?"

"I sure have." The sheriff raked his dark hair with his hand. "He had a show here a few years ago. I'll grant you, it was pretty strange stuff. A whole family that looked like they'd died in the belly of a beast. I didn't much care for it myself. My wife hated it. But I'm not your artsy-fartsy type either, so what do I know? I like pictures of sunsets, and elk with seven-point racks. The kind of stuff you probably think is garbage," he said with considerable good nature.

"The reason I ask," Lauren said, "is that *all* of his work is concerned with pain, terrible pain."

"I know, but all of it's also concerned with family. Everything he does is about family. He's got that whole series of his, *Family Planning* one, two, three, all the way up to eight. My chief detective spent a whole day looking at his website and reading up on him. See, we've thought about all this stuff, but where's the family here? The girl's mother and father will be coming in here any second to see me. And besides, you can't confuse the artist with his art, right?"

"Sometimes you can't separate them," Lauren replied.

"You really think so? Then we're really in trouble," the sheriff said gravely, "when you think about what we're seeing on TV and in the movies."

"I wouldn't call most of that art," Lauren said.

"What about Stassler? You're a professor, do you think what he's doing is art?"

Lauren paused, tried to hold back, but couldn't: "No, I guess if I'm going to be completely honest, I don't think it's art."

"What do you think it is then?"

"I think it's a travesty of questionable intentions."

"Really? Now that's an answer I don't get every day, 'a travesty of questionable intentions.' But then I don't get a professor in here every day either. I'll have to think about that one. Are you going out there to talk to him?"

"I plan to."

"You might want to call first. We've had reports over the years that he doesn't take too kindly to people showing up on his doorstep."

"How would you feel about us talking to Nielsen?" asked Ry.

The sheriff's hand worked his chin, but as soon as he started to speak Lauren decided it was an act, that he'd figured this chess move out long before he opened his door to them.

"I can't stop you, but remember, if I scratch your back, you scratch mine."

"You're on." Ry made a scratching motion with his fingers. "Where do we find him?"

"The El Dorado, room 256."

Ry stood to leave as a woman's voice called from the doorway.

"Sheriff Holbin, I'm sorry to interrupt, but you said to come in as soon as we got here."

Her eyes were teary, and the sheriff walked right past Lauren and Ry to lead the woman into the room. Her husband appeared behind her.

Lauren thought she looked a lot like Kerry, the same dimple in her chin and big eyes, the same youthful appearance too. She must have been young when she'd had her, a realization that reminded Lauren that she herself could have raised a child by now. In those brief seconds, the years of her early adulthood seemed to have vanished as swiftly as the girl they were all determined to find.

Jared Nielsen was loading his blue mountain bike on his Expedition when Lauren and Ry intercepted him in the parking lot of the El Dorado motel.

"Where you going?" Ry said.

"What? It's against the law for me to go riding now? Who the hell are you? Another cop?"

"No, I'm a writer," Ry said, pulling out his narrow reporter's notebook.

"A reporter!" Nielsen spat. "I've got nothing to say to you. Any of you." His eyes landed on Lauren with no less reproach.

"I'm not a writer," she said evenly. "I'm Kerry's sculpture professor."

"*You're* Lauren," he said. "Lauren Reed?"

"Yes."

Jared glared at Ry. "What are you doing with him?"

"He's a friend."

"I don't care. Tell your friend to put away his notebook. I'm sick of reporters and their questions. You read the papers around here?"

"Not yet."

"They make it sound like I did something horrible to her."

"I'm not a newspaper reporter," Ry said. "I'm writing a book."

"One of those quickie things? Bet you're hoping she's dead."

"No on both counts," Ry said calmly. "It's a book about sculpture, and I was working on it long before Kerry disappeared."

"Where are you going now?" Lauren eyed the bike on top of the Expedition.

"I was going out to look for her, the same damn thing I do every day. I've been over every inch of trail we ever rode together. I've been back up Onion Creek twice now looking to see if maybe she took a detour, got herself stuck in some quicksand, but I haven't found a damn thing. And come on," he scowled, "she didn't do some header into quicksand. That's bullshit."

"Header?" Lauren said.

"An endo. You know, flying headfirst over the bars."

"You heard they found her bike?" Ry said.

"Yeah, I heard, and that's the one place I wasn't going because that's a place she never would have gone. The detective was out here early this morning banging on my door, and I told him the same thing I'm telling you, that it doesn't make any sense, her riding her bike all the way up that crappy jeep trail. For what? She liked single track, the gnarlier the better, and slick rock. The jeep trail's nothing but a grinder for the altitude hounds. That wasn't her style, any more than falling into a mine was. She never said word one to me about that either. I don't know where they're getting all this bullshit from. You'd think I would have heard something about abandoned mines from her, seeing as I'm the one she was spending all her time with."

"Not all her time," Ry said carefully.

"You got that right. She was working with El Creepo. You know that's what she was calling him? Why aren't they going through *his* stuff?"

"They did. They didn't find anything," Ry said.

"I've got a mind to go out there myself and look around."

"He doesn't like strangers. I've been warned," Lauren said.

"Yeah? Well, I don't like the coolest girl I've ever met disappearing, and I sure as hell don't like being made to look like the asshole who did it to her. Mines? Some stupid jeep trail? That's a bunch of shit."

"So where would you look?" Lauren said.

"The trails we rode, the ones I know she knows."

"What do you think you're going to find?" Ry said. "It's not like you're going to be riding along and there she'll be."

"But maybe I'll find something of hers, like her watch or one of her earrings. You know, something that'll lead me to her. I stare at the trail the whole time I'm riding. I'm not giving up."

"So that's where someone should look, the trails you two rode?" Lauren said.

"Someone? Or you? Because it depends on what kind of shape you're in." He looked her over.

"I haven't been on a bicycle in years, but I run three or four miles every morning. Sometimes more."

"You could handle it. But you got to have bikes. Unless you feel like doing a marathon. You want to rent them?"

Lauren eyed Ry, who nodded.

"Sure," she said. "That sounds good." Trail time with this young man might reveal more than an edgy conversation in a parking lot.

"I'll take you down to Rolling Thunder. It's a great bike shop, and I'll show you what to rent. Then I'll show you the trail I was going out to today, and then maybe somebody'll start believing me."

"Let's do it," Ry said, "but I'd like to ask you something first."

Jared bristled.

"I was going to ask if you have a lawyer?"

"A lawyer? What for? You sound like my father. He wants to send out the family lawyer. I refused. No way. I'm not guilty of anything. I'll answer a cop's questions any time of the day or night. I told them I'd take a polygraph too."

"They ask you to?" Ry said.

"No, *I* insisted. I told them, 'Hook me up and quit beating around the bush.' "

"What'd they say?"

"They said they would."

"When?"

"I think it's tomorrow. I'm supposed to call. I don't know why. They got that guy," he pointed to a white car parked across the road, "watching me all the time. Him or someone else. Only time they're not watching is when I'm on my bike. I think they're too lazy to ride. They said the state police are sending some guy with the lie detector stuff from Salt Lake. I can't wait to take it."

"You've got a lot of faith in it," Lauren said.

"More than I've got in them," he said with one more glance across the road.

By the time they walked out of Rolling Thunder Bicycles, Lauren had bought a pair of bike shoes, bike pants, sunglasses dark enough for the desert, and the single most garish shirt she'd ever seen. Jared had assured her that she'd want it.

"Cotton'll kill you. Soaks up your sweat and gives you the chills every time you start going fast." He fingered the sleeve. "This stuff's kind of techy but it's worth it."

She also rolled out a bike with a front suspension system to absorb the bumps.

"Don't we ever look like the tourists," Ry said.

"You two do look a little geeky," Jared laughed. "Tell you what, I'll just meet you at the trail head." He made to get away quickly, and then laughed again. "Don't worry, you look like everybody else who comes here, including me."

They loaded the bikes on the Expedition, and headed out of town.

Lauren found herself enjoying the company of this brash young man, and couldn't help wondering if he was really capable of murdering Kerry. Then she remembered that psychopaths succeed precisely because they are convincing, not because they go around casting suspicion on themselves. This little reminder did not prove particularly comforting, considering the doubts that Sheriff Holbin had about the young man. But why would Jared forego a lawyer, or volunteer for a polygraph test, and spend all of his free time looking for Kerry? Just to make it seem as if he's innocent? If he were guilty, wouldn't it make far more sense to accept his father's offer of the family barrister, and stonewall at every opportunity? Everybody who saw the OJ trial, or grew up hearing about it, had learned its most painful lesson: if you're rich enough, the only way you're going to pay for your crime is when you write out a check to your lawyer.

As they hit the highway, she learned that his father had started a chain of stores specializing in imports from Asia and Polynesia. She knew the chain well; she'd furnished her first apartment with a lot of that ticky-wicky junk. Part of it had undoubtedly paid for Jared's pricey education at USC. Film major. He and Ry shared the common ground of the camera eye, though Jared's view of the news business had grown greatly jaundiced by his recent experience.

"You know one of those Salt Lake stations actually had a helicopter follow me up a ridge trail two days ago? You know how dangerous that is? They could have blown me into the canyon, and that's about a thousand-foot drop. I gave them the finger after they got so close a gust had me death-gripping the handlebars. So guess what they used that night on the news, right over the words that I was the 'prime suspect'?"

He glanced from the road to Ry.

"I'll tell you, it pissed me off plenty. That's why when I saw you pull out a notebook I thought, *No way, not another one.* I tried talking to them at first, but I learned my lesson."

Jared turned off the highway, eased the Expedition over railroad tracks, and parked next to a VW Vanagon.

"This is the trail we did last week. I've been back over it once, but I want to check it out again. At first it's nothing but desert riding, and you'll be wondering why we even bothered, but in about two miles we'll hit slick rock, and it gets totally fine."

He said "fine" the way Lauren's first sculpture professor used to say a student's work was "fine," with the accent on every letter, practically spelling it out with appreciation.

She'd hit her water bottle three times already, but otherwise she felt pretty good. The helmet was snug, but not suffocating, and riding a bike made her feel like a kid again. The shifters took some getting used to, but she was accustomed to working with tools, and got the gearing down easily. Ry must have done some riding at some point because he experienced no adjustment at all.

Now they began a switchback that filled her legs with lactic acid, and notably dampened their enthusiasm for talking. After the turn, they climbed until she saw formations of red rock that appeared to stretch all the way to the horizon.

"Wow," she said.

"Kerry loved it up here. Made me promise to come back with her. I told her I would. I never thought I'd be coming back looking for her. I'll show you why she liked it so much, what made it so special to her. It's a little farther."

A little farther in young Jared's case turned out to be about five miles of moderate uphill riding before he veered off the main trail, and took them down a dogleg. It ended at a clear desert pool hidden behind boulders as big and brawny as earthmovers.

"That's so beautiful," Lauren said. She pointed to a five-foot waterfall, more a trickle, really, that ran down a length of moss hanging over the rippled surface.

"Cool, huh?"

Lauren had to restrain herself from hurling her hot, sweaty body into the water.

"I'm amazed no one's here," Ry said.

"It's not on the tourist maps, and the locals want to keep it that way. The day we came out, we had the place all to ourselves for a whole hour. Nice and private, if you know what I mean."

Another young man might have made that comment sound sleazy, but to Lauren's ears, Jared seemed mournful.

They returned to the smooth sandstone trail and rode for another hour, mostly uphill again, but without too many leg-cramping climbs. Jared jumped off his bike as he came to the edge of an abyss that looked out over the Colorado River, which could have been a length of loden ribbon drifting across the land.

"This is it?" Lauren said between breaths.

"We've been riding for over two hours," Ry said.

"We have? You've got to be kidding." But she checked her watch and was surprised to see that he was right. She would have guessed half that much time. "I can't believe it."

Jared smiled. "Riding's great, isn't it? Look at that." His hand took in what looked like miles and miles of incredible mountains.

It *is* great, thought Lauren, who stayed a good five feet from the edge of the canyon wall; any closer and her palms would have turned into ponds.

"When Kerry and I came up here, we sat over there." He looked at a rock roughly the size and shape of a bench.

Lauren watched him swallow deeply and turn away. He's no more guilty than I am, she said to herself. Guilty only of having been one event in a long series of them that brought Kerry to whatever and wherever she is.

"Sometimes I think I'm going to look up, and there she'll be telling me to get the lead out of my butt."

"Did she say that to you?" Lauren asked softly.

"Yeah, she was one helluva rider. She could smoke my butt. No way she went riding into some abandoned mine," he said with sudden vehemence. "Or went flying off some cliff." He kicked a rock the size of a baseball off the edge, and watched its long flight down to the river.

"You see that out there?"

Lauren tried, but could not make out what he was pointing to.

"Here, hold on." He shrugged off his small backpack and took out a monocular, then stood like a pirate as he focused the lens. He reached back and handed it to her.

"Look below that peak at about ten o'clock."

She saw a house, barn, and a flat brick building. "Is that Stassler's place?"

"It sure is. She was so stoked about working with him at first. You know, I met her the first day she was here, and she practically bragged about him to me. But by the time we made our ride up here, she said she didn't care if the whole place blew up."

Lauren continued to study the compound through the monocular, but privately wondered why Kerry had never shared her misgivings.

"You see those hills by the compound?" Jared said.

She nodded. They looked like hefty humps rising from behind his house, though with the monocular's compression of distance she doubted they were that close.

"A lot of that is his land too."

"Is that a river running through there?" she said.

"Yeah, that's the Green River. This time of year it gets some mondo rapids."

"Do you know if they ever did any mining on his land?"

Jared put his hand out for the monocular. "I've heard that they mined all over. I guess they could have mined there too. It's a huge ranch. She could be anywhere."

"Anywhere there?" Is that what he was saying?

"Could be. Whatever happened to her was done to her. You know how you can feel something like that in your bones?"

Lauren nodded. So did Ry. The three of them stared silently into the distance.

On the way back down, Lauren almost flew off a five-foot drop, which was precisely what Jared had done, racing off its lip and landing some twenty feet beyond without even a wobble of his wheels.

Lauren braked, skidded, and managed to follow Ry as he

threaded down an easier route. They didn't catch up to Jared until he stopped by the dogleg that led to the pool.

"I thought you guys might want to hit it. I'm going to go back, but you should do it while you can."

"What about getting back to town?" she said.

"That's easy. Just go back to the highway the way we came and hang a right. It won't take you more than fifteen minutes, and it's almost all downhill. Believe me, it's worth it."

Is he smirking, Lauren wondered, or smiling?

"What do you think?" Ry said to her. "I think a dip in the pool would be great."

"I do too," she said with finality. She reached for Jared's hand and thanked him for the ride. "And for talking to us."

"You still think I'm guilty?"

Ry shook his head.

"What about you?" he pressed Lauren.

"The jury's still out." But she was smiling, and was sure the young man knew what she was really thinking. She could feel it in her bones.

When they rode up to the pool, Lauren looked around for signs of bikers, hikers, anyone who might intrude on their privacy. No one.

They stashed their bikes between two of the boulders, and hurried toward the trickling sound of the water streaming from the hanging moss. Ry stripped down as naturally as Joy had in the studio. Lauren took a deep breath and also peeled off her clothes.

The water felt cooler than the air temperature, but by no means cold, and she felt pleasantly weightless in its soft formless bosom.

They drifted separately before his foot touched her leg. An accident? She didn't think so; when she opened her eyes, she found him smiling at her.

"A penny for your thoughts," he said.

"They're worth a whole lot more than that," she teased.

He eased over to her, and she ducked playfully beneath the surface, eyes open to the silly sight of his penis lolling freely in the water.

She had to resist the impulse to reach for it. She came back up into his arms and kissed him, and then when she did reach down she found that he wasn't quite so limp as he had been moments before.

His hands encircled her waist, and drew her close. It felt as natural as their buoyancy for her own hands to settle on his hips, her fingertips on the tops of his buttocks. All the tension she'd felt the night before had dissolved somewhere between the start of the trail, and this moment. She'd have to thank Jared for suggesting so strongly that they stop here, if she ever got to know him well enough for such a confidence.

Ry took his turn ducking down, kissing her belly and breasts before taking each nipple in his mouth and suckling her softly, then with an urgency that surprised her.

He broke the surface gasping for air, his face a magnificent picture of water droplets and desire. She reached down and took him again in hand, pressing him close, not sure if this would work. She felt excited, very excited, but the only time she'd tried this with Chad it had been painful, and they'd both ended up lurching for shore.

But Ry slipped right in, and she realized that her own wetness was more than equal to the water.

He cupped her bottom as she wrapped her legs around him and filled with pleasure. She squeezed him, hungry for his hardness, and forced herself forward. Their hands swam all over each other, finding pleasure, and then groping impatiently for more.

Her back settled against a mossy rock, and she arched her spine to consume every bit of him. The trickle of the stream fell beside them as his hands finally rose to her face. He kissed her repeatedly, and her mouth opened as readily as leaves in the desert to an early morning mist.

Her fingers dallied over each of his features, and she kissed his wet nose and eyes, feeling his lashes on her lips as the softest of burrs, and tracing the tip of her tongue along the curlicues of his outer ear, listening to him moan, growing more excited by the pleasure she gave, squeezing him as he moved in and out, the motion growing rapid, more fevered.

"I can't stop myself," he confessed.

This excited her even more, to see the helplessness on his face, to feel him so out of control, and to know that she alone had done this to him, was doing it even now, squeezing him, kissing him, pressing her eager breasts into his chest as his thrusts grew desperate and deeper still, and then to feel him all the way up inside her, his pelvis hard and flat and muscular against her own, the sweet friction that would not cease, not even after he came and made her come too, with his interest, his desire, his unwillingness to do anything in these sweetly private moments but hold her tightly away from the world.

# CHAPTER

## 17

O YE OF LITTLE FAITH. I stare at the monitor and repeat these joyous words to myself because I have underestimated Diamond Girl, and I couldn't be more pleased.

There she is cuddling, embracing, *kissing* Her Rankness, the two of them like furtive lovers huddling behind a bush. The sight leaves me almost paralyzed with pleasure.

This revelation comes at the end of a very long twenty-four hours, and I rewind the tape to six this morning, when I dragged Sonny-boy out of there and left them alone with each other for the very first time. Were they kissing even as I turned my back to them and took his impression, as I tried mightily to make the boy mature, to outgrow the narrow, narcissistic concerns of childhood?

I must know. I hit PLAY when I see Diamond Girl whispering into Her Rankness's ear. I can't hear a word. Her Rankness whispers back. Sweet nothings? From the evidence, what else could it be? Now the tape reveals the first truly intimate moment: Diamond Girl looks into her lover's eyes, caresses her shoulders, and Her Rankness—this *does* surprise me—offers no resistance, not even at first. Instead, she succumbs with a smile as Diamond Girl's touch drifts to her chest, her hips, her firm round bottom.

It *moves* me. It's as if Diamond Girl—and it must be at the instigation of Diamond Girl, so inconceivable is it that Her Rankness could ever initiate anything so supremely, delightfully depraved as to have sex in the immediate presence of murder—has once again reached into the most fertile of my fantasies and flooded them with desire, brought them to bloom with this raw, indulgent, highly explicit display.

Fingers, yes, now at this very moment her nimble eager fingers are down in her own underpants, knuckles bulging against the satiny fabric. She must know that if I see them I won't be able to look away, that I will be struck motionless by the sight of them. Indeed, I do stand here like those legion of husbands who cannot grow excited but for the image of their wives, their homely conservative wives, on their knees receiving with their papery lips the boldly erect penis of a stranger as another man lifts her decorous skirt and prepares to couple her rudely from behind. Husbands—and I have read the research and know there are many who are mad for such a lewd, sluttish show—who imagine their wives growing wanton, crazed, uncontrollable from such untoward attention.

This is my Diamond Girl, whore and harlot, seducer and strumpet, igniting in me the same storied emotions, the desire to see her taken, mounted, making even Her Rankness erotic by association. Her Rankness! Whose top is up around her throat like a necklace, and whose breasts I see—yes, I *do* see, cannot look away, even from her—are firm and pointy in the manner of all the small-breasted young women around here who ride their bikes until their buttocks are hard and round and randy.

I feel I could be hallucinating, such has been my final experience with the Vandersons. I did create a Frankenstein with Jolly Roger. After I dispatched June, he became wholly unruly. Those bowls he pounded into the earth could have filled with his tears, so struck was he with grief. He was yet another sharp reminder of how unpredictable the human animal can be. I had him pegged as a pushover, a cipher, but in the wee hours I realized that he was one of those creatures who couldn't believe in darkness until he'd stared into the deepest shadow. Then he underwent a change so profound that it was frightening. All his dopey-headed optimism, his enduring belief in the ultimate safety of himself and his family, of my ultimate goodness, I suppose, once all that had been torn from his chest and left to drip before his eyes like a heart on a bloody stake, he became a beast who swore and stomped and tore at the cage as if to slam it to the ground and march across the room and kill me. His fury was far more powerful than anything I could have conjured up with words, and I realized that in his dying moments I would not have to coax resistance from him as I did from June and from so many others because he had found his own true rage for the first time in his life, and as with any other fresh discovery the rules of display—the boundaries and borders— had yet to be drawn.

No, the challenge with Jolly Roger was getting him on that table, strapping him down. He would not accept the lie of Sonny-boy's survival in exchange for his own skin (yes-yes, another pun. Enjoy!). He held Sonny-boy against him like a shield, and Sonny-boy held him—surely I can say this—in a *death* grip.

So there I was, tired, impatient, cranky, with a huge workload ahead of me, all kinds of details to attend to, and there were Jolly Roger and Sonny-boy clinging to each other while Diamond Girl and Her Rankness looked on, Diamond Girl in visible amusement, and Her Rankness in what I would have described at the time as horror. But I question this now, question both her state *and* my perception of it, so unsteadied am I by the girly sex I am witnessing on these screens.

I had to threaten Jolly Roger with the worst abominations to Sonny-boy's body, and point the gun right at the boy's crotch before he willed himself to the side of the cage and placed his hands behind his back.

There was still the problem of Sonny-boy clinging to his leg like lice. I was all but ready to shoot him off (bullet holes be damned), as you would a locked door handle, when Diamond Girl led him away. The boy, perhaps as shocked as I was by his sister's sudden display of kindness, let himself be comforted. He buried his face in her chest and began to wail as I reached in and cuffed Jolly Roger, placed him in leg irons (I was taking no chances), and locked the cage behind us. I even saw Diamond Girl whispering to him as I spoke to their father.

"I don't want your kids," I assured Jolly Roger as I strapped him to the table. "They're pawns for you and June."

I didn't disabuse him of this until I had the last strap as tense as a steel cable, and the black ball in his mouth. Then I told him what I really had in mind for Sonny-boy, the pride and joy of his progeny.

Frankenstein.


When Sonny-boy's turn came, he never fought me, and there was little I could do to kindle a real fire in his flesh, only the reflection of pain, a pallid substitute for scorching terror; and if that's all my work can show, then why bother? But that's always the problem with kids: they simply don't have enough life experience to appreciate a truly terrifying death. Terror thrives on the bottomless pit of the imagination, and the imagination comes to life with the passage of time. Time is its vintner, the family its fertile field. Only as a child comes of age, passes through puberty with its rude surprises and brute understanding that all he knows of life can be replicated ad nauseam—the mother, the father, the sister, the brother, the aunts and uncles and grannies and grandpas with their wet kisses and smothering hugs and suffocating smells—only then can he refract pain through the undying prism of terror, only then can the shadow skin come to life, the one that

I urge into the unknowing unconscious of the viewer, that invisible organ of agony that hovers just above my sculptured bodies and makes you *feel* every inch of them, and tremble when you do so. My *Family Planning* series has made the invisible to the indelible the shortest of journeys.

Their "skins" lie next to one another in the foundry: June, Jolly Roger, Sonny-boy, green lengths that seem to me as if they are my greatest work to date. I can't be sure of this until I cast them, but when I look at June's twisted pelvis, or Jolly Roger's arms, so newly developed, veiny and embossed with raw muscle, I am hopeful. As for the dreary appearance of Sonny-boy, I can say only that he looks no worse than the other children in the series. Maybe it's enough to simply depict their pain, though I have not given up, have read scores of studies about children and terror, many of them about children in war, and expect to make some significant breakthroughs in the future.

I severed the head of each green figure with a long serrated kitchen knife, perfect for cutting crispy baguettes and alginate necks, and carefully laid them aside. I'd love to have Ring Ding see them. The detail is exquisite. I'd even contemplated having him help me build the molds. I was taken with the idea of a newsman, even an erstwhile newsman, laying his eyes and hands on the biggest story in art history, and not knowing it. But I have come to accept that it would be far too risky, and that I'll have to pass on this particular perversity, however grand the reward to me personally. Even more tempting would be casting their faces with him, especially because he had the temerity to dredge up the only criticism that's ever dogged me: to wit, that I can't "do" faces.

Only a few second-rate writers have carped about this, and I know I should let it lie, but it annoys me unceasingly. The faces for the entire series are forged wholly from my hands and imagination. That these extraordinary creations, the beneficiaries of my artistic touch—the highest honor of all—should have to bear the only criticism of note, is a wound that will not heal.

The real faces, the ones I actually peel from my subjects, have given rise to my great collection of masks, the ones that will remain hidden until my death. But I'm about to make an exception for Ring Ding. I'm going to show him real faces in real horror. I fear that if I don't, I will have to endure a replay of all that useless carping in a book (bad enough when disparagement, thoroughly undeserved, appears in an art journal).

It's a safe exception, completely devoid of risk. I will use the real faces from *Family Planning #2,* a family from Dover, Maryland. No one will remember them. No one ever did (no one of note). And no one but Ring Ding will see them anyway; there was never a single news report about their disappearance to trigger even his dim memory. Not a one. Can you imagine? It was as if they never existed. But in many ways it was predictable, and the reason was so simple, so obvious. Why? To hear the answer is like solving a riddle: they were black! Blacks, I might add, who were eager to let me visit my cherished "childhood home." I rather suspect that they saw a white man at their door making this request as something of a pathetic vindication of their own rise from whatever squalor their ancestors had known.

Despite my inexperience back then, I got a lot out of those black folks from Dover. Not nearly as stoical as their history of suffering would suggest. But #2's all I'll show Ring Ding. I certainly don't intend to take him down into the catacombs for the full tour of the masks, but with the faces of two adults and three children he should see how terribly unfair that criticism is. Perhaps I'll allude to the idea that the Dover faces might inspire another addition to the *Family Planning* series. He's not going to know that they came from bodies that have already been cast and seen by millions.

Faces are to my sculpture as Rembrandt's notebooks were to

his paintings. I'll tell Ring Ding that the faces inspire me to create the families, that I cannot do the bodies until I see the faces before me (and there is truth to that, much more than he'll ever know). The faces *are* my notebooks, the ones I write in the studio. Or to put it another way, I am like a novelist who cannot devise a plot until he has his characters, who must know their fondest thoughts and desires and their back story before he can plot their future.

Now I should stop, take my rest while I can, but I stand before the monitor as Diamond Girl stiffens with a flood of orgasm, and begins to shake, the fragile appearance of a young woman at play with her body, with the thrill of a newfound friend.

She removes her hand from the cleft that she treasures so, and reaches for her underpants, which have ended up down around her knees. Her Rankness rolls off her side and on to her back without so visible an experience of pleasure; but she's smiling, touching Diamond Girl, and I wonder, I can't help myself even though it is a most subversive thought, subversive to my whole belief in Diamond Girl's depravity, but nevertheless I wonder if it's an act. I wonder, more to the point, if it's a trap. If the two of them think they can actually seduce me into forming a threesome, a merry ménage à trois. And just that insistently my prick speaks up, for the danger is now conjoined with titillation, its sexy Siamese twin. A deadly kind of game, perhaps, to find myself between them both, the meat in their sweet sandwich. As I stand here I begin to feel breasts against my back and chest, handsome young nipples, proud and peaked, and hands, an endless stream of fingers and palms and hot horny holds that leave me to satisfy myself, which I do with inordinate haste. As I clean up, I remember that this was how it all began with Diamond Girl, with my fixation on her body, with her posing in the cage. I had hoped to see my obsession slacken, but now in her uncanny way she's raised the stakes in the strange game she's playing.

. . .

Ring Ding is clumsy. He almost drops the mold of #2's mother, and I have to resist the urge to slap him. He has that kind of face. I have seen it countless times sitting next to a weatherman, or a woman who reads the news with him, or an aging athlete who smiles a lot and laughs even more as he reports the latest scores and mishaps on the court, the field, whatever ridiculous game they're playing.

And he's so serious, even pausing to take notes, that when he asks why each of their mouths is slightly open, I'm tempted to joke about the hard rubber ball. I do think the reference would go right over his head; but I restrain myself, and explain as I would to a child that I sculpt the mouths into such agonized positions to show how the American family's attempt to speak honestly is muzzled by the *brutal* constraints of convention. Therefore, when I do faces—and I remind him that I always do faces first—I want the strain to speak to be apparent to even the most noodle-headed (like you, I want to add, but don't). Even more than speak, they want to shriek in pain. "Can you see that," I ask him, pointing to the curled lips, the clearly tortured contortion of the mouth.

He nods. That's it. A nod. I have just given him the vast moral implication of my work, and I get a nod. No wonder he thinks nothing of including those half-wits with me, of enfolding my genius into pages that will include a plasterer, a poseur if there ever was one. At least the others work in stone or metal, but she avowedly eschews "permanent" materials, valuing instead the "intransigent impermanence of plaster."

It's enough to make me retch, and it's all right there on her website. I shouldn't say *her* website because, no, she's far too modest for that, but on a website put together by her devotees. That she has them is criminal. Read all about it! She's doing a show next winter on "slowness." Slowness? What the fuck is that supposed to mean? Honestly, the more I learn about her, the more driven to distraction I become by this pompous woman with her amateur notions of art.

She says her work is about the body. No, *my* work is about the body. Hers is about a sculptor too inept to get it right, so she renders the space the body occupies.

How can you get that wrong? Shapes it like a canoe, and says this is her shape when enveloped, or bends over and says—this gem is on the website, so you can read it if you don't believe me—"This is the space between my legs and my torso and head."

I allude to her by telling Ring Ding that *some* sculptors have lost faith with their art, have taken to distorting the gifts they *might* have had, that Michelangelo certainly would never have turned his back on the real challenge of the body. Rodin wouldn't have either, nor I, and that it's unfortunate, even shameful the way these lesser artists engineer publicity for themselves.

Who are you thinking of? he says, suddenly bolder than I would have expected.

I name names, dropping hers in the middle of a long list with no emphasis whatsoever, but he keys in on it, and the moment he does I wonder, just as I did when I questioned Diamond Girl's desire for Her Rankness, if he fucks his subjects. If he does, then I am helpless to stop him from including her. She's using her witchy little tail to gain success by association, and there's nought to be done but suffer the indignity of her presence on those pages. But still I am hopeful, because if they are not having some sordid little dalliance, then with the right answer I could dissuade him from including her, and if I can do that, perhaps I can also make him see the deeply embarrassing error he'll make if he includes the others as well.

But this must be danced around, dealt with delicately, diplomatically. I don't want to appear to be some petty jealous artist when my concerns are so much larger than such craven considerations would suggest. I will have to pick my moments carefully, cultivate his interest in my own work, and by its rarefied standards let him view the others anew. I do have one decided advantage: I am the last of the sculptors he's interviewing. Let them all pale by comparison.

"She is," I tell him, "a classic example of the old axiom that those who can't do, teach."

This he doesn't write down. Perhaps I have underestimated him by using such a platitude.

"It's not as simple as that," I concede, "but neither is it terribly complex. Her work, if we're to be honest, could be 'executed' by any high school student competent with plaster. She may offer artful explanations, but text does not constitute art. Text is text, and as such is suspect in every manner possible."

I can see I'm losing him with the allusion to deconstruction-ism. "It's like this," I add quickly, "it's as if she's recognized the limitations of her hands, her eyes, her vision, and imbues her work with an intellectualized air that it does not, in actual fact, possess."

Still not the See-Jack-run school of news writing, but I think he gets it. Then he surprises me by biting back,

"Couldn't the same claim be made of your work, with the lengthy 'exegesis' (I am stunned that he uses the word) that accompanies every show?"

"Yes," I concede, "but my explanations are necessitated by the limited purview of so many patrons who might otherwise see only pain, and not the larger excrescences of culture that are represented in the work, which does not simply occupy space, but *dwells* in it."

"That," he notes with stunning insight (stunning for him, any-way), "sounds a lot like Heidegger, whose work also inspires Lauren Reed."

"I assure you," I tell him, "that I share no such ground with her, nor she with Heidegger, no matter how grandiloquent her claims."

And that finally shuts him up so we can begin the pour.

After the bronze fills the molds, even before it cools, he reaches in his pack for a camera.

"No," I tell him firmly. "No pictures. As I said, these faces are my notebooks. If they inspire a new family in the series, then the whole world can see them. Until then, they must remain private."

He tries to appeal to my ego by saying that the art world deserves to see these "amazing creations" now, even in their present form, and while he's undoubtably correct, I see right through this ploy and turn it to my advantage by saying that I have no further need to impress the cognoscenti.

"Did Kerry help you with these?" he says, the first time today that he's brought up her name.

"No, no one has ever worked on these before. No one has ever even seen them before."

He looks up from his notebook and asks what I thought of her work. I can't believe this. In the midst of an interview about my art, I'm being asked to offer a pronouncement on some student's scribbles.

"I never saw it," I say with all the genuine indifference I feel.

He returns to his notebook for another nagging question about the faces: "Why did you show me the new ones?" His own face is noticeably blank. I imagine he's just smart enough to play a good game of poker.

"Because you're writing a book, and I wanted you to see *all* of my work, my very latest creations, which I think may be the best faces I've ever done." I don't believe this for a second, but I must humor the notion.

He scrawls in his notebook and snaps it shut. We are done. I sense that this is what he's saying, that he will leave here today and I will never see him again. I search desperately for some final suasion in my unstated assault on the insult of Lauren Reed and the others, but I would appear too full of effort, and even Ring Ding would see right through it.

. . .

I feed Diamond Girl and Her Rankness a good meal, veal with potatoes and asparagus. Her Rankness brightens when she sees her plate, but this is not intended to flatter her: I've already seen how Diamond Girl shares her food, and I have no desire to see her lose so much as an ounce of her succulent flesh to Her Rankness.

They have the easy physical familiarity of athletes in a locker room. They brush past each other without worrying about touch. They must know that I know, but Diamond Girl still makes a display of hooking her finger around the waistband of Her Rankness's jeans.

"I see you're happy together," I say with the unease that only Diamond Girl succeeds in wringing from me.

"We are," says Her Rankness forcefully, a little too forcefully to be convincing. A little too . . . strained.

Diamond Girl has a smoother ploy. She draws Her Rankness to her and kisses her neck from behind while she trains her beguiling eyes on me. Diamond Girl's tongue makes an appearance, too, before she says that they need a bath.

"I'm sure you do. I'll get the water and soap."

They bathe while I watch them on the monitor. Her Rankness manages an enterprising degree of modesty, but not Diamond Girl. She did this to me before with the bath, the arch posing. All of this has the tread of familiarity, but I watch as eagerly as ever because it also has the same quicksilver excitement.

It is only then, in my postorgasmic glow, that I remember what I said to Ring Ding about Her Rankness's work. My stomach tightens, my face actually twitches because I said I'd never seen it, but I'd told him the first time he came out here that her work showed promise.

I force myself to breathe. It is but a small inconsistency, and Ring Ding is unlikely to catch it, and even if he does I can ascribe it to the pressure of the pour. But the fact that I've put into proper play every other detail magnifies this nettlesome oversight. I rehearsed for the sheriff, knew my lines as well as the most accomplished thespian, then revealed her interest in abandoned mines, knowing that I needed to lead them away from me by degrees. I also knew that as soon as they found her bike, they'd think abduction; and with details that I let slip about her beau, they'd think of him in the next breath. Yes, all of it was so smartly accomplished, drawing them farther and farther from here, drawing their thoughts to roadways, to maps, to all the lines leading all over Utah and well beyond its borders, radiating from me, from the epicenter of the girl's true distress. Perfect, perfect, perfect, until this admittedly minor error. But still it bothers me. It is the speck of dust that makes your eye tear, and if you tear enough the world becomes a blur. When the world of the artist becomes a blur, he might as well be blind.

# CHAPTER
## 18

LAUREN LAY UNDER THE SHEET, eyes still shut, willing away the demands of the day as she savored the scent of the night before. She could feel Ry's warmth beside her, the gift of his presence, for that's how she thought of him, a surprise to the solitude of her body. He lay on his side facing away from her, a marvelous position for viewing his shoulders. Her eyes came alive on his smooth, tan skin, so delicious to taste, if memory could be trusted this early in the morning. Two days of lovemaking had left her sleep deprived and yet still unsated, and not a little guilty too, for feeling so good with Kerry still missing.

The girl's name formed a hard ball in her belly, a dark circle amid all this tender light. She worried that her pleasure might somehow shortchange the search, but it hadn't. While Ry went out to Stassler's yesterday to work in his foundry, to cast faces of all things, she had canvassed the entire town, posted more than fifty copies of a new photograph of the girl, and experienced a painful encounter with her mother outside the grocery store. The woman had pointed to Lauren and said in the saddest voice imaginable, "You sent her here. *You!*" Her father had shook his head, as if to say, Don't worry, she's just very upset. But hearing those words had rekindled Lauren's misgivings, fed them as surely as tinder feeds a match.

She listened to Ry's sleeping breath, those soft expirations such a contrast to his passion. Hers too. They'd been behaving like a couple of teenagers with a fresh infusion of libido. They'd made love seven times (she'd been keeping track, though there had been moments when counting to two would have proved a dizzying affair), and though she felt sore, she experienced this as a minor discomfort hardly capable of chilling her ardor. Even now she was snuggling up to Ry and kissing his shoulder.

He moaned, and she filled with pleasure. Her hand slipped under the sheet and squeezed his firm bottom. She couldn't believe her hunger for him. It was almost embarrassing, and she'd told him twice that she'd never been like this before. But she was thirty-nine, in her prime, right? Giving license to her desire even now, rolling him toward her, finding him as stiff as a sixteen-year-old, his eyes yet unopened, but his mouth smiling mischievously.

For the first time their lovemaking assumed a relaxed rhythm, and gentle moments passed between them as easily as the dappled light that filtered through the motel room drapes. Absent was the frenetic groping of the previous two nights, but scarcely gone for good because he soon rolled her on top of him and buried his face in her breasts and began to make love in earnest. Her breath lost any semblance of control as the pressure of his pelvis enforced a small but spreading pleasure.

She yelped when she came, at least it sounded like that to her. To Leroy too, apparently, because he raised his sleepy head and groaned, not growled, mind you, but groaned as if in terminal envy.

Ry had that impish grin that often appears on a man's face after a woman comes. She squeezed his chin and told him not to be so smug; but she was laughing, and so was he, laughing and fondling every bit of her that he could reach. And she was all too happy to accommodate him, to luxuriate in the feel of his hands on her chest and buttocks and back and belly, swimming over her thighs, reaching up between her legs to their rich contact, and then back to her face, where they'd first held her weeks ago on the porch outside her house.

"Tell me how you feel," he whispered.

She forced aside her deepest concerns, and in response kissed his ear and neck and cheek and mouth, and rubbed her breasts against him. She felt him stiffening beneath her, climaxing almost as loudly as she had, his face suddenly so taut that it could have been cast, so stark were its lines, so pronounced were its features.

"You're good," he said when he caught his breath.

"Yeah? You're just saying that because you've got me where you want me."

"And I'm not letting you go."

She raised herself up and looked down at him.

"You have to. There's lots to do. You," she poked him playfully in the chest, "are supposed to call that helicopter place to confirm that we've got a pilot, and I'm," now she poked herself in the chest, "going to take a shower, and then I'm going to take Mr. Bad Bad Leroy Brown out for his morning constitutional."

She rushed off to the bathroom, threw open the faucets, and stepped under the nozzle before the water had a chance to warm up.

Now that the day had begun, she couldn't move it along fast enough.

The water had finally warmed when she turned it off and grabbed a towel. She dressed quickly, and told Ry she'd be back in ten minutes.

"And then I've *got* to go by my place for a change of clothes."

Al Jenkins sat at the front desk doing a crossword puzzle as Lauren and Leroy breezed through the lobby. They'd left Ry to scout the eateries to see if it was possible to find a decent breakfast in this town. Jenkins didn't look up until he spoke.

"Never came in last night. I was worried about you. Thought

you might have gotten yourself sucked into one of those abandoned mines."

"No, nothing like that," she said as she hurried up the stairs.

She unlocked her door and tossed off her clothes almost as hastily as she had the night before when they'd entered Ry's room. She found fresh underwear, and a clean pair of shorts and a top that *kind* of matched. It would have to do. She brushed her hair, which had dried rapidly in the desert air, and spiced her lips and eyes with touches of makeup.

Sensible shoes, she told herself as she kicked aside a pair of mules for her cross-trainers.

She took the stairs two at a time on her way back down to the lobby, and was almost out the door when Al said,

"Hold on. Is Prince Leroy going to the spa today?"

"No, he's going to hang out with us, aren't you, buddy?"

Leroy wagged his stump appreciatively.

"Okay, just checking. I thought I'd offer to dog-sit, if you wanted me to."

"That's really nice," Lauren said, genuinely touched. "Thanks, but we're going to keep him with us. The other day we had so much running around to do that I figured he'd be better off in a kennel, but he's getting with the program now."

She turned to leave once more.

"May I have a word with you?"

Al sounded serious. She looked back at him. Very serious.

"Sure."

"You remember what I said about those people getting themselves pushed into mines?"

She nodded.

"If I were you, I'd go down to the County Building and check with the state Division of Mines. I'd find out if Stassler has an abandoned mine on that property of his."

"You would?"

Now it was Al's turn to nod. "I sure would."

"And what do you think I'll find?"

"No telling what you'll find." His hands rose in a helpless gesture, as if he really didn't know. "But the folks that owned that place before him were peculiar as all get out, and about as private as he is. No surprise that he bought it. They were ranchers, but they might have done some mining out there in the early days. They had the whole spread in the family for four generations. Some of the mines in these parts have more shafts running through them than New York City has subways."

Lauren walked up to the front desk. "Are you saying that you think I'll find—"

Al's hands shot up again, this time in the universal sign of surrender. "I'm just telling you what I'd do. I wouldn't assume anything when it comes to the old Johnson Ranch. Strangest bunch of folks ever lived around here."

"You don't like Ashley Stassler either, do you?"

Al shrugged. "Can't say as I care for his so-called sculpture. No, can't say as I care for it one bit. He had a show here a few years ago, and made a big to-do of standing up and telling us what we were *supposed* to see when we looked at his 'art.' But you want to know something? You don't need to tell people what they're supposed to see. People can see things well enough on their own. I know what I saw. It wasn't any of those big ideas he claimed for himself. It was just some poor folks who looked like the world had gotten its teeth into them and never let go."

"The world?"

"That's right, the world. Or someone in it. So I'd check with the Division of Mines. You might have to find the plot number for the ranch. That's over in the tax department."

Lauren let her elbow find the counter.

"What were you doing before you bought this place?"

Al smiled. "I was a professional busybody. And I was nobody's best friend."

He let her think.

"I was the county tax assessor." Now his smile spread across his crinkly face. "Why do you think I run a business catering to strangers? I've got no friends around here. But I know more secrets than Paris has parks."

His smile turned into a wheezy laugh, and he smacked the counter with a hand as wrinkled and mottled as the skin on an old peach.

"I guess we could check it out," Ry said after they'd picked up their drive-through breakfast; they'd settled for fast food because they were running late for the helicopter flight. "But I'm not all that optimistic."

"We'll do it later," Lauren said. "We've got to move."

They'd reserved the flight in her name so Ry's link wouldn't be obvious to Stassler, if he took umbrage over another aircraft flying over his land. The chopper's owner, Bob Flanders, had assured them that Leroy would be fine at the hangar.

Ry handed Lauren the headphones and helped her put them on, positioning the attached mike so it was right in front of her mouth.

She'd taken the front seat next to Flanders, who said his own first ride in a helicopter came at the behest of Uncle Sam more than thirty years ago.

"Mekong Delta. They dropped us off and said 'good luck.' "

Lauren's stomach did its elevator dance as the chopper roared off. The ground fell away as if it had been kicked free.

"It's a Bell Jet Ranger," Flanders explained over the headphones. "We can cover a lot of territory quickly in one of these."

"We don't want to go *too* quickly," she said.

Flanders acknowledged this with a nod. "You're the third group I've taken up to look for that girl."

"Who were the other two?" Lauren looked at the town far below them, spotting mountain bikers teeming on the slick rock like brightly colored ants. She forced a breath and tried to adjust to the exposed feeling of the chopper, the bubble of glass that seemed to barely enclose them, that made her feel as if she were flying on terms a little too intimate with the sky.

"First time up it was with the sheriff and his chief detective. They didn't want to wait for the state police to free up a bird, so I had them up for four hours. We practically plowed up Stassler's ranch that day. Second group, oh, that was a sad one," Flanders shook his head, "the girl's mom and dad and grandfather. I let them pay for fuel, that's all. I can't imagine losing one of my girls out there." His eye swept over the spread of canyons, mountains, and desert.

"You have daughters?" Lauren said.

"Two of them." Flanders perked up. "Both at the University of Utah up in Salt Lake. The oldest graduates next month with a degree in biology," he said with pride.

"Congratulations."

Flanders flew them over Stassler's compound at about four hundred feet, which was, he explained, a violation of air space, "but the hell with him. What's he going to do? Send me back to Vietnam?"

Lauren was beginning to note a distinctly chilly trend in the feelings locals had for their famous neighbor.

"That must be the foundry." Lauren pointed to a square brick building to their right.

"That's it," Ry said from the seat behind her.

"It's big," she added.

Flanders swung the chopper around so they were facing the foundry. "I heard it said that he built that place himself, brick by brick. I got to hand it to him for that. Not every rich son of a bitch is willing to work that hard."

Lauren agreed. A foundry was a huge undertaking, and this one was larger than most, even bigger than the one at the university.

The foothills that had seemed so close to his compound when she'd viewed them during her bicycle ride, now appeared a good two miles away. As they approached them, she made out lovely wave patterns in the petrified sandstone, along with immense boulders and slender stone towers that rose to dizzying heights. Miles beyond the first of these natural marvels, she spied the chasm for the Green River.

"Can we go over there?" She pointed to the canyon, wondering if Kerry had been curious about the river. She herself would have been.

"You want to go down in there?"

"Can we?"

"It'll be a squeeze, but we can do it. I don't think you're going to find much."

As soon as Flanders dropped the Jet Ranger into the river canyon, the narrow corridor seemed to grow perilously tight. A gust of wind shook them, and she flinched when she saw his hands tighten on the controls. He looked over and told her not to worry.

"This is nothing."

He flew the chopper up river. They were low enough to make out the waves.

"Where do you end up if you capsize a boat down there?" Ry said.

"You don't want to capsize down there. You can try and ride it out, but you're going to take a devil of a beating on those rocks. We've lost more than one boater in there."

"No run out?" Ry said.

"Not for about nine or ten miles. That's nine or ten miles of hell, if you're caught in there. Course, you're not going to be caught in there unless you know what you're doing. That's the theory anyway."

"The reality?" Ry said.

"The reality is we've lost more than one boater in there," Flanders repeated.

They flew in silence before Lauren realized that Flanders was right: they were unlikely to find anyone, living or dead, in such swift currents. She asked him to show them where bodies had washed up in the past.

Flanders pulled back on the controls, and the chopper rose up so swiftly that the bright canyon walls blurred. As they lifted over them, they saw two hikers waving. Lauren waved back, envious of their innocence.

They hurtled downriver to the first run out, where the canyon bled into the desert, which looked as wide and flat as the rock gorge had been narrow and steep.

"Chances are, if she ended up in the river, we'd have seen her body hung up on something by now. For the first few days, I'd check this area each time I went up."

Flanders turned the bird to the west and roared back over Stassler's compound.

"You ever see any evidence of a mine on this land?" Lauren said.

The pilot shook his head. "No, can't say I ever have. Course, after a mine's closed down, it's nothing more than a little hole in the ground, if that. Now, if they close them up like they're supposed to, that's different because then they fence them off, but I've never seen anything like that here. This was ranch land. Seen some cattle skulls."

They flew two more hours, covering Moab and the immediately surrounding environs. But the longer they were up, the more hopeless Lauren became. Looking down reminded her of what a huge job it was to find someone in mountain and canyon country. You could spend weeks at it and cover only a fraction of the possibilities. What were you thinking? she asked herself. That you could succeed where the sheriff and state police, with far more experience in search and rescue, had failed?

She imagined it must have been much worse for Kerry's family, to feel so small above land so large, and to know that somewhere out there was your daughter. Dead? Alive? Dying? To feel so powerless when so much was at stake.

"Let's go check the Division of Mines," Lauren said to Ry after they were back on terra firma.

"You think your hotel guy really knows something?"

"I don't know if he's being cute or cagey, but maybe he's on to something that no one else has thought about."

"I doubt it."

"Ry, come on. What can it hurt?"

They paused only long enough to grab lunch at a burrito wagon parked in the shade of a cottonwood tree. A female German shepherd walked by with its owner. Leroy checked her out, but didn't bolt. Lauren nudged Ry, "Look-look-look-progress!"

Ry chuckled. "I doubt he sees it that way."

The Division of Mines hunkered, appropriately enough, in the basement of the county building. It was run by Barbara Hershing, a woman in her sixties with a florid complexion and a dress that might have fit her twenty pounds ago. She was cheerful, if not discouraging.

"I've never heard of a mining claim on the Johnson land. I guess you'd call it the Stassler land now," she corrected. "You know the Johnsons were descended from Brigham Young himself? Are you LDS?"

"No," Lauren said, hoping the woman would remain helpful anyway. She'd already done them the favor of looking up the tax number instead of packing them off to the assessor's office upstairs.

"Let's see what we can find," she continued as she pulled out a pair of dusty volumes from a shelf. "We never did get these on the computer. We got all the new mining claims on it, but that's easy," she snorted, "only get a few of those a year."

She flipped through a volume, paused over a page, and ran her finger up and down columns of numbers as she shook her head. But then her finger froze.

"Well, I'll be a chicken in the Sunday pot! There was a mine out there after all. A claim filed way back in 1910. Can you beat that?"

She looked up, amused by her finding.

"What kind of mine?" Lauren said.

"That's the interesting part," Hershing replied, "a silver mine. We had a few of them around here. Never amounted to much. I'll be darned."

"Does it say anything about the mine? How deep it is, anything like that?" Ry said.

Hershing looked down, then spoke hesitantly. "It does, but you can't trust these old claim descriptions much. A lot of these old miner types didn't want anyone knowing how they had their mines laid out . . ."

Lauren wondered if the same could be said of Stassler.

". . . but it does say that it had a main shaft about a hundred feet down, and that it was about a half mile long."

"That sounds big," Lauren said.

Hershing shrugged. "Like I said, I wouldn't put too much stock in this. Back then no one bothered to check on them to see if they were confabulating."

"Can we get a copy of that?" Lauren said.

"Honey, that'll cost you."

"How much?"

"Oh, about a dime."

As they walked upstairs to the main floor of the county building, Sheriff Holbin spotted them and strode right up.

"I heard you were down there."

"We were. We were looking up something in the Division of—"

"Have you seen Jared Nielsen?" he interrupted.

"The last time we saw him was on Wednesday. We went riding with him."

"I know all about that," Holbin said. "I mean since then."

"No. Why?"

"Because he was scheduled to take a lie detector test this afternoon, and he never showed up."

"I thought that was scheduled for yesterday," Ry said.

"It was, but the examiner couldn't make it down here till today, so we postponed it. Now Nielsen's gone."

"What do you mean, gone? Did you check his room?"

Sheriff Holbin gave her a weary look. "Yes, ma'am, we checked his room. He's still got some of his stuff there, but his bike's gone and so's his SUV."

"I thought you had him under surveillance," Ry said.

The sheriff crossed his arms. "We did. But he took off during a shift change, which makes me very suspicious. It's like he waited for the one time when we might not be looking. We still shouldn't have lost him, but we did. I've got an alert out to the state police."

"So you really think he took off?" Lauren said.

"I think he broke a promise to me, and I've got a warrant out for his arrest on flight, and I aim to use it too. So if you do happen to see him," Holbin eyed them both closely, "tell him he's made the biggest mistake of his life, and he'll be a lot better off if he turns himself in."


Jared Nielsen didn't feel that he'd made a mistake, much less the biggest one of his life. He felt the damn sheriff was dragging his feet, putting off the lie detector test, expecting him to sit tight and be a good little boy. Enough of that. He could take the lie detector test any old time, but time was running out for Kerry.

He drove the Expedition slowly across the desert to keep his dust trail down. More like creeping. After about twenty minutes he saw the Green River off to his right, and the steep gorge from which it rushed. He'd ridden his bike across this same stretch of land when he'd reconnoitered early yesterday morning. He knew that on Stassler's side of the river, there was a cave where he could stash the Expedition. A few caves, actually, but the one he had in mind looked like it had been bored into the rock with the nose of a 747.

He drove the Expedition right in, as if it were a garage. It was about thirty feet deep, and would certainly hide the SUV from all but the most serious search. The ceiling was high enough for his bike, up on the roof rack, to clear easily. He planned to ride it across the ranch to the compound.

The dashboard clock said five after three. He'd timed this as carefully as he could, but he'd still got way ahead of himself. Too eager. And he needed to hide: once he'd slipped away from the cops, he couldn't sit around sipping espresso drinks downtown. He planned to wait for the sun to go down, ride his bike in with the last of the light, and spend the night looking for Kerry. He would have preferred to search during the day, but according to her, Stassler sometimes didn't leave the compound for a week at a time. At least at night he had to sleep.

Jared lowered his bike from the rack, and checked his day pack to make sure he had all his gear, water, food. Enough for two days, if he had to lie low. If Kerry was in there, he was going to find her. The newspapers said the sheriff had been out here and looked around, but Jared wasn't going to "look around." He'd comb through every inch of the place. She hadn't fallen into some mine, and she hadn't been up on that crappy jeep trail, so in his mind that didn't leave a whole lot of possibilities outside of El Creepo and his ranch.

At a little past seven Jared pulled on his pack, mounted his bike, and headed out across the desert. Shadows from the foothills darkened the dusky light, turning him into a spectral figure. His camouflage clothes and the layer of mud he'd painted on his frame and handlebars added to his cover. He rode with great care because all of the territory ahead was new to him.

Rugged terrain challenged him for more than an hour before the silhouette of the compound grayed the dying light.

The foundry stood closest to him. He ditched his bike by some purple sage, and lowered himself for a series of sprints from the sparse shelter of one desert bush to the equally sparse shelter of another. No sign of El Creepo.

He drew closer to the rear of the foundry. He wanted to check it out first because he considered it the least likely place to run into Stassler at this time of day; Kerry had said that he liked working in the morning, and that's why she'd always had her afternoons free.

After the foundry, he'd search the main house. That's where he'd spend the night too, find a spot to keep an eye on Stassler, and in the morning when El Creepo went to work, he'd slip into the barn and guest quarters. That would be the weirdest part. The thought of taking such an enormous risk with Stassler so close made his groin tighten. But he might not have to. He might find Kerry long before he ever had to enter the barn.

As he drew closer to the foundry, he was grateful that Stassler didn't own a dog. The last thing he needed right now was for some big old hound to start barking, or worse yet, to start trying to eat him. He had no weapons, unless you counted his Swiss Army knife. He wished he had a gun, wished this even more as he crouched no more than twenty feet from the foundry's rear door.

Before scrambling up there, he looked around one last time. She's out here. Jared had an almost unshakeable faith in this. Then his eyes rested on the ground, and he feared that she was already dead, stuffed into a crude grave. But that possibility seemed too cruel. You don't wait all your life for a Kerry, only to have her taken away. He refused to believe in anything so bleak. And he'd refuse to believe in Stassler's innocence only after he'd had a chance to scour every inch of the compound.

He made the dash to the foundry, and crawled all the way to the corner. He wanted to see if the creep's Jeep was parked by the barn. It would be a great break if he'd taken off. Kerry had said that when he did go into town, he'd do it in the early evening.

The Jeep wasn't there. Jared wanted to shout with joy, before it occurred to him that Stassler might have parked it in front of the barn. The only way he'd know was to work his way to the front of the foundry.

Think about it, he told himself. If it's out there, is it going to change anything? No, it's not. So stick to the plan. Get inside the foundry, and see what you can scope out from there. Then if he's gone, you can decide if you want to go for the barn and guest quarters tonight.

Jared retreated to the rear door, metal, the kind you find in a warehouse, and locked. No surprise there; she'd said he was secretive. There were double-pane windows too, with thick metal mullions, but they were also locked. This was proving grimmer than he'd thought. Before breaking glass—and it could take serious pounding to smash through two layers of tempered glass—he'd check out the roof. He'd been a climber since his dad had taken him to Yosemite when he was twelve, and he'd brought enough gear to scale anything in the compound. A foundry had to have a furnace, and a furnace had to have a chimney. Usually the brick kind. He was slim and strong. It might be doable. Plus, from the roof he could scope out the front of the barn for the Jeep.

On his first attempt, he snagged the grapple at the end of his climbing rope on the edge of the flat roof. He did this as smoothly as a fly fisherman hooks a trout, although as he started up the wall, suspended on the end of the rope, he had no thought of himself as the creature who'd been caught. Instead, he felt the first rush of success, especially when he hoisted himself up and spotted a skylight that was cracked open.

Excellent, he said to himself. Totally, totally excellent. He gathered up his rope and pack, and crept across the roof. He peered through the skylight, but made out only shadows down in the foundry.

He scurried to the front of the roof, and looked across to the barn. There was Stassler's Jeep. An ill feeling muddied his belly. Not until that instant had he realized how much he'd been hoping El Creepo would be gone. And not until that instant had he recognized how much fear could flood his system.

It's no different than you thought it would be, but reminding himself of this didn't make him feel any better. He inched away from the edge, uneasy with the knowledge that for all his precautions, Stassler could spot him by simply looking out a window in the guest quarters, which were on the second story of the barn.

Better move.

He lifted the skylight open and laid it on the roof. After hooking the grapple on the skylight's metal frame, he lowered himself into the still shadows. But as his feet hit the floor, he was gripped with the fear that one of them would reach out and grab him.

To calm his breathing, he took a few moments to look around, to let his eyes adjust to the dim, uneven light. That's when he spotted a man crouched in the corner.

Is that Stassler? What's he doing? Then Jared realized—no, he *hoped*—it was a statue, sculpture. He peered as intently as he had ever looked at anything, and saw a glint of the day's dying light on the form's metallic arm. Jared bit the back of his hand in relief, a nervous habit from his boyhood, one that he hadn't resorted to in at least ten years.

He ripped his hand away from his mouth. He wouldn't want Kerry to see him like that. He was not without a hero's fantasies, imagining her gratitude when she finally saw him, her open arms and thankful tears. She had trusted him with her secrets, and he, Jared Nielsen, would make that trust his cause.

Glancing to his side, he saw a movable crane, and chains hanging from its six-inch pulley. A few feet beyond the crane was the pour area with its metal grate and earthen floor. A faint chemical odor lingered in the air. Not unpleasant, but pungent, like the waft of wood after it's been burned and left to smolder.

When he looked to his left, he faced the furnace, round and as tall as he, with dials and switches. The crucible stood several feet away. So much so close together. Why so large a room? He knew only what Kerry had told him about casting, the process of mold making, and then the heating and cooling of bronze, how nothing could be hurried. Nothing. You had to make every movement count. That's why foundries were designed so carefully. See, there are the window fans, sinks, the mold-making table. All right, all this makes sense, but what's over there, in that space behind the partition?

Jared took his first steps across the concrete floor slowly, careful not to bang into anything, one more shadow in the growing night, edging closer and closer to the partitioned area. He definitely didn't want to knock over one of the tall metal tanks of oxygen, $CO_2$, or argon gas. Knock the valve off one of those things and they could turn into a missile, blast right through a brick wall. That's why they're supposed to have those dome-shaped metal caps, but Kerry said sculptors sometimes got lazy and didn't bother to screw them back on.

He stepped on a small, hard object, stooped, and picked up a shard from a shattered mold. A table stood to the side. This must be where Stassler pounded the molds off once the bronze had cooled.

Wait! He drew himself up at the sight of three bodies lying on the table itself, one of them a woman. Unmoving. As rigid as he found himself once again. But their skin was . . . greenish. He could see their pallor even in this lousy light. He touched the one closest to him, the largest of the three. It felt hard and brittle, and Jesus . . . they were headless. Except for their size, and the hump of their sex organs, they lacked any distinguishing features at all, more like mummies than anything he'd ever seen. To judge by its shape, he'd put his hand on the figure of a man. The one next to it belonged to a woman, and the last was of a boy. They were horrible. *Headless*. He felt a sickly presence and became acutely aware of his vulnerability, standing there alone, looking at these three decapitated creatures.

As much as they repulsed him, they intrigued him. He took a single finger and ran it along the arm of the male figure. His finger hooked under the edge of the hand, and he felt all the details of skin and bone and muscle. It was what Kerry called an impression.

He looked behind him. No window, just wall, so he dug into his pack and took out his headlamp. He set it for the narrowest beam, and switched on the batteries, holding it as he would a flashlight. As he eased himself down, he lifted the arm and trained the light on the inside of the hand. What he saw made him gasp, so real was the appearance of pain. The hand had clutched at air, he could almost see the desperate motion as it grasped the empty promise of nothingness, each finger extended, stretched, bones and tendons so distinct they protruded like thorns from a prickly bush. But it was the surface of the arm that shot an eerie current through Jared, that made him suddenly feel as if his hero's quest were so compromised by fear that he would never save Kerry. The arm was rank with terror, pocked with dimples in each of the muscles where the strain of survival had lost its human roots, had assumed a primate's jungle shriek, when an appendage is no longer a tool for travel, feeding, breeding, but a weapon to be used in any and all ways. But this weapon, Jared could see, had failed; and it was this sense of doom that he saw most clearly in the raised biceps, ropy forearms, and clutching hand that might as well have been a claw for all its brazen primitive hunger.

The brittle material shattered. He'd dropped the arm. He stepped back, alarmed by the sound, feeling the world inside himself as fault lines, great shifting plates of foreboding. He swore softly, reflexively, without real meaning, then slipped on the headlamp to free both hands, and looked at what he had done; but his eyes caught on the boy's feet, snagged by their torturous, twisted shape, as if the child had been squirming in place, trying to escape whatever terror he had known by screwing himself right into the earth.

Jared had the sudden feeling that he was in a slaughterhouse, a butcher's haven. His eyes finally moved back to the remains of the man's arm, a crumble of shards and dust. *What have I done?* Even now, even after the suspicion of nature's deepest violation had risen from beneath his skin, when he sensed that he'd entered the undying presence of murder, he felt a proper young man's guilt over breaking another man's work, of laying it so visibly to waste.

The arm had shattered along dozens of ragged lines, and his headlamp picked up motes already swirling upward, a rich green-gray cloud rising toward him till he smelled its dusty scent.

He'll know something's wrong. He'll know it the minute he sees this. You're going to have to do all of it tonight, because he's going to see it tomorrow. Jared knew he wouldn't face arrest for breaking and entering, he'd face murder. His skin bubbled with the feeling of death that surrounded him. Truly, he could feel it in his bones.

Across the room stood his destination, the partitioned area he'd started off to before the impressions of the bodies had stopped him, transfixed him, and finally horrified him. He made his way past a table saw and a pair of saw horses, tool racks, and two more fuel tanks for an oxy/acetylene torch.

When he moved behind the partition, he broadened the head-lamp's beam. Dust covered everything, a table, tools—mallets and chisels—and the floor, where his eyes settled last, spotting shoe prints that looked fresh, distinct. They led up to, and then away from a wooden box the approximate size of a four drawer file cabinet. But what was strange, very very strange, was that one forward shoe print had only the heel, as if the front of the foot had stepped directly into the box, as if the wood were no more than illusion, a wall that could be walked through.

Without thinking about his own trail, he inched up to the box. As he braced himself to try to move it, his fingertips found a seam that betrayed a door. It swung open with little resistance.

His headlamp revealed the floor, no longer of concrete with dusty prints, but of hard earth, and a few feet away, rising from a hole in the ground, the top of an aluminum ladder.

It looked . . . yes, it looked like the opening to a mine. But it was no more abandoned than the airport back in L.A. She's here, he told himself. Down there.

He crawled inside the wooden box, drawing the door closed. He stared into the blackness of the hole, his headlamp revealing little more than the length of the ladder and the dark dirt at its base.

Down he climbed, clammy with fear, but excited too. The cops didn't know about this place. Nobody knew about this. He'd go in, find her, and get her the hell out. Then later tonight he'd come back with the sheriff, take this son of a bitch away for good.

At the bottom of the ladder, he did indeed find himself in a mine shaft. The ceiling grazed his head lamp. At five-ten, he figured that meant it was about six feet high, and as wide, to judge by reaching out his arms in both directions.

Every few feet wood beams as broad as railroad ties braced the planked ceiling. When he rapped them, dust spilled from the seams, but they felt solid. He worried about a cave-in, then found short-lived consolation by reminding himself that a cave-in was the least of his concerns. His biggest worry lay down this dark tunnel, in whatever festered in the nether reaches of his headlamp's throw.

Damp cool air moved past him, came alive on the sweaty exposed skin of his neck and arms. As he penetrated the darkness, as he forced its black borders aside, he glanced back and saw how illusory was his victory, how brief, for his wake had already been enveloped by air so empty it held nothing, no light, no sound, no life. It had rushed him from behind, and now pushed him forward. He could feel its iron hands, and see the shadows shifting before him, the fragile beam flickering nervously on the walls and ceiling and cold earthen floor. From all around him rose an unmistakable urge. It was as if these walls were trying to give birth to a complete and final darkness by forcing him deeper and deeper into the void of an ever more malevolent world.

His toes pressed against the tips of his running shoes as the downward slope steepened and drew him farther from the surface. In this thick, almost feral blackness, he wondered if what we called the night were no more than the insides of the earth rising relentlessly to the surface, an insatiable animal burrowing upward to spill out over the land, draping it in darkness, choking it with chills. It was a bizarre thought, and Jared knew this; but it held to him as a nightmare holds to sleep, unwilling to surrender to any thought of light.

Where would it end? How much farther? He thought of running back, of fleeing this tomb. That's how he thought of it now, as a vast vessel of death. He'd failed to check his watch before he'd climbed down that ladder, so when he saw that it was nine-thirty, it meant nothing. Had he been descending into the earth for half an hour, an hour?

Kerry, he said to himself, Kerry. He tried to cling to her name, but his heroism had been thinned by his fear, and to its awful bounty he added a new one: that his headlamp would go out, the batteries would run down, and he would be left to navigate in absolute blackness. This fear stilled his feet, and as the beam steadied its stark gaze he remembered the night-light he'd kept in his bedroom until his junior year in high school. Every morning he'd stash it in the closet in case any of his buds dropped by. But his night fright had been that deep, that persistent, a predator with a constant hunger. He felt its teeth once more.

It's not going to go out, he assured himself. The batteries are good. The beam is strong. See. As he ordered himself to look forward, he saw iron rails that came to an abrupt end about fifty feet from where he stood. He approached cautiously, but with the smallest spark of hope too. Maybe the rails would lead to the end of the tunnel, and he could return to the foundry, to the safety of earth and all those—even Stassler—who lived above it. So great was his fear that all the threats he had known now paled.

When he stepped close to their terminus, he saw large openings on both sides of the mine shaft. Warily, he looked to the right first, and startled at the sight of a ghoulish bronze face staring back. No body, just a man's face hanging on the wall about ten feet away, glowing in the light of his headlamp, the empty eyes fiercely set, the mouth twisted in fury, or pain.

Jesus H . . . but he never said Christ, so fearful had he become of alienating the only ally he might find down here, the God of his childhood that he'd started to call upon.

With his heart raging, he turned to look across the rails, and in the recessed space behind him spied a woman's bronze face with the same paralyzed appearance, the same deformed features. It also showed the same ghastly pain he'd seen in that man's hand and arm in the foundry. His head swung back around, and he studied the male face again. Maybe that *is* his face. Jared's fear had started asking the cruelest of questions.

She's right, he said to himself. Kerry's right. He's a creep, a total creep. No more "El Creepo." Stassler was no longer someone Jared could joke about. Stassler was a cold, cunning creep, and Jared almost bolted back to the ladder, actually saw himself climbing up into the foundry where he saw not the night, but the brilliance of the desert day.

But he held firm because he believed she was near, and that he had to move on. If there was a single moment of real courage in his entire effort to save her, this was it.

It did indeed mark the beginning of the end.

Each step forward sounded resonant and alone. And each step filled him with greater doses of the dread that had been building all along.

A line from a song came to him, one of his father's CDs. The old man listened to some heinous stuff, but that line had stuck with him. It was about how you had to be willing to fight for what you wanted most in life.

Okay, he was ready to fight, though with what he didn't know exactly. The Swiss Army knife? Your hands? Your feet? It had been a long time since he'd studied karate. A phase he'd gone through when he was ten. He could barely remember the kicks now.

These were his thoughts, some comforting, most not, as he moved along the rails. He walked about two hundred feet before the shaft abruptly broadened, and he triggered a motion detector light, which illuminated a room to his left that was filled with bronze faces like the ones he'd seen minutes ago. They sat on shelves that climbed to a ceiling at least ten feet high. Across from him, rising well above his eyes, was a bronze family, one of Stassler's families, but with terrible tortured faces, so much worse than the ones he'd seen in the *Family Planning* series that Kerry had shown him pictures of. A mom, a dad, a little girl maybe three or four, and a boy a year or two older looked down at him with haunted faces that were all but screaming. They looked like they'd lost all of love and life and hope and prayer in a single terrifying instant.

He looked away, and began to search for *her* face. He felt like a man who'd been led to a morgue, and now had to make the grisly identification. His eyes moved along each shelf, left to right. He saw every manner of visage, some beautiful, some not, but all twisted by seizures of agony. Why does he hide them here? As soon as he asked that question, Jared knew. Jared knew that Ashley Stassler hid the faces because Ashley Stassler really was a killer, and that every one of his sculptures was a sepulcher, in spirit if not in flesh. That whatever he did with the bodies was an afterthought to the man, because it was their lives he had stolen, and their bones, their skulls, and all of their blood were the waste matter of his work.

Jared, who hadn't prayed in years, who had only a vague memory of the Methodist service, offered words to God that would have made sense to all who had fallen here, because they, too, had come to prayer, to seek its soft embrace in a brutal world. And this is what it had earned them: these shelves, these walls, from which to stare vacantly for all eternity. This was their hell, deep in the earth. Yours too, he whispered to himself. The corrosive fear of dying in such absolute darkness pierced him the moment he became aware that the motion light might well be an alarm.

Still, he forced himself to search the last of the shelves, but before he could finish his grim task the light went off, and only the beam from his headlamp cleaved the darkness.

*What's going on?* His head whipped from side to side, but he found no answer. Neither could he glimpse where the shaft continued, *if* it continued. But his beam landed on an old cart on the rails. It was pressed against a rock wall. That's it, he realized. *The end of the line.* He rushed over to see if an axe, a pick, any tool with lethal points or sharp edges had been left to rust, but the cart was empty. Then he heard the first of the footsteps, as distinct as hammer blows, resounding from the shaft where he had crept so quietly.

He snapped off his headlamp and listened intently. Those footsteps were moving closer, as deliberate as the rise of day. No rushing. No hurry. And then another noise, like a stick thumping the earth. Or was it the ceiling? It sounded sharp, provocatively so. Made by someone who didn't know Jared's fear, who didn't care if he heard him. Who walked without a light.

Step, step, thump. Step, step, thump. Step, step, thump.

Jared dug out his Swiss Army knife, unfolded the biggest blade, which couldn't have been more than a few inches long. Nevertheless, he held it in front of him like all the knife fighters he'd seen in movies and on TV. But he felt weak with fear, not strong; vulnerable, not invincible. More so as the footsteps grew louder, and that stick, or club or whatever it was, began to thump madly, gaining a horrible rhythm of its own, a staccato *thump-thump . . . thump-thump-thump-thump*.

It had to be Stassler. Jared wanted to hide, but where the hell could he hide? And wouldn't it be better to face off with him? Kerry had said Stassler was about his size, but he was a lot older, and probably not as quick or strong.

As the footsteps grew louder, nearer, and the *thump-thump-thump-thump . . . thump* madness began to beat in his brain, the young man took little comfort in his own counsel. He even considered climbing into the rail cart. Then he thought of placing himself behind it. He pulled it from the wall with a plan to roll it right into Stassler.

He was imagining the damage it could do when the lights came back on, all but blinding him with their brightness. He didn't see Stassler until the sculptor stood several feet away wielding a baseball bat. Jared couldn't even push the cart into him: Stassler wasn't on the rails. It was a stupid plan. All Jared could do was try to keep the cart between them, and even this idea, as hopeless as it was, failed when Stassler pointed a gun at him.

"You are an idiot," he said.

"I'm sorry," Jared said.

"For what? Your idiocy? Or for violating my property rights and destroying my work?"

"I'm sorry about that. I didn't mean to."

"Oh, you didn't mean to. Well, in that case, go on. Leave. Come on, get moving."

Stassler tried to wave him out from behind the cart, but Jared was having nothing of the man's game.

"You don't want to leave? You want to stay down here with all of my friends?" Stassler looked at the bronze faces. "How do you think they died?"

Jared risked a glance at the shelves, and at the family standing to his right. He wondered if he could push them over and crush Stassler.

"I don't know."

"Tell me, Brilliance, do you think they had a good death? Do you think they died happy?"

"I don't know."

"You're being obstinate, Brilliance. What is your name anyway?"

Jared told him.

"I thought so. I would have been disappointed if you'd been anyone else. Why are you here?"

"I'm looking for someone."

Stassler smiled. "And who might you be looking for?"

"Kerry Waters."

"Kerry Waters? Tiny tits? Hard round butt? Red hair? Used to be my *intern*," he said with a roll of his eyes.

Jared offered a barely perceptible nod.

"Come on, I'll take you to her, but first I want to know how you got here."

"Got here?"

"Yes, how you arrived. Did you walk, flap your wings and fly? How did you do it, Brilliance?"

"I drove. And I rode my bike."

"You drove *and* you rode your bike?"

Jared stared at him.

"Where's your car?"

"Out by the river, in a cave. One of those big sandstone caves."

"Did you park it in there?"

"Yeah."

"What about your bike?"

"It's behind your foundry, maybe a half mile."

"Who knows you're here?"

"Everyone."

"You're such a bad liar, Brilliance. The truth is, no one knows you're here. Do you want to know how I know? Because I listen to the police band, and they're looking for you right now. They have a warrant out for your arrest. As far as they're concerned, you've disappeared. Get in there." Stassler smacked the rail cart with the baseball bat. The noise made Jared jump. "I'll give you a ride."

"No." Jared shook his head firmly.

"You don't have a choice, young man. You're either going to climb in there, or I'm going to shoot your balls off."

Jared climbed in the cart.

"It works ever time," Stassler said, as if to himself. "Now kneel, with your head by your knees."

"What are you going to do?"

"I told you, I'm going to take you to see Kerry Waters."

Jared did as he was told, holding his knife close to his chest, waiting for a chance, any chance, to use it.

Stassler pressed the gun barrel to the base of his skull. He never made an effort to push the cart, never so much as touched it; but the old wagon began to rattle on its iron wheels, rattle like a bag of bones from the boy shaking inside.

"What did you do to her?" It took the last of Jared's courage to ask.

Stassler laughed. "What did I do to her? What do *you* think I did to her?"

"I think . . . maybe . . . you . . ."

"'I think . . . maybe . . . you . . . ' Really, try to speak in sentences, *please*. If I understand your mutterings correctly, the answer is yes, I *do* have her somewhere. We call her by a special name. Would you like to know what that is?"

Jared tried to nod. The cart shook even more loudly.

"Her Rankness. She smells so bad that that's what we call her. What should we call you?"

"I . . . don't know," he blurted out.

"Should we call you Brilliance? Or should we call you Dead?"

Jared heard a metallic click.

"Please don't . . . please?"

"You really don't think you're going to die, do you? Admit it. That's okay. Nobody does. Every last one of you thinks that something, or someone, is going to intervene. Am I right?" He prodded him with the muzzle, but got no reply. "You all think that some deus ex machina will descend from the ceiling or the sky or walk out of the shadows and save you? I know that kind of thinking. There's far too much of it nowadays. I blame it on the culture. It's sad, all this gusto for garbage. Do you want to say a prayer? I advise it, buys you some time. More than that Boy Scout knife you're holding."

"They're going to figure it out," Jared said in a voice barely above the rattling cart. "People can't keep disappearing out here."

"But you're not 'out here,' Brilliance. You've fled this jurisdiction, and you're the number one suspect in the disappearance of Kerry Waters."

Jared started to speak, opened his mouth to say something, but the horrible truth of Stassler's words stunned him into silence.

"Flummoxed, aren't you? Try prayer. It really does buy you some time. But do it out loud. I love to hear these things. Maybe if you pray hard enough, your God will save you, your own little deus ex machina."

"I'm . . . Our Father, Who art in heaven, hallowed be Thy name. Thy—"

The gunshot echoed up and down the shaft. If it had been a beam of light, it would have crisscrossed the tunnel a thousand times and left brilliant zigzagging trails behind. But it wasn't light. It was darkness, and it left only a dead boy.

When the echoes fell silent, the cart began to roll up the shaft, and a creaking filled the void.

DEAD WEIGHT. BRILLIANCE HERE IS the very definition of it. I'm guessing he's a hundred sixty, a hundred seventy pounds, and I'm definitely not a power lifter. But I've got to get him out of this cart.

I slip my hands under his greasy armpits, tighten my stomach muscles to protect my lower back, and give him the old heave-ho. He's almost as sluggish dead as he was alive. He's certainly not thinking any less clearly. He was *such* a cretin.

There, I've got him about halfway out, but I have to stop for a breather, get ready for the next move. I want to swing him over to the shaft as smoothly as possible. The more he bounces around, the more I'm going to have to clean up. As it is, I'll have to come back down here with a broom, dust pan, and a rag and bucket for the blood drips. But I must say I'm feeling good, almost giddy, despite all the setbacks and adversity.

This young fool's appearance and predictable demise make me feel like I'm doing a high-wire act without the net.

Actually, he's the one who could do with a net right about now.

I've moved him right to the edge of the shaft, right under the steady gaze of Harriet from Mineola, New York. *Family Planning #3*. Say hello to Harriet, Brilliance, she's the last face you're ever going to see.

I give him the boot, and as he falls I listen to his body bouncing off one wall and then another. I'm guessing it's a hundred-, a hundred-fifty-foot drop. Not a straight shot by any means, and he smacks off the walls the whole way down.

There, I heard him land. Land? No, I don't think so, but I do hear his flight, let's say, suddenly arrested. Satisfying to the ear. Richly so. Like the snap of a stem when you pluck a flower in full bloom.

I dust my hands and head up to the foundry. So much to do, so little time, and I need to get some sleep.

The first hint of the sun wakes me, and I'm up and about in seconds.

It doesn't take me long to find his bike, but I'm lucky: I literally stumbled upon it. It could have taken an hour or more to troll through all the desert a half mile behind the foundry. I have to hand it to him, he did a commendable job of coating it with mud; it could easily have sat out here unnoticed till the first rain.

I ride it back to the foundry, take off the wheels, the handlebars, and seat. I feel like I'm running a chop shop, but it's the only way to fit that bike through the hole that goes down into the mine. I lug the parts down to Harriet, and return the bike to its rightful owner. No thief am I.

Now I'm faced with the far more daunting task of dealing with his car. There'll be no taking that apart and stuffing it down a mine shaft. No driving it away either. Better I should write "I am guilty of murder" on a Post-it note and stick it to the end of my nose. Neither can I afford to have his car sitting around in the open anywhere near here.

I'm going to have to ride my bike all the way to the mouth of the canyon, a conclusion I am loath to endorse. I dread the toil, but if I do have to move his car to a less obvious site, if that pestilential little twerp was lying about leaving it in some sandstone cave, then I can't have my Jeep out there begging the most uncomfortable of questions from anyone who happens by.

Before departing, I run upstairs to check on the monitor. Look at them, cuddling like a couple of kittens. I'm sorely tempted to wake Her Rankness with the news about dispatching her boyfriend to the bottom of a mine shaft, but frankly fear this would upset the delicate balance of these two young bodies. I've no time for her grief when she delights me so by cavorting with Diamond Girl, who sports her basest desires with the abandonment of the determinedly doomed.

Reluctantly, I drag myself away from the sight of their mostly unclothed but chastely clutching bodies. This means turning from flashes of thigh and hips and back so luscious that I am all but driven to run down there and lick them. But I can't do that. I can't even afford to dally for the lavish memories that fire my fantasies.

It takes an hour and a half of hard pedaling before I arrive at the mouth of the canyon. I'm dripping with perspiration, and I've chafed myself where it hurts the most.

The good news is that Brilliance did not lie about where he parked his car, which is actually a behemoth SUV. I filched his key fob first thing, but I won't need it; he drove the Comanche or Trail Smasher or whatever it's called all the way into the cave. Only the back remains partially visible, and I can cover that up much as he camouflaged his bike.

This too is work, make no mistake about it. I have to use my shirt to haul mud from the riverbank. It's a healthy hike back to the cave, and I have to tread this path six times before the exposed flank is completely smeared. The entire time, mind you, I'm worried about helicopters and planes. What would I tell them? That I'm taking a mud bath? It would appear that I have, but appearances at a time like this do not equal plausibility.

By the time I finish, you'd have to walk right into the cave before you'd see that vehicle. I swallow all but the last few ounces in my water bottle. The sun is strong, and I've a long way back. The only good to come out of this mud hauling, besides the obvious benefit of hiding that hulk, is that my shirt and shorts are the color of the earth. I am no more conspicuous than dirt on dirt.

It's a grim ride back, but a lonely one, and for this I am grateful.

When I arrive at the compound, I'm as weary as a priest among the pagans. It's ten o'clock, a little after to be precise, and the sun is beating me up. I shove the bike over, sincerely hoping I never have to endure its torture again. My crotch feels like it's been worked by a vengeful virgin with a power sander. The shower raises a sting that leaves me gasping. But after thirty seconds or so the pain passes, and a few minutes later I feel much better: clean, refreshed, renewed.

I towel off, carefully attend to the afflicted skin, and return to my bedroom and switch on the monitor. There they are, awake, but not particularly frisky. They look sullen, which in my view is the dank opposite of sexy. I've never found pouting all that appealing.

Then it hits me: they must be starving. So I put together a wholesome breakfast tray: melons and yogurt, green tea and cereal, and two big bran muffins.

Diamond Girl brightens at the sight of me. Or is it the food? I slip the tray into the cage and ask how they're doing. My first mistake of the day.

"How are we doing?" Diamond Girl says with a swagger. "Oh, just swell. We're living the life down here. Club Med has nothing on this place."

She looks, let me say, not as cheerful as she has of late. Not as sexy either. She better watch out. If she loses her appeal, she loses her life.

"You need nourishment," I tell her.

"You're *so* right, Ashley." She tosses a bran muffin in the air, catches it neatly. "Something to keep me regular. Who wouldn't want to use that thing every day." She glares at the kitty box.

Yes, she's in rare form today.

This time when she tosses the muffin, I have to duck.

With her insolence, her sneering rejection, she has me in her thrall again. And she knows it. I can see it in her eyes. The way they light up, the way they *burn*. And she knows I know, because she smiles, stretches, yawns, and turns to Her Rankness, who has remained in the background.

I stare at Diamond Girl's rump, and my stream of desire runs as deep as ever. I'm revisited by the powerful urge to open the cage and join them, but I stop myself from such foolishness, recognize that I'm far too tired to think clearly. Yet as I force my feet into retreat, I still can't resist looking back. No, it's more than the act of looking, I'm scavenging for an excuse, any excuse, to lose my discipline, my remarkable restraint. If Diamond Girl were to kiss her girlfriend right now, or lift her top and suck her breasts, I would lose all control. I am so close that I teeter, bone china on the very edge of a counter.

But they are whispering, and as I approach the stairs my foot crushes the bran muffin. The last I hear of them is laughter.

Phone messages. Eleven since I checked yesterday. It's actually slowing down. I would change my number but what good would it do? It's already unlisted. These reporters must pay someone off at the telephone company. Or maybe they sell it to one another. If they were a real plague, they'd wipe out the planet.

I delete one after another, soothing myself with the electronic waste basket.

My finger freezes when I hear that voice. I don't believe it. It's Lauren Reed. She's come to Moab looking for Her Rankness. The little media whore. It's not enough that she gets to butt her way into a book with me, but now she's come up with some desperate gambit to glean even more publicity. She's "insisting"—who does she think she is, insisting on *anything* from me?—that we meet. "It's urgent," she adds redundantly, though I doubt redundance would register in the doldrums of her brain. That woman is as common as clay on a potter's pants.

I haven't the stomach to return her call, but knowing she's here makes it all the more likely that she really is having a career-enhancing affair with Ring Ding the reporter. I'm surprised she's had time to come up for air.

Delete. I wish I could do the same to her.

I also wish I could nap, but every time I think of what Brilliance did to Jolly Roger's arm, I get agitated all over again.

There's no replacing that arm. It's not as if it's some uncle's favorite beer mug that can be glued together. There's no gluing together hundreds of shards and millions of particles of dust. He mangled my art, mangled my sculpture, mangled months of planning and careful execution, and all he could say was I'm sorry.

*I'm sorry.* What pitiable words they are. If I had a dollar for every time I've heard them, I could start up a cruise line to rival Cunard's.

It was nothing but joy to wash my hands of him so easily. His fate was shaky from the start. I knew it the moment I saw him cringing behind the cart, whimpering like some worthless dog. He should have considered himself lucky, and he would have if he'd known the fate of the others. Any number of those fools would have exchanged their immortalization for his immediate demise. Most would have done it in a heartbeat.

# CHAPTER
## 20

ONE MORE SIP AND SHE thought she'd spit. Lauren eyed the murky brown microbrew suspiciously, as suspiciously as she'd eye Ashley Stassler, if she ever got to see him. She put the glass down on the table, adding to the water rings that she and Ry had been making for the past half hour. What she wouldn't do for a nice cold Budweiser. Heresy to admit, very politically *in*correct, but there you go, the result of another deeply discouraging day in the desert.

"It's the temperature," Ry offered, reading her disgust, appraising his own dark gloomy glass. "They don't want to overwhelm the taste by serving it too cold."

"Please, overwhelm the taste. By all means," Lauren said. "Do you think they'd throw me out if I asked for an ice cold Bud?"

Ry laughed.

"Look," she said, "I'm going out there. I'm not going back to Portland without seeing that guy."

They'd been talking about Stassler before the brew's bitter taste had set her off.

"Fine. I'll go with you," Ry said before pushing his own glass away.

"No, you won't," she said so firmly that Leroy, lying at her feet, opened one eye. "You'll just end up blowing your whole relationship with him, and that could blow the book. What's the point in doing that anyway? I'm a big girl. I can take care of myself, and your book is getting better all the time."

"For all the wrong reasons."

"For whatever reasons, it's turning out to be a lot more interesting than you could have figured."

Not only did Ry have the strange disappearance of Kerry Waters to include in his account of Ashley Stassler, but Jared Nielsen had also been missing for two days now.

"I still don't buy this thing about him taking off," Ry said.

Neither did Lauren. The two of them had told Sheriff Holbin about the young man's stated desire to go out to Stassler's ranch to look for Kerry. They'd also told Holbin about the mine. It turned out the sheriff already knew about it, and he bridled when it became clear that they'd assumed he wouldn't think of checking with the Division of Mines on his own, as a matter of course. Their bit of investigation, in the sheriff's dour view, was barely noteworthy. As for Jared's pronouncement that he wanted to go out there, the sheriff said it was as "common as tumbleweed" for a killer, crook, or crackhead to offer to solve the crimes that they themselves had committed.

"Does the name OJ mean anything?" he'd said. "They all do it. 'I'm going to find the killer.' Or 'I'm going to find the guy who stole my mother's TV.' Meanwhile, they're out playing golf, or smoking up some more drugs. I've heard it all before."

He probably had, but it still didn't dampen Lauren's belief that the sheriff should get a search warrant for Stassler's ranch.

"Do you think they'll ever go back out?" she asked Ry.

"You mean with a warrant? Tear the place upside down?"

Lauren nodded.

"Nope." Ry picked up his glass, apparently thought better of it, and put it back down. "I seriously doubt it. Holbin really does need at least a shred of evidence linking the disappearance of at least one of those kids to Stassler."

"He's got that!" Lauren said. "Kerry worked there, and Jared said he was going to go out there."

"This is property rights country down here, and they're not going to run roughshod over some man's land on a whim. Especially the local celebrity's."

"So a judge needs one piece of evidence?" Lauren said. "Like a bloody shirt, or a bloody pair of underpants?"

"That's a bit dramatic, but something on that order."

"How about a pair of bike pants with the crotch missing? Something," her hands put together an imaginary puzzle, "that fits the pieces they found?"

"They would call that a smoking gun."

"I'll keep my eyes open when I go out there. Maybe he's got it hanging on the clothes line."

"Lauren," Ry said with exaggerated patience.

"No, that's what you're saying, right? That without that kind of 'evidence,' Mr. Ashley Stassler is off limits."

She spoke so loudly that a table full of twenty somethings with goatees and nose rings stirred at the sound of the famous name.

Ry leaned forward and spoke softly. "*I'm* not saying it. Don't confuse me with Holbin. I'm with you. But how are you going to get in there? He keeps that gate locked."

"It's not a fortress. You said it's a barbed wire fence with a cattle gate. And you said he left a key stashed behind the fence post."

"Because he knew I was coming, but you don't really think he keeps it out there all the time, do you?"

"Then I'll climb the damn fence and walk in. It's only a mile or two, right?"

Ry shook his head, but he was smiling. "You got game, girl."

He took her hand. She pulled away and leaned back.

"Not really. I don't want to go out there, but I can't leave without seeing him. When I go home, I have to believe that I did what I could."

That night their lovemaking assumed a new urgency, as if it were both the last time they'd be together, and the first time too. It felt pure and driven, intoxicating and intimate, like she was opening the deepest recesses of her body to him, letting him find her heart in all that he kissed and caressed. The intensity of his touch, and the earnestness of his emotion, felt fundamentally different from what she'd experienced with other men. They had made promises with their bodies, and broken them with their words. Artists mostly, too in love with their own delusions of grandeur to ever fall in love with love itself.

She received Ry's hands on her face as she had received all of him, with a gratitude she'd never known before. His fingertips stroked her cheeks, and his lips lifted away her tears, the ones that had fallen at the very moment when they'd spent the last of their desires, when they'd collapsed into each other's arms and he'd looked into her overflowing eyes and told her that he loved her.

# CHAPTER
## 21

I SLEPT THROUGH THE ENTIRE night again, from eight to six-thirty. It's been years since I've slept this well. It must be the relief I feel over resurrecting *Family Planning #9*, my dear June, Jolly Roger, and Sonny-boy. It came to me in a most gratifying inspiration that I needn't lose them at all, that Jolly-Roger's mishap will lend *humanity* to my series, a humbleness to undermine the "hubris" that some of my lesser critics have complained of. Millions of men have lost a limb. It's only natural that I'm sensitive enough to represent them. As for the Vandersons' entirely superfluous flesh, it has joined the rich lime bath where I disposed of all the others, while their skeletons have assumed their rightful places in the parade. Proud additions, each of them. So yes, their earthly selves are already forgotten, but their individual forms will rise forever.

Only a man at peace with himself can sleep as I do, though there was a dream, a strangely violent one. It didn't last long, but it's what I awoke to. A man had been threatening his wife, maybe beating her. She had a boy by her side, he couldn't have been older than eight. But somehow the man tripped, landed on his butt. She pulled a shotgun out of a closet and walked up to him. He crawled backward like a crab until he was against a wall, I think in a kitchen. He was moaning horribly, almost bellowing in fear. She shoved the barrel right into his chest. I saw the two big openings at the end, and she pulled the trigger.

Click.

Nothing.

Click.

Nothing again. She turned to run away, grabbing the kid as the man stood up. Now his moans became a roar. He was going to get even with her. He grabbed a handsaw, the kind you'd use on two by fours, and started after her. He was going to cut her to pieces, the thug.

What's with that? I'm sure some shrink would have a field day figuring that one out. I abhor violence. What I do down in the cellar has no more to do with real violence than do birds when they build their nests. I'm creating art, and I need my materials. Everyone has to die, but these people get to live into the *un*foreseeable future. Long after this young century is over, long after this ranch has been turned into another subdivision or strip mall, every one of my subjects will be alive in the eyes of the world, which is a lot more life than any of them knew before I came along. Except for Diamond Girl, they were all as numb as ice.

The remote is on the nightstand, and I reach for it to check on the Bobbsey twins. That's the real reason I'm as stiff as a pear cactus, not because of some thug with a saw.

I punch in the extremely elaborate code, and there they are. Diamond Girl—the demons must be dancing again—is naked, sitting in side view talking to Her Rankness, who is clothed. I haven't captured the spectacle of her nudity in real time yet, only that single instance when Diamond Girl was fondling herself and the two of them were kissing, when they christened my fantasies with the enticements of voyeurism, its everlasting lure of participation, though how could I ever do it safely?

The question suggests the depth of my desire, doesn't it? That I would even contemplate myself with both of them at the same time. Already I have started to consider the obstacles, which more than anything means the possibility, however remote, that they would try to disable me. And though I am hesitant to admit it, I do have to accept that those two girls could indeed disable me if I were to lie with them, if I were to *open* myself to them.

Diamond Girl brought out a little of this fear, but I grew relaxed with her until we began that damnable chat, with her riddles and ridicule, the *Yes, I fucked my father. No, I didn't. Now do you think you know me?* routine. But I am drawn to the idea of both of them. I find pleasure even in the prospect of squeezing the athletic limbs of Her Rankness.

My sheet has the appearance of a tent, and I am of the mind of a three-ring circus with these two, the simultaneous sex that only a threesome can inveigle. I've done it before. What artist or musician of any fame hasn't? You'd have to be empty of imagination not to try. But never have I craved it. What are these two? My very own sirens? That's what worries me finally, that they will lure me to my death.

I switch cameras to better reveal Diamond Girl from the front. Yes, the full frontal nudity that so entranced Sonny-boy when he first saw his sister blazing naked. As I settle down to this, resting against the headboard, lifting the sheet, Her Rankness walks into the picture. Diamond Girl rises to her knees, and begins to wrestle Her Rankness's jeans off. Her Rankness offers no resistance. She just stands there as her jeans come down, and then her panties. Neither does she move when Diamond Girl presses her face against her muff. I cannot see exactly what my wicked little witch is up to with her mouth, her lips, that lascivious tongue of hers, but her hands are clutching those full round cheeks, pale as milk, and I can see her fingers flexing and unflexing in some strange rhythm that absolutely transfixes me. It is no longer the mystery of the mouth that I find so engaging, but the graphic possession of those hands. Diamond Girl is a miracle of longing. A blind man could see this. She squeezes, she kneads, she pleasures.

The bed is behind me before I realize just what it is that I'm doing. I take the stairs three at a time, throw open the door to the barn, the one to the cellar, bound down those final steps, and run past the bone parade.

My erection is enormous, straining upward, as if to split its own skin. Both girls pause to stare at it, and Diamond Girl—who but Diamond Girl?—waves me in.

The keys! I've left the keys upstairs. In my rush I have left without them. And do I dare enter this cage without my knife? Do I dare enter it at all?

I try to calm myself. I consider relieving this urge, this grilling need, as I stand apart, but cannot bear this awful thought for more than a miserable moment. I am tired of my own touch when all I want is theirs.

Then take Diamond Girl out. Take her out and take her upstairs, but *don't* . . . don't go in there with the two of them. For fleeting moments my caution prevails. I know without question that this would be the greatest risk I have ever taken, and for what? For nothing more than I can have at the opening of any of my shows. But I delude myself. At my openings I have middle-aged women admiring me, making their lewd allusions. I don't have Diamond Girl, and I certainly don't have the body of a young bicyclist whose most intimate urgencies have been anointed with the sweet emollient of her own sex.

This debate, these wildly frantic words cause me only to pause, but the admonitions that I offered myself only seconds ago now feel as weak as doors made of reeds, and I trample them easily as I climb the stairs. I even tell myself that I will get the key just for Diamond Girl, when I know this is no more than the permission to move, to linger no longer, for surely I know better. I know that Her Rankness is part of my desire too, that when I saw Diamond Girl's hands on her flesh it was as if a blessing had been bestowed on those hard haunches, those athletic buttocks, and that they would rise to desire as easily as I. Now I see them both all over me, and I can see myself all over them. I even see Her Rankness's mouth closing over mine, the sleek feel of her young tongue so eager to learn, so willing to please.

The key is in the . . . bedroom. Yes, in my trousers. I race back, this ungainly protuberance still bobbing up and down, smacking my belly, my legs, hurling itself about in a madness all but heedless of its master.

I fumble with the keys, fumble them badly, but at last I have them in hand. There on the monitor I watch them return to their pleasures, Diamond Girl always the initiator, and Her Rankness always so passive. It's often like this at the start. I've read about the bulls in prison, how the one enforces the code of pleasure in the other until a new link is formed in the chain that binds them all together in the rich treason of their own sex.

That binds me to these two young bodies.

I hesitate over the knife, hesitate for long seconds, feel even a diminishment in my member when I consider the use of the blade. See, truly I am a romantic and care nothing for violence. I doubt my heart registers an extra beat when I work, even when the final ball of alginate finds its home at last; but now my heart races, races ahead of me, and I am out the door without the knife, with the assurance that they will give me pleasure, and I will do the same for them.

Down the stairs I sprint again, back into the barn, down the first step when I hear the pounding on the door. Not a knocking. No, this is a *pounding*. This is the sound of men.

I freeze. I don't mind telling you that for two or three seconds I do, in fact, freeze with fear. Then I draw a breath and creep back up into the barn.

More pounding. The door is locked. I will never suffer that oversight again, though in the moments that have so immediately passed I was thankful for the rashness of Her Rankness, for all the succulent possibilities she has brought to life.

I close the door to the cellar, spread the straw back over the stall, and enter the house, locking the door behind me.

When I look out, I could scream. I could kill. I could take a claw hammer and pry out her eyeballs. It's that nympho media whore, that poseur, that *plasterer* standing there looking like the harridan I've imagined from the pictures on the website.

Control yourself. Absolutely control yourself. I am so full of rage I could easily drag her into the basement and strap her down, enact the most wicked of dreams, and she without even an empty shotgun to save her.

But this is out of the question. I urge caution upon myself as the pounding resumes behind me, as I climb the stairs and go to the window above the front door.

You must endure this, I tell myself. You must. You have no choice in the matter.

The window, though little used, slides open.

"What are you doing on my property? And who are you?"

Let's see how the nympho media whore introduces herself.

"I've called you over and over," she shouts, the stentorian wench. "I'm Lauren Reed. We have to talk."

We *have* to do no such thing, I all but shout back at her. But again, I force aside the urge to batter her. It would be much better to get this over with.

"I'll be down in a minute."

I close the window, and as much as I wish I could close her out too, I go to my room and dress quickly, my penis as limp as string. I hate her for this. I look at the monitor where Diamond Girl has her lips on the perfectly tiny teat of Her Rankness, and I hate her for all that I am missing.

# CHAPTER
## 22

LAUREN HADN'T FOUND THE KEY to Stassler's gate, just as Ry had predicted, and she'd been forced to climb the barbed wire fence, at one point perching precariously over the top strand as she negotiated shaky footholds for which there could be no failure.

Then she had to pull mightily on the bottom strand while commanding and cajoling Leroy to crawl under it. Her dog showed a real reluctance to bellying along the ground, and she realized that while he might be charming, he was no commando. No endurance hound either: the forty-minute hike from her car to the compound had left him panting by her feet in the hot sun. Whatever security she'd hoped to find in his presence had been rapidly displaced by the reality of his discomfort.

Now she stood by Stassler's door realizing that she was going to have to ask him for water, which she regretted bitterly. She wanted nothing of his favors because she had demands, but they would have to—

Stassler threw open the door, interrupting her thoughts. He

looked every bit as lean and muscled as most of the men in his *Family Planning* series. They might have been modeled after him, except Stassler looked harder, somehow, than even his bronze figures. He wore a sleeveless shirt, and with the sun angled low, the morning shadows threw the taut muscles of his shoulders and arms into sharp relief. The body, she saw, of a young gymnast. Had she read that he had once performed on the high bar and rings, been capable of an iron cross?

"I've been calling you," she said with far less anger than she'd felt when she'd pounded on the door and shouted to him at the window. She'd been softened, as she often was, by meeting the object of her scorn. Ashley Stassler was no longer simply words and ideas, no matter how offensive.

"Yes, that's what you said. But I don't check phone messages anymore. They're tiresome." He spoke as if he were stifling a yawn.

"I want to talk to you about Kerry, but first I need some water for him." Her eyes fell to Leroy, who still lay beside her, panting heavily.

Stassler looked at the dog as if he hadn't noticed him. Lauren detected a slight movement of the sculptor's head. Disgust? Possibly. Nothing approbative, of that she felt sure. But then he walked past her and turned on a spigot protruding from the barn wall. The water sparkled brilliantly in the sun.

"Go on, Leroy," she said.

Her dog rose heavily and walked over to the lush stream, biting at it to drink, his mouth a cavern opening and closing with each attempt.

She thanked Stassler.

"I'm very busy. What is it that you think I can do for you? Or Kerry?"

"You can show me where she was staying, where she slept, where she worked. She was my student," Lauren said with feeling. "I can't have her disappearing. I've got to know everything I can."

"So you can find her? Do you really think you can do that?"

"I don't know," she said earnestly.

"I don't see how I can help you. I've extended every opportunity to the sheriff, and I've talked to more pinhead reporters than the president. I have a lot of work to do. This is a very busy time for me right now. I was in the middle of starting a new project when you interrupted me, and I need to get back before the materials start to cool."

Incredibly, he turned to walk away. She took his arm.

"Please. I'm trying to remember all I can about her, because in the end that's all we may have. Can you at least show me her room, her bed, where she ate her meals, where she worked? This is important."

He withdrew his arm, and strode toward the house. He spoke without looking back at her. "I'll give you the tour. And then I'd appreciate it if you'd let me get back to work."

Lauren tried to soak up every detail as she entered the foyer with its copper ceiling. She had a powerfully eidetic memory, and had first understood its blessing in childhood after her father had taken her to the famous boat show at Madison Square Garden in New York City. She'd come home with a great desire to draw, and had spent hours that night sketching the sailboats with photographic precision.

The same powers of observation came to her now as Stassler led her through the lofty living room and down the hall to the bedroom that had been Kerry's.

A change of clothes lay on the floor. A foot away, the girl had left her panties strewn across a pair of flip-flops, as if she'd been in a rush to leave, to pull on the bike pants that would be torn so brutally from her body.

"I didn't touch a thing," Stassler said. His voice, the gesture of his hands, were dismissive.

This offends him, she realized. The violation of order. Underpants, just lying there! What a priss.

Lauren looked through each of the drawers, and under the bed. She opened the closet, having no idea what she might find. Not much, as it turned out. A single dress, a few pairs of pants, jeans mostly. Certainly no "smoking gun," as Ry had put it.

"Are you ready?" Stassler's tone revealed a trace of impatience.

She glanced around once more as she backed out of the bedroom. He showed her the kitchen, ample enough for a team of cooks.

"That's where she ate." He nodded at the breakfast bar. "Fascinating, isn't it?"

She hardly noticed his sarcasm, or the hand that herded her out the door.

"Okay?" he said.

"Thank you." She looked bewildered. She was. Seeing evidence of Kerry without seeing the girl herself had finally unmoored Lauren.

He walked her out of the house and toward the road.

"No," she said, feeling as if she'd snapped out of a fugue. "I want to see where she worked."

Now Stassler appeared perplexed, but it was all for effect:

"You mean *you* want to see *my* foundry, *my* workplace? You've got to be kidding." He circled his finger in the air as if to say, Guess again.

"I'm not kidding," she said grimly. "And I'd like to take her portfolio with me. Do you know where it is? I didn't see it in her bedroom."

"I don't know. I haven't seen it for a while."

"What do you mean? You were supposed to be helping her."

"I don't suppose she was here long enough to benefit from my counsel."

This infuriated Lauren, his casual disregard of the compact, the girl, and now her.

But before she could speak up, he pointed to the foundry.

"You want to see it? Fine. Let's go."

He led her to the brick building, the one she'd first seen from the helicopter.

Lauren settled Leroy in the shade of the front wall and followed Stassler inside.

She'd been in a lot of foundries, but none as large as this. Cranes, chains, grates and tanks, tables, tools, cabinets, and crucibles spread out before her. He had the luxury of space.

Stassler waved his hand at the room. "Look around. Maybe her portfolio's in here."

It's not in here. She felt this as clearly as she felt the surprisingly cool air that greeted her. Every item in the foundry had its place. Ashley Stassler was a sculptor who would know where he'd placed every last bolt or chisel. Or a portfolio.

Still, she would look. She'd try to add to the paucity of details from which she might construct a portrait of Kerry's final days.

She walked past a bench with a mallet and clamps hanging from a rack right above it, and stepped into a partitioned area. He walked up behind her. A boxy wooden cabinet stood against the wall. Why bother with the partition, she wondered.

"You don't like my sculpture anymore, do you?" Stassler said.

"What are you talking about?" Stassler's personal tone, after so much chilly distance, startled her.

"You liked it at one time. You *adored* it. You sent me the review that you wrote for your campus newspaper. 'Ashley Stassler not only understands the underbelly of our age, he comprehends its dark cousin called the future.' Overblown, but that's typical of an undergrad."

She was flabbergasted that he could quote from a review she'd written some twenty years ago. It took her a moment to respond.

"You're right. If I'm going to be honest, I'd have to say I'm not a fan."

"I can always tell."

"Do you really care?" She couldn't imagine that he did. But then why bring it up?

"Of course not," he replied quickly. "But I'm curious to know what changed your mind."

She shrugged. "Tastes change. I used to like the Dave Clark Five, but that doesn't mean I do anymore."

Her hand fell to the cabinet. She rubbed the fine silty dust between her fingers. It felt familiar, good.

He shook his head, more noticeably this time, and she understood that she'd nicked his ego with her reference to a schlocky sixties band, placing him by implication in a tacky milieu that would never square with his inflated notion of his own importance. But again, she couldn't understand why he would care when the art world was full of sycophants ready to sing him choruses of praise.

"Seen enough?" he said.

"I suppose." Her hand fell from the cabinet. A ripple of air, cooler than the room, coated her fingers; but if she noticed the sensation, it was quickly lost as she followed him out, once more recording every visual detail. But why bother, she asked herself. If this is all that you can piece together of her life here, then you have nothing at all. And it's not as if he's got Kerry's body stashed behind a table. He's got only these. Her eyes had taken in the three alginate forms, eerily headless. Then she saw that the male figure had a shattered arm.

"How did that happen?"

He glared at her, as if she had no right to ask. "It was a mistake," he said icily. "And it'll never happen again."

In moments they were back under the bright sun. When they reached the barn, she opened the spigot for Leroy, who bit off half a dozen more mouthfuls before he quit. She cupped her hand and drank as well. Stassler never offered to get her a glass, but he did surprise her by saying that he'd give her a lift back to the gate.

You must be in an awful hurry to get rid of me. But her first thought quickly succumbed to her second, which was the desire to save herself and her dog from the hot trek back.

"Thanks. I'll take it."

He led her past the corner of the barn to the Jeep. The padlocked doors caught her eye.

"What's in there?"

"Nothing."

"Then why is it locked up?"

"I don't want mice and every other rodent in the desert running around in there."

"Could I see it?"

"This is my *house*," he said. "I can't believe you're asking to go through my private quarters."

"I'm not asking for that. This is the barn. Your home is upstairs. I have respected your privacy. I never asked to see that." Though she wondered if she should have pressed that point too.

"You knew better." His words suddenly sounded strident, spiteful. He seemed to notice this too; his lips pinched closed. Then he recovered, saying, "There's nothing in there. You're going to be disappointed," as he walked past her and unlocked the doors.

She didn't reply, but felt he was probably right; she'd been disappointed time and again in her search for Kerry.

The barn was as barren as he'd said. Straw in the stalls, that's all. Maybe a dozen of them, but no sign of horses: no bridles, saddles, not a thing. Empty as a cave.

But if he's so damned worried about mice, why's he leaving them all this straw to make nests? Who knows? She was through asking him questions. Not one of them had produced a satisfying answer.

Lauren turned and took two steps toward the entrance when Stassler said, "Come on, boy, let's go," and clapped his hands.

She looked back and saw Leroy pawing the straw in the last stall on the left.

"Leroy," she commanded sharply, "come."

Stassler stepped away as she walked up to her dog.

She grabbed him by the collar at the very moment his claws hooked an O-ring, snapping it upright before it fell with a clatter.

Lauren, honestly perplexed, turned to Stassler; but he was already beside her, grabbing her arm.

"Get your hands off me," she shouted, and Leroy turned his head from the O-ring to the man who had seized his master.

His growl alone released Stassler's grip. Leroy backed him into the opposing stall as Lauren, stiff with tension, looked from Stassler to the O-ring and back again several times in two or three seconds.

Then as she reached for the handle, he yelled "No!" and lunged forward. Leroy bit him right on the thigh.

Stassler swore in pain as Lauren lifted the thick wooden door. She shouted, "Anybody down—" but before she could finish, Kerry screamed, "I am! I am! Get me out of here."

Lauren looked once more at Stassler, pinned against the wall, bleeding through the tear in his pants. Leroy had released his bite, but at a price no man would want to pay: the dog's seething muzzle, white teeth bared, was right up against Stassler's crotch. The sculptor looked ashen.

Lauren raced down the stairs, saw the bone parade and cage, and sucked in a breath that could have been her last for all the confirmation of death it contained.

She ran across the cellar to where Kerry gripped the bars. A naked girl stood next to her.

"The keys," Kerry shouted. "He keeps them on him. He's always got them."

Lauren took the stairs back up to the barn, frightened by what she might find. Stassler with a gun? Stassler gone to get one? But Leroy hadn't conceded an inch, and Stassler stood as frozen as any of his sculpture, evidently fearful that to move at all would be to concede far more than a mere inch.

"I want the keys," she yelled, inciting Leroy to growl louder.

"They're upstairs, in my bedroom," Stassler said nervously.

"Empty your pockets."

"He'll bite me."

"No, he won't," Lauren said, not knowing and not caring if this was true.

Stassler reached a hand into his left pocket with agonizing slowness. He pulled it out in the same fearful manner, trailing only the dull fabric.

"The other one," Lauren snapped.

"I can't," Stassler said, his eyes dropping to Leroy, as if to engage her in an unspoken understanding; but she wanted no part of it.

"Do it or he'll eat you alive." Again, she had no idea if any of this was true and didn't care as long as Stassler did exactly what she told him.

He reached in, and this time when he unfolded his pocket a set of keys came out.

"Throw them here."

He made a weak toss that fell short of her reach. She scrambled forward, scooped them up, and tore back down the stairs. As she ran across the earthen floor, she realized that from this day forward her acute visual memory would no longer be a blessing, but a curse: the bone parade, with its grotesquely clothed skeletons in their grisly postures, would haunt her forever.

She tried three keys before she found the one that worked. But as soon as she swung the door open, the naked girl tackled Kerry and pleaded with her to stay.

Stay? She must be out of her mind. Lauren hurled herself on top of them, trying to pull the naked girl off. It would have been so much easier if she'd been clothed. The girl surprised her by releasing Kerry, and Lauren made the mistake of letting go of her.

The girl bolted out the cage door and tried to slam it shut. Lauren threw her shoulder into the metal, bruising herself and knocking the air out of her lungs, but saving them from this prison.

She watched as the girl fled up the stairs. Kerry helped her to stand, and the two of them hobbled past the skeletons.

The burning pain in Lauren's shoulder started to fade as they climbed up into the barn. They found Stassler still pinned to the wall, but no sign of the girl.

Kerry turned on him, screaming, "I hope you die, you son of a bitch. Die!"

Lauren pulled her away. "Come on. Let's go!"

They ran out of the barn, right toward the Jeep. Lauren tried to yank the driver's door open, but it was locked, and the keys . . . Christ, the keys were in the cage door!

She turned back, intent on one more trip down the stairs, when she saw Leroy bounding up. Looking past him, panic rising, she spotted Stassler hunched over, but hurrying out of the horse stall.

Lauren spun back around, grabbed Kerry, and dragged her to the right, toward the uneven plain of the desert.

"We can't take the road," she gasped. "He'll drive after us."

She led the girl toward the rugged terrain, the dry washes and sinewy trees that would stop any vehicle. But even as they stumbled down sudden dips and slogged through sandy stream beds, Lauren knew that Stassler would track them down by foot, if he had to. He could never let them get away, no matter how hurt, although she doubted he was truly hobbled: Leroy, for all his power, had not torn his femoral artery. Lauren had looked for gushing blood, but seen only a seeping wound. Stassler could still move, and that meant that she and Kerry, and the dog at their side, would soon be at odds with the harsh land that would have to hide them.

# CHAPTER
## 23

I TORE AFTER THEM, AND I was no more than twenty yards back when my leg seized up. In an instant, I found myself stumbling, humbled by a grotesque pain, as if a serrated knife were having its way down there. Then I realized that even if I did catch up with them, that goddamned dog would turn on me again if I didn't have my gun. I also realized that I needed a painkiller if I was going to chase them down.

That filthy animal ripped right through my thigh. Now I've got to keep my eyes on them, *and* I've got to quickly scrub out this wound. An infection from that filthy beast will finish me faster than those two harridans.

They're making it tough on me, heading for the foothills, but it'll be murderous for them. They have no water, no food. They're finished. It's their fate. It plays out in every step they take. I can find joy in this, and I do, but I rue the loss of Diamond Girl. She saw me at that goddamned dog's mercy. She stopped and looked me right in the eye. I thought she'd help. I thought I'd have this beautiful young naked damsel coming to my rescue, but then she fled out the doors without ever looking back. My last view of Diamond Girl was of her glorious ass, those hard round cheeks that I'd pressed my face to, whose valley I'd traveled so eagerly with my tongue.

I have no idea where she is now. I cannot see her. But if I'm given this grievous choice, to chase Her Rankness, who paused too, but only to swear her ignorant anger at me, and nympho media whore, or Diamond Girl, I must let my little lover go. She's the least likely to turn the state on me. If I know her at all, she'll prevail in her own perversity, and to do that she must grant me mine. It's the silent code we share, that we've always shared, the marvelous seeds from which we root: hers in bud, mine in bloom.

The disinfectant burns. Oh . . . oh . . . it *burns*. It bubbles over the wound, forcing eruptions of blood from the purpled, savaged skin.

I keep my eye on them as much as I keep it on my wound. I spread ointment over the damaged flesh, tape gauze over it, and throw on my shorts and a shirt that will cover my shoulders. I grab my hat, day pack, and water bottles. I fill them both from the refrigerator tap. Icy water, thirty-four degrees. I look for Tylenol with codeine, but I'm out. I pop three Advils, and hope they take the edge off the throbbing in my leg. Then I stuff trail mix into my pack, along with two bananas. I'll be traveling light, but not nearly as light as they are. I long for the moment when I'll find them suffering in the sun, their throats as swollen as sponges, as dry as dust.

As I head out the door, I grab my gun, but I warn myself not to get carried away. It would be a terrible mistake to kill them out there, because then I'd have to carry or drag them back. My Jeep could never navigate all the dry streambeds and drop-offs. So as much as I revel in the rich rewards that await me, I must control myself until I have them safely in the cellar. Gratification must be delayed.

Their footprints angle across a dry streambed about twenty feet wide. It appears that already they're flagging, although I'm willing to grant that this may be mostly desire on my part, for surely they can't be weakening so quickly. Two healthy young women. I expect they'll be good for at least a couple of hours out here, and many more back in the cellar. And if they're not, if they're the sort who want to give up easily, then I'll use methamphetamine to return them to the nightmare of consciousness.

Even as I track them, I'm planning, getting all the details down. Perhaps I'll even use the needle myself so that all three of us can properly enjoy the extremes that inevitably ensue. There's no need to tire when the effects are so dire.

The giddiness again. I'm definitely working without a net now. The variables are many. A plane could fly overhead. A mountain biker could have the ill fortune of trespassing, and the good luck to get away. All this frames my focus in an adamantine manner. It's as if I'm nothing now but the pure force of vengeance, and there's beauty in this, as there's beauty in all purity. Don't let it be said that I don't appreciate beauty in every one of its manifold manifestations.

The foothills rise before me, and the La Sal Mountains beyond them, but between the hills and the mountains lies the river, and they'll go no farther than the cliffs that form its precipitous bank. They won't jump. No sane person would ever do that. This isn't *Butch Cassidy and the Sundance Kid*. This is the Golden Gate Bridge they'll be staring down from, and all they'll see are rocks and whitewater a thousand feet below. Of course, they could be insane with fear by the time they get there, insane with heat prostration, insane with the crude mechanics of escaping a man who will hunt them down wherever they go, unless they *do* choose to jump into the river, an eventuality that would not be entirely bad. The fall would kill them, and their bodies would wash down to the run out. I could scarcely be blamed for their foolishness, though I'd grieve privately for the loss of such rich opportunity.

I can't see them, but I cannot avoid spotting their tracks, which appear before me as clear as paint splatters. Already the dog lags behind, confirming my delightful suspicion about his wretched demise. Look at those paw prints. Any moment now I expect I'll find a single long line between them from his tongue dragging in the dirt. What a beast. What a bite. What a bounty he'll be.

My water bottle is slick with condensation. I swallow my first drink with a smile, with the added satisfaction that after what—twenty, thirty minutes?—I need water. They've been out even longer, had a good ten-, fifteen-minute lead. The sour taste of thirst must be coating their tongues. I expect they're no more ready to survive the desert than a couple of penguins.

When I do catch them, I'll have to monitor them carefully. I really don't want them dropping from the heat. I might even have to give them a drink, make them kneel like communicants with their mouths open, seeking the sweet wafer of water. More likely it's the position assumed thrice daily by nympho media whore to wheedle her way into a book with me. I wonder if he'll include her after she's gone, a posthumous honor, as an honor it certainly will be if she's still sharing those pages with Ashley Stassler.

Now, only now does it occur to me with the clammiest of feelings that if anything happens to her, anything at all, the authorities will be all over my ranch. As long as I get Her Rankness back, her escape changes nothing. She's the biker who was abducted from a jeep trail four thousand feet above Moab. Brilliance's disappearance follows because he remains the suspect. But nympho media whore cannot disappear. This stops me, stops me faster than a rattlesnake on my path, so deadly is the threat of this possibility. For the first time I ask myself, what am I going to do? I've been in such a rush to doctor myself, to set off after them, that I haven't considered these monstrous implications. And then as quickly, the answer comes to me: she'll survive long enough to announce to the world that she's abandoned her paltry career to live with me. She'll make telephone calls at my behest, to her college, her friends. She'll even joke that she's like that graduate student who showed up at J. D. Salinger's house and never left. It'll surely make sense to the perspicacious eyes of the art world because her sudden devotion to me will testify to the greatness of my work, even as it implicitly devalues all the junk she did on her own. Best of all, only a fool would include her in the book after such a frank concession. It might even force Ring Ding to reconsider the other three mediocrities with which he intends to cloud those pages.

All of this will come to her easily with a knife to her eyes. Why, the phone will seem like a savior to her by then, a means to bargain for her literal vision. Don't I know my subjects? Don't I? She won't be the first woman to abandon her own vapid ambitions for a loftier association with a man. No one will question it. They'll forget her. As well they should anyway. I'll simply hasten the inevitable. And a day, a week, maybe a month after the calls, she'll take a fall. A tragic accident. *We were so in love.*

I hum an old Beatles song, and remember her snide remark comparing me to the Dave Clark Five. Tastes change? Yes, your taste will change. By the time I'm through with you, nympho media whore, you'll love the promise of bronze, the death it will hold. You'll *scream* for its salvation, all twenty-one-hundred degrees of molten metal to drape over your hapless form, to quiet your grief, to shock you into eternal redress.

But you won't get it. I'll hold out on you even then. I'll pump your vein with another injection of methamphetamine. Life, I'll whisper in your ear, is *so* precious!

I'm surprised at the extent of my desire for revenge. Never have I felt such simple, unadulterated blood lust. I feel like a cultural anthropologist as I observe these seething emotions in myself, their raging presence. Part of me remains so distantly cool, analytical, and honestly amazed that the other part wants all of this to turn out as perfectly as possible for the madness of my hands.

Odd, isn't it, what we learn about ourselves if we're truly willing to listen?

I'm closing in on the foothills now. The land ahead rises and falls in undulations not unlike the face of a shar-pei. Dogs are certainly on my mind. No surprise there, given the day's grim experience. I've always hated dogs. Even as a child I thought they were despicable with their slobber and shit and constant shedding.

Oh, look at this: one of them tore her shirt on a prickly cactus. I can see a swirl of footprints where she must have spun around. It probably stuck her too. I'm utterly delighted to see this. Who wouldn't be? They're struggling already. They can sense my presence.

I've heard about women driven insane by stalkers, those urban idiots who track every movement of the women they imagine to be theirs. While I share nothing with those cretins, would execute them instantly if it were left up to me, I do take heart at the extent of terror that can reach these two at such a remove. It's likely, now isn't it, that Her Rankness has told nympho media whore about all that she's witnessed, the slow death of the Vandersons, the playful plugs of alginate? Remembering this, sharing the details, will heighten the horror for Her Rankness, and hearing it for the first time will make her near and dear professor sick with dread, with terror. It'll foul their judgment, compound their errors, and in the end deliver their sorry selves to me, the only one of us who can take true delight in the offerings of this day.

More water. So cold I can feel it wash down into my belly like a cool cloth. Again, I eke out the additional pleasure that comes from knowing their deprivation.

Two hours have passed, and still their tracks show no pause. I had expected them to grow weary by now, to shuffle along. The sun is right above us, and I can feel my head baking inside this hat, but how much worse it would be without its shade. Or clothes. If Diamond Girl is out in the desert, she'll expire first. But she could be anywhere. She could even be hiding in the compound, in the foundry, the house. But perhaps she's not hiding at all. Perhaps she's waiting for me. But I don't really think so. I saw that look on her face. She's left me. She's gone. Her absence makes me want to murder nympho media whore. If that wretch hadn't shown up, I would have been basking in the pleasure of both girls right now. Instead, I'm out here tracking.

I don't want to give the impression that I'm some great white hunter, because I'm not. I've never shot more than stray dogs and rattlesnakes, and only at close range. I'm not even a target shooter. I've never actually hunted anything before, not out here. My excursions to the cities and suburbs are really nothing more than trolling. And yet I'm beginning to understand the appeal of hunting. You follow the tracks, and when you've succeeded, you get your reward—the kill. Or in my case, the capture of what I'll slay at my leisure.

Would that I could make more of their deaths. What I'm thinking of is how appropriate it would be if I could make an example of them, one that I could show the entire world so everyone would have a fair warning of what it means to cross me. But then I tell myself that this is its own blessing because for the first time ever I'll understand killing not in the abstract, not as part of a greater design, burdened as it were with ulterior motive, but in the immediacy of the moment, in the eternal present of hearts that have been seized and silenced. I suspect I'll then understand the essence of death. This is all very Zen, this type of insight, and I'm willing to accept that it has come to me at this time because I've traveled my path straight and true for so many years, never wandering, never growing weary. I have been faithful. So few are.

It's mid-afternoon, about three, and I've just opened my second water bottle. While it's hardly tepid, the water has lost its chill, and I try to put aside the hard fact that really cold water hydrates a body much more efficiently than this dishwater.

But this is hardly a crisis. They're the ones in crisis. The main problem facing me is that I've reached the point where the foothills turn almost entirely to sandstone, and their tracks have disappeared. All along they've been shrewd enough to take to rock wherever they could, but I still picked up paw prints and footprints in the patches of dirt that they had to cross. There's no likelihood of that now: ahead of me are miles of nothing but red-colored stone. It rises and falls like ocean swells, and there are boulders as big as boats. But surely their lack of water will stop them soon, sap their strength and leave them crawling across this wasteland. Their thirst has become my greatest asset.

I look around and see that they could have gone left or right, or straight ahead. With every rise, though, I still expect to find them all prostrate. I've even entertained the thought of their beloved bowwow betraying them for the water he'll smell on me. That would be sweet.

But I haven't come upon them obviously, and I estimate that I'm only a few hours from the cliffs that tower over the Green River. I try not to think about this, but a painful possibility does creep up on me: What am I going to do if I haven't found them by sundown?

The deliverance of this thought leaves me bitter with resolve. Not finding them is not an option.

And that's when I see him. The goddamned dog. The first to falter, just as I figured. What with his black fur, he must be miserable out here. He's stuck his huge head under a rock overhang. It's the only part of him in the shade.

I draw my weapon carefully, and approach him with as much reserve. Remember what he did to you, I tell myself, though I need no reminding; my thigh has throbbed throughout this hunt. So now it's time for this beast to throb for the remainder of his time on earth. I'll do what I can to make sure it's as excruciating as possible. I really will, for I have no desire to see him escape my wrath.

"Hi, pooch."

He growls. No fool he. But his growl isn't the terror I faced in the barn. This is the growl of a drunk in an alley who wants only to be left alone. Too bad.

I pick up a rock the size of a baseball, and strike him hard in the hindquarters. He howls. His heads whips around and he snarls, but he makes no move to charge. Instead, he lies there squinting at me.

This will be great fun. I can walk right up and shoot him in the legs, a bullet for every joint. Give him back the agony that he gave me. But even before I can begin my approach, I realize the foolishness of this impulse. In the silence of this desert, the gun will sound like the heavens crashing. There's no telling if some self-flagellating fool is hiking along the cliffs on the other side of the river. Or a lost mountain biker is floundering across my land. And why give away my presence to the targets of this hunt for the cheap pleasure of tormenting a dog?

I look at him. He really is suffering. He's thirsty. His tongue is as limp as mud. He pants loudly. More than anything, I understand that if I don't give him water, he'll die before I ever have the chance to kill him. This is a dreadful thought. I look for some way to give him a drink, and I'm pleased when I spot a depression in the rock only a few feet from him. But will he rise to the occasion?

He can't possibly know what a water bottle is, or can he? I pull it from my pack and shake it. He eyes me carefully. I approach. He moans, doesn't growl, but moans. He senses the water. I dribble out no more than two spoonfuls. I don't want to waste it if he won't come. But he does. With another moan, he oafishly drags his hind end up, the one I took such pleasure in bruising. He walks up to me completely defeated and drinks the water. He keeps licking the rock long after it's gone. I give him more, about half a cupful, and he slurps it up too, then he stares at me. I point my gun right at his muzzle. "Go back," I tell him, "lie down." He just keeps staring at me.

I pack away the water bottle and start to move on. He stands over that depression as the sun burns away the last trace of moisture.

"I'll be back," I promise him. "Just you wait and see."

LAUREN AND KERRY WERE STILL within earshot when Stassler discovered the ailing dog. Their own parting with Leroy had been tearful, and cut short by the urgency of escape.

They'd listened from behind a boulder as Stassler greeted the heat-stricken animal, the "Hi, pooch" that spoke nothing of kindness and everything of cruelty. And they'd heard the awful confirmation of this in Leroy's painful howl.

Lauren almost bit through her bottom lip when the bastard struck him. She'd briefly debated over waiting to see if Stassler would walk past their boulder so they could double back and rescue Leroy, try to carry him to her car, but the risk of being spotted forced them to move on.

For three hours they'd scrambled over the smooth red rock that formed the foothills, passing through waves of heat so strong they could see it rippling the air. Their thirst had grown desperate, and now they could hear the river hundreds of feet below. The sound of the water was torture enough, but in minutes Lauren knew they'd look down and actually see the foaming rapids in the early evening shadows. All that coolness, all that comfort. They'd be staring at the single substance they needed to survive, and they'd be faced with the certain knowledge that any direct attempt to descend the canyon wall would surely end in death.

They clambered up the final stretch, looking back several times as they had throughout the afternoon. They'd spotted him twice, which had led them to angle to the northeast, while Stassler had continued climbing straight to the cliff. But Lauren strongly suspected that their lead in time and distance had increased only slightly, an advantage more than mitigated by Kerry's shaky condition. The girl's confinement had left her unsure of herself. Lauren didn't know how else to put it. She'd had to hold her hand most of the way, and about an hour ago she'd even been forced to slap her when she'd refused to move from the scant shade of a scrawny desert tree.

Lauren had never hit another person, but there had been no time for discussion.

Now she worried the girl had grown delirious from thirst. Lauren's own tongue felt as hot and swollen as a grilled sausage, as if she'd awakened in the middle of the night with a sore throat that extended to her lips. How they'd survive another hour to sundown was an agony she could not afford to consider. And this wasn't even summer. This was spring in the desert. Temperature of about a hundred degrees. Temperate by local standards.

The edge of the cliff appeared before them, and the river grew louder with every step. She saw her hands dipping into the fierce current, scooping up mouthfuls of icy water, a wish made fervent by the sun baking through her white top. She expected her shoulders and back to blister; cotton provided the equivalent of SPF 14, hardly sufficient for all-day exposure in almost entirely treeless terrain. The few spindles they'd found looked ready to die, and as her thoughts had grown crazed by the unrelenting heat, she decided that if you were a tree, this would have to be your hell, to be rooted through crack-ridden rock to dry dusty soil, to drink but rarely and never enough, and to hear from the birds and the wind that far away were lands so sweet and moist and green that anything could prosper, even you.

If he looks this way, he'll see us. She was seized by this thought. But still they had to search for a way to the water. If they couldn't find one, they'd face at least three or four more hours of trekking before the foothills spilled down to the desert, where they could finally reach the river. A good nine to ten miles, based on what that chopper pilot had said. Without water, she doubted they could do it.

He'd given water to Leroy, though. Maybe he'd give it to us. Stassler's strange act of kindness had puzzled her, as much as his stoning her dog had ignited her weary rage. But she didn't trust his kindness, and now she didn't trust herself for surrendering to the temptation of it, if only for a second.

She inched over to the edge, and saw the river far below. Her incorrigible fear of heights turned her palms damp, and she had to lie on her belly before she could look down for more than a moment. Kerry, on the other hand, came to life as she gazed from the towering precipice. She sat on her heels with the tips of her running shoes hanging over the abyss. It made Lauren's stomach swirl just to glance at her.

They both looked south, scanning the waves of rock for him. They saw nothing but shadows, for this was the time of day when stones no bigger than soccer balls threw shadows as long as football fields. Somewhere in the dark mix, he could be staring at them.

Lauren forced herself to study the wall below them. Her eyes glided far to the right, then far to the left, moving as a giant pendulum might if it were suspended from the violet sky; but everywhere she looked the wall appeared as sheer as plate glass. She defied her fear by inching forward until her head and shoulders protruded over the chasm. Then she reached down and flattened her hands against the rock. It felt frighteningly smooth, with nothing to grip. As her eyes fell from the rock to the river, the tailspin in her stomach forced a fast retreat.

A few feet to her right, she spotted a one-inch seam that ran down the wall for a good fifty feet before it was lost to the shadows and dusky light. But she was no rock climber, and Kerry shook her head.

"We don't even know where it goes," the girl croaked.

Lauren agreed, glad to hear Kerry making sense.

They climbed to their feet and moved on, looking for a drainage in the rock where a spring would feed a tree or a cluster of flowers sprouting from the wall. Anything that might speak of life, of moisture. They'd both seen these growths of green leaves and colorful petals on rides and drives in canyon country. Maybe they'd see one now, when they needed it most of all. The imperative of finding water eclipsed every other concern, including the need to escape Stassler. Without ever saying so directly, both women acknowledged that death would come to them soon if they couldn't find water.

A half hour of suffering later, Kerry hissed at Lauren to stop. She pointed ahead to a break in the clean edge of the cliff. Instead of the near ninety-degree face, a section of rock about thirty feet long and twenty feet wide was missing, leaving behind a roughly shaped rectangle with a fifty- to fifty-five-degree slope. Scary enough that Lauren kept herself several feet away. Kerry, however, stepped right up to it.

"It's steep, really steep. I meant it's steeper than anything I've ever snowboarded, but if I can find some footholds—"

"For what?" Lauren said. She saw nothing but air, seemingly miles and miles of empty air beyond the lower portion.

Kerry didn't respond. She crouched and studied the rock.

"It looks like a funnel, doesn't it? See those mineral deposits?" She pointed to a barely discernible cleft near the center, noticeable only because of its thin, ribbony shadow. "Those are from water. If there's any water falling around here, it would flow right there."

"But," Lauren rasped with both palms flattened to the sky, "there's *nothing* falling around here."

Kerry nodded. "But it could collect around here. There could be a spring. I'm just going to climb down there and take a look."

"Down there!" Again, the only thing Lauren saw beyond the steep slope was her greatest fear: empty space high above the hard crust of earth.

Kerry walked along the upper part of the angled rock. Lauren followed, but maintained her distance from the edge.

As they neared the center of the section, Kerry lowered herself to the rock, looked around until she found some dust, and rubbed it over her hands. Then she dropped her feet and legs down, as if to descend from a roof to a ladder; but as Lauren noticed all too sharply, there was no ladder, and there were definitely no rungs. She felt she was watching the girl commit suicide.

"Don't do this! I'm telling you not to do it."

Kerry had just enough spit and vinegar left to shake her head. "I've got a good grip. Besides, what would you rather do? Die out here?"

"I'm afraid you *are* going to die."

"I'm not going to die. It's—"

"Famous last words."

"It's no big deal."

The girl dug the toes of her running shoes into the slope. Her fingers, filthy from their dusty bath, clenched the rock.

"Now would you please let go."

Without realizing it, Lauren had taken hold of Kerry's wrists.

"This is crazy. You don't even know if there's a spring."

"There's a crack, goddamn it, and I'm going to go see."

Her eyes looked wild, or was she boldly determined? Lauren didn't know, but she finally released her.

Kerry inched down the sharp face, keeping her body flush with the rock wall. Her fingers sought out and clutched the slightest protrusions. Lauren had seen calendars with pictures of rock climbers, their arms and backs ropy with lean muscles, but she'd never seen the extreme exertions demanded by such—

"No!" Kerry blurted.

Her grip had failed, and she was sliding, gaining speed rapidly, heading straight for the brink. The girl clawed at the rock as she slipped, as if to rip it open; but she found no purchase, and the edge came up on her faster and faster.

"Christ-Christ," Lauren pleaded.

Kerry's feet flew over the side, then her body, head, arms . . . But . . . yes! She clutched the cliff with her left hand and held on. Lauren could see her ferocious grip, knuckles as rigid as the rock itself. "Thank you, thank you," she muttered.

And then Kerry fell. Lauren moaned. Tears would have run from her eyes, but her body had no moisture for grief.

Kerry never shouted, never screamed, never betrayed Lauren's position to the man hunting them. Lauren could not fathom her courage, the restraint it took to fall that distance without shrieking in horror, in final gruesome terror.

Then, so softly that Lauren thought she was experiencing an auditory hallucination, she heard these words: "I'm okay. There's an outcropping. And there's water."

Kerry sounded like she was drinking. No words passed between them for at least another minute.

"Come on," Kerry said. "It's only a trickle, but it'll fill your mouth if you wait a little."

Already she sounded refreshed, her voice stronger. But "Come on?" No way, thought Lauren. Not in this life. Only moments ago Kerry—an athlete, no less—had lost her grip, and would have died if there hadn't been this outcropping thing to catch her. It never occurred to Lauren that Kerry might have seen the ledge and chosen to let go.

Not that it mattered because Lauren had no faith whatsoever that she could slide down this slope and then drop—*drop*—to another rock. Forget it. It would be insane to even—

Kerry's face rose above the lower edge of the cliff. Her mouth and cheeks were wet. And she was smiling.

"It's only about a four-foot drop, once you're hanging, and there's," she paused to look down, "a good three feet of rock to land on."

Three feet!

"We could stay here tonight and climb out in the morning. Or we could drink till we're ready to burst and then climb out."

Lauren didn't care one bit for either of these options.

"I'll be here to help you. I can grab you. Just do whatever you can to slow yourself down. Really dig your body and toes into the rock."

"What if I take you with me?"

"You won't. I'm not going to go flying off this thing for anyone."

Which meant that flying off was a distinct, not a distant, possibility. That's all Lauren could conclude. Even so, she knelt as if in preparation, or prayer, turned around and began to lower her feet over the upper edge. But no, no way, she . . . could . . . not . . . do . . . it. Then she spied Stassler several hundred yards away, a dark figure moving among the shadows.

"Stassler!" she hissed to Kerry, who nodded and waved frantically for her to come.

Never had she been so frightened, but the fear of falling during these critical seconds paled ever so slightly when placed against her fear of a man who kept skeletons in his cellar, and who'd tortured and murdered three people, including a child, in front of Kerry.

Her hands were so wet with perspiration that she wanted to swear at them for cheating her mouth of such precious moisture, and to swear at herself for not taking a cue from Kerry to cover them with dust. She understood the strange washing now, how the dust coated the sweat and oils of the hand and made your grip a little surer. But it was too late to go back up. She had to go down.

She held the edge of the cliff and lowered her legs, digging the tips of her cross-trainers into the rock. Then she reached down with her right hand, found a lump distantly resembling a hand hold, and clenched it so tightly her fingers throbbed. Now her left hand released the upper edge of the cliff, committing her to the steep climb down. She scoured the rock for a hold, felt the sudden weight of her body, and jammed her index and middle fingers into a tiny indentation, arresting what felt like a free fall, though in truth she'd moved only inches. Her legs were shaking so badly they felt like pistons turbocharging terror.

"Don't look!" Kerry warned, but only after Lauren, frozen on the face of the cliff, had turned her head to gaze into the shadow-filled gorge that waited to swallow her.

Her fingertips, slick as dim sum, lost their slender purchase, and her own slide began. Raw panic drove her chin into the rock, and her head began to chatter as she moved toward the open maw of the canyon. The tips of three fingernails exploded, but there was no slowing down, only the horrifying acceleration of her body. Then her feet shot over the edge. Her belly. Her head. And for a brief, wrenching second she saw the outcropping, narrow as a coffin, and the harrowing backdrop of whitewater and monstrous looking boulders.

For an instant she felt no contact with anything, and the world, her life, and everything she knew stood in stark suspension. She filled with no flood of memories, only an intractable, infinite fear of death.

And then she hit the ledge. Hard. On her bum. Her hands reached out instinctively, glancing off rock, grasping only air. She teetered on her butt before toppling toward the void. Her right hand caught a rough ridge as her legs spilled over the side and dangled in space, hinting of what could await her. She reached desperately for Kerry. The girl grabbed her arm, and Lauren scraped and scratched her way to safety. She didn't stop moving until she'd pressed herself against the wall. Still shaking, she realized she'd peed her pants. Not a lot, there wasn't much water left in her, but her pants were unmistakably wet. She was too frightened to care.

Kerry leaned over. "You okay?"

Lauren couldn't respond, not right away. Neither could she look to her left, her right, or straight ahead. Each glance brought the emptiness rushing at her once again. She couldn't bear its penetrating presence, and yet it all but surrounded her.

"The water," she whispered.

Kerry helped her to her feet, and as Lauren straightened she saw the glorious trickle. It proved surprisingly bountiful when she pressed her parched lips against it.

She drank for minutes without stopping. Then, as if in another ugly dream, she heard Kerry's soft words,

"He's up there."

A footstep, then another. He, too, had paused by the oddly shaped section of cliff. The two women stood as still as the rock that held them. Lauren wondered if he'd have the temerity to lower himself down, and if he took a tumble, as she had, if they'd be able to use his momentum to push him off the outcropping.

But why would he bother, she asked herself. He must have water, and only water could have made them stop. Water *and* fear, she corrected herself, the one so scarce and the other so abundant; but she realized that if either of them had been denied her, she might be dead. Her greatest fear had been him, and it had driven her here, to her greatest need, water.

His footsteps continued, then stopped. He was walking back. They heard him sit down.

Lauren eyed Kerry, and used her hands to make a pushing motion. Kerry understood immediately. Had any plan to murder been hatched and agreed upon so quickly? Lauren doubted it.

Kerry leaned forward, and drank silently from the trickle. Below them they heard the river, but Lauren no longer found the sound torturous. Indeed, she found it comforting, and decided that water, like so many other things, could make you magnanimous, once you'd had your fill. But how then, she wondered, do you explain him? Stassler had achieved more success than any other living sculptor. In the eyes of some critics, he'd already risen to the exalted ranks of Constantin Brancusi and Henry Moore. But Stassler wasn't big-hearted. Stassler was a stone-hearted killer.

A pebble struck her head. Another fell on Kerry's shoulder. Like a child, he was rolling pebbles down that steep slope.

Like a child? Maybe not. Lauren thought it likely that he was listening for their report, to see if there was an impact, or if they fell soundlessly into the canyon so far below.

Now a rock the size of a golf ball fell. Lauren surprised herself by catching it and tossing it on. Kerry appeared puzzled. Lauren whispered,

"He's trying to figure out—"

Kerry's finger rose to her lips. She understood. Both of them stared at the cliff edge several feet above them.

A rock the size of an orange came next. Kerry fumbled it, but managed to deflect it over the outcropping.

He's incredibly methodical, thought Lauren. They're getting larger.

And larger still: one the size of a grapefruit rolled angrily off the cliff. Lauren smoothly—so smoothly it shocked her—half caught and half heaved it toward the river.

She feared he'd roll a boulder that would crush them. But his game stopped as suddenly as it began.

They listened to him climb to his feet and walk away. This time he didn't return. Lauren's mouth had dried, and they spent the next half hour taking turns with that trickle. Each time she pressed her lips to the wet rock, she thought of Ry.

When they could drink no more, they sat with their backs to

the wall. Lauren experienced a dreadful flush in her groin as she looked out and saw nothing but air between them and the opposing cliff, a sensation worsened by the reality of the sparse space she shared with Kerry: with her right side pressed against the girl, she still had only two inches of empty ledge to her left. She wanted a mile, would have taken a yard, and felt as thoroughly undone as a windowpane in a hurricane.

"Okay, Spider Woman," she nudged her student, "what now?"

# CHAPTER
## 25

FOR THE FIRST TIME IN my life, I'm forced to consider the unthinkable. Even now, I try to find hope as I look over the darkening land; but simple-minded optimism is nothing more than denial in its shabbiest guise, and I have always taken just pride in my unwillingness to seek such cheap deceits. Her Rankness and nympho media whore have escaped me, and the implications are enormous. When they show up, wherever they show up, it will mark the end of my life as a sculptor, at least for the foreseeable future. There are actions I can take, actions I *will* take, but nothing can stop them from harming me in the short term. This appears as likely now as the setting of the sun, whose cusp is losing its weak hold on the horizon.

I sniff the air, sage and juniper, though where these scents originate I have no idea; there's so little that lives on this rock. Perhaps these are merely olfactory memories, the first of my senses to long for the loss of all that I'll have to leave behind.

To have sacrificed so much, to have come so far, only to leave it all in the hands of the Philistines is an insult whose force I could hardly have anticipated. I can't even afford to mourn, not now. If I don't move quickly, they'll figure out my methods and seek to discredit the entire body of my work. They'll refer in headlines to the methods of my madness, coining the term anew ad nauseam, and all because of that nympho media whore, though I recognize that I do share some blame. I should never have let that dog on my land. I should have shot him on sight as I have every other dog that ever wandered up. I should have let her go screaming to the authorities. Whom would they have believed? That miserable wench, or me when I said the beast tried to attack me? Rottweilers are biters—don't I know—and she would have gotten nowhere with her complaint.

It's all so bitterly ironic that she, in her bumbling, has brought all this down. The greatest sculptor of the last several hundred years forced to run into the night like a refugee because a hack like her happened upon my life.

Isn't that always the way it is, the humble seeking to enslave the proud? It's my very definition of democracy.

To dwell on her demise, the exquisite means by which I could dispatch her slowly, is my greatest wish; but I can no longer afford such self-indulgence. As I head back, I need to review all that must be done. I consider, for example, that blowing up the mine might be my best course of action. It would seal the graves of dozens, along with the faces, the real faces of all whose lives I've taken. I would grieve this loss deeply. After my death, I did want those faces to look out on the world, but they must be buried too. It is the only hope for my possible return.

I've planned my artistic doomsday carefully, though I would never take my own life, only the lives that have already been left in my hands, entrusted to me by fate, you might say, to be their master. I will have to carry the bone parade up from the cellar and over to the shaft. This could take hours, but in the end they'll all join Brilliance, who joined so many others.

The mine will become a wasteland, but once I'm done the physical evidence they could use against me will be destroyed. No sheriff will authorize hundreds of thousands of dollars to excavate a mine cave-in when there's no knowledge of its treasures. No one alive knows of them, certainly not nympho media whore and Her Rankness. They know only of the cellar, the cage. Let the authorities make of it what they will. There's no crime in owning a cage, and I imagine that more than one law enforcement official will admire its rugged construction.

And then I'll wait, as the coyotes out here wait. I'll wait years, if necessary, to see how it all plays out. There'll be the angry words of those two wretched women, their statements to the sheriff and the press, but without the corpora their words will gather dust. As the months turn into years, and the attention of the press and police turns to the thousands of others who are routinely murdered in the most wasteful ways, I'll have my say with those two, and they'll experience the deep suffering and death each of them deserves.

The tabloids will remark upon their sudden absence . . . perhaps . . . but again there will be no suspect in sight, only the notable disappearance long ago of the renowned sculptor. The sheriff, whoever he is by then, will make his measured pronouncements that the case remains open, but privately he and his investigators will know that with no bodies and no witnesses, statements given years earlier will not be terribly useful.

So within a decade I think it's likely that I'll be able to resurface. I'll still be a young man. I'll tell the world that the horrors of that era drove me to seek solitude, and given the constructs of contemporary culture, I expect I'll not only be forgiven but I'll be more sought after than ever before. There'll be rock bands named Stassler, and my sculpture will sell for several times its original price. I'll be welcomed back because such is the nature of commerce. I'll work again in the medium of flesh, and next time it will be with infinitely greater care.

This is the solace that soothes my bruised spirit as I start the long hike back. But these are also the consolations afforded a man prudent enough to have paved any number of possible futures. I don't need a great deal of time. I expect I'll make it back to the compound by midnight when I can begin to close down my life there. I have all the identification necessary for a new one, and more money stashed away in foreign banks than I'll ever need. Yes, I'll have ample time to grieve in the days ahead, and to plan the means by which those two will eventually die.

The sky splinters to the north, far above the La Sal Mountains, and I hear the thunder many seconds later. It's true, thunder *does* sound like bricks tumbling down. I look up at the night sky, pleased that I can still take pleasure in its simple beauty, its random boisterous wonder, that my joie de vivre has not been unduly blunted by the most unpleasant events of this unfortunate day.

A sudden rush of coolness chills my skin, as if I'd just cracked open the cabinet that leads to the mine. Her hand had settled on the false door when she toured the foundry. I'd been ready to fillet her right then. But she'd stepped away, and my hand strayed from the pocket where I keep my knife. I read the emptiness of her eyes and knew how little I needed to worry.

But I was wrong, wasn't I? Wrong to overlook her insistence, and the blunt-nosed curiosity of her dog. How many dogs have I killed, both on the ranch and during my forays, like that Border collie that I used as bait? Two dozen? Three dozen? Each one a pleasure, I assure you. And along comes as dumb-looking a brute as I've ever seen, and he slipped right past me when he got in the barn. Or perhaps she'd planned it that way. Kept him out of the house, out of the foundry, and when my guard was down let him wander past those doors. But no, that's giving her too much credit. She did no such thing. The beast was in a barn; it was appropriate, I suppose from her eyes, that he should be free to roam around. I never gave him a thought myself until he began his burrowing.

I have other regrets, deeper ones. It's impossible not to second-guess myself now. I should never have taken the time to clean that noxious wound. I should have grabbed my gun and run. Better to have risked infection than the chance of their escape. But what chance, I thought then. What chance did they have? I had them in sight the whole goddamn time. It was only after I ran down the stairs and back outside that I lost them. Even then I expected them to flounder, perhaps even to die out here. Any reasonable man would have thought the same. I didn't expect them to make it to the rock and use its impenetrable surface to hide their tracks. It's even possible that they are racing back there now, in which case I'll simply have to flee without any hope of destroying the mine, and thereby someday resurrecting the career of one of history's greatest sculptors.

The storm veers ever closer. Lightning brightens the land like beacons, bleaches it white for stuttering seconds, and then the bricks tumble once more.

The wind hits me, and I suck it in, smelling the ozone. Rain will soon follow. With every illumination, I see vast sheets falling to the north. Rain brings the desert to life, a hoary beast rising to its legs. The rock on which I stand will shed it like the wings of water fowl, spilling the flood onto the parched land that surrounds my compound, filling the dry streambeds with brown roiling currents of water and sand and mud. It will lap at the boulders and drain into the beds of quicksand that have lain as dormant as the spadefoot toads, those ugly cat-eyed creatures that bury themselves in the dirt until the rains lubricate their furious urge to procreate.

All manner of the desert will soon surge to life with its own fierce face. These nights are a madness, a glorious insanity, and if the storm is strong enough, and this one feels unrepentant, it can shake the sky, rattle the earth, and rip the rootless from the land.

I peer toward the compound, the many miles I have endured. I study the flanks of these hills and wait for the lightning to come again. I could be struck by a bolt, but I don't believe this will happen. Isn't that odd, at my most vulnerable moment to feel so supremely protected?

Long white crooked fingers claw open the darkness, throwing shadows and brilliance over the hills, a chiaroscuro worthy of Caravaggio. I stand amazed by the depths to which perception can lead, grateful for this unbending moment in time. And then I see them. It's as if this godless, barren universe is saying, There they are. Take them. Take them both. They are yours. You deserve them. You have earned them with your anguish, your unfeigned despair.

They are not five hundred feet away. Two females fleeing across the rock. I turn my face to the sky and my arms reach out to embrace the growing fury. The first pregnant drops splash against my cheeks. Thunder barrels past me, swept by violent gusts of wind. The rock on which I stand shudders, and I scream an unrepealable oath, a sound so pure and primal that it can mean only one thing: murder and survival, the one born of the other. Both born of blood.

# CHAPTER
## 26

THEY'D RESTED ON THE COFFIN-shaped ledge for more than an hour, though not long enough for Lauren to grow comfortable with her uneasy roost. Eternity itself was not up to that task. She'd remained in absolute awe of Kerry's easy willingness to stand and drink from the trickle of stream without, apparently, giving their chancy circumstances much thought.

Lauren took a few more drinks too, but only after Kerry rose, extended her hand, and held her close. She quickly reached the point where the ratio of her need for water and her acrophobia fell firmly on the side of fear.

But then a storm broke over the mountains to the north, angry clouds, their huge muscles bursting in the purple glow of twilight, and Kerry said softly that they had to go.

"Why?" Lauren didn't want to move. She wanted to root.

"This is probably the worst place in the world for us right now. If we don't get off, we could get washed off."

Lauren looked up. Grimly, she understood: When the thunder and lightning hit, the entire section of angled cliff above them would collect the rain and form a powerful cataract.

"How much time do you think we have?" Lauren didn't want to stir or stand any sooner than absolutely necessary.

"None, really. There's no telling how fast that storm'll move. Can you imagine what it's going to be like if we have to climb out of here with a lot of wind and rain whipping around, and—"

"Stop," Lauren pleaded. It was painful enough to imagine climbing out at all, much less while knocked around by all the angry elements of this forbidding desert.

"You should go first," Kerry said.

"Why me?" Lauren snapped, as if accused.

"Because if I'm behind you, I can help you."

Lauren cringed over her cowardice, how it mistook generosity of spirit for its rude antithesis.

Kerry stood, and made a stirrup of her hands.

"I'll give you a boost up. Then I'll get under you, and with your feet on my shoulders you shouldn't have any trouble climbing up there. There's a tiny shelf on the bottom part of the cliff that you can hold on to." She nodded at the lower edge.

"How tiny?"

"It's a couple of inches. Enough."

"Two inches?"

"That's a lot when you're climbing."

"Maybe for you."

"You can do it too, Lauren. You *have* to."

"How are you going to get up?"

Lauren, still sitting, still clinging to the outcropping, had forgotten that Kerry had climbed up on her own during those sorrowful moments when she'd thought the girl had fallen silently to her death.

Kerry reminded her of this, then said, "I'm sure you could do it too, but if you go first I can help. Besides, getting up there won't be the problem."

"What's going to be the problem?" But Lauren really didn't need to ask. The problem would be scaling the steep rock slope that lay between the lower and upper edges of the cliff. Slowly, she pointed up. "That's it, right? Once we get on the bottom part."

"Well . . ." Kerry stalled. "I'm thinking it *should* be easier climbing up than it was going down."

Christ, it better be.

"We'll see," she added cheerily.

*We'll see?* Lauren wanted better odds than that.

Kerry's next few words proved no consolation whatsoever: "It's not like we have a choice."

Lauren stared at the trickle.

"You want another sip before we get started?" Kerry extended her hand again, and Lauren forced herself to stand one more time. She took a drink, then another.

"You ready now?" Kerry asked.

"I guess."

Kerry braced herself just to the side of the slim stream. Lauren raised her left foot, and placed it in Kerry's cupped hands.

"Don't let your leg shake so much."

"I'm trying," Lauren pleaded.

"Because we don't want to be doing this more than once. It's a little risky, and the more we do it the more chances we're taking that you could—"

"Stop! Don't say it. I'll do it, I promise."

"Okay, cool. On three."

Kerry counted off, and as Lauren felt herself lifted upward, she straightened her leg and tried with all her will to drive her hands to the two-inch shelf on the lower edge of the cliff. It meant trying to disregard all the open space behind her and to her sides. In effect, it also meant trying to transform herself in seconds into someone she'd never been—a woman whose palms didn't turn sweaty from a mortal fear of heights.

She rose higher, higher—don't look down, *don't!*—groaning with real terror until her right hand grabbed the shelf. Then her left hand took hold, and she felt the endless weightless depth of the world behind her. She wanted to cry.

Kerry said she was going to let her go, but just for a minute, long enough to get her shoulders under Lauren's feet.

"All right," Lauren whispered.

She hung there with her breasts squashed against the wall, knowing that if she fell she'd be lucky not to go bouncing off the ledge to the rocks and river below.

Kerry eased her shoulders under Lauren's cross-trainers, and the pressure on Lauren's hands eased.

"Breathe," Kerry ordered.

Lauren hadn't realized that she'd been holding her breath.

"Now get up there," the girl said.

With Kerry pushing, Lauren managed to jam her elbows up on the narrow shelf of the lower edge. She craned her neck until she could see all twenty feet of the rock wall rising above her. It seemed an unbridgeable distance.

In spite of that, she raised her belly up to the shelf by pressing down on her hands until her arms were fully extended. The edge now cut into her like a tight belt, but the pressure on her arms was far more grueling. To take her weight off them, she'd have to get her knees up on the shelf as soon as possible.

With a stomach-swirling wave of panic, she realized she was out of Kerry's reach, and on her own a thousand feet above the river.

Her struggle turned utterly frantic as she raised her right leg, and wedged her knee onto the slender shelf shared by her hands. Now she had to get the other leg up. She reached high above her, plastering her face and arms to the wall. Consciously, she held her breath, balanced all of her weight on her right knee, and gingerly moved her left one into position.

Success left her kneeling, but trembling, on the tight lower lip of the cliff. Her arms were outstretched, and her fingers felt like claws. She noticed that her nails—the few that hadn't snapped off on her unruly descent—were trying to scratch holes in the rock.

"Lauren, you've got to start climbing, or get over to the side so I can get up there."

Both choices horrified her, but heading straight up sounded marginally safer because if she did fall, Kerry would be there to catch her. Right?

She clung to this tissuey illusion long enough to make her first move, which was to stand with her feet turned outward like a duck's until the whole of her body pressed against the rock.

"Go!" Kerry urged. "It's raining in the mountains. Can't you smell it? This rock'll be slicker than shit when it gets wet."

Lauren nodded with her eyes closed, every bit of her trying to turn into glue, into any substance sticky enough to stay stuck to this rock. She tested the purchase she could get with her duck's feet. Shockingly, it worked! She actually moved up the wall a few inches. Kerry offered immediate encouragement.

"Keep going. You're doing great."

Kerry spoke from right behind her. Lauren still did not dare look back, but she could tell from the sound of the girl's voice that her head must have risen above that dangerous lower edge.

Lauren's hand and feet found nicks and niches in the rock, and quarter-inch protrusions to clamp on to. In this unwieldy and fully terrorized fashion, she gained two more feet, constantly forcing herself to unfreeze from the fear of sliding backward into the great emptiness.

"Don't freak," Kerry said, "but I'm going to put my hands on your feet and push. Okay?"

Lauren nodded as Kerry, kneeling on the bottom edge, placed her palms against the bottom of her shoes and started pressing upward. Lauren rose quickly on the wall, her fingers combing every inch for holds. Then Kerry stood, and repeated the effort until she'd stretched to her limit. Lauren now found herself in a wholly petrified state—just out of Kerry's reach, but still a good eight feet shy of the top. She was afraid she'd never gain another inch, that she would cling to this spot until her muscles gave in to the greater force of gravity.

"I'm going to climb around you," Kerry said.

Lauren didn't respond, convinced that any break in her concentration would send her tumbling to her death.

Kerry, using the same duck-footed stance, inched past Lauren on the right, never pausing to even look over. She kept her eyes trained on the surface directly ahead of her, studying the rock so intently that it appeared she might immolate the cliff with her gaze.

The girl climbed without pause until she reached up and clutched the top edge. Only then did she look down at Lauren.

"We're going to make it."

Lauren could hardly believe that Kerry had ever been her student, so indebted did she feel to her now.

In moments, she would feel an even deeper debt. Kerry pulled herself up, and then promptly pulled down her jeans. She hung the top third of her body down the slope, and lowered the pants to Lauren.

"Grab them. It'll be easier than holding on to the rock."

Lauren wrapped her hands around the legs, placing all of her faith in Kerry's judgment. With the girl inching back and pulling hard, Lauren rose to the point where her hands could reach the top edge.

As she struggled to haul herself up the last two feet, Kerry gripped the back of her waist and dragged her to safety.

Both women were breathing hard. Kerry stood and pulled on her jeans. The wind ruffled her dark red hair.

"We made it just in time. Look at that."

After crawling a few feet farther from the cliff, Lauren worked up enough courage to glance back. Lightning continued to flash over the La Sal Mountains. Together, they counted, an odd chorus of whispered numbers, but when the thunder finally broke, it spoke in the lowest tones.

Lauren looked up at Kerry. "I want to thank you. You saved my life."

"Come on, we're not even close to being even. You saved me twice today. You got me out of that goddamn cage, and then when I wanted to roll up and die out here, you wouldn't let me. So I still owe you, prof."

"No, you don't."

Kerry pulled her to her feet. Now they faced the crucial decision to continue along the cliff till it eventually descended to the desert, which lay about nine or ten miles away, or to double back toward the compound.

"I know which way I want to go," Kerry said. "He went that way." She pointed along the cliff toward the desert. "So I want to go thataway." Her finger revolved like a tank turret back to the direction they'd come.

"He *might* have gone that way, or he might have turned back, figuring we'd already done the same thing. It's been over an hour since we heard him."

"Let's hope it's the last time we ever hear him." Kerry cast an uneasy eye over the dimming landscape that enveloped them on three sides. Not that it was likely either one of them would spot Ashley Stassler, not if he'd hidden among the boulders, or down in the valleys between the gently rising swells of rock.

"I think we should head back," Lauren said. "Not to the compound. We'll just use it as a reference point so we can hike out toward the highway and flag someone down. It's shorter, and if we do go the other way and get down to the river, we still have to hike out. I don't know where it goes. Do you?" She'd seen nothing but desert from the helicopter.

Kerry shook her head, and eyed the storm clouds gathering across the chasm.

"Even if he does go back," Lauren continued, "I'm thinking we might beat him there, and I'm also thinking Ry might be at the compound by now. If he is, he could help us; but if we don't see his car, then we stay away and head for the highway. I told him I'd make sure to be back before dark."

"Lauren, it's just getting dark now."

"I know, but by the time we get there it's going to be real dark. Maybe he'll even call the sheriff."

The thought of the sheriff, of rescue, sealed their decision. They started down the smooth rock they'd climbed hours before. Miles of it spread out before them.

Thunder rose from the north, growling louder with each burst. They expected the storm to overtake them any minute. Lauren figured they'd find cover when it hit. For now, they hurried. Not running, not exactly, but moving quickly up and down the rocky slopes, past balls of tumbleweed and boulders the size of trucks.

Lauren felt the rain on her arm first, then the back of her neck. A crack of lightning struck so close that they both fell to their knees. They smelled the burned edge of earth, and heard the thunder roar a second later.

"Whoa," Kerry said.

They spied a corner between a boulder and the smooth rock that they were scampering down. They sprinted for it, and huddled as another bolt broke about a hundred feet behind them, so close they heard the electricity singe the moist rock, smelled it again too, a startling mix of moist wool and sulfur, and all the hot points of a campfire all at once. An overwhelming odor.

"Shit!" Lauren said.

Kerry nudged her. "Don't worry. It'll probably pass in a few minutes."

"No," Lauren gasped. "Him!" She pointed to Stassler moving toward them, seemingly oblivious to the storm that raged all around him.

"Let's go," Kerry sputtered.

Both of them started running for the first time, much more frightened of him than the storm. It might have been Lauren's imagination, but the footsteps she heard were not her own or Kerry's, and they pounded like the thunder itself.

They scrambled up and down the rocky swells, tripping, stumbling, banging their arms and elbows; but they kept moving, two fit women using their last reserves of energy, surviving mostly on the sudden strength of adrenaline.

Lightning stunned the slope they were crossing, and both of them dove like soldiers launched into the air by a mortar attack. But these two were not riddled with shrapnel, maimed and unmoving. Lauren was already rising to her feet, looking back, seeing Stassler loom ever larger. He was gaining on them, a hundred feet away, maybe less. She spotted the gun in his hand.

"We've got to split up," she shouted to Kerry. "He can't go after both of us at the same time."

They ran off still holding hands.

"You go right," Lauren yelled between breaths, "and I'll go straight or left, depending on what he does."

Kerry was shaking her head. "No-no. We stick together."

"He's got a gun. We stick together, he'll kill us both."

For the first time in hours, Lauren read terror on Kerry's face. She could see this even as they raced on, and felt it in the young woman's tight grip. They looked back to find that Stassler had disappeared; but then his head rose up from behind a rock, and they saw that he'd never slowed down. He was screaming words they couldn't possibly understand through the rain, wind, and thunder. In the instant that followed, he fired his gun at them, a wild shot that had only the slimmest chance of finding its target, and most likely was intended only to scare them into stopping. If so, it failed miserably in its mission because at that moment Lauren squeezed Kerry's hand and pushed her away. The two of them scattered like sparrows, Kerry indeed veering right, rapidly widening the gap between herself and Lauren, who was darting straight ahead, then cutting between a wall of boulders and shooting out from them like a pinball.

Lauren glanced over her shoulder as Stassler leaped up on a rock. He looked toward her, then Kerry. She rejoiced over his indecision. Then, with a heartfelt sense of what she had to do to save the girl's life, she waited till he turned to her once more, and that's when she ran five more steps and fell. She rolled onto her back, grabbed her ankle, and screamed. She lay there gripping it fiercely as lightning stung a pinnacle only fifty feet away. Rain lashed her, washing the dust and sweat from her face, leaving only the turmoil and terror she wanted him to see.

He actually raised his arms in triumph, the gun silhouetted against the flashing sky, before jumping from the rock and racing toward her.

# CHAPTER
## 27

I'D BEEN TRAILING THEM FOR all of five minutes when they spotted me, but I didn't care. I knew that seeing me in the middle of that storm would leave them witless, a loss of nerve and intelligence that neither could afford, given the perilously fragile state in which it existed in both of them under the best of circumstances.

What did I need to worry about? They were running off holding hands like Hansel and Gretel, and in my imaginings at the time I wondered which one of them played Hansel and which one played Gretel in their professor-student fantasy. The point was they were *together*. I needn't have worried about them getting away, and as I looked at them fleeing like children I could feel all my earlier concerns misting into the breath of this chilly thunderstorm. And then they shocked me by separating. It was an intelligent ploy, and so surprising that it was like watching a play, believing wholly in its verisimilitude, only to have an actor suddenly come out of character by turning to the audience and asking for a beer. I would never have guessed that they were up to such a stratagem, such self-sacrifice. I would have bet the compound on their fear of me keeping them together. Their sudden separation drove me to stop and choose, but what I wanted most, what I absolutely required, was no such choice: I needed them both. My only remaining option was to kill one of them as quickly as possible, and to immediately hunt down the other.

But then I forced myself to reconsider. Perhaps not. Perhaps the hard bounty of a desert storm would do my work for me. I took comfort in that, but only a fool bets on chance when certitude lies by its side. I could gun them down, collapse the mine with the murder weapon in it, and flee. They'd never find the gun, and I would begin my waiting game, for the years to blur memories of the deed, though not, of course, of me.

So all was not lost, but I needed to work swiftly. And I did, as soon as I saw nympho media whore fall and roll around like a toddler thrown from a trike. Amazing, I thought, how instantly our problems solve themselves when we don't panic.

I set off for her, keeping an easy eye on Her Rankness too, though I did lose her among the shadows and rock. Still, I knew her direction, and the night was only beginning. I also knew what Her Rankness would face as she ran into the darkness, if not soon, then in all likelihood later. It would terrorize her as much as I could. And she had to be greatly weakened from not eating and drinking. She was only now getting her first taste of water. She wouldn't run for long before stopping to drink, and if she was like most of the desert's near fatalities, she would prove gluttonous and barely able to move by the time she'd had her fill.

What I didn't anticipate in my newfound equanimity was nympho media whore's deceptiveness. As soon as I ran toward her, she rose like a cripple at a televangelical's rally, and took off with a burst of speed, wholly unhampered by injury.

This was abominable behavior, like a mother bird faking a broken wing to lead a fox from her nestlings.

Now I'm facing difficulties again. She's keeping the distance between us so constant that I'm certain that she's intentionally luring me farther away from Her Rankness. Why else would she turn back so often? Fear is an obvious answer, and though I flatter myself in thinking so, and willingly grant that it does play a role, I would be delusional if I didn't recognize that the success of her deception seems to be spurring her on as well. Yet this deceitfulness, this disgusting dishonesty, has been such a distinctive feature of hers that I should never have been surprised by this twisted turn of events. The only surprise is that she found a victim for her cheap treachery in me. Why I let this happen is a question that I'll have to resolve eventually, if for no other reason than to make sure it never happens again.

Yet, as long as she continues toward the compound, I'm not overly concerned because I know what awaits her. She can't possibly anticipate the wonders of the desert night, the transmogrification wrought by a storm of this magnitude. She'll be more than a bird faking a broken wing, she'll be a bird whose wings are clipped entirely, a bird forced to watch a fox feed on her nestlings. There'll be no compound tonight. No road. Not for her. How do I know? Because the rain is a relentless, truculent ally. It's drenched me. It's drenching her. Wild sheets of it lash the rock and sting the eyes. I see her soaked hair whipping in the wind, and every time she looks back I see lengths of it snaking across her cheeks and brow. But best of all, I see her fear, genuinely stark fear. I want her face to overflow with it, to grow even uglier and more contorted for all the toil she's given me.

But I get even more than I asked for because she slips and falls hard. No cheesy trick this time. She's really grabbing her knee, rubbing it fiercely. She gets up, but she's limping, bent over, holding her knee and trying to run at the same time. Not so fast now, is she? See how suddenly it all changes? I'm almost within shouting distance. I want to tell her to stop, spare us all this effort. Then I realize that most assuredly I am within shooting distance. All I have to do is "wing" this bird, and she's mine. She'll crumple like foil.

I raise my left arm, rest the barrel of the revolver between my elbow and wrist, and steady my aim. I lead her as I would a dove or a duck, a deer or a dog, and shoot.

She jumps from the impact, but is not hit, at least by the bullet. I see her smacking her leg as she runs, as if to brush away chips of rock that have sprayed her skin. Close, very close.

I want to get closer before I try again, so I maintain my runner's stride. She's no longer babying her knee, so I assume that my latest injection of fear has inoculated her against whatever pain she might have felt. I'm beginning to think that she's a runner of long standing. I know something about this. I ran cross-country in high school, and several twenty Ks in college. I haven't run a race for many years, but I recognize serious runners when I see them, and I have to say that she's a serious runner. I suppose if you're as deceitful as she is, you'd better be. She has the practiced stride of someone who doesn't waste a lot of energy flailing her arms and legs in useless motion. This would give me pause, if I didn't need to keep pace myself. I have to admit I'm beginning to tire, and as I do my thoughts about her blacken. Though she doesn't know it yet, she'll also be forced to slow down, and eventually stop, if not from fatigue then from the desert's own deceitfulness. She has no monopoly on duplicity. The desert, she'll soon see, is not always what it appears to be either.

Till then, I can only try to keep up. She's widening the distance between us, no doubt figuring that we're fully afield of her little friend. She's right about that.

I'm probably a hundred fifty, maybe two hundred feet back, and still she shows no signs of flagging. But I have to keep up, keep her in sight. Just in case. But this is growing increasingly hard to do. She's like that idiotic bunny on television, the one that never winds down. I can't even calm myself with thoughts of her death. It's all I can do to keep her in sight.

And then I hear it, and ease up, take an extra breath. Yes, I hear that glorious sound. It's there. It comes to me as the most benevolent of saviors. I don't even have to run now, but I do because I'm not taking any chances. I need to see if she throws her life away. I wish that upon her, the blend of desperation and stupidity necessary to make her attempt the impossible. It would serve my interests well.

The sound grows louder. The first time I heard it speak, the roar was so animate it chilled me. Then I drew closer, felt the ground beneath me shake, as if evil spirits—if you believe such pap—were rising like wraiths to take over the darkness. And then I saw it. The moon was out, three quarters full, and it reflected off the surface with the intensity of chrome.

There it is now. I can see it again. And yes, I see her as well, stupefied by the sight, paralyzed by its bold presence. She's standing there, staring at it. Doesn't know what to do. Better not get too close, nympho media whore, it'll eat you right up.

She's looking at me. My smile grows in the fractured light that spills from the sky. To settle my shooting arm, I slow to a walk. I missed last time because I was too far away and out of breath. I'm going to keep it simple now and gun her down at *point-blank range*, as the newspapers love to say. That's why it's critical to convey supreme confidence, to let my smile prosper with every step, to give her the unbreakable impression that she's cornered in one of the desert's own cul-de-sacs.

I take heart in the fact that she's not moving, not going anywhere. Where can she go? And she's got to realize that Her Rankness is stymied too, trapped as it were by my greatest ally, whose long thick arms come alive in a sudden rain, whose dry washes run deep and fast with water, currents so strong that they rip boulders loose and send them tumbling into the empty reaches of the far desert.

That's it, nympho media whore, stare at that torrent all you want, but if you try to cross that roiling water, you'll die. You've come to one of the desert's phantom rivers, and now you stand upon its unsteady bank.

She edges no closer. I see her looking left and right. She could run along the bank, but to where? To go right is to lead me to her friend, the one she thought she'd die for, and to go left is to run toward the maw of this widening river of madness, all the water and waste now starting to eat at those sandy banks. Look, there goes a chunk—she jumps back—consumed by the hungry current. She glances at me. The distance between us narrows to thirty, thirty-five feet. Now she's the one forced to choose. Does she die in the river? Or does she fall to her knees and beg like a mendicant for the measly alms of her life?

Her eyes sweep back to the river. How deep? I can almost hear her thoughts. Deep, my dear, deep by the parched parochial standards of the desert. Six feet, seven. It may not sound like much, but once you get in the water whips you around with the frenzy of a washing machine. I have found the bodies of man and beast after these storms, their skin and hides bruised and gashed from the beatings they endured. So little different, really, from the raging floods that surge through our cities. In Los Angeles the wide, concrete-lined river comes alive with everything imaginable—bed springs and old cars, fifty-foot trees and refrigerators—but most of all, it comes alive with people who are dying. You can never imagine just how swift a flood current is until you've seen an arm rising from that churning muddy mass as it sweeps out to sea. A lone arm reaching up, as if to be plucked to freedom. And then that lone arm sinking down, never to be seen again.

If she takes the dive, I'll applaud. She'll drown of her own accord, and I'll have only Her Rankness to hunt down.

But if she doesn't, I'll force the issue. This is even better than having her fall from the cliff. There are always questions, annoying and protracted, when someone falls from way up on high. But a flooding desert claims lives every year; the ignorant and learned alike grow fascinated with the violent juxtaposition of seething water and barren land, the ancient and venerable constituents of earth and sky. It's hard not to become mesmerized by the manner in which one consumes the other, gobbles up big bites and carries it away. But the desert always wins. Always. Because the sun always shines. I remind myself of this as I approach her. No matter what else, the desert always wins.

CHAPTER
28

THE SURGING WATER TORE OFF another chunk of bank less than two feet from where Lauren stood. It happened so fast that it was as if the earth had simply vanished. If she hadn't felt it in her feet—the rude awakening of roots and rocks and soil—she might not have believed her eyes at all.

She'd hesitated for moments, caught between the river racing constantly away, and Stassler moving relentlessly closer; cocky enough to slow down, as if he no longer had a need to hurry. Even at his best, she knew she could outrun him, but his gun, his bullets? The only cover rushed by in the raging water, and after backing up over the last few inches of bank, after drawing close enough to be swept away in the slightest surrendering of land, she charged upriver, refusing even now to compromise Kerry's safety. She sprinted along the very edge, tempting fate with her feet, deciding in the odd clarity of her panic that if he did shoot her, she'd cast herself into the flood rather than let him seize her bleeding body.

Her resolve had hardly been reached when the first bullet fractured the air so close to her face that the backwash pulsed against the tip of her nose. She started to dart as randomly as the drops of rain that spattered against her skin. She heard two more shots before his gun fell silent, and he too began to run.

There was so little light left in the sky that she stumbled twice and almost fell. She could not suffer a twisted ankle, not now. But if it's this bad for me, she thought, then it's just as bad for him.

He yelled at her. She had no idea what he'd screamed. A command? A plea? It didn't matter. She wasn't negotiating.

Always her eyes came back to the river, looking for passage—quick passage—to the other side. She hoped for a rock arch. There were so many of them here in the desert, their great gaping windows chipped open by the chisels of ice and snow, water and wind. She could climb an arch, bridge this furious river, and head toward the compound. Maybe she'd find Ry, certainly the road and rescue.

But . . . there might be more of these floods, a veritable maze of rivers and streams crisscrossing the desert like a glass of water spilled on a kitchen floor, reaching out in the many arms of Kali.

One battle at a time, she told herself, and then you win the war. She sought simple solutions, their comfort and hope. But the simplest of all—the arch—was a fantasy, and she knew this even as she searched for the easy passage it would promise.

The lightning had passed on, and with it a more innocent fear, one born of nature, brute and direct; but the storm's crooked fingers still lit the distant sky, and threw open the darkness to the boulder field she was about to enter. They looked as big as cars, as moving vans, boulders stacked on boulders; but no arches anywhere.

She ran among these obstacles, and dodged their smaller, spectral, shadowy brethren, the spindly trees and sharp-toothed cacti, the hump-backed stones and sudden gullies. Stassler fell back, and she took pride in her strength, her endurance, her besting of a man so clearly impressed with his fitness; but his was the self-consciously sculpted shape that comes from a gym. She'd seen this in her first glance, when he opened the door in a tank top and shorts, and the morning sun on his shoulders and chest threw sharp shadows across his smooth skin.

Lauren had earned her fitness running through the streets and parks of Portland, and down the dusty fire roads of the Angeles National Forest. Now she would conquer the desert, because to fail was unthinkable.

Eventually, he would have to quit. She'd run him till he dropped. And the longer she ran, the easier it would be for Kerry to escape. That had been her hope, to draw him farther and farther away from her student, to make him commit to her; but Lauren's success had buoyed her, broadened her goals, for now she saw herself united with Kerry in a studio at the university, at work again in plaster or stone, hardwood or marble. At *work*. The very sound of it wildly pleasing, to work at what you loved, to get paid for doing something you'd be doing anyway.

These thoughts fueled her. She'd found her rhythm out here in the darkening night as she had found it over thousands of miles of trails. She heard her breath fall into its natural cadence, so clearly at peace with her flight that it seemed a wonderment to her, these rich endorphins coursing through her brain like the river through the desert.

She'd moved a good twenty feet from the bank now that his bullets had failed. So at ease in her stride that she had to blink hard at the sight of the boulders rising from the water, blink the rain from her eyes to see them piled randomly across the river, or perhaps not so randomly at all. Some of them were huge, one and two stories high.

When she looked back, Stassler had become a plodding, far-away figure. She hurried to the bank and studied the boulders. A bridge? Yes, possibly, though not as she'd envisioned one. More like a series of stones that let you step across a creek. But this was not a narrow creek you could clear with a few skips and a jump, and these were not mere stones. These were boulders caught in a flood powerful enough to sweep them away.

She froze as she imagined herself clinging to one of these massive rocks as it started tumbling down the river. She'd read about the thick-trunked pines that washed up on the Oregon coast, stripped limbless by the stronger arms of the sea. Every summer children played on them, and then died when "sneaker" waves turned the friendly looking trees into giant rolling pins that spilled their young visitors into the surf, and crushed them on the sandy bottom.

Stop it, she hissed. You can do it.

As she scanned the boulders one final time, she realized they'd formed a pinnacle, a tower rising incongruously—as all pinnacles do—from the desert floor, thick and brittle and broken apart by its fall, then smoothed and sanded by the abrasive elements of the earth itself.

Only three feet of water separated her from the first and largest boulder, and she claimed it quickly. The rain, as heavy as a winter cloak, beat her back and shoulders, and turned the rock slick; but she clambered to the top seconds later. She found herself twenty feet above the river; not so high as to instill fear, but high enough to survey the lesser boulders that awaited her, and to spy Stassler as he closed within two hundred feet.

More daunting was the five feet of water that swirled between this boulder and the next.

She eased herself down from the modest summit, studied the edge, then ran and leaped. She landed with inches to spare, emboldening herself further.

The third boulder waited a short distance away. Stassler, she saw, had drawn close to the bank. So let him. Run your own race, not his. But this was the worst kind of silliness, and she knew it as soon as she said it. Her only goal was to remain free of him. Anything less was suicidal.

She cleared the modest span to the third boulder without further pause, and descended to a saddle in the middle of it. After scampering up the opposing slope, she gasped at the gulf she now faced.

It did not look possible. At least eight feet. She swore, and the wind and rain carried her epithet away. She turned to check on Stassler, but couldn't see him. Where *is* he?

She decided to jump to a lip protruding from the left side of the fourth boulder. If she failed, as she fully expected she would, she might at least grab the outreaching rock. And if she failed at that too? She would fight the current until she reached land, or drowned.

Still, she held back. Possible death, or certain murder? The decision might have seemed easy to anyone not faced with that dark, foaming chasm.

What made the jump even more frightening was the takeoff: it inclined about fifteen degrees, so rather than gain the momentum of a downward-facing slope, she would have to compensate for the added demand of an uphill run, however slight.

She could dither no longer. She pumped her legs and bent her knees and sprang into the cold darkness. While in the air her arms reached out, her legs too. She was the picture of athletic desire. But during that first second of soaring, she knew without question that her feet would fall short. An instant later she felt the cruel indifference of stone smash into her chest, knocking the air out of her.

Her hands froze on the outreaching lip as the rushing water sucked at her legs and the bottom of her torso, and tried to sweep her downstream. She battled mightily to hold on. The sounds that issued from her throat were the same horrified groans she'd made on the cliff, for this was very much like hanging in the air, only now the gravity that had tried to rip her hands from the rock had been replaced by the surging water that tried to wrestle her into the deep.

She had only seconds to lift her legs out of the current, or it would tear her loose.

Fighting for air, for handholds, fighting for her life all over again, she inched her right leg up onto the curved surface of the boulder, then brought her left up beside it. Now she clung almost horizontally to the stone, a burden she couldn't bear a moment longer.

With a wrenching effort, she wedged her armpit up on the lip, and grabbed desperately at the rock until she found a hold. From there it was an awkward, painful, but successful effort to pull her legs up too.

Glancing back, she spotted Stassler on top of the second boulder trying to steady his gun in the wind and rain.

She sprang up the rock she'd gained with such difficulty, and dove for cover down the other side. He never fired.

The jump to the fifth and penultimate boulder proved easy, but as soon as she landed she felt it shuddering from the violent flow. Then it did move—a good foot or two! She ran toward the far edge, determined to jump without pause to the last and smallest of them, but stopped short when she saw that it was shaking too, as if caught in a quake of its own.

Her hesitation solved nothing, and as soon as she understood this she leaped over the four-foot gap. Seconds later she would have made a slightly shorter jump to land, if she hadn't spied a wide crack in the bank about ten feet to her left. In the darkness she couldn't see how far the crack cut into the bank, but it appeared on the verge of cleaving off a broad section of earth. Then lightning flashed, and she saw floodwater bubbling up from the crack all along a ragged line that extended at least eight feet from the river, confirming her worst fears about the bank's stability. She worried that if she jumped, her weight would knock the bank loose and plunge her into the water, along with a pummeling cascade of rocks and soil. She also worried that if she didn't move immediately, the bank would rupture on its own, leaving her at a dead-end.

From one unsteady roost to another. The boulder beneath her shook and rocked like a boat about to snap its anchor line.

Hit the bank and never stop, she urged herself as Stassler shouted. She couldn't understand his words through the storm, but he sounded perilously close. He was. He'd dragged himself to the top of the fourth boulder, the one that had almost defeated her.

She did hit the bank running. Vibrations from the flood raced up her body until she'd cleared the crack. She gave thought to kicking at the eroded edge, to trying to break the bank loose; but her legs carried her beyond even these considerations in the next few seconds. Her only concession to this vengeful impulse was the prayer she offered as she raced off: that the land would indeed fail and dump Stassler into the murderous wash.

Kerry had trailed the river for miles, never venturing close, never challenging its raw authority. She saw no need. It appeared to roughly parallel the road that led to the compound, and as long as its course remained constant, she'd end up at the state highway, which would deliver her from Stassler, the storm, hunger. She was sure of this.

She'd run for the first half hour, but fatigue had slowed her down, and now she found herself walking, though it seemed that every easy footstep betrayed Lauren's well-being by eating up seconds that might save her life. This spurred Kerry to hurl herself into a jog, which was all she could manage in her famished condition.

At once she saw the small sparkle of headlights, and called to them in a hopeless voice. They were so far away. She wept miserably as they passed into the night. She staggered to a walk, furious with herself for growing weaker. She felt like an ingrate. Lauren had lured that monster from her, and she couldn't muster the strength to run to a highway no more than a mile or two away.

She closed the distance by jogging for a count of fifty, and walking for a count of twenty-five. Alternating in this torturous fashion brought her to the road far faster than she would have ever thought possible.

For some godforsaken reason, a barbed-wire fence prevented her from simply climbing up the five-foot embankment. And here comes another car. She could have screamed. She scaled the barbed wire anyway, snagging her hands and jeans but managing to race up to the road before the headlights blinded her. To the driver, she must have appeared as she was, the victim of a horrible crime. Streaks of blood ran from her upheld hands and arms. Her clothes were ripped, her entire body soaked by rain, and her eyes were wide with fright.

The car, as if reflecting the alarm on the girl's face, screeched to a stop. Kerry shielded her eyes from the headlights as she staggered toward the open door of an SUV.

She climbed in, anxious for safety, for shelter from the storm; anxious as well to sit, to rest, to be rescued. And ever so grateful that a woman had stopped. She glimpsed this before she reached for the door, pulled it shut, and thought about how willingly she'd traded her fear of Stassler for the Russian roulette of flagging down a stranger. And it had turned out okay. A woman had pulled over. What a relief. So much safer than a man.

As it might have been, if the driver hadn't been Diamond Girl.

# CHAPTER
29

I FALTERED. I FALTERED SO often that I lost faith in my own fury. How could it fail me now, the fuel I need to sink my hands into her stringy neck and choke her till her blue eyes bulge and her hands fall limp by her sides? Such mundane imaginings, and yet all during this pursuit I've found myself reveling in the most common renditions of murder—choking, beating, bludgeoning—as if each were a secret indulgence, a psychic slumming.

All my patience with the slow, delightful deliverance of death has deserted me. And with its flight went a few degrees of caution. This is the luxury I will grant myself, the absolute catharsis of an anger unbridled any longer by artistic considerations or impulses. This will be murder for its own sake, the sweet purity of singular purpose.

*Murder for its own sake.*

I've repeated this mantra for more than an hour. It sustained me as my fingers turned bloody from those rocks, from saving myself from the black hole of that flood.

Twice I was almost killed crossing that river. Twice! I could only imagine the torture it must have been for her. I smiled only once during that entire time, and it was when I realized that if I was barely surviving, then she was doomed to die.

I see her stumbling. We're closing in on the compound, maybe two, two and a half miles. She's tiring. No more than a hundred feet separate us. I want so desperately to shoot her, to *wound* her. I want this so powerfully that I can see the bullet's damage, the ripped organs and shattered bones, as I have seen my hands crushing her windpipe.

But I've wasted three bullets, and that has left me with only three more. I thought I'd shot her back by the river. That bullet came so close. I saw her head snap back, but then she was running again. Thirty feet was all that separated us, but thirty feet is a great distance with a handgun, and I have never been sure with its aim. I've had no need. I've always worked up close and personal. For this creature I need a deer rifle and scope.

So I'm keeping the gun in my belt and forging ahead. We're so close to the compound now that I can see the light above the entrance to the guest quarters, like a single star in the vast black firmament.

What does she think she's going to do once she gets there? This is like the spider chasing the fly into its web. It's too easy, but just as I'm taking delight in the image of myself as an eight-legged creature that devours its prey, she deviates from the path. We're but a mile from the compound, and she's heading right. It looks like she's planning to parallel the road. This is a smart move, a very smart move. It forces me to stay on her track or risk losing her. I want nothing more than to herd her into my lair, shove her filthy wretched body into my cellar where I can begin to extract my vengeance, balancing as I will, my need to destroy the mine and all the evidence it holds with my desire to destroy her with my hands, to bludgeon this nympho media whore with my bruised flesh.

But this is strange. She's cut back again toward the compound.

And now I see why. There's a man under the light by the guest quarters. It's that goddamn idiot, Ring Ding.

I *must* catch her. I'm driven by the inescapable need to reach her before she warns him. I already have one loose end unraveling over the land. I have no need of another. And then I notice my Jeep is gone, and know that Diamond Girl has taken it from me, has logged the first leg of her journey in it. Under normal circumstances, I'd want to leave Diamond Girl rigid with remorse; but Ring Ding has arrived, and that means his equally anonymous Land Rover is moored around here somewhere. It's precisely what I need to set off on the first leg of my own journey, the one that I had thought would eventually lead me back to Her Rankness and nympho media whore, the only witnesses with eyes that still see and words that still speak.

But I won't have to wait so long for the whore, now will I? She's barely fifty feet from me, and still a quarter mile from him. She's shouting, but I can barely hear her, so he won't hear anything at all. The wind and the rain muzzle her as furiously as the hard rubber ball that I've rammed into the pleading mouths of so many, whose smooth surface long ago grew pitted with bite marks upon bite marks, little pictures of pain for the album of their final anguish. I have often considered casting that ball, and the strap that holds it so securely in place, for it would speak so clearly of the alginate, as the alginate speaks so clearly of them. If I fail in this regard, if I don't find a way to preserve the gnashings that I alone have gathered, then the work that I have recorded on that marvelous ball will have no more meaning than the hoofprints of a herd on a long dusty trail.

I've got it down to thirty feet, two car lengths. That's all that separates her from my furious hands. She's so intent on him that she doesn't even hear me closing in. She's waving her arms, which slows her down even more; but she's still a couple hundred yards from Ring Ding, and he isn't even looking this way. No, Ring Ding, that cur, is too busy trying to jimmy the lock on my door.

She looks back, startled to see me *so* close. She's wild-eyed, and starts to backpedal. Her hands are up, no longer for him. For me! To stop me. I tackle her. I drive my head into her belly as hard as I can and slam her into the muddy earth. I can't restrain myself, I savage her face. There are only dull wet sounds escaping us. Her own screams, though eager, are muffled by the force of my fists. Little grunts, that's all. Like a piggy. Are you a piggy, nympho media whore?

She's unconscious. She lies there like a lump. I smack her face. Blood flies loose from her lips. Both of them are split, but I have yet to knock out any teeth, and strangely her nose looks straight. I'm dearly tempted to perform some cosmetic surgery on her right now. In fact, my hand is already on my knife; but Ring Ding is shaking the handle on the door, and I'm forced to accept that there's no time for play. I must go about my chores as soon as possible, all the cleaning up that I have to do before leaving. People, possessions, the like.

I slap her face hard. Then the backhand. Her eyes flutter. I smack her again, sparing my knuckles this round because her eyes have opened wide in gratifying fear. She also opens her mouth to scream, and I slam my hand over it.

"Shut up!" I whisper with more dignity than she deserves. "Shut up and listen to me. I want Ring Ding over here. You," I jam my finger into her chest, "yes, *you* have to call his name. Do anything else but call his name and I will kill him *and* you. But first him. He's dead if you betray me. Do you understand?"

She's not responding. Perhaps she can't breathe. Poor thing. I'll admit to having enjoyed the suffocating spasms that have punctuated our little talk; but I do need her alive if I'm ever going to enjoy her death, so I slip my hand off her nose, and watch her suck blood and snot and the minutest amount of air into my favorite targets.

At that very moment, I look at my watch and see that if I hurry there's enough time to melt all the bronze I'll need. I'll make Ring Ding help. It'll speed up the cleaning immensely. But I need him under my control, not out there screwing around with my locks.

She snorts madly, and I keep my hand pressed firmly on her mouth. She's getting some air, but nature's own alginate is doing its duty handsomely.

I let this continue for another minute, so enamored am I of the efforts she makes to breathe. And it may be years before I can do this again. To set up a studio, to find such a cellar, all this takes time. I check my watch once more.

"Yell his name. That's all. Do you understand?" And then I add the coup de grâce, the most compelling threat to any artist: "Or I'll rip out your eyeballs."

I form a wicked pair of pliers out of my thumb and index finger, and press the tips into the corners of her eye.

She's all struggle now, to clear her nostrils for breath, to close her eyes to try to save her sight. She's insane with fear. I recognize this, appreciate it greatly, but I have to bring her back to the land of the living. I take away my prying fingertips, and ease my hand from her mouth so she can suck in enough air to feed her lungs, her blood, her rabid brain.

"Okay, now. Are you ready?"

She nods.

"Just his name. Yell 'Ry,' and that's all."

Again, she nods. She's a good girl.

I take my hand all the way off her mouth, and she screams, "Ry, run!"

I'll kill her. I reach for her eyes but stop because Ring Ding has been startled from his hapless burglary, and is starting to run this way, toward us, lured by a wasteful, chivalrous impulse. I love this. This is so sweet. I take my hand away again and whisper, "Go, girl, go."

"Run!" she screams again, as predictable as a windup toy.

It works like a magnet. He's barreling toward us. Don't stop. I give her another go, and she complies richly, hastening his effort. He's bounding into the darkness, blind as a beggar in Bengal.

Come on, I whisper as I pull out my gun. Come on. I cock the trigger, release my hand, and she screeches, "Stop-stop." It's the most soulful beseeching. So . . . unselfish of her, isn't it? So . . . self-sacrificing.

Her mouth widens as she starts to scream again. It's simplicity itself to jam the gun into its warm, wet recesses, the barrel resembling in notable respects the organ upon which she bestows her most profane favors.

Here he comes. I can see him now, the wild animal panic on his face is a reflection of her raw fear, which I feel in my gun hand, in the squishy spastic tremblings of her tongue and gums and teeth and tonsils, the guttural protest of her gagging.

"Stop!" I yell at him.

He obeys. He sees me pointing to her face, her lips stretched wide, refusing the barrel as I imagine she'd refuse me. He puts his hands up, as if I have any need of his tedious sign of surrender. I want only his help, and I shall have it. I shall have his dutiful brawn and dumb willingness to take direction. There are tasks before us, and they'll fill the length of the night. And when they're done, I'll smile at the dust drifting up from that mine, and the thought of her body glowing deep within its grasp. And then I'll greet the dawn with the recognition of my own new day.

CHAPTER
30

A BURNING PAIN DEEP IN Lauren's throat clawed her
awake. The gun. She remembered the barrel jammed into her
mouth, the spasms before she'd blacked out.

Stassler was dragging her to her feet. Rain pelted her face. She
felt herself shoved, caught. Words she couldn't decipher floated
past, thin as rumor. And then Ry gathered her in his arms, and
they were trudging toward the compound, her eyes on the ground,
studying the desert soil soupy with rain, and the way plants with
stems no thicker than wires had fattened and stored what they
could for the day so long in coming.

Lauren had nothing she could store. She'd been emptied of
everything but fear and hunger. The desire for food gnawed at her,
even as she imagined the agony of swallowing.

Stassler forced them at gunpoint to the front of the barn, and
threw on the lights. After so much darkness, she had to squint.

He herded them down to the last stall on the left, where the
door to the cellar stood open from her escape with Kerry.

"Get down there," Stassler ordered in a voice so calm it was jarring. "You're going to work, and if you slow down for even a second, I'll take you apart."

Even his threat came softly to her ears, and it took Lauren a moment to register the overriding menace: not *I'll kill you*, but *I'll take you apart*. It's what he's done to the others. It's what he's going to do to us too.

Ry extended his hand, and helped her down the stairs. She saw the cage and wondered if Stassler planned to imprison them after they'd finished whatever work he had in mind. Then she spotted the stainless steel table with the straps, and lost all hope in bars and locks and old car parts.

Stassler pointed to the skeletons.

"You're taking every one of them up to the foundry. Now move!"

Neither she nor Ry spoke. She couldn't, her throat still throbbed from Stassler's assault; and Ry seemed stunned by the ghastly collection that he was seeing for the first time.

Then he surprised her by turning to Stassler and saying, "I've reported about war criminals and murderers, and all of you come out of the same shitty mold." Ry glanced at the skeletons, and his eyes widened, as if seeing the extent of the slaughter had become a physical challenge. "There's nothing you do that's worth any of—"

Stassler silenced him by placing the barrel of his gun against Ry's head.

"One more word, and you join them. Now get moving."

Stassler kept his gun level as Ry approached the skeleton of a little girl in a blue corduroy skirt and pink sweater. The sweater had the face of a teddy bear on the front. Toddler clothes. He carried it over to Lauren.

The soft details sickened her. She was terrified of touching it, of sensing the life it had known; but she clutched it to her chest, as if to comfort the child it had once been, and moved numbly back to the stairs.

Her legs were so weak that she had to focus on each step to keep from collapsing.

Stassler was extracting her last few ounces of effort, and for the first time the thought of death brought a glimmer of relief. The tide of pure horror had receded, and she felt drained of all hope.

She stepped up into the barn with no thought of fleeing. Hours ago she'd tried to run away, and the entire journey, with its vast inventory of fears and pain, had led back here. The physical impossibility of another escape was so thorough that she didn't need to think it. It had become as real as air, darkness, and the deadening night.

Stassler must have known this too because he made her lead, and kept his gun on Ry, who bore the burden of two skeletons, one under each arm. Stassler carried only his gun.

They walked out into the rain. It had never stopped pouring. Through the fat pearly drops and gusty winds they crossed to the foundry, where Stassler showed them the opening to the mine.

Lauren realized that if she'd been a few degrees keener when he'd given her the tour, she could have died so much sooner. Her only solace was Kerry, believing the girl had escaped; but even Kerry's survival seemed terribly compromised by Ry's entanglement, as if no matter what Lauren did, someone was destined to die with her.

When she dropped the skeleton into the dark hole, the leg caught on the ladder about halfway down, and the little blue skirt bunched up around the hip bone. Ry had to reach down and yank it free. The sound of bones scraping against metal proved grisly. She looked at Stassler, and wished it was his skeleton they were stuffing into the mine. But even this sharp desire was dulled by the hard labor that followed.

When they walked back down for the last three skeletons, Stassler made them pause.

"These are the Vandersons," he said with a theatrical sweep of his hand, as if Lauren and Ry had come to a grand party, and he had the honor of introducing them to their hosts.

"June the Cleaver, Jolly Roger, and Sonny-boy, I want you to meet nympho media whore and Ring Ding."

So that's what he calls me, she thought. But the name was confusing, it meant nothing. Then *all* the names took on meaning for her, the only meaning that mattered: he'd stripped each of them of their real identity, and replaced it with a cruel moniker. He'd probably done it to every person he'd ever abducted, dehumanized them long before he'd actually killed them. No different from naming his series, *Family Planning #1, 2, 3, 4, 5, 6, 7, 8,* all those numbers that added up to no more than brute-naked anonymity.

"When you were in the foundry, you saw the impressions I took of them."

His eyes landed on her again so suddenly that she felt stung, attacked by a wasp. She looked away as quickly, but saw only those fully clothed skeletons striking oddly animate poses.

Yes, she had seen those dull green forms, and this made it far too easy to imagine them alive; easier still to look at these bones and imagine their pain, to sense in an instant all they'd lost of life, and the thistles of love known to every family.

Ry gently handed her the boy, dressed like a mannequin in jeans and a red T-shirt; and as she climbed the stairs, her eyes, though tired and tested by all she'd seen, began to absorb the details around her, and to sense, even in the midst of all this horror, the joy of vision, the manner in which it revealed textures and surfaces and shapes—all the forms, simple and complex—that had inspired her hands and imagination for as long as she could remember. She'd been born to be an artist, and an artist she had become. This consolation was not so small as it might once have seemed.

She walked to the foundry with her eyes rising from the trail of mud to the stars poking through the cloud cover, and she looked in wonder at the thick drops of rain racing past the outdoor lights that burned with a strange beauty.

More than anything else, this incandescent awareness of the physical world, the way it seemed to light up from within, and to radiate from without, made her understand that death had become as imminent as breath.

She hoped she *would* die quickly. Not like the others. But when she entered the foundry and smelled the melting bronze for the first time, she knew its slow, torturous threat. The time had come, she decided, to take her fate in her own hands, to plan her own death. Not his gun. He would want only to wound her, to drag her bleeding to his desires. No, her death needed to be swift and sudden. Her death needed to be sure.

# CHAPTER
## 31

IT'S TIME TO ADD HER bite marks to that hard rubber ball, the one with the straps that I've clamped so tightly around so many skulls. I don't have the time for the alginate, but I can still take an impression of her pain. Maybe she'll even rip the ball in two. I've been waiting a long time for one of them to fill up with enough raw terror, enough hormones to tear the rubber apart with their teeth.

She might be the one. I certainly never did to the others what I'm about to do to her. I was never the least bit inclined to waste the bronze. But what better use will those bars ever have? It was either leave them behind, or harness their molten fury to force all of her pain onto the ball, because in the end the ball's all I'm going to have. I can't take the bone parade or faces with me, but I can take the ball and the straps and the bite marks. Small enough to stuff in my pocket. And some day, it may be years from now but some day I'll make a mold from that deeply pitted device, and I'll cast it in bronze. I even have a name all picked out, one that will carry on a rich tradition: *Family Reunion #1*. Isn't that perfect? All of them together at last.

At first I'll admit that I suffered terrible regrets over not having the time to use the alginate on her, but I've come to see that a greater wisdom is at work here. The fact is, she doesn't deserve such an honor. She was never intended for the afterlife of art. She's flesh to be burned and destroyed, to cower, cringe, and scream, to become nothing more than teeth tearing into that black rubber ball till they bleed from their roots and snap at their tips, and crumble like mortar too long at their bricks.

I was so preoccupied with my plans that I almost overlooked the videotapes. Years of them. A catalog of crimes that has to go. So I drive the two of them back out into the rain, and make them carry boxes of tapes to the foundry. I tell Ring Ding to pour them down the opening to the mine, and I stand over him listening to the clatter of a thousand images rising from the darkness.

I also have them carry the impressions of June, Jolly Roger, and Sonny-boy over to the partition wall. I can't bear the thought of having such exquisite forms tossed into the darkness, of destroying them any sooner than I have to.

Before we go down the ladder, I check the fuses running into the mine. For this I put on Brilliance's headlamp, and force them to sit about five feet away. The fuses are fine, as neat and dry as the day I put them in.

Now I tell Ring Ding to climb down the ladder. She seems too petrified to move. That's fine with me. Right now I don't want her to do a thing.

I wait till he clears a path through the bone parade and tapes, and then hand him the impressions of the Vandersons. First, Sonny-boy the guttersnipe, then June the skeptic, and finally, Jolly Roger. No one's ever greeted me quite like him. Come in, come in, come in. I can still feel that big meaty hand of his, and hear the door clicking shut behind us.

Nympho media whore ruined the plans I had to cast them, and it's all I can do not to reach out and rip her face off right now. But I exercise great restraint, and tell her to get down in the mine with

334 • Mark Nykanen

"lover boy." She doesn't flinch, and that's when I know my suspicions are true: she really has been using sex to get into the book. She's *earned* her name the old-fashioned way. And now she's going to *earn* her death.

She gets up slowly, moving like a geriatric, and I realize that she's on the verge of total exhaustion.

I have Ring Ding drag three skeletons away, a mother and son from *Family Planning #7*, and a father from *#3*. I recognize them as if they're my own children. She makes a feeble effort to help.

Move, I tell them. He turns on me.

"Back off." He's shouting. "We're moving as fast as we can."

*Back off?* Me? This is too rich, this outburst of his, this little display of bravado for his lady dear; but rather than shoot him in the groin, which is my most immediate urge, I let them move on. I need his muscle, and his life can be measured in minutes. I'll have his humiliation in the end. He'll see.

Back and forth they go, ferrying the bone parade to the same shaft that has received so many others, disposing of these marvelous creations beneath Harriet's tortured gaze.

Watching this is painful to me. No, it's much more than painful, it's excruciating. The bone parade was the shadowland of my great success, the perfect balance to the bronzes that went to art collectors, museums, and galleries. I spent thousands of hours on it. Thousands! I had to weld the bones together, and shape every skeleton to strike the subject's most characteristic pose. And I did it brilliantly, from the first to the last. The Vandersons are perfect examples of this. I look at their skeletons slumped against the wall, and I can still see June's insolence, Jolly Roger's insipid lazy posture, and the way I captured the puling of their sniveling son without the benefit of sound or tears.

The beauty of the parade inspired me every time I took off in search of new subjects. I could always tell how they'd look stripped of all flesh, their clothes hanging from their bones, with only the empty caverns of their eyes looking out at me. This wasn't hard to envision. I'd carved away so much flesh, removed so many eyes, that I was practiced in the art of the unimaginable. I could even sense the longing in them when they took their places in the parade. I felt it as intimately as I felt the hot breath of their final exertions. And now, to toss them all away so unceremoniously, to consign them to such an ignominious end, with the likes of Brilliance and his bike, no less, hurts me as nothing ever has. As nothing ever could.

But it must go. The whole parade. It's a forensic nightmare, a veritable keyboard of clues to all the families.

The last in line are the Vandersons. I have Ring Ding haul them down to the shaft, and then I make him carry the impressions one at a time; they are far too fragile for her shaky hands, and I can't stomach the thought of her carelessly smashing them. They must be disposed of too, but not with the taint of her touch.

I have a soft spot for the Vandersons, I recognize this now. I'm going to miss casting them. But what I'm going to miss most of all is Diamond Girl. Even now, with the theft of my Jeep, the betrayal of my trust, I think kindly of her, and hope that some day I'll catch up to her again. Maybe it's sentimental, maybe not, but I see Diamond Girl at twenty, or twenty-one, and me still in my prime, walking hand in hand down a beach in the sun, gazing at the bodies on the blankets, watching the signals that fly among mothers and fathers and children, seeing the little ones at play in the sand, their smiles, their soulful expressions; and from this cornucopia of eyes and arms and hands and feet selecting the families we'll sculpt, the bite marks we'll add to the ball.

As I say, maybe it's sentimental, but it's also immensely satisfying—and consoling—to imagine the two of us knitting our lives together as tightly as honeysuckle knits its sweet summery fragrance to a fence.

At my command, Ring Ding stands before Harriet and tosses June, Jolly Roger, and Sonny-boy into the shaft. The last of the bone parade. Then I have him drop their impressions down there too, and we all listen to a strange tinkling sound rising from the depths. It's the alginate, shattered and falling through the skeletons, playing the bones like a xylophone.

There's one chore left, and it's critically important to me. I want them to move the stainless steel table from the cellar up here to the foundry. We have time. Ring Ding may be no brighter than a fruit fly, but he's a hard worker, and he's gotten a lot done. And besides, I simply can't imagine that Her Rankness has found her way out of the desert yet, not in these conditions. But if at some time in the next hour or two she does manage to stumble out to the highway and hitch a ride into town, what's the sheriff going to do? He'll be getting a call in the middle of the night from some foggy-brained dispatcher who's going to tell him that the missing girl has just wandered in the door with a bizarre story about the world's most gifted sculptor sticking her in a cage and snuffing an entire family with some green gunk.

Sure, he'll respond. He has to, but first he's going to drive down there and question her long and hard until he's sure that she hasn't spent the past week eating peyote soup with a bunch of wannabe Indians.

Then he'll wake up his deputies and work out a plan. But he's going to move cautiously, and who can blame him? Not me. This is rural America, and you never know if you're about to walk into another Ruby Ridge or Waco, or some other kind of nut factory.

The one thing he's not going to do is shake the sleep from his eyes and come racing out here in the middle of the night. It'll take him an hour or two to question her and get all of his deputies organized, and another hour or so to set up a perimeter. All of that adds up to more time than I need, and a whole lot more than nympho media whore has left to live.

So I'm not about to deny myself the single pleasure I have left to me here. They'd have to be beating down my door before I'd give that up.

                                   . . .

She's so tired she's barely able to walk, and not much help to Ring Ding, who's having to lug the table up the stairs almost entirely by himself. I'm definitely going to have to give her a shot of methamphetamine. She's not going to be any fun like this.

Once they drag it into the foundry, I wipe it down. I save a towel for her too. They both look soaked as sponges, but she's the only one I'm willing to waste a towel on. His work is almost done. All he has left to do is strap her to the table. Then, when she's staring at him most intently, pleading with her eyes—I've seen this a lot and know what to expect—I'll shoot him in the head. It'll be the first shock to her system, and the gentlest by far that she'll face.

But for now she must take off her wet clothes and use the towel because I need her dry, though they're never truly dry, not when they're scared. Their palms and brows dampen, and puddles form. Yes, *puddles*. Bodies lose control of their functions at exactly the same rate that they lose control of their fears. Everything I've ever seen in the cellar testifies to that fact. It's a lesson I'm anxious to pass on one more time.

# CHAPTER

STASSLER ORDERED LAUREN TO "DISROBE." He said it softly, as if he were a physician getting her ready for a physical exam, instead of a killer with a deadly plan.

A tremor in her legs spread rapidly to her belly and chest, and her hands fluttered upward, as if sprouting meekly in the face of death. She felt a grinding desire to plead for their lives, but couldn't force herself to speak. It wasn't the throbbing in her throat that stopped her, it was the fear that words—any words at all—would incite him to start shooting.

She took a last look around, saw a hammer, tongs, tools, but nothing within reach.

"Take them off," he said evenly, as if she needed the definition of "disrobe," as if the humiliation he planned wasn't apparent enough.

She complied, but slowly, stalling with the hope that somehow the darkness outside would explode with red, blue, and amber lights, with rescue vehicles and sheriff's deputies and the end to all this horror.

He raised his hand to strike her with the gun. She cowered, and hastily pulled her drenched pants all the way down. Then she lifted her soggy T-shirt over her head and looked back at him. He pointed the gun at her underpants and bra, conducting her nakedness with movements that made him smile, but not with lust. There was no lust in those eyes, not even the hard spark of its sudden violence. As he peered at her underpants, translucent from the rain, his eyes were grim veils that revealed nothing of life. A deadening.

She lowered her panties and laid them on her T-shirt and pants. Then she unhooked her bra and placed it down there too, before rolling her clothing into a neat bundle

Stassler nodded, as if he approved of her fussiness. Perhaps for the first time he glimpsed a quality in her that he considered redeeming, a tidiness so ingrained that it could prevail in the face of such stark uncertainty.

Her nudity felt like a sickness as she stood with her soaking clothes at her feet. She shivered, not from the cold but from the threat of the scalding heat that rose from the furnace and crucible. The yellowish glow lit the salty beads that gathered on her face and arms and chest, and dripped to the floor. She imagined a puddle forming around her, and wished more than anything that it could be a moat, a magical ring of water to douse all the flames and the worst of her fears.

Stassler threw her a rag that had once been a towel, and told her to dry off. She did, not out of any wish to obey, but to try to stop the shaking that taunted her so. After she'd dried her legs, he pulled it from her and tossed it aside. Then he ordered her to lie on the steel table, and any thoughts she still had of magic or moats immediately surrendered to the hard shiny surface with its macabre arrangement of straps.

"Don't do it," Ry said.

"You," Stassler turned on him with cruel calmness, "say one

more word, and your hand will go in that." He snapped a quick look at the glowing crucible, not ten feet away.

"Why do you want me on that thing?" Lauren had finally managed to speak, but with no real hope of an answer, only the penetrating knowledge that the liquefied metal was intended for her, to curse her with its bone-bending pain. To carve her to the core.

No matter what, she wouldn't get on that table. She'd rather be shot or stomped or stabbed to death than let him do anything to her with twenty-one hundred degrees of liquid bronze.

He ignored her question, and waved his gun at the table.

"No," she said flatly, and then she repeated herself.

He aimed the revolver at her leg. She expected him to grow angry, maybe strike her, scream, vent some of the fury that had to be pent up inside him. But he did none of these things, and he showed no emotion. Nothing. He simply fired the gun, and it was she who screamed as screeching pain ripped through her thigh, and blistering heat tore through her entire body. It was as if she'd touched an electric rail and couldn't let go.

The foundry turned fuzzy and her ears rang as she staggered and collapsed on the other side of the table. Her leg had a scorching hole the size of a dime. How could such a small hole make such a horrible pain? She held this thought without the gentility of words, with the piercing clarity that the worst pain brings.

Stassler turned to Ry, who was standing beside him and shouting, remonstrating wildly. Lauren was sure Stassler would fire on him too, and that this time he'd shoot to kill. Despite spasms of agony, she grabbed her bundle of clothes, the whole big wet ball, and hurled it at the white hot crucible.

Ry saw this, and lunged for the steel table. In that startling instant, he must have remembered the warning she'd given him in the university foundry, when she'd told him to leave his water bottle by the door.

Stassler whirled around as Ry pushed the table on to its side, and launched himself over the upended edge. Lauren pulled him to the floor behind this makeshift barrier as the crucible exploded from the shocking assault of cold water.

A terrifying BOOM shook the foundry. Harsh, hissing sounds, like tracer bullets, whirled around them as molten bronze splattered against walls, tables, ceiling, shelves; and then the first of the fuel tanks for the acetylene torches exploded, the argon and $CO_2$ and oxygen—*BOOM-BOOM-BOOM*—turning the tall steel canisters into the lethal missiles they so strongly resembled, blasting them through the brick walls as if they were made of tissue paper.

An anvil smashed into the end of the steel table with so much force that it whipped wildly away from Lauren and Ry, and he had to haul it back as the brick wall to their right crumbled. Seconds later the ceiling began to fall in sections, as each failure triggered the one that followed.

It felt like an earthquake. Support beams toppled, and walls cracked around them. Three thick wooden posts slammed down on the edge of the table, forming a crude triangular shelter as the ceiling continued to fall, and fires began to feed on the tools and workbenches and debris.

An insistent hissing crept above the sound of the flames.

"What's that?" Lauren whispered, still worried more about Stassler than the collapsing walls and ceiling and flames and fumes.

Ry tried to climb to his knees to look over the edge of the table, but Lauren pulled him back down.

"The fuses," she shouted, no longer caring about the other threats, for this one loomed so much larger. "The ones going into the mine! The ones he was checking."

The hissing, sputtering sound raced on for five seconds, ten, as Ry draped her protectively with his body. Lauren felt his whiskery cheek next to hers; his face was pressed to the floor while hers looked up.

She jolted at the sight of a bloody, bronze hand reaching over the table, gripping it tightly. And then she saw Stassler's head rising too, his eyes on hers, his features parboiled with the liquid metal. It coated his cheek and lips, and had melted off half his nose. A hollow had been carved into his temple, and she spotted a small circle of exposed bone above his ear.

All of his ghastly wounds had been cauterized by the extreme heat of the bronze, which now contained gruesome swirls and splotches of blood, dark red spottings that appeared frozen despite the smoldering metal.

Stassler's mouth, no more than a rigid oval from its sudden casting, issued a grunt that she couldn't understand. His other hand now inched above the table, and it still held the gun. He pointed it straight into her face. She watched petrified as he nodded, and though his mouth couldn't move, and his eyes were dark with pain, he smiled. She was sure of this, smiled and slowly wrapped his finger around the trigger. She squeezed her eyes shut, refusing to accept that the last vision of her life would be the horribly mangled face of this murderer.

An explosion nearly shattered her eardrums.

She feared she'd been shot again—the same painful ringing shook her ears—and didn't know better until her eyes opened to a powerful blast ripping through the remains of the foundry. It leveled the last of the brick walls, and sent debris flying hundreds of feet into the air.

Beneath them the earth rumbled as loudly as the thunder that had chased her hours before. She felt the implosion of the main shaft, and feared that at any moment the earth would open up and swallow them too.

Rocks and soil and bricks and glass poured down on their crude shelter; and she became aware, though only dimly, that the rain itself continued to fall, and that it had been warmed somehow by the explosion.

Stassler's hand still gripped the table's edge, but his head was gone, decapitated by the blast, and what she saw now would never leave her: a fountain of blood sprayed from the stump of his neck, and she realized that the warm drops that fell on her face were not the rain at all.

She wiped madly at her skin, forgetful of her own pain, then saw Stassler's body slump. The movement seemed ponderous amid the explosion's furious aftermath. But his fingers still clung to the table, and now she saw why: they'd been moist with molten bronze when he'd grabbed it, and now were welded to the surface where he'd tortured all of his victims.

Ry moved the beams that had formed their rough shelter, their crude triangle of life, and they saw that every wall had fallen. Flames flared from an opening in the floor where the furnace had stood only minutes ago. Several smaller fires burned around them, lighting the darkness with a frightening red glow, while the flames themselves seemed to sneer at the weak insult of rain.

"I want to get out of here," Lauren said in a voice so shaky it might have been shattered forever.

Ry placed his hand on her back, as if to reassure her; but she felt his fingers trembling, and knew he was scared too.

Another rumble raced beneath them, shaking the earth, shaking them. It was as if the hollow ground were once again preparing to swallow them whole. Thirty feet away, where the entrance to the mine had received the bodies of so many men and women and children, the earth belched a great cloud of caustic black smoke.

In seconds it drifted over Lauren and Ry, and they started to cough. He took her hand, and she climbed to her feet, weighting her good leg. She was naked, bleeding, and blackened by the dust and smoke. Her thigh no longer shrieked for attention, but the pain was severe, and she held it for a moment to try to ease the agony. She couldn't.

She hobbled with Ry's help, unaware of the tears that streaked her dark face. She was far too concerned with navigating the rubble-strewn floor of the foundry, stepping over beams and bricks and twisted, charred canisters.

"We're getting out of here," Ry said. "We'll be okay."

She wanted so much to believe him, and might have if she hadn't looked over and seen Stassler's head lying but a few feet away.

Lauren fell fully into Ry's arms, and screamed for the first time, a harrowing sound that could have been heard for miles. The pain in her throat had given way to a pain so much greater. Her fingers raked his back as she stared at the sky and screamed until her voice grew weak.

Even then she could not shake her final sight of Ashley Stassler: the blast had sheared off the side of his skull, and driven lengths of bone as thin and sharp as knitting needles into the dark knots of his exposed brain.

Her hands clutched her stomach as the smell of his seared flesh filled her nose, and before she understood what was happening, Ry picked her up and carried her away. She might have heard a groan, an expiration, and while she knew it could never have come from Stassler, she didn't feel safe denying this fear either. So much was dying right then that it would have been impossible to say exactly what had made that haunting sound. The earth itself had not fully sealed, and its secrets were still escaping.

# CHAPTER
## 33

"SLOW DOWN!" KERRY SMASHED THE dash with her fist. She wanted to smash Diamond Girl, but not with this crazy chick driving niney-five miles an hour down a rain-slick, storm-whipped highway.

"Stop trying to get out," Diamond Girl responded coolly, "and maybe I will."

"What do you think I'm going to do? Jump out and kill myself? Slow down!"

Kerry *had* tried to open the door the second she'd seen who'd stopped for her; but Diamond Girl had thrown the childproof locks and floored the accelerator, forcing them into a wild, fishtailing sprint to ninety miles an hour. Kerry had spilled onto the floor mat, and been forced to concede, if only to herself, that flight, at that point, was fruitless and no doubt fatal.

But she hadn't given up. A half hour later, when Diamond Girl's attention flagged, and her foot eased up on the gas pedal, Kerry tried the door again.

Diamond Girl glanced at her, shook her head as if she, Kerry, were hopeless, and sped back up to the ninety to one hundred mile an hour range.

Kerry had also tried screaming, *screaming* at her to stop the goddamn car and let her out; but this had brought a response that made her want to smash her head, along with her fist, against the dash: Diamond Girl had looked at her with the same vacant expression, and in a voice wholly devoid of emotion, said that Kerry didn't really want to leave her.

"You have fun with me. I'll bet it's more fun than you've ever had," Diamond Girl said as she eased up on the speed long enough to execute a U-turn across all four lanes.

"Fun? Fun!" Kerry slammed her elbow into the door so hard she bruised herself and didn't care. "I didn't have fun. We were in a goddamn cage. I had to watch three people get murdered. Your own mother! Your brother. Your father. What the hell was fun?"

"I didn't want all of that stuff to happen, but fucking with Ashley's head was great."

Kerry blinked hard, not once, not twice, but three times. She could hardly believe what she'd just heard, and had to think that if her ears were deceiving her, then her eyes could not be far behind. A hallucination, of course. But no, Diamond Girl was right where she'd been all along, behind the wheel, and the words she'd said were as real as the rain.

"So now you're fucking with *my* head? Right? Tell me that. Tell me you're just fucking with my head?"

Diamond Girl looked over and put her hand on Kerry's knee. "Don't you dare!" Kerry pushed it away. "Don't even think about it. That was an act, remember? To get him in the cage. You . . . you . . ." Kerry stammered, enraged and appalled at how completely in control Diamond Girl appeared. ". . . you *are* doing it to me now. You're fucking with my head. You were doing it then, and you're doing it now."

"You and Ashley, if you really want to know the truth."

"That's bullshit! I was trying to help you get us out of there."

"Poor girl. And now you feel . . . violated?"

Diamond Girl shook her head and exhaled audibly, as if she'd been challenged by an especially unruly child. Which infuriated Kerry all the more. She'd put up with that bi-girl routine to try to lure that . . . that *asshole* from hell into the cage, so maybe they could beat his balls blue and escape. But the whole time they'd been gaming Stassler, Diamond Girl had been gaming her too.

Kerry had hung out with some outrageously cool bi-girls, riot grrl chicks like herself, but none of them had been insane, until Diamond Girl.

"Sometimes things start out to be one thing, and turn into another." Diamond Girl spoke as evenly as ever. "Just ask Ashley." A smile crept across her lips.

The hand again. The knee. Kerry groaned, and threw it off.

"This didn't turn into anything. Nothing. You hear me?"

Diamond Girl stared at her. The eerie green of the dashboard lights reflected off her eyes.

"The road," Kerry said nervously. "Look at the goddamn road!"

The Jeep hit the shoulder. Pebbles rattled the undercarriage. Diamond Girl didn't seem to care. She kept staring at Kerry with the same blank expression.

Kerry launched herself across the seat and grabbed the wheel. The car skidded as she turned it back toward the road, and the rear wheels started to swing around until the Jeep felt like it was sliding sideways down the wet shoulder.

"Slow down!" Kerry yelled even more frantically than before. Her hands turned rigid on the steering wheel. Vibrations from all four tires jarred her wrists.

Her heart thumped louder than the Jeep when it jumped back onto the highway. The vehicle began to straighten.

Diamond Girl didn't fight her, but she did press harder on the gas.

Kerry screamed as the speedometer clocked a hundred and five. Then she felt Diamond Girl's hands creeping onto her chest.

She swore, and elbowed her off. Diamond Girl had messed with her mind, but Kerry would be damned if she'd let her mess anymore with her body.

Diamond Girl slowed to a more reasonable ninety, and her hands returned to the wheel.

"I'll take over. The car," she added pointedly, the first emphasis any of her words had claimed.

"See," she eyed Kerry, who now sat cross-armed against the passenger door, "you do have fun with me."

"Let me out," she demanded.

"Here? This is the middle of nowhere."

Nowhere sounded fine to Kerry. Nowhere, she figured, was anywhere but here. She'd gladly take her chances with another car passing in the night. What were the odds of a second crazy pulling over? Two in one night? The odds had to be in her favor, right? But when she looked into the darkness, she found no comfort there. The world suddenly seemed filled with crazies.

"I'm taking you back." Diamond Girl interrupted one set of fears by introducing another.

"Back where?"

"To the road, the one that goes to Ashley's."

"No! Don't take me there."

"I'm going to drop you at the gate, and then I'm taking off. We're real close to Ashley's road, and if I don't get you a few miles from here, you'll be waving at some car just like you waved at me, and calling the sheriff before I can get away."

Hope, real hope, had dawned at last. Kerry said nothing, unwilling to snap the spell.

Diamond Girl turned the wipers on high as the rain thickened. The gesture was so . . . normal. It made her seem, well, not normal—nothing could make Diamond Girl seem normal—but sensible? Maybe.

"Why don't you go to the cops with me?" Kerry ventured. "You haven't done anything wrong."

"I've got plans, and that's the last thing I want to do."

"Plans? What are you going to do?" Kerry wanted to encourage the conversation because Diamond Girl sounded almost sane. After all, if she had plans, then she was thinking about the future. Maybe she passes through phases, Kerry thought, like the moon when it glows and grows, and then darkens and shrinks.

Diamond Girl offered an authoritative nod. "You're definitely going to be hearing about what I'm doing, and when you do you're going to know it's me. It has nothing to do with Ashley." She waved her hand as if she were dismissing a pesky autograph hound. "I've got my own plans now."

"What are they?"

But Diamond Girl's attention was grabbed by a distant fire.

"That's got to be the compound," she said.

She turned down the road.

"Please let me out," Kerry pleaded.

"Stop whining. I told you I'd let you out by the gate."

The fire seemed to grow larger as they sped toward the compound. The gate, much to Kerry's horror, stood open, welcoming, which must have been how Diamond Girl had left it when she'd stolen the Jeep. But she kept her word, braking quickly. She cut the engine, and jumped out with the keys. The moment the locks disengaged, Kerry kicked open the door and backed away. But Diamond Girl wasn't even looking at her. She climbed up on the roof, towering over the flatlands that surrounded them.

"It looks like the foundry," she reported. "It's gone. All I can see are some smaller fires where it used to be."

Kerry kept backing away. She didn't give a flying fig about the foundry or the fires. All she cared about was her freedom, keeping it at any cost, bolting into the damn desert, if need be.

As she considered this, Diamond Girl spun toward her and raised her arms, as if reaching to the stars.

"Yes," she whispered, and even with the rain spattering the Jeep, the damp earth, Kerry heard her. A stage whisper, a cunning sibilance that embraced her ears as Diamond Girl's hands had embraced her body.

She lowered her arms until both of them pointed straight to Kerry. A red glow lit the side of her face.

"I can't make you go with me. That was Ashley's mistake, thinking he could make me do something I didn't want to do. Like my parents."

She paused, and Kerry saw a strange look appear on Diamond Girl's face. Wistful? She wasn't sure, and it passed so quickly that she wondered if she'd imagined it.

"So I'm not going to do that to you. But I'm going to make you *want* to come with me. You'll see. Someday you'll want it more than anything in the world. You'll hear about me, and you'll let me know. You'll find a way, and I'll come back for you then. I promise."

What the *hell* is she talking about? Kerry backpedaled madly, trampling brush and stumbling; but never, *never* taking her eyes off Diamond Girl, who jumped down from the Jeep and threw open the driver's door.

The dome light filled in all the shadows on her face, and she looked as excited as a child about to board a roller coaster for the first time; a child eager to begin a long scary plunge with a great scream of joy, of delicious, delirium-inducing fear. A child about to grow up in ways that she has only begun to imagine.

Kerry stood by the gate unmoving, unsheltered, long after the Jeep's taillights melted into the night. When she felt certain that Diamond Girl was gone for good, she forced herself to walk toward the highway. She might be hours from rescue, but each step, she assured herself, was bringing her closer to a warm drink and final safety.

She hadn't moved fifty feet when a pair of headlights coming from the compound stole her shadow from the blank darkness.

"Oh shit!"

She raced back to the slim refuge of the gate and tried to hide behind the post. As the headlights grew brighter, she bundled herself into the smallest possible ball, and shut her eyes, as if this could add to her cover.

Behind her lids, the lights enlarged, and the pixels of fear expanded. The tires grumbled on the road, and then stopped.

She burst from the gate post and ran into the soggy desert, suppressing the screams that wanted to rip from her throat.

A horn sounded, and a man yelled, "Kerry. Kerry! Stop."

The only man she knew around here was Ashley Stassler, and she'd run until her legs dropped off before she'd stop for him. But then she heard a dog's deep bark, and a woman with a wounded voice trying to shout to her.

Kerry halted. Ashley Stassler never called her by name, only Her Rankness; and the only other woman who'd ever been out here, besides Diamond Girl and her murdered mom, was Lauren, though it didn't sound like her.

"It's me, Ry Chambers," the man shouted. "There's nothing to be afraid of. I've got Lauren in the car."

The cute older guy with all the wavy hair. She remembered him. But she was still too wary to rush back to the road. She took light steps, fully prepared to pivot and flee if this horrifying night took one more dark turn.

It wasn't until she drew within twenty feet of the Land Rover that she could make them out.

Ry helped her into the front passenger seat, which she had to share with Leroy. Lauren herself lay stretched out under a blanket in the back. She was gripping her leg, and her face looked severely bruised and bloodied.

"What happened to you?" Kerry said.

"Stassler shot me in the leg, and it hurts like hell."

Ry started driving toward the highway. "Do you know the way to the hospital?" he said to Kerry.

"Sure. Take the road to town, and I'll show you from there."

Lauren shifted on to her side. "We found Leroy out here too. I wonder who else we'll find on this road."

"As long as it's not Stassler, I don't care," Kerry replied.

"It won't be him," Lauren said in a strained voice that immediately broke. "I promise you . . . it won't be him."

# CHAPTER

A SALVATION ARMY SANTA RANG his bell in the rain. Lauren reached into her wallet and stuffed a ten dollar bill into his red bucket. She rarely passed one of these Santas without donating at least a few dollars. She'd been feeling exceptionally generous since she'd survived her ordeal in the desert. Generous *and* grateful. Never again would she take any aspect of living for granted. Smells, sights, sounds, all her senses teemed with intensity.

Might be love too, she said to herself with a smile. For months now love had been weaving its wonders into almost everything she did and thought. Ry had been a marvel, helping her through all the physical rehabilitation, and holding her through the long nights when the ghostly visage of Ashley Stassler would invade her dreams and destroy her sleep as surely as he had tried to destroy her life.

They'd rented a small house with a big fenced yard three blocks from the university. The single-car garage had become her studio, and while the view wasn't nearly as impressive as the one she'd known in Pasadena, the company she kept—Ry and Bad

Bad Leroy Brown—had proved so much better. A starter house, she thought, for a starter family. She hoped.

She all but skipped up the steps to Bandering Hall, immensely pleased to feel so much strength and spring in the leg that had been wounded. Last week she'd started running again, amazed at how the body and mind healed. She'd been extraordinarily pleased to see both coming together in her work, transforming tragedy into sculpture. Her pieces had never been edgier, or better.

The door to Bandering swung open, and she moved aside for a young woman carrying a brightly colored painting cloaked in clear plastic.

Lauren hurried inside, and took the stairs to her office, beaming when she unlocked the door and saw the tiny Christmas tree sitting on the corner of her desk. Tree? She knew that was a stretch. More likely the top foot or so of a pine that Ry had lopped off, and then decorated for her with dozens of bulbs the size of BBs: red and gold and purple and green and silver, all those wonderfully lurid colors that heralded the season so boldly. She loved them. She loved the tree. Most of all, she loved the man who'd given it to her.

He'd brought it by this morning, and promised to rendezvous with her after lunch. He was busy on the last chapter of his book. Not the one he'd planned on writing, but the one dictated by the gruesome evidence that had surfaced in Stassler's compound. Ry was exploring the links—and they were legion—between Stassler's sculpture and his insanity. Other authors were writing books about Stassler too—his murderous methods had become sensational news—but none of them possessed Ry's firsthand knowledge of the man and his madness.

As she sat down, her computer screen came to life, displaying a schedule delightfully unencumbered. Even Dr. Aiken, the curmudgeonly chair of the department, had been moved enough to lighten her load. Not that she'd ever forgo teaching entirely. She derived such genuine pleasure from lecturing, showing slides, and working with her students in the studio. And they appeared more receptive than ever to her guidance. Kerry's work, in particular, had evolved in ways unimaginable for most undergrads. But then the woman herself had endured the unimaginable. She was no longer a girl, and Lauren would never think of her that way again.

Ry strolled into the office with mischief in his eyes. It was as visible to Lauren as the mauve scarf that hung from his neck.

She'd been so surprised and flustered the first time he'd walked in. What had she been expecting? A Mr. Peeps maybe, or a twenty-something burning with misplaced literary ambition. Certainly not a desirable physical specimen with a head full of intelligent questions. That just didn't happen very often in a university, or anywhere else for that matter, now that she thought about it. Brains or brawn? Take your choice, and take your chance. But with Ry she'd never had to. She'd lucked out. She knew it. And she wasn't about to let this opportunity pass her by.

He kissed her and squeezed her hands, and this moment, above all the others, sealed her decision.

"I have an idea," she said.

"What's that?" he asked as he sat in the chair next to her desk.

"Let's get married."

"Married?" he repeated, as if the word were an especially dangerous allergen.

"Yes . . . married," she said, though with less assurance than she'd felt a moment ago. Only last Christmas Chad had backed away too, and for the same reason.

"I think . . ." Ry paused, "you should see what Santa brought before you say another word."

Santa? For a moment all she could think of was the Salvation Army Santa she'd seen on her way back from lunch. But then her eyes settled on the outstretched arms of the tiny tree. Below the glittering bulbs she spied a small package in white tissue paper, hidden behind the skinny trunk by a scheming hand.

"Should I open it?" she teased.

"No, *don't* do that," he replied as playfully.

She picked it up and peeled away the tissue paper slowly, savoring the full romance of the moment.

A red velvet box appeared, and when she opened it she saw the ring, and the sparkle of the stone.

"I can't believe you beat me to the punch," he said with a laugh. "I slipped it under there this morning when you weren't looking, and I was going—"

She put her finger to his mouth to silence him, and then replaced it with her lips.

# CHAPTER
## 35

A WOMAN IN A BLACK, knee-length coat knocked softly on the door of a single family home in East Alton, Illinois.

Within moments, a dark-haired girl no older than eight answered.

"Is your mommy home? Or your daddy?" the woman said.

"Mommy," the girl sang out, "there's someone here to see you."

Her mother walked to the door, drying her hands on a dish towel. She looked friendly, and smiled when she spoke.

"Can I help you?"

"Yes, I hope so. I used to live here when I was about her age," the woman's eyes alighted on the child, "and I wondered if I could take a look around before I leave town today. I just . . ." and now her voice broke, and when she began to cry she appeared less like a woman than a child herself. ". . . I just came from my mother's funeral."

# ACKNOWLEDGMENTS

I want to thank Elizabeth Mead, a sculptor who gave so willingly of her time and expertise. She sat for numerous interviews and opened her classroom and studio to me. She's a fabulous artist and a remarkable woman.

Thanks also to Tim Burton, a sculptor and old friend whose tales of travel in Nepal sparked some of my earliest thoughts for this book (and whose work, *Garden Spirit*, presides over our seedlings).

If there are errors in my account of the arts, they are mine alone, and would have been more numerous but for Elizabeth; Tim; and Steve Comba, a superb artist whose work graces my walls.

Thanks as well to Laura Makepeace, DVM.

I have been fortunate in having a long-standing circle of readers whose encouragement and criticisms have helped me immensely over the years. I want to begin with a great thanks to Ed Stackler, who read my earliest ideas for *The Bone Parade*, a sampling of chapters along the way, and the novel in its entirety. He always provided the most incisive of comments.

My other readers have all offered keen thoughts and assistance, and if I could I would embrace them all every day: Dale Dauten, Tina Castañares, Lars Topelmann, Catherine Zangar, Christopher Van Tilburg, and Steve Comba.

My deepest thanks to my agent, Luke Janklow, for his instincts, passion, and humor. What a pleasure it is to work with him.

And special thanks to my editor, Leigh Haber. It's also been a joy to work with her. She's possessed of a sure hand and a light touch.

# AUTHOR'S NOTE

All the characters and events in this book are a product of my admittedly twisted imagination. I do want to take a moment to note that the fictions extend to the restaurant and pub offerings of Moab, Utah, where I have, in fact, eaten some very fine meals, and where I understand the local brew is excellent. Forgive me my fun, foodies. Forgiveness, too, for the liberties I've taken in my description of the geological features of southeastern Utah.

If you enjoyed *The Bone Parade,* be sure to catch Mark Nykanen's newest thriller, *Search Angel,* coming in June 2005 from Hyperion.

An excerpt from the prologue and chapter 1 follows.

# PROLOGUE

PAUL SIMON'S SONG is in my head. The one about the mother and child reunion. Nothing new in that. I could probably sing it in my sleep. In fact, I probably have.

It's a beautiful day. They were calling for rain, but there's not a cloud in the sky. There'll be plenty of rain soon enough. It's already October. I tracked Katie down in August, but it took me a while to work all this out. When I first came up here, the lawns and trees were green. Now I'm looking at leaves as big as my hands all over the sidewalk.

She lives on a pretty street. It could have come straight out of a Frank Capra film. There's actually a white picket fence on my left. Not hers, but it's nice anyway, and I can't help running my hand over it.

In some ways I feel I already know Katie Wilkins. I've seen her from a distance, and even photographed her with a telephoto lens. I'm good at the sneaky shot. And she's a great subject, really cute. Everything about her is cute: her hair, figure, clothes. She's cute like Katie Couric's cute. The same kind of look. It's easy to see why this Katie got in "trouble" in her teens. Why she could still get in trouble.

I've done my homework on her. She's single, no kids, lives alone. It's better this way, for her and for me. There's not going to be some husband standing there all bug-eyed, or kids asking a bunch of stupid questions.

When I spot the house, the one I've driven past nine times, it's all I can do to keep from running up and pounding on the door. That's what anticipation does to you. It builds and builds and builds until it's ready to explode.

But I'm not going to make a spectacle of myself. The neighborhood's too quiet. I've walked three blocks from my car and hardly seen anyone. Not a single kid. She sure hasn't surrounded herself with what she never wanted.

I can't help wondering if she's going to see herself when she sees me. The same nose, maybe? Or mouth, eyes? Her own reflection in my features? It's not unusual for birth mothers to notice this stuff right away.

Three steps up and I'm on the porch. The doorbell sounds unfriendly, shrill, as if it can't decide if it's a bell or a buzzer.

She opens the door. This is the moment, the one I've been waiting for.

"Hi, Mom." I let those two words linger as her brow knits a thousand questions. Then, with her lips quivering and threatening to slice the silence, I say, "I'm your son."

"I don't have a son."

Her immediate denial makes her look ugly. A better man, a less bitter one, might feel devastated; but I've searched and planned and rehearsed this over and over, and I'm not going to be denied.

I force a smile, and my words come more easily than I might have imagined.

"Yes, you do. You had me thirty-two years ago at St. Vincent's in Cincinnati."

She all but doubles over, her hands gripping her gut. It's as if the memory of labor is ripping her apart. She knows she's not lying her way out of this one. I've got the details. She may have lied to lovers, to the husband she had for three years, but she can't lie to me.

"Look, I know it's a shock, but I had to see you. I had to. It's nothing to be ashamed of, and I haven't told anyone anything about you. If you want, I'll go away and never come back. You'll never have to see me again."

She shakes her head, a little less uncertain.

"No, come in. Come in."

She closes the door behind me and raises a hand as fluttery as the notes of a flute. It takes me a second to see that she's gesturing to a sofa where she wants me to sit. But I don't want to sit down. She's the one who sits, flattening her pants with her palms as if she's straightening the memory of a skirt.

"I knew this would happen one day. How did you find me?"

"I followed my heart," I tell her, "and it led me here."

She starts to cry. I hear the word *sorry,* then "I'm so sorry." She says something else, too, but I can't make it out.

I use the breakdown to put my arms around her and raise her to her feet. She reaches up to be hugged, comforted. I indulge her for a few seconds before I begin to lead her to the back of the house.

We take only three short steps before she freezes.

"What are you doing?" That look is back, the one she gave me when she tried to deny her own motherhood.

"I'm taking you back there so you can lie down."

"I don't want to lie down." Her eyes narrow and dart to the front door, and I wonder if she's going to try to run.

"Sure you do. It's okay. Relax a little."

I reach into my jacket and show her the knife. I let her see it up close. I tell her not to say a word, not even to think about screaming. Or running. The blade speaks, too. Volumes. It has the shape of a wiggling snake. It's like a dagger out of *The Arabian Nights.* Form does follow function, especially in matters of the flesh.

I nick one of her belt loops. Just that quick it's in two, the ends sprouting loose threads. I nick another one. Her eyes are plenty wide now. She backs against the wall. Here comes the best part. I bring the blade down the front of her blouse, popping buttons off like grapes. They clatter on the tile. They sound loud to me, but I bet they sound even louder to her.

She's trembling. "Who are you?"

I shake my head. "You tried to deny me once before, Mom. Don't do it again. That hurts."

I point my blade down the hall. She backs along the wall, afraid to look away. That's okay, I like the eye contact when I remind her of the details: "St. Vincent's, the fifteenth of May. Ten-twenty in the morning. Eight and a half hours of labor."

She begins to sob. She's a slave to memory. Aren't we all?

The first door opens to her bedroom. I herd her inside and tell her to take off her clothes. When she starts to say no, I slice open the front of her pants. I can see her white underpants, white like her skin, the secret skin that hides her womb. Then I see a little button of blood. I've nicked her. Didn't mean to, but the effect, if nothing else, is undeniable. She disrobes, defeated. She discards her clothes as if they no longer belong to her.

I take mine off, too, but fold them carefully and lay them on a dressing table. You could look at her clothes and mine, and they'd tell you the whole story. They'd even tell you the ending.

She weeps and shakes and tries to pull her hand away, but I'm very persuasive, and I've had lots of practice. Lots of mothers. I adopt a new one whenever I feel the urge. And I'm feeling it right now. I've felt it for months, ever since I saw Katie's name on the registry of birth mothers. Katie Wilkins: Does a name get any more American than that? Then I saw her picture, and I knew she'd like nothing more than to meet me. They always want to meet their son.

# 1

A BED OF NETTLES, this business of telling secrets, and Suzanne found herself tossing and turning on it as they began their approach to Chicago. The landing gear lowered, and she realized the shudder that radiated from the wings to her window seat could just as easily have arisen from her body: She was on the verge of making the most painful confession of her life to the biggest and most important audience she was ever likely to face.

She spotted the blue-capped, blank-faced chauffeur with the "Suzanne Trayle" sign standing just outside the security checkpoint and had to fight an impulse to walk right past him to the nearest ticket counter for a return flight home to Oregon. She'd come to Chi-town to give the keynote address to the annual conference of the American Adoption Congress, but after reviewing her speech for the umpteenth time on the plane, she felt as keyed up as a long-suffering understudy about to take the stage for her first real performance.

The convention organizer had told her that they wanted her to speak about opening adoption records. Suzanne had been so flattered—and had agreed so quickly—that the personal implications hadn't been immediately apparent: How can you talk about opening adoption records if you're not willing to be open yourself?

So she'd resolved to come out of adoption's darkest closet, a decision that had been much easier to reach when she was still about two thousand miles from the podium. As she wound down the Chicago lakefront, peering through the smoky windows of a limousine at the whitecaps surging to the shore, her uneasiness prompted assurances that by nine o'clock it would all be over; but then she recalled how many times she'd used this tired—and ineffective—gambit to try to weasel her way through a pending crisis.

And it's not going to be *over*. Don't kid yourself. It'll just be starting.

Red, white, and blue pennants snapped in the breeze as they pulled up to the City Center Complex, an unimaginative name for an uninspired-looking convention hall and hotel.

The driver hustled around the stretch to get her door, and she managed a smile as she remembered a famous photographer saying that the outdoors was what you had to pass through to get from your cab to your hotel. But these were tonier times for Suzanne, and the cab had turned into a limo.

Before she made it to the reception desk, a short man with freckles all over his bald head intercepted her.

"I'm Douglas Jenks, and I'm *so* glad to see you." His smile burned as bright as those spots on his polished pate.

"It's good to meet you, too."

The convention organizer. She shook his hand, as cool and limp as raw salmon—and so at odds with his animated face—and thanked him for the invitation.

"No, don't thank me. Do *not* thank us for one second. We want to thank *you* for coming. This is so great having you here. And the timing with that story in *People*? It couldn't have been better. Like you planned it. The—"

"I didn't, really."

He went on undeterred. "—ballroom is absolutely packed. We're sold out, *and* we've had to clear out some chairs in the back so we can make room for the overflow. Lots of TV, too," he added with even more delight.

Suzanne barely had time to consider the gratifying—and intimidating—size of the audience before he was reminding her of his invitation to join him for dinner.

"I'm so sorry," she said. "I can't. I have to beg off. I really need some time to get ready." The truth? She didn't think she could hold down dinner.

"Okay," he said slowly, drawing out both syllables skeptically. "Well, we do want you at your best. You're feeling all right, aren't you?" He frowned, and in an instant fleshy cornrows traveled up his brow and the front half of his spotted scalp.

"I'm fine. Don't worry." Suzanne touched his arm reassuringly. "I just need to get settled from the plane ride."

She edged toward the reception desk and handed a credit card to the young man waiting to check her in. The Congress was hosting her, but there were always incidentals to pay for.

"All right. Come down when you're ready. We'll be waiting. Ciao-ciao."

As he turned away she had to stifle a laugh because with that silly good-bye, and his orange spots, he suddenly reminded her of Morris the cat in those old commercials.

She just managed to bite her lip—pain the moment's preferred antidote—when he executed a spirited and surprisingly graceful spin to wheel back around.

"Sorry, almost forgot." He dug through a three-ring binder and pulled out a note. "A distinguished-looking man with silver hair gave me this earlier and asked me to give it to you."

One glimpse at the crisp penmanship confirmed that it was, indeed, from Burton. But distinguished looking? Silver hair? She'd always thought of it as gray. He'd made her husband sound like a Supreme Court Justice, which he definitely wasn't. Not yet anyway. Try administrative law judge for the Oregon Construction Contractors Board. He'd applied for a circuit court judge pro tem position, but was still waiting for the governor to promote him to the bench. Despite his steroidal ambition with the gavel—or maybe, now that she thought of it, *because* of it—His Honor had suffered a serious lapse in judgment in following her here. Hardly the first such lapse, and far from the worst, but can't an estranged husband stay estranged? At least for a while?

The note proved blessedly brief: "Good luck, sweetheart. I'm with you."

But not brief enough to keep her from seeing that he could have chosen his words more carefully, too, made them less susceptible to sarcasm. *I'm with you.* Where were you a few months ago? And where are you now?

A quick, furtive look around the lobby assured her that he wasn't haunting its remote corners. Thank God for small favors.

She took the key card from the receptionist and handed it to the bellman.

They stepped off the elevator on the sixteenth floor, and she trailed him to a plummy suite with a large bedroom. Nice. The Congress was treating her well.

She heard the bellman opening the drapes and turned to take in a view of Lake Michigan as wide as the horizon itself.

Two weeks ago clocks were set back an hour, and though it was still early evening, the blackening sky, with its gray filaments of cloud, looked like an eerie reflection of the dark, windswept water.

A chill prickled her arms, and as she rubbed them, the bellman, more alert than most, pointed out the thermostat. He turned it up, and as he left she handed him a five.

She unzipped her laptop case and reviewed her speech, double-checking the most painfully revealing lines.

The words she'd written over the past few weeks left her stomach feeling as if she'd never left the elevator, and more glad than ever that she'd declined the invitation to dinner. Hardly tempted in any case by the morel-stuffed mahi-mahi that was, at this very moment, taking its final bow on terra firma.

The bellman had hung her garment bag in a closet with a full-length mirror on the door. After slipping on a cerulean blue dress that highlighted her eyes, she gave herself a once-over, fluffed her honey-colored hair, which promptly deflated in palpable protest, and called it good.

Not quite. In deference to the harsh lights that seemed to bear down on every podium she'd ever commanded, she reluctantly applied mascara, lip gloss, and enough blush to enliven her pallid Portland complexion. About as much as she'd concede to the dogs of demeanor. But she'd learned the hard way that when you went before your public, you really did ignore your appearance at your own peril. That hideous photograph of her in *People*? Taken at a speech she'd given in Orlando two months ago. All the proof—and impetus—she'd ever need to primp.

She returned to her laptop, checking the time on the screen. Fifteen minutes and counting. One more look at the speech, even though she'd committed every last pause to memory.

Second thoughts? "Try third and fourth ones, too," she murmured. *But you're not turning back now.*

The title sounded simple enough, "Opening Records in the Era of Open Adoption," but simplicity in all guises is pure deception—ask any magician worth his wand—and this surely proved true in the scroll of words her eyes now scanned.

Minutes later she made the trip back down the elevator and glanced in the ballroom as she headed to the backstage entrance. Packed! Camera crews choked the aisles, including one from *60 Minutes* and another from *Dateline NBC*. Both shows had been hounding her for interviews. Ed Bradley himself had called, not some assistant to the assistant producer. She'd liked his manner on the phone, very smooth, yet chummy, but supposed that every reporter had learned to give good phone, a skill as necessary to their success as it was to the practitioners of another, more bluntly seductive art. He was so good she'd almost asked him what he was wearing.

All the attention was a sign, she supposed, that she was truly emerging into national prominence and mainstream interest, coming as it did only three weeks after that cover story in *People*. The headline? "The Orphans' Private Eye," a gussied-up way of overstating the humdrum nature of her work, which typically entailed hours of web searches and visits to the dustiest removes of distant libraries. She had allowed to the reporter that occasionally she did the work of an actual gumshoe—surveillance, interviews, impersonation—and evidently that had been enough to earn her the colorful sobriquet. But danger, the kind often associated with PIs? Not a bit. Her world was no more noirish than a cheese blintz.

The initial blip of publicity had occurred two years ago right here in Chicago when she'd appeared on *Oprah*; but she'd shared that hour with birth mothers and their children and had been featured only briefly, which had been fine with her. But *60 Minutes, People, Dateline NBC*? This was a whole new level of fame, and she wasn't sure it was good for the open adoption movement to be wedded so closely to one person, even if that person happened to be her.